A HARD DEATH

Jonathan Hayes is a British-born forensic pathologist. After medical school in London, he studied pathology in Boston, then became a medical examiner in Miami. Arriving during the cocaine wars of the late 1980s, he investigated drug murders in Miami and in the Everglades. In 1990, he moved to New York City, where he's a senior medical examiner. Since the mid-1990s, he's been a prolific freelance journalist, writing mostly about food and travel for the *New York Times*, *Food & Wine*, *New York* magazine and *Gourmet*; until resigning to concentrate on fiction, he was a contributing editor at *Martha Stewart Living*. He teaches forensic science nationally and internationally, and has been a visiting lecturer at the American Academy of Forensic Sciences, the New York Police Department Homicide Investigation School, la Société Française de Médecine Légale, the National Institute of Justice and the Federal Bureau of Investigation.

Also available by Jonathan Hayes

Precious Blood

A HARD DEATH

JONATHAN HAYES

arrow books

Published in the United Kingdom by Arrow Books in 2009

1 3 5 7 9 10 8 6 4 2

First published in Great Britain in 2009 by
Arrow Books

Arrow Books
Random House, 20 Vauxhall Bridge Road,
London SW1V 2SA

www.rbooks.co.uk

Addresses for companies within The Random House Group Limited can be
found at: www.randomhouse.co.uk/offices.htm

The Random House Group Limited Reg. No. 954009

A CIP catalogue record for this book
is available from the British Library

ISBN 9780099538646
Export ISBN 9780099517559

The Random House Group Limited supports The Forest Stewardship
Council (FSC), the leading international forest certification organisation. All
our titles that are printed on Greenpeace approved FSC certified paper carry
the FSC logo. Our paper procurement policy can be found at
www.rbooks.co.uk/environment

Typeset by SX Composing DTP, Rayleigh, Essex
Printed and bound in Great Britain by
CPI Bookmarque Ltd, Croydon, CR0 4TD

A HARD
DEATH

1

SOUTH FLORIDA: THE WESTERN EVERGLADES:

The airboat was nearing the edges of the Glades, wending its way through a series of small sloughs. The dry season had been unusually harsh, and parts of the swamp where Tony could normally have flown over the sawgrass at full speed were still shallow-water mazes of protruding sedge and dried marl.

The airboat, bought from a local tour operator and souped up with a Chevy big-block engine, had a flat aluminum hull that could glide over the shallowest marsh. Tony was perched high up, on the stick, in front of the safety cage around the six-foot carbon fiber propeller that powered the airboat.

The going was slow. The airboat was always tricky – the stick controlled the two vertical rudders, but there was no way to slow down, no reverse, and the slower you moved, the harder it was to steer.

With six passengers, the airboat was near capacity. Smith was boss for the day, Bentas his second in command, and Tony was on the rudder. And Brodie had sent Tarver, that boil on the ass of humanity, along for the ride. Finally, their cargo, the two Mexican prisoners – the whole reason for the trip.

Smith shifted the shotgun into his left hand and

3

scowled, turning to make a cutting gesture to his pilot. Squinting into the setting sun, Tony nodded, then throttled down, tapping the stick forward gently to send the airboat scudding left, missing a rotting tree limb.

The Mexicans sat in the front row, each hooded with a white plastic bag that read "Delfine Piglet Feed" in red. The shirt of the heavier one, Gordo, was soaked in blood – Tony's handiwork. A coarse yellow nylon rope hung slack between their necks, tying the men together in life as it would in death. Their wrists were lashed behind them; Smith hadn't bothered shackling them to the seats: where were they going to go? They knew he'd shoot them if they went into the water – shoot to wound, leave 'em for the gators to finish off.

Smith wondered what he'd do in their place. They knew what was going to happen: when a worker finally won entry into the inner circle, while they were still high on how much money they'd be making, they had to watch the special videotape, to learn what happened when someone broke the rules; the sight of a man's legs kicking wildly in the air always made an impression. But maybe not *enough* of an impression, Smith thought.

He looked at the Mexicans again. Maybe they thought they'd get another chance. Maybe they thought he'd just take them out, give them a beating, send them on their way, telling them he'd kill them if they ever came back to Douglas County.

No, they knew – the fat one wouldn't quit blubbering, the sound so loud that even the noise of the prop couldn't drown it out. Smith was sick of that shit, but if he just gave in and blew Gordo's head off and dumped the body,

4

there'd be nothing to show the other workers, no way for them to understand that the rule was the rule, and the rule must be obeyed. No way for them to learn from the bad mistake Gordo had made. And it was too bad that Joaquin had done nothing: Smith couldn't kill Gordo and just let his brother go.

The hell with it – this had to be done right.

Smith leaned over, tapped Bentas on the arm to get his attention. He yelled "Shut him up!", and jabbed his finger toward Gordo.

Bentas bent forward, smacked Gordo's hood hard with the butt of his rifle, and yelled, "*Oye, puto! Sigue así y vas a echar las entrañas. Y si vomitas ahí, te vas a ahogar!*"

Gordo's head jerked forward and stayed there, craning away from the unseen club. Smith couldn't hear the blubbering anymore.

"What did you say?"

Bentas grinned. "I told him if he keeps it up he'll puke, and if he pukes in that bag he'll drown . . ."

He scanned the horizon, looking for the big island of trees. He wondered if it had a name; Tony claimed to be an eighth Miccosukee – maybe he knew. But that was probably bullshit, anyway.

The airboat was almost idling now, slowly edging forward. A snowy egret roused, skittering across the surface of the water before launching itself awkwardly into the air.

They swung into a wide curve; Tony whistled and nodded to the right. The humped shape of the hammock, rising like the back of an elephant out of the marsh, maybe a quarter-mile further. A couple of acres of dark loam covered by thick swamp forest.

As the boat drew closer a handful of vultures rose from the canopy and flapped high into the air to wheel and glide over the treetops.

As Tony let the airboat glide in toward the bank Tarver lifted up the camcorder and shouted, "Guys, guys! Let me out first so I can get them coming off the boat!"

Before Smith could stop him, he'd scrambled out and jumped onto the island, almost sliding to his knees in the mud before grabbing a branch and hauling himself up onto the solid ground. He turned, lifted his camcorder to his face and yelled "OK! Come on!"

Tony climbed down from his seat and stepped nimbly up onto the bank. Smith pulled the hoods off the two men, who looked around wildly, blinking in the light. Gordo's black hair was now slick with blood, probably from when Bentas had hit him.

Bentas prodded the two Mexicans to their feet with his rifle, nudging them toward the front of the boat. Wrists bound behind their backs, their necks leashed together by rope, they hobbled forward clumsily, overbalancing frantically as the boat tipped gently and slid under the moving weight. They slowed to a shuffle, so Bentas gave Gordo another tap.

Joaquin got down first but missed the bank, his feet slipping backwards and out from under him as he fell face forward against the slope, toppling Gordo who fell on top of him. The two writhed together in the mud, Joaquin kicking as he slid back slowly toward the water.

Tony pushed Tarver out of the way and reached down to haul the fat one up onto solid ground, while Bentas stepped down into the muck to grab Joaquin.

Smith let them catch their breath before going on toward the clearing.

They moved in single file through the thick undergrowth, crashing through the tangles of muscadine and devil's claw as the ground firmed under their feet and began to rise. They squeezed past tall gumbo-limbo trees and into the heart of the island, where the gumbo-limbo gave way to a few dozen towering mahogany trees. At some time in the distant past, timber poachers had carved a hollow into the island, leaving a moss-covered clearing at the center; the deep green shadow flickered with light when the wind stirred the canopy high overhead.

As they reached the clearing Gordo slipped on the moss, pulling Joaquin down to his knees. Gordo lay there rigid on the ground, not moving as Bentas and Tony tried to get him to his feet, Joaquin dragging back and forth as they struggled. Finally Bentas swung the butt of his gun into Gordo's head one more time, connecting with a low, hollow *pock*! that resonated dully through the dead air of the clearing.

Joaquin muttered, "*Tenemos que hacerlo, vamos ya de una vez. Como quiera, nos van a matar. Haz tu paz, mi hermano.*" It's going to happen. Let's get it over with. They'll just hurt you more, and then kill you anyway. Make your peace now, brother.

Bentas grunted, "*Hazle caso a tu hermano, cabron. Es inteligente.*" Listen to your brother, asshole. He's smart.

But it didn't take, and Gordo began to wriggle and kick again as Smith and Bentas dragged him forward across the moss. Joaquin scrambled forward on his knees as best he could.

Tony had set the chairs against a big mahogany tree,

the rust-pitted metal of the backs pressed firmly against the thick gray trunk. He stepped forward and, with Smith and Bentas holding Gordo down, quickly loosened the rope. He pulled the noose tight around Joaquin's neck so that he couldn't run, then dragged him over to the tree.

He motioned for Joaquin to get up on the chair.

When the Mexican hesitated, Tony wordlessly pulled out the knife he'd used to cut Gordo earlier.

Joaquin straightened. They had lost, and now it would happen, but he was a man: he wasn't going out like some little bitch.

He was calm now, the clearing hovering around him like water, distant and separate. He was moving through the air, he was stepping up onto the chair, he was leaning forward to steady himself against the trunk, he was turning to watch them drag Gordo to the other chair, punching him and clubbing him as they went. He was. He was. He was.

Tony threw the free end of the rope up and around a thick branch, looping it over before retying the noose. The others wrestled Gordo to him, Smith yelling at Tarver to put the camcorder down and help. Tarver, muttering, slung the device round his neck and walked over to the foot of the tree, where he stood and watched them try to control Gordo.

Tarver sighed, opened a folding knife, and stabbed the blade deep into Gordo's flank. Gordo bellowed and flailed, but backed onto the chair; it took Tony a second to get the noose around his neck, and then to knock the chair out from under Joaquin. After that, Gordo's body rose more easily as they lifted him. Tarver had the camcorder out and was filming before the Mexican was fully suspended.

Afterwards, Tarver whined about how he'd missed Joaquin's drop. But when he watched the tape, later he admitted that it wasn't the end of the world.

2

PORT FONTAINE, DOUGLAS COUNTY, SOUTHWEST FLORIDA: TWO WEEKS LATER

Jenner watched the old man push the shopping cart across the motel parking lot. The guy wore shorts and sneakers only, his shirtless chest leathery and nut brown, fading blue military tats scattered across his torso and arms. There was no way he'd get the cart's wheels up onto the concrete sidewalk in front of the rooms – the curb rose barely three inches above the parking-lot tarmac but the man was so drunk that Jenner was amazed he'd made it across the lot without falling.

He rammed the wheels against the concrete lip, the foraged cans in his cart rattling like tin maracas. He kept ramming until Jenner put down his copy of *The Kite Runner* and stepped off his porch.

"Hey, sir. Can I give you a hand with that?"

The man eyed Jenner warily; his jutting jaw and small, toothless mouth made his face look skeletal. He looked Jenner up and down, squinting at his grubby T-shirt and running shorts.

Jenner waited.

Finally the man nodded. Jenner pushed the shaky cart onto the pavement, then followed the old man's directions as he wheezed along behind, mumbling about immigrants and liquor stores and respect.

They stopped at the man's room, next to the icebox and vending machines under the stairs. The old guy nodded at Jenner again, turned and disappeared through the door.

And just like that, Jenner had been accepted. He now *belonged* at the Palmetto Court Motel.

The Palmetto Court, Jenner's home for two weeks now, was a strip of two-story concrete buildings, flanked by a cluster of weather-battered cottages in front of a dismal little creek. While Port Fontaine's famous beaches had made it a playground for the wealthy since the 1920s, the Palmetto Court was in the Reaches, the part of the town closest to the mosquito jungles that rimmed the Everglades.

The motel was classic faded Reaches chic, the sort of place that would be shot by hipster photographers for ironic coffee-table books about rotting Mid-century Americana. The buildings were a garish green that made the place look like a fun-house ride, and Jenner was sure it was only a question of time before he found a dead snake in the pool.

He sat on the porch of his cottage and picked up his book. But he couldn't concentrate; he just sat there in front of his Chrysler Sebring, staring at the dented fender that had earned him a thirty per cent discount on his rental.

And he needed the discount. His New York license suspended, his reputation as a medical examiner a topic of heated debate in the forensic community, stone-broke . . . If Marty Roburn, the Douglas County medical examiner, hadn't hired him to cover for three months, he'd have been out there picking up cans, too. Jenner had been lucky.

Still, as he looked across the motel parking lot towards State Road, out over the battered sedans and pickup trucks – all American-made, most of them with bumper stickers variously praising God, the U.S.A. and the Grateful Dead – he wasn't feeling particularly lucky.

There was a soft rattle, and Jenner turned to see the old man emerge from his room, dressed now in long black slacks and a yellowed but clean and pressed white shirt, its long sleeves buttoned at the wrist, its collar closed. He waited at his open door, and then a tiny old woman in a powder-blue pants suit and marcelled black hair plastered against her scalp stepped out. She took his arm and they walked along the sidewalk, their gait unhurried and stately.

As they passed Jenner, he gave a friendly nod at the gentleman; the old man ignored him.

Jenner watched them pass. *This,* he thought, *will be the moment when I finally realized my career was finished.*

They moved toward the end of the lot, out of his sight.

Jenner put the book down. It was already gone noon, and it would only get hotter and wetter. He should run before the rain started.

3

Out in the Everglades, Jenner ran along the old canal road, pounding the four-mile stretch in the early

11

afternoon heat. He'd done it most days for almost three weeks. At first, each breath had ripped out of his chest, jagged and wet, but now his body had its own rhythm, and his feet matched that rhythm, steadily beating the ground, pistons smoothly working the bellows of his lungs. He felt his body tightening, distilling down to muscle, sinew and bone, an increasingly elemental structure moving over the earth, through the air, by the water.

And he could feel himself healing – not healing physically, the way the knife slash across his left arm had become a smooth purple scar, but the other type of healing, his body fusing with whatever particular metaphysical energy powered it across the surface of the planet. He was integrating, becoming whole again.

It was a Wednesday, and Jenner had told the staff at the medical examiner's office that he'd be available by cell phone if they needed him. But they wouldn't need him – Douglas was a place where old money went to die, a place where no one ever died violently. At least, according to Marty Roburn.

Jenner saw no one for two miles, not even a fisherman. The Faxahatchee Canal was a straight line carved across the Everglades to contain the wilderness, to signal the beginning of civilization. But on the other side of the dark canal the bank was crumbling and overgrown, barely recognizable as man-made. The Glades fought back against the imposition of order, spilling over the edges, forcing itself through the boundary of concrete and tarmac. On his runs he'd pass white herons hunting frogs in the shallows, and packs of cormorants posing in the branches, facing the sun immobile, black wings like widow's weeds draped wide to dry. And occasionally, on the far side, where smaller tributaries trickled slowly through the undergrowth into the canal, he'd catch sight of a gator, half-hidden in the dark, glassy gaps in the pale green lace covering of water plants.

Most days, though, he ran blind, seeing nothing but the man he'd killed. Jenner carried the dead man awkwardly, trailed him along like a sagging helium balloon, the cord somehow entangled around his neck.

It was a kind of stress manifestation, he knew, some hysterical yelp from his unconscious that something wasn't right. But Jenner didn't understand why. He wasn't afraid of this man, nor did he feel guilty for killing him: Robert Farrar had been a monster. They'd called him the Inquisitor, and he'd killed many people, killed them horribly. He'd killed Jenner's friend Joey Roggetti, had cut Rad Garcia's throat, had done it while Jenner lay gasping in front of them. And he would've killed Ana de Jong too.

Ana. Farrar kept her prisoner in the warehouse for days, then hunted her through the decaying space like an animal. Jenner remembered her afterwards, lying there on the couch, too weak to cry as he plucked nails from her filthy skin.

And when he thought of what Farrar had done to Ana, it got easier for Jenner to remember how he'd killed the man. How he'd driven that spike through his chest, how he'd nailed him up against the wall and held on as Farrar coughed out his last bloody breaths. The way the spike shook from Farrar's agonal twitching. The heat of Farrar's blood as it had coursed down the iron to slick Jenner's fists, locked white-knuckled to the rusted shaft.

And the thing was that, sometimes, it actually felt *good*.

The path ahead was empty, spattered with shallow puddles from the recent rains. Jenner liked to run alone, liked listening to his own footsteps. If there'd been other runners, he might have lost his pace, become distracted by their clatter.

He'd been alone for a while now, alone since the relentless media scrutiny – the paparazzi stationed outside his loft apartment in New York, the shocked articles about Jenner's relationship with Ana, an Inquisitor victim almost half his age, and most of all, the episode of *American Crime Prime Time* where Amanda Tucker had referred to him as *"that creepy, creepy sexual opportunist"* – had driven Ana away.

Since she'd left him it had seemed that his life was unfurling slowly, like a battered old umbrella, tears visible in the fabric, the spokes now bent and broken. Because of what he'd done to catch Farrar, he'd lost his New York license and there was a movement to expel him from the National Association of Medical Examiners, driven by supporters of Steve Whittaker, the newly minted Chief for New York City, former colleague, now his dedicated tormentor.

Jenner heard a feathery squeak and turned to see a blue heron take off, swooping low over the water, its long legs ticking the surface to set spreading ripples in motion. Or was it an egret? No, a heron: the guide at the Everglades park had said that herons flew with their necks bent.

In the distance he saw the East Farm Road bridge. He'd stop there, catch his breath, look for alligators in the water below. Act like a tourist.

After Farrar, people treated him differently; Jenner's

friend Jun Saito said he should write an article titled "Things Change When You Kill A Guy". It wasn't that people thought killing Farrar was wrong – quite the contrary, in fact. It was that, by killing, Jenner had crossed a line: he had become a killer.

The worst had come one night at a forensic meeting in Detroit, where a documents examiner from Dallas, a willowy blonde in her early fifties, had drunkenly hit on him in the elevator, slurring to him how much it turned her on that he had killed, that he had killed for a woman.

He'd come home to New York to find a message from Marty Roburn, who'd been his mentor in forensics in Miami: "Hey, Jenner. I hear you need a job . . ." Marty and Bobbie were taking a long-promised world cruise, and Marty needed coverage for three months. The salary was small, but it was a salary nonetheless.

Up ahead there was something going on. Jenner was nearing East Farm Road, which crossed the canal and went on to merge with Pelican Alley, which cut all the way across the Glades to Miami. As the canal path rose up to East Farm, he slowed to a walk.

A sheriff's department Special Response van was parked on the far side, and beyond it an olive-green SUV with the Florida State Parks logo. A large tow truck was backed up to the water's edge. Next to the tow truck a uniformed deputy was shouting down into the water.

Jenner walked up onto the bridge to get a better look.

In the canal a diver was bobbing next to the tow-truck line. The line disappeared into the water, plunging toward a pale, ghostly shape that billowed faintly beneath the surface.

They were recovering a car.

The diver had attached the line to the frame or axle. Jenner watched him swim to the other side of the sunken car, grab another line and swim down with it into the dark green water.

The driver backed the tow truck closer to the bank to swing the boom further out over the canal. The hoist motor howled and the steel cables tautened, but the car didn't break the surface. The diver popped up again to yell to the deputy on the bank; the driver cut the hoist motor. The park ranger spoke to the tow-truck operator, gesturing sharply toward the bank, probably warning him that he was too close.

"Doctor Jenner! Doctor!"

The deputy was waving up at him, the diver looking up too, treading water as he floated over the pallid shadow of the drowned car.

"We got a body!"

Shit.

Jenner lifted his hand to them, thumb touching index finger to make an OK sign.

The diver slipped backward as the motor began to grind again. The cables snapped taut, then the car's rear end lurched visibly under the water and began to tip up, setting off a series of sucking currents.

Jenner climbed over the concrete barrier and scrambled down the embankment. It was an unpaved feeder road, a quiet place where people from the Reaches came to drink Bud and fish for bluegill and tilapia. There was no fence or wall to separate the road from the water, just a shallow concrete lip at the top of the pavers that lined the canal.

Jenner recognized the deputy from a motor vehicle accident out on Pelican Alley the week before.

"Deputy Nash, is it?"

"Hi, doc." Nash looked at Jenner's sweaty Pixies T-shirt and worn Nike shorts, and grinned. "Good thing you were in the neighborhood."

Jenner joined the deputy and the park ranger at the bank and peered into the water. He could see the car clearly – a light-colored, late-model compact. The boom slowly pulled up, the hoist whining away as the trunk rose, the rear bumper finally breaking the surface in a rush of eddies.

The driver edged his truck forward, the grinding turning to a howl as the car continued to rise, now tipping vertical.

The diver raised a flat palm abruptly; the deputy relayed the stop signal to the driver. The diver dipped and swam down to the rear passenger window. Through the canal's shivering surface, Jenner saw him bash the window repeatedly until it was riven by a web of fracture lines. The diver pushed in the shattered window, then shoved off, kicking away from the car.

He bobbed up to the surface, then repeated the flat-palm wave. He swam to the bank and, aided by his partner, climbed the rope ladder up onto dry land. He sat down heavily on a flat-topped log.

Jenner and the park ranger watched him catch his breath. The ranger turned to Jenner and said, "Excuse me, doctor? Were you at the visitor center over at Magic Bend park yesterday?"

He nodded. "My day off."

She held out a hand; Jenner noticed a pistol on her hip. "Deborah Putnam, senior ranger."

The diver slipped off his weight belt and began to unstrap his harness. Jenner approached him.

"So, what can you see, deputy?"

"You're the M.E.?" He blew into his regulator a couple of times, then slipped the harness off his back and eased the tank to the ground. "Doctor . . .?"

Nash said, "Doctor Jenner. Doc, my partner here is Norris."

They shook hands. Norris took the Mountain Dew that the ranger offered, popped the top and chugged it down in big gulps. He breathed out, and grinned. "Thanks, Deb."

Deborah tipped back her baseball cap, and Jenner noticed she was pretty. Blue-eyed and freckly, blonde ponytail, leggy, tan – a Florida girl.

Norris turned back to Jenner. "Looks like you were in the right place at the right time. We've got a big ole swelled-up son of a gun in there, floating around in the driver's compartment."

"Is the body intact?"

"It's so murky down there, I can't hardly see him through the window. Best I can tell, he's by himself." Norris shook his head. "Don't see any damage to the car, though."

He took another swig of soda. Jenner turned back to the diver. "Why did the tow-truck operator stop? With the hoist, I mean?"

Nash jerked his thumb toward the car. "That thing is just a two-ton bucket holding another ton of water, doc. Deputy Norris will go back in, unroll the windows so it can drain right as it comes up."

"Why didn't you just break all the windows?"

Norris shot Jenner a reproachful look. "And lose all those fingerprints? The sheriff would not be happy . . ."

He grinned, wiped some of the water off his face. "It's probably just another drunk driver – we fish at least one out of the water every summer – but until we know, better not take any chances, right?"

He finished the last of the soda and crushed the can, then tossed it to the ranger with a belch. "You'll want to recycle this, right, Deb?"

"Norris?" Deborah smiled sweetly, then lifted her hand gracefully, one finger raised toward him. She held on to the can.

Norris stood, smirking, and without hesitation jumped into the canal and swam to the car. He took a breath, pulled the mask back over his face, then dipped down to wiggle through the broken window. It was a snug fit, and Jenner understood why he'd shed his tank.

Nash shook his head. "So, doc, you're from New York, right? You're going to find Port Fontaine pretty boring – the only people who die here are either old folks or drunks. Occasional drowning, not much more than that."

He thought for a couple of seconds, then added, "And then, mebbe two, three times a year, we get a stabbing up in Bel Arbre – you been there yet?"

Jenner shook his head. "What's Bel Arbre? A prison?"

"Ha, no!" Nash mused for a second, then his face assumed an expression so thoughtful that it bordered on soulful. "Although I guess, in a way, you could say that – Bel Arbre is where the migrant workers live, about forty miles north of here. Mexicans, mostly. Dirt poor. Guatemalans, Peruvans – uh, people from Peru. A few Haitians. Mostly illegals, but unless there's trouble we don't interfere – who'd pick the strawberries if we got rid of the illegals?"

He grinned brightly.

There was a yell from below. Norris had both rear windows fully down and was giving the thumbs-up. Nash signaled to the tow-truck operator and the hoist began to grind.

It was slow going. The trunk took forever to rise from the water. It was a generic sedan, a Ford or maybe a Chrysler, the color of cream gone bad.

Behind Jenner, Deb Putnam was leaning against the cruiser with Nash, the two of them idly watching Jenner over on the bank.

She said, "Hey, Tom, the doctor looks familiar – I feel like I know the name, too . . ."

Nash became animated. "Those college-girl murders in New York this winter? Doc Jenner is the one that killed the guy."

"Oh my gosh!" She stared at Jenner, remembering the enthusiasm with which the news anchors had presented the details of each horrific murder. "Didn't he end up dating one of the victims?"

"Yep. Big fuss about that." Nash grinned at Deborah slyly. "But I think he's single now – want me to tell him you're available?"

"No, thanks." She laughed, and looked Jenner over. "Although maybe I'll tell him myself . . ."

Watching the car rise slowly, Jenner remembered his first dead body in a vehicle. It had been back in Miami, with Roburn. A young doctor, taking his brand-new Saab convertible for a test run on the Don Shula Expressway, had made the mistake of flipping off the wrong car; Crime Scene had counted thirty-two bullet holes in the side panels, and Jenner had found seventeen more in the doctor.

They'd towed the car into the mortuary garage just before dark, the victim covered with a shroud, still strapped into his seat. The doctor's father was a deputy police chief in Miami Beach, and the victim's body arrived accompanied by a throng of detectives and uniformed cops. The detectives crowded around Jenner as he tried to examine the body, peppering him with questions, and becoming testy when he stopped answering.

Then a voice boomed out: "Officers! Step away from the damn car! Step away from the damn M.E.! Give that boy some room to breathe, for Christ's sake!"

There was some shuffling of feet, and Jenner looked up to see Roburn in his vest and fisherman's weathered hat, the madras plaid band bristling with lures, trolling rods at his feet in a green Frabill case. It was a Wednesday, and every Wednesday Roburn took his boat out to go sunset fishing.

Roburn put one hand on Jenner's shoulder, then turned to the cops and announced, "Doctor Jenner needs room. You're slowing him down; only one detective and one uniform can stay with the body."

For almost six hours, Roburn stayed with Jenner, watching him work. He nodded approvingly from time to time, and once or twice he leaned in to show Jenner a technique or explain a finding. But mostly he just sat back and let Jenner work.

Afterwards, he took Jenner for a Blizzard at the Dairy

Queen by the river. They sat at a picnic table by the oily water at midnight, sweating in the heat and humidity of a Miami summer, Roburn chattering away about casting and lures, Jenner, exhausted, nodding occasionally as if he knew what the man was on about.

Then Roburn announced, "I want to show you something."

They walked back to his car. Roburn's twenty-fifth wedding anniversary was approaching and he'd had a jeweler make something special. "Bobbie knows I got her something, and it's driving her nuts! She's tearing the house apart, but she's not going to find it . . ."

He leaned forward, and reached deep under the dashboard to feel along the steering column. His eyes lit up, and with a wink and a flourish he produced a small white cardboard box.

He said, "It's my own design", then spilled the contents onto his palm: there were two platinum fish hooks, each on a fine chain. Roburn fiddled with them for a second, then showed Jenner how the two hooks fitted together to form a heart, the point where the barbs met hidden by a large diamond. The plain hook, he explained, was for him, the one with the diamond for Bobbie.

"Doc."

Jenner looked up. The car was mostly out of the canal, the passenger compartment draining quickly as water gushed from the open windows. A huge gray mass of sodden clothing and slippery pale flesh was plastered down against the front window, now just above the water.

The crane motor shrilled as the car rose faster, and soon the vehicle was clear, swaying slightly over the canal, water sieving from the hood and radiator.

They waited on the bank for the car to drain.

There was a loud thump as the tow truck pulled the car onto and over the lip of the canal. Inside the car, the body, impossibly inflated by putrefaction, had become wedged over the front-seat back, the splayed legs pressed up against the front window, the upper trunk sliding into the back seat.

Norris, now stripped to the waist, was at the driver's-side door.

"Shall I do the honors?"

Jenner nodded. Norris reached through the window and felt gingerly for the handle, his body leaning away from the car as best he could. There was a soft clunk, then Norris jumped back as the door swung open, water gushing from the footwell.

The four of them stood by the open door and peered in at the car's occupant.

4

Nash produced a yellow emergency blanket, the sort used for covering traffic-accident victims along the highway, and Jenner laid it out carefully by the driver's-side door. Jenner stripped off his T-shirt; he wrapped his cell phone and iPod in it, then tossed it onto the gravel at the shoulder of the road. He was momentarily self-conscious about his pallor, then realized that the others were looking at the livid purple scar slashed across his left arm.

He pulled on the gloves that Nash handed him, then turned and said, "So, who's going to help me?"

23

With the door open, the reek of decomposition became more intense. There was silence for a second, then Norris grinned, and said, "I hope neoprene rinses out OK . . . What do you need me to do, doc?"

"I'll drag him forward, back onto the driver's seat, as best I can, then we'll pull him out the side together. You stand to my left: if he starts to come out too fast, just grab him and help me support him so we can ease him down."

Deb Putnam asked, "Anything I can do?"

Norris shook his head. "We got it, Deb."

He zipped up his wetsuit top and called over to his partner, who was now lolling against their patrol car. "Nash, you owe me, buddy. You owe me big time . . ."

Nash shrugged. "Eh . . . You're a natural for this kind of work, Swamp Boy."

Jenner leaned into the compartment. The body was swollen, the arms spread wide as if reaching to embrace someone. He grabbed the left wrist but lost his grip as the skin slipped off beneath his fingers.

He grasped the forearm a little higher with his other hand, and tugged it forward. The body jerked towards him, then slid quickly onto the front seat.

He straightened, breathed fresh air into his lungs, then reached inside again. He held the left upper arm, then leaned backward, putting his weight into it. The body started to slide towards him. Norris braced to support the torso as the body moved faster, but as it cleared the door well he misjudged the slipperiness and lost his grip. Jenner's feet slipped on the shroud and he fell into a sitting position, his back against the car. He tried to pull himself back but was too slow, and the body slithered across his lap onto the shroud.

24

As Jenner shoved the body quickly off him and got to his feet cursing, Norris shook his head in apology. "God, doc, sorry! It came out too fast. I really wasn't ready for it."

Jenner lifted a hand. "It's hardly the end of the world. It's just . . ." Norris jumped out of the way as Jenner swung his arms, casting off the brown fluid.

"Unpleasant."

Jenner walked to the lip of the canal wall, kicked off his running shoes and peeled off his socks, then jumped feet first into the water. He plunged deep into the cool and the dark, feeling the fast current flow over him. Then he swept his arms down and rose slowly; when he broke the surface, the water had washed him clean. He climbed the rope ladder with difficulty – Norris made it look easy – and Nash helped him to his feet.

Norris was squatting on the shroud by the body, peering down at it. He looked up at Jenner and said, "Looks like the fish were feeding on him, right, doc?" He was pointing to a series of vertical gashes in the skin of the chest.

Jenner shook his head slowly. "We need to call Crime Scene – these are knife wounds."

He straightened. "You guys got a camera?"

Nash, now somber, said, "No, sir, just the dashboard video." Deb Putnam shook her head.

Jenner found his T-shirt and pulled out his cell phone. He stood over the body and took photos to document the condition of the body.

Norris said, "You think he was killed, doc?"

Jenner ignored the question. "Do me a favor? Flip his shirt closed? He's way too bloated for it to fit, but I want to see how it would've looked when he was wearing it."

As Norris struggled to pull part of the shirt from under the body, Jenner stepped back to get an overall sense of the victim. The swelling made the body look like every other badly decomposed body, the bloated features round and generic, like an overinflated basketball.

The victim was a man, possibly heavyset, maybe five nine, five ten. Caucasian – at least, nothing left to suggest he was any other race. Whatever hair he'd had on his head had slipped off; the chin still had clumps of white stubble. An older man, then. The eyes were bulging and leathery, the irises ruddy brown – who knew what color his eyes had been in life?

The cuts on the chest were covered when Norris flapped the shirt closed around the man's torso. At first Jenner had assumed that the man had lost a knife fight, but his shirt had no holes – it had been open when the man was cut. Jenner nodded, and Norris flapped the shirt open again.

There were a dozen or so roughly parallel raking cuts on the chest, vertical to oblique, each one about eight to ten inches in length. The incisions were very clean, obviously made with a sharp blade; since they were of different lengths, it was clear that they'd been inflicted by multiple separate cuts of a single-bladed weapon. During their time under water they'd flared open, and the bases of the wounds were bloodless and pale, filmy like some weird white algae. None of the cuts looked deep.

The furthest-right wound was different: it descended along the victim's flank as a straight line, but just above his hip it curved off suddenly toward his back, leaving a pattern of scrapes interrupted by fine parallel lines. The knife would've been big, with a regular cutting edge on the lower side of the blade and alternating serrated and smooth sections on the upper. It had to be some kind of Rambo weapon, but the wounds it had inflicted were unusual, even for a survival knife. One thing was certain: if Jenner ever saw the blade, he'd recognize it instantly.

Jenner tipped the head back; it moved freely, almost as if hinged, to expose a yawning slash across the upper throat.

He heard Deb Putnam murmur, "Christ . . ."

He turned to her. "You okay?"

She nodded quickly, slightly irritated at the question.

Jenner looked down at the neck. "The poor bastard – it looks like they tortured him, then cut his throat."

Norris called over to Nash, who was by the patrol car, talking on the radio. "What's the ETA on Crime Scene?"

"At least an hour – they're all the way over near Dade, processing a burglary."

"Tell them to move it – we got a Signal 7."

Jenner turned out the victim's shorts pockets – empty, no wallet, no ID. No defensive injuries on the hands – most likely he'd been incapacitated somehow, bound or restrained in some other way. The legs and feet were also unremarkable.

A low, stuttering snore welled up behind Jenner. The tow-truck driver had draped a sheet between the roof of his rig and its open door; he was napping under his canopy, his tan calves and sneaker-clad feet sticking horizontally out of the cab.

Jenner felt a fleck of water against his cheek and looked up. It had grown darker, and the breeze was picking up. On the far side of the canal, over the Glades, the sky was a bruised purple-black, and the bare trunks of battered cypress trees, lit by the western sun, were bone white over the brilliant green sawgrass.

"Nash, tell Crime Scene they can just do the basics out here – we'll take the whole car back to the M.E. Office and examine it there."

The rain wouldn't destroy anything that the river hadn't already taken care of. Fishermen were constantly using the feeder road, and, because it was summer, it rained every afternoon; judging from the victim's degree of decomposition, the vehicle had been in the water for a couple of weeks, so any relevant tire-mark evidence was long gone from the road.

A quick glance inside the car told Jenner nothing. A coffee cup and some pieces of white paper floated in the flooded footwells, but there was no obvious weapon, no bindings, no bloodstains – nothing but the sweet, dank odor of decay and oily black mud.

Norris was shaking the driver awake, Nash was still on the radio. Jenner peered again into the back seat: nothing there except a broad sheet of sloughed skin, curling like used carbon paper stuck to the driver's headrest.

Jenner started toward the cruiser, then stopped and leaned into the driver's compartment to press the trunk lock.

The first spatters of warm rain were tapping the trunk lid as he popped it open.

The body of a woman was stuffed inside the trunk. She was an older woman, probably Caucasian, with straight white hair, her dark, bloated flesh strained against the taut clothes and the loops of duct tape that bound her. Jenner caught a glint and looked closer: spilling out of her filthy brown shirt was a fine necklace. He reached into the trunk to lift the chain. A pendant hung from it, an elegant platinum fish hook, a gleaming diamond hiding the barb.

Jenner stepped back and sank to his heels, hands to his head, oblivious to the staring deputies and the ranger and the gawking tow-truck driver. Oblivious to the sheeting rain.

5

Adam Weiss was thinking: This is bullshit. This guy is lying to me. He's telling me this story because he wants money.

The man wasn't in front of him just then: a couple of minutes earlier, he'd stood abruptly and stumbled quickly to the restroom, and now Adam could hear him puking. The man was puking because he was drunk, very drunk. No, more than drunk: this guy was *high* – coke or speed, one of the two. The man had to be coked out of his gourd to be telling him this story, to've been snorting speed for days to get this fucked-up, this fucking paranoid, this fucking out of his mind . . .

What was Adam supposed to do with that story?

He looked around the sorry excuse for an office – a desk, a desk chair, two battered armchairs salvaged from God knew where, all crammed into one end of a double-wide so decrepit that it made the chairs look fancy. Behind the desk, a stand fan feebly stirred a big wall poster showing farm workers striding bravely across the fields, arms linked in proud solidarity.

From the bathroom the heaves and choking gasps reached a crescendo that rose over the roar of rain pounding the corrugated roof.

Christ. Why the hell did this have to happen when Ricky, his supervisor and the founder of the Workers' Solidarity Movement, was away?

Adam looked at the generic Commie worker poster again, and wondered if the socialist propaganda meant anything at all to the workers who attended the meetings. When Adam addressed them he felt completely ridiculous – a rich twenty-two-year-old summer intern from Barnard, standing in front of a few exhausted field hands, urging them on to unionization and freedom. The workers actually stood and cheered when Ricky spoke; to Adam, the applause of five or six men sounded tinny and feeble in the shabby trailer.

He fought a sudden urge to run out of the trailer, to get on his bike and pedal. What the hell was he still doing here? Leave the drunk *campesino* to the toilet – it'd probably be less embarrassing for the man! Adam would just head home to his little shack in Bel Arbre. It'd take him twenty minutes, tops, twenty minutes and he'd be home and dry. He'd play videogames on his laptop, then text with Tiffany Coen.

It was Tiff's fault that he was even in that fucking dump; he'd thought he'd impress her by getting a hard-core fieldwork internship, but when he told her that he was spending the summer in Florida organizing migrant farmers she'd dismissed it as some romantic ego trip, and said that she and Andy Willet were actually helping to *change* immigration policy. So now Andy and Tiff were working for a plush PAC in DC – cocktails in a different embassy every night – while Adam was stuck in the middle of a fucking monsoon, listening to some Mexican or Guatemalan or something spew his guts out in the shitty bathroom of the shitty trailer.

God, he was so fucking far out of his motherfucking depth. What could he do? Surely it was money, the guy just wanted some money . . .

But he hadn't asked for money.

What do you do when an anonymous farm worker staggers into your aid office and tells you that at one of the estates, if you screw up, the foremen take you out into the Glades and shoot you in the head? That they record your execution on video to show new workers so they get the picture?

It was insane, it was *insane*! What the hell can you screw up so badly that they kill you?

Drugs. Oh, Christ, Adam thought. It's drugs. It has to be drugs.

He suddenly realized that the vomiting had stopped.

He waited.

Silence.

He looked toward the bathroom and called out, "*Señor? Que tal?*"

No answer.

Shit. He pushed himself slowly to his feet, the creak of the floor suddenly loud in his head.

What if the guy had died, just keeled over from the coke and the drink?

But he would've heard something.

Adam didn't want to have to deal with this.

Then he started thinking: If this was drugs, if there really were men willing to kill workers just as a warning, these men would be vigilant. They would watch their employees like vultures, waiting for them to slip up. And this guy had just slipped up big time.

Adam pushed the door to the hallway open gently. Light in the bathroom peeked through the crack in the frame. Something behind the bathroom door was clattering and banging, the sound loud and arrhythmic.

He took a step closer, then tapped on the door.

"*Señor?*"

Silence.

He rapped harder; maybe the man hadn't heard his knocking above the sound of the rain and the hollow banging.

"*Señor?*"

There was no sound other than the rain and the clattering. Adam had no choice: he grasped the doorknob, and pushed.

The door swung open slowly to reveal an empty bathroom, rain pouring through the open window, the wind smacking the window and storm shade against the frame. Adam saw the boot mark that the man had left on the toilet seat when he pushed himself through the window and out into the night.

The rain soaked him briefly as he pulled the window shut. As he went back to his office he realized he was trembling.

If the man was so scared he'd climb out a window rather than leave through the front door, it meant that he thought he'd been followed. That the man thought these men, these killers, were watching him and waiting for him.

And he'd led them straight to Adam.

6

It was well after dark when Nash drove the patrol car past the municipal building to enter the back morgue entrance. The barrier lifted, and as the headlights raked the parking lot Jenner saw a crowd in front of the garage. Word had spread through the building, through the sheriff's department, the fire department and emergency medical services: despite the hour, many people stood silhouetted in the municipal building windows, and at the mortuary the entire staff was waiting for the Roburns in the bucketing rain. They huddled under the eaves in their yellow county rain slickers, some brightly lit by the parking-area floodlights, others near-invisible in the shadows. Several held glowing white candles; the candles kept dying, snuffed out by the rain and the wind despite makeshift paper-cup shields.

Jenner got out and stood uncertainly, shivering in his wet T-shirt and shorts. A bulky male figure in a dark poncho detached himself from the group and ran to him, the umbrella he held opening with a pop. Richard Flanagan, the morgue director, held the umbrella up, threw a bearlike arm around Jenner's shoulder and walked him toward the garage. As Jenner approached he saw that many of those waiting were crying.

There was a loud buzz to his right and the security gates at the main entrance ground open slowly, revealing the hulking shadow of the tow truck in a fizzing halo of light and rain.

As the truck crept into the lot people moved out to greet it, singly and in forlorn little clumps, letting the truck pass so they could gather around the towed car.

Several reached out to press their fingers to the bodywork; Jenner didn't have the heart to stop them until Norris muttered, "Doc, should they be doing that?"

Jenner shook his head and moved forward, calling, "I'm sorry . . . We can't . . . Please don't touch the car . . . We have to think of it as a crime scene."

Jenner felt a tap at his shoulder: Flanagan, back with his umbrella, now holding a dry scrub suit.

"Doc, c'mon, you better change. You're soaked – go inside, dry off, put these on. We'll look after Mrs. R." He looked at his colleagues standing mutely around the car in the rain and shook his head. "You know when they're bringing in Doc Roburn?"

As if on cue, the garage walls began to flicker blue as the ambulance carrying Marty Roburn's body rolled through the gate, hazard lights flashing, behind it a column of patrol cars, the blue and white turret lights revolving silently. Behind the police cars Jenner saw a long string of civilian vehicles stretching out, a ragged cortège of cars and trucks, SUVs, even motorcycles, all with headlights blazing, a staggered line of brilliant white light puncturing the dark and the rain.

The back doors of the ambulance swung open and two morgue techs climbed up, motioning aside the para-medics so they could take Roburn down themselves. They rechecked the belts securing his body bag, then eased the gurney back, unfolded the rear strut and let the wheels take his weight before extending the front strut.

They wheeled the body past the line of employees to the morgue entrance, then stopped in front of Flanagan.

"Doc, if it's OK we'd like to offer up a few words in prayer for the Roburns."

Jenner nodded. The morgue staff, now joined by a motley group of deputies and civilians, gathered around the gurney as Flanagan opened his arms wide, looked up through the rain, and said, "Father, we beseech you, look after our good friend Doctor Martin Roburn and his beloved wife Roberta. Thank you for blessing us by sending him to us. I know I speak for everyone here when I say that he was the best of the best. He was a father to many, and a friend to all, and we're going to miss him."

Jenner was listening to the sound, the loud *pack! pack! pack!* of raindrops smacking into the stiff black plastic of Roburn's body bag.

Flanagan paused, then looked at Jenner. "And thank you for sending us Doctor Edward Jenner from New York City. We know he's a good man, and a good pathologist. We ask you to guide his hand as he investigates the tragic killing of our friend and brother Doctor Martin Roburn."

There was some head-nodding in the crowd, and some amens, and then Jenner realized that they were all looking at him.

7

The deputy sat inside the car, watching them move the bodies into the morgue. He'd figured it would've taken them longer to find them.

It was funny how a life changed. You start out with the best intentions, wanting to help people just get along, live peaceful lives, free of fear, free of violence. Then life gets complicated. You buy a house, get a mortgage, have to make payments each month. You meet a girl, and you marry her, and you have kids.

But she falls in the kitchen and injures her back, and needs therapy and pain meds, and soon she doesn't like to get up too much, but now she needs pain meds just to lie in bed and watch TV. And your kids go to school, and it's a public school in a good district, but they need clothes, and they grow so quick. And the $50,000 a year that you're making as a cop suddenly doesn't go as far as it should.

But you go on busting bad guys, laying down the law, carting lowlifes off to jail. You are not one of them, you are better than they are. One day you bust some scumbag coke dealer and he has a brown paper bag with $25,000 in hundreds in it, old, new, worn, intact, just thousands and thousands of dollars in hundreds. And he says take it, just take it and let him go. And you need a new roof, and a new water heater, and the boy's birthday is in a week, and that money would let you breathe for a second, just a second, help you get your head above water.

But you say no. And you arrest him, because he's a scumbag and you're the law.

But now it's different. You know it's out there, that little brown paper bag or one just like it, that one-inch-thick wad of untraceable hundred-dollar bills. Or one just like it. You coulda had it, but you said no.

But it's still out there.

And things don't get better. The real-estate market tanks, and you can't sell the house, and you can't afford to fix the roof. Your wife is drinking, but not as much as your thirteen-year-old. He's dropping out of high school, but you're not there because you're working overtime to save up for the roofing, doing details, working security at the parties of the rich, or guarding convicts as they edge the lawns on the Port Fontaine Polo Club driveway as part of some political back-scratching program. And you sit there watching blonde high school girls go past, driving German sports cars that cost as much as your house, laughing and tan and carefree.

And your wife is now a sucking hole of need, a festering ulcer in your bed, and as you lie next to her you want to gnaw off your arm, hack it off, anything to escape, you want to be parked off the sand at Grand Turtle Beach, slipping the bra off that sixteen-year-old blonde in the back of her Mercedes convertible, breathing in the smell of million-dollar perfume on her neck as you slide aside those silk panties and start fingerfucking that rich little pussy.

And you discover that busting bad guys is like watching the tide – they just keep coming, sliding in, going down, always more mopes to take down. And the funny thing is that you get to know them, you see they have families, people who care about them. And one day you realize they're just like you – screwing up their lives trying to make a fucking buck, trying to make enough to keep their own heads above water. And it occurs to you that the problem is the scumbag customers: dealers just give the customer what he asks for, a product that in some countries isn't even illegal anymore. You've learned that the users will *always* find drugs, and if they can't buy from one scumbag then they'll buy from another. And you finally understand your life is some picayune shit, measuring out the ocean with an eyedropper.

And then one day someone offers you a thousand dollars; you don't have to do anything, you just have to not be somewhere. All you need to do is make sure your patrol route doesn't take you past a particular intersection during a particular hour.

And this time you say yes.

And after that it's all over.

He picked up the cell phone; it still had another eighteen minutes' credit before he had to chuck it. He answered on the second ring.

"They found the car in the canal and identified the body."

He listened.

"Yeah, I know it was fast. The new medical examiner recognized the wife's jewelry."

He shook his head.

"No, they did. But she was wearing a small necklace, and I guess they missed it."

The parking lot was mostly empty, now. As the cars began to trickle out of the lot the radar gun mounted on the dash sporadically flashed the speeds – 7, 12, 8 – the digits splashing pale green light on his face.

The deputy shook his head firmly. "He's sharp – we need to be careful with this one. You still have people inside, don't you? Well, tell them to keep a close eye on him."

He hung up. Sixteen more minutes and this phone would be history. Fuck it, he should just trash it now, pick up the next one.

What he was doing wasn't so bad – it was just information.

The rain picked up again, and the last of the mourners scurried in to shelter. The deputy liked the sound of the rain on the car, liked being quiet and dry while it poured down around him. Tonight he'd lie awake in bed a long while, listening to the sound of the rain drumming against the terra-cotta tiles that covered his beautiful new roof.

8

Jenner had asked all staff other than Flanagan, and Bunny Rutledge and Calvin Major, the mortuary technicians who'd be assisting him, to leave the morgue area. He followed the employees out of the autopsy room, crossing the breezeway into the main office facility so that he could change into his scrubs.

Marie Carter, the office manager, put up a fresh pot of coffee in the break room, then disappeared, returning a short while later with four dozen doughnuts from the Dunkin' Donuts on Country Club Road. Bucky Rutledge, another technician and Bunny's twin brother, arrived with an almost full bottle of Jack Daniels. He set up at the opposite end of the room to Marie, with the bottle of Jack and a line of mugs swiped from the sink.

When Jenner got back to the autopsy suite Flanagan was prepping the table while Bunny and Calvin positioned Marty's body for photographs. As the Crime Scene technician photographed the unclothed body, Calvin hung Roburn's shirt and slacks in the drying cupboard. Then Flanagan wheeled the body into the radiography suite to X-ray the head and chest. Jenner asked him to do dental films, too – with both Roburn and his wife dead, a legal identification could be tricky. Visual identification wasn't an option – Jenner had seen Roburn alive barely a fortnight before, and hadn't recognized his corpse. There was no ID on Roburn's body – no wallet, no cash; the fish-hook necklace had either been removed or been lost in the water.

As Bunny rolled the body Jenner noticed an area of discoloration on the right buttock; he wiped the deteriorating skin, and the top layer slipped off to reveal an orange and green tattoo of a white ibis with a football, pristine in the underlying dermis. It was the University of Miami Hurricanes logo, from Marty Roburn's alma mater.

Jenner helped support the body as the tech photographed the tattoo. Flanagan said, "Yep, that's Doc Roburn, all right." The techs all nodded in agreement.

Flanagan murmured sadly, "Sebastian the ibis", and the techs nodded again.

"You've seen it before?"

Flanagan shook his head. "Hell, no! But Doc Roburn was nuts about the 'Canes." He shook his head. "It's him."

Jenner said, "Yeah. Well, we'll do the dentals anyway, nail it shut."

"Of course, doc – everything for Doctor R. Both him and the missus went to Dr. El-Bashir – he's our odontologist. I'll give him a call in the morning, and I bet he'll walk the dentals over himself. Heck, he'll be pounding down our door as soon as he hears."

The three lifted Roburn's body onto the autopsy table. The corpse's size and condition made its difficult to hold, and when they eased it flat the body started to slip off the sides of the autopsy table. They were still placing support blocks to secure the corpse on the table when the door flew open.

40

A thickset, heavily freckled blond man, maybe forty years old, strode over to the table and stood there swaying. He jabbed a finger at the body and said, "Is it him? Is it really Roburn?"

Jenner said, "Who are you?"

"I'm Tom Anders. Sheriff Tom Anders . . ." He looked Jenner up and down, then added, "Your boss." He gestured impatiently toward the body. "Is it really him?"

Jenner could smell the alcohol.

"We need to confirm with dental in the morning but, yes, I think it's Dr. Roburn."

"Oh, Jesus Christ!" Anders looked around wildly, struggling to focus, then blurted, "I *liked* that old guy . . ."

He was leaning against the cabinets, breathing fast. Jenner turned to Flanagan and raised an eyebrow; Flanagan shrugged.

Jenner said, "Sheriff, you don't have to stay for this – I can stop by your office first thing in the morning to discuss my findings."

In a heartbeat, Anders's gaze shifted from dazed to suspicious, his eyes like teeny ball bearings in his chubby baby face.

"No! I'll stay! I want to stay." He looked around the room, spotted a stainless steel stool, and pointed at it. "I'll be right there, out of your way. No need to worry about me, Mr. Jenner! I'll be right there . . ."

He walked carefully towards the stool, then sat down hard and slumped back against the drying cupboard. Jenner was pretty sure he'd pass out soon.

When they were back at the table, Jenner muttered to Flanagan, "Rich, we've got to get this clown out of here.

A guy that big, if he slips and hits his head, we'll be mopping up blood for hours; I don't need the hassle tonight. Anyone we can call to get rid of him?"

The morgue director thought for a second, stroking his moustache. "Well, none of the deputies – he scares the crap right out of them. Maybe Detective Rudge? He's out in the loading area, talking with Crime Scene."

"Okay, good. Can you take care of that?"

Flanagan nodded and left the room.

Jenner looked over to the techs. "Bunny, Calvin? I'm about ready to start the autopsy. Are you okay with this? If you don't want to stay, that's all right, I can manage."

Calvin said, "We want to see it through, doc."

Jenner nodded.

He turned, stood directly in front of Marty's body, scalpel in his hand.

How he was supposed to feel? He knew pathologists who said you could do no higher honor to an old colleague than to perform his autopsy, but he'd always thought that was affected bullshit – he would choose for his friends what he'd choose for himself: leave my body alone. Just burn it, scatter my ashes somewhere I loved. Don't cut me up, and don't put me in the fucking dirt to rot.

But there he was, about to cut right into the heart of a man he had loved – his mentor, his friend. The only person who'd helped Jenner, when things were bad, when everyone was talking about just how badly he had fucked up.

He felt a nudge at his elbow and turned to see Bunny. Behind the face shield her eyes were pink and puffy.

"Doc, you okay? You think maybe you should take a break?"

He shook his head. "No, I'm okay."

He looked at Roburn's body.

He was my friend.

But that wasn't true anymore, was it? This wasn't Marty, this was some spongy, rotted husk that had once been wrapped around his spirit. Christ, the bloated form on the table looked barely human . . .

No, this wasn't Marty Roburn: Marty had left the building long ago, and what lay festering on the autopsy table was nothing but evidence. And Jenner would read the evidence and document the information perfectly.

He smiled at the technician. "I'm fine, thanks, Bunny. How about you? You really sure you don't want to wait in the break room?"

"No, doc. I'm with you here."

She was crying. Jenner looked away.

In the corner, Sheriff Anders began to snore. In his pale blue Lacoste tennis sweater and pink Polo Grounds shirt he looked like a big three-year-old dozing off after a busy day playing with toy trucks.

Jenner turned to Bunny and grinned, and she began to giggle, the tears streaking down to her mask.

Jenner looked down, shut his eyes tight for a second, and then made his opening incision.

He would get whoever did this, get them if it was the last act of his whole fucking disaster of a career.

9

Cause of death wasn't an issue – anyone could see that Roburn's throat had been cut with ruthless efficiency, the blade slicing cleanly through the carotid arteries and jugular veins, even severing the windpipe from the Adam's apple. This would have been the final injury, the *coup de grâce*.

And Marty would have needed a *coup de grâce*: he had been tortured systematically – long, shallow cuts had been made into his chest, carefully and methodically inflicted. Since the wounds were roughly parallel, Jenner could tell that Marty hadn't moved much during or between each injury; he'd have been restrained, either with bindings or by force. He'd have bled more with each cut, and anyone holding him would've got bloody, so Jenner figured that they'd probably bound him.

Jenner made incisions to explore the wrists and forearms; there was no evidence of a ligature, but a soft or broad ligature could leave no marks.

Flanagan showed up in the doorway.

"Doc, Detective Rudge from Major Crimes."

Jenner had heard about David Rudge; everyone in Port Fontaine apparently thought that Rudge walked on water – sharp, driven, stellar arrest record, the sort of guy who could nail down the truth in seven questions. Jenner knew enough to take police legends with a grain of salt, but Roburn had said that if he ever had trouble he should find Rudge. And Marty had been a good judge of people.

In person, though, Rudge was hardly the All-American Brylcreem-and-Vitalis jock that Jenner had imagined. Rather, he seemed like a man on the cusp of undistinguished middle age, gently pear-shaped, with a shabby gray suit and a grubby white shirt. The expanse of shirt that covered the slope of his belly was dotted with droplets of what appeared to be ketchup, and his tie hung loosely; apparently Rudge didn't believe in wasting a decent knot when a tie could be easily slipped off over the head and put back on the next day with minimum fuss.

The other surprise was that he was black – Jenner had just assumed that an African-American wouldn't have reached that position in the South. No one talking about Rudge had ever hinted at his race – score zero for Yankee stereotypes of what life was like below the Mason-Dixon line, he thought: this was the New South, not the TV South.

Whatever his expectations of Rudge had been, the moment the detective looked at the body Jenner knew he was the real deal. Rudge stood in the doorway, nodding absently at Jenner while staring at Roburn's body; it reminded Jenner of one of those Fifties sci-fi movies where the alien robot scans an earth object – a car, maybe, or a dog – its gaze tracking in a beam over the body, centimeter by centimeter, measuring, gauging, analyzing.

He stepped back so that Rudge could get a better view.

The detective came closer, shaking his head. "So, what, you think they tortured him, then cut his throat?"

Jenner nodded. "Yes."

"Shit." Rudge shook his head sadly. His lip curled. "Nuh-uh." He paused, then shook his head again. "That ain't right."

Jenner nodded again.

Rudge looked at the incised wrists and forearms. "Did they tie him up?"

"I can't see anything, but I think they probably bound him, yes."

"And Mrs. Roburn?"

Jenner stepped back and tore off his plastic gown. "She's in the X-ray room. We can look at her now."

His face solemn, Rudge followed Jenner down the hall.

Bobbie Roburn lay on a gurney next to the X-ray table, clothes and duct tape bindings undisturbed. Decompositional swelling had stretched her clothes tight, her body bulging through the mesh of silver tape. Her blouse was stained with purge fluid but there was no blood, and Jenner found no hole or slashes in the clothes, nothing to suggest a stabbing.

Her wrists were taped in front of her – whoever had bound her had felt she'd posed little threat. They'd wrapped the tape in loops that completely encircled her torso, securing her arms to her sides. Her ankles were taped together, and her thighs and knees.

Jenner put on gloves and reached for the gag.

"Doc, want me to get the photographer?"

"We've already taken over-alls."

He focused on the gag. The duct tape wound between the lips and around the head, but they'd left her nostrils exposed.

Jenner cut the tape with scissors where it passed behind Bobbie's ear, then peeled it up carefully from her hair, gradually rolling it around to where it entered her mouth. Here, he gently opened her lips and slipped the tape out of her mouth; there was nothing stuffed inside the oral cavity. He hung the tape in the drying cupboard with clothes pegs; the way it had been applied seemed pretty random, without any particular elaborate pattern. He looked the tape over carefully but could find no hairs or fibers; the Crime Lab might still be able to recover fingerprints or DNA.

He opened the mouth wider, tilted the head to examine her neck. There were no injuries of the mouth, no bruising or cuts on the lips. No visible hemorrhages in the bulging eyes. Bobbie's neck was clean, free of any obvious injury.

"Christ."

Rudge took a photo of the neck, then looked at him. "What is it, doc? Find something?"

"No, the opposite: there's no injury at all."

Rudge wrinkled his brow.

"So how did she die? You think . . ."

Jenner tore off his gloves and said, "I think they just fucking threw her in the trunk and let her drown."

10

Jenner walked out into the steel-gray morning, blinking in the bright haze. Barely eight a.m. and he couldn't believe the humidity – stepping out of the air conditioning was like being immediately wrapped in a heavy wet wool sweater.

The patio was empty. He sat at the picnic table with his vending-machine breakfast – a can of Coke and a Snickers bar – and stared vacantly at the puddle-splashed lot as he ate. There was still a handful of cars in

47

the lot, probably belonging to people who'd worked for Marty since the beginning – Jenner had avoided the break room after the autopsies. Rudge had left around four a.m., waking the now-docile sheriff to drive him home.

Jenner's eyes burned; they kept tearing up. He told himself it was just the fatigue. His back muscles were buckled up tight, and every bone in his body throbbed. The highest-profile double homicide in Douglas county history . . .

His friend.

He had just autopsied his friend. He wiped the sweat from his forehead, rested his elbows on the picnic table, then sank his head into his hands and began to cry. He struggled to stop the tears, to still the shaking of his shoulders. He propped his elbows on the table top, then pressed his face firmly into his open palms, tried to be less obvious.

He gave up, and let the tears flow. His friend was dead.

There was the clack of an opening door; Jenner looked up, but the door had already shut again.

He pulled himself together. He was finished now, done. He'd labeled the clothes and hung them in the drying closets, completed the autopsy notes and wound diagrams, put the blood and tissue samples in the refrigerator, dictated both cases for transcription, readied the death certificates for signing as soon as the dentist confirmed the ID.

He should go home, back to the motel – he could feel his body coming apart from lack of sleep, the muscles raw and ragged, about to pop, the bones on the point of shattering.

Jenner washed down the chocolate bar with another acid blast of lukewarm Coke, wiped his damp face, then glanced around to make sure the coast was clear. He forced himself to his feet, then stood with his hands on his hips, leaning slightly backwards to stretch.

He heard steps on the gravel behind him and turned to see Marie Carter, the office manager, pale, eyes puffy, clutching her black cardigan to her body as if the temperature were in the forties instead of the high eighties.

"Doctor . . . is it true? I heard that Bobbie . . . drowned?"

Jenner nodded.

"And Bucky Rutledge is saying that Doctor R was tortured."

"Yes. I'm afraid that's true, too."

He thought Marie was going to cry, but she just nodded and said, "I'm glad I caught you, doctor. I was able to reach Sheree Roburn, the daughter; she'll be here tomorrow. And Detective Rudge left you a message early this morning, but said I should wait until you'd finished the cases before I disturbed you. When you have a second, can you give him a call to discuss your findings, please?"

"Sure."

"The number's on your desk." Mazie hesitated a second, then said, "And Doctor Jenner?"

"Yes?"

"You should go home and get some sleep."

11

Adam Weiss leaned back against the tree, his ear still warm from the cell phone.

How *could* she? Tiff knew damn well what she meant to him; didn't they have an (unspoken) agreement that they'd be faithful over the summer? He'd known there'd be temptations – more for Tiffany, in DC, with its clubs and bars, while he was out in the middle of some stinking fields, knee deep in cow shit, ministering to a bunch of fucking wetbacks. But still – that she'd do it after less than a month?

And with *Andy Willet*? It didn't make any sense at all!

Maybe if Adam hadn't picked up, if Tiff had had more time to think about it, she'd have realized it was just some dumb mistake. After all, they'd been to an embassy party, then fucking Willet had taken her out to a club with some of his other embassy buddies, and somehow, miraculously, they'd ended up at Andy's place, with Tiff too drunk and tired to get in a cab, too drunk to offer any resistance as Andy's fat fingers dropped the zip on her Zac Posen party dress.

And what was killing Adam – no, really, just *killing* him – was that she sounded happy. She'd called him at 10:30 a.m. on a Sunday, sounding happy, to say that she'd just fucked Andy Willet, and that Adam was the only person she could tell. What the hell was she even thinking?

The line at the taco stand was shorter now. Adam looked to see that his bike was still okay over against the tree. He was behind a couple of Guatemalans, next to a battered hand-lettered sign that read *Desayuno Mexicano:*

Papas con Chorizo $1 then, in English, *Brkfst Tacos $1 ea.*

Tiffany had picked up on Adam's silence, had tried to prod him into a response, but he'd remained stoic and mute. Finally she'd said she just didn't understand him, she'd thought he'd be happy for her because he knew how much she liked Andy (that last bit just about blew his mind). Then she'd hurried off the phone, saying, "Okay, talk later, buddy," hanging up before he could think of a smart or cutting reply.

Then it occurred to him: she was probably still drunk! It was 10:30 a.m. now, they'd probably got in maybe 3:30 or four a.m., some drunken fumbling, then the Act, fall asleep at five a.m., wake up at 9:30 a.m. for her little Walk of Shame . . . Yes, she could very well still be drunk.

The thought buoyed Adam and, by the time he'd pedaled back to his little white clapboard box on the north side of Bel Arbre, he was imagining how their make-up conversation would go that night. She'd cry and say she was sorry, and he would be cool at first, but eventually would give in and tell her it wasn't her fault – she'd been drunk, she hadn't known what she was doing. Tell her to tell Andy fucking Willet that the next time Adam saw him on campus he was going to beat the crap out of him.

He stopped.

Someone had smashed in his door. The flimsy slab of fiberboard hung lopsided, buckled around the doorknob by multiple kicks, canting steeply into his living room.

The events of the night before – the fucked-up *campesino* who'd disappeared into the storm, the fears he'd laughed off when he woke safe and sound in his own bed – all came flooding back.

They'd come for him.

Too late, he heard the soft clink of the gate behind him, turned to see two stone-faced men blocking the path. One held up an arm and motioned Adam forward, gesturing into the shadow of the doorway, the house now a ghastly white face, the door a mouth gaping to swallow Adam whole.

The man pointed into the shack again. He had a cane machete at his hip, a long, wicked blade, curved on one side, gaping saw teeth on the other.

Adam did as he was told.

12

Jenner sent his Fontaine Burger Shack Special back twice. The first burger had been overdone, the second drowning in fake orange cheese, despite him specifically saying that he didn't want cheese on the burger. The manager delivered the third himself, with an air of finality.

"I hope you'll find this to your satisfaction now, sir . . ."

He stood over Jenner, a plump man with thinning gray hair plastered to his scalp.

Jenner took a bite; it was like swallowing packing material.

"Fine, thanks."

The manager nodded curtly, then headed to the hostess stand to sort out the traffic jam at the register.

Though it was still late afternoon, the storm had turned the world outside black. A stab of lightning lit the bare trunks of cypresses beyond the parking lot; through the curtain of rain, Jenner saw a young man and woman running hand in hand across the lot to the shelter of the awning, laughing. He watched them enter the restaurant, watched the way the woman swept the raindrops from her hair, the way the man's hand casually pressed her wet white shirt against the skin of her back. They were in their late twenties – a fairly new couple, he guessed. He watched the hostess lead them to the best table, watched the way their fingers lingered entwined for a while before they separated to sit.

The wind picked up and spattered the rain against his window.

Jenner looked down at his book; he'd started *The Kite Runner* the week before but was getting nowhere with it. The police shrink he'd seen after he'd killed Farrar had told him that he might have difficulty concentrating.

The notion irritated him. He had no regrets about killing Farrar. He'd had no choice – he'd killed the man to save Ana de Jong, to save his own life. Besides, Farrar was barely a man: he was something bestial, the Inquisitor, a compulsive predator who'd killed many. Not a man but a monster who would have continued to kill. Jenner had done the world a favor.

"Even so," the shrink had said. Jenner remembered the slow, deep tock . . . tock . . . tock . . . of the pendulum of the grandfather clock in the office. "Even so, you may find you punish yourself for your actions."

He'd paused for a second to polish his glasses, then added: "It doesn't matter that you know you did what was right. The thing is, Jenner, the heart speaks louder than the mind."

The heart speaks louder than the mind.

Fatigue washed through Jenner in waves – his eyes burned, his shoulders ached.

He looked around the room. Families, mostly young, with kids. And couples. Mostly young, kids on the way in the next year or two.

The manager stood at the register, the Fontaine Burger Shack Code made flesh, his maroon apron every bit as infested with pins, slogans, clips and tags as those of his teenage employees. He spoke with two girls and looked on as they recruited another girl and a boy and then lined up in front of a table that had two middle-aged couples and a pair of chubby kids sitting at it. The servers clapped and sang "Happy Anniversary" with manic enthusiasm. Afterwards, everyone in the restaurant applauded and cheered, and one of the men stood to announce that it was their twentieth anniversary. There were more cheers, and the manager sent over a free order of chicken nachos, giving a jolly little wave when the couples toasted him with their umbrella drinks.

On the jukebox, Bo Diddley died away and was replaced by Buddy Holly tremoloing "Not Fade Away". There was a bright flash of lightning, and an almost immediate ear-splitting crash. Several diners screamed; the lights dimmed for a second, then came back up to sheepish laughter. The jukebox fell silent as it rebooted.

The manager went out to the parking lot to investigate. As he opened the door, there was a blast of hot wet air and Jenner saw palm trees, brilliantly illuminated by the awning's spotlights, swishing wildly in the torrential rain.

"Are you still eating? Anything else I can get for you?"

Jenner looked up at the server, then down at his burger. He shook his head.

"Just the check, please."

"If you'd like, I can package it up so you can take it with you."

"No, thanks. I'm good." He leaned back and stretched stiffly.

The server cleared the table, then disappeared. Jenner pulled out his wallet, stretched it wide open.

Eight dollars.

Christ. He had just a few hundred left in his bank account. The county needed two full pay periods before Personnel could let him have his wages; he'd get his first Douglas County money on Thursday. He placed his MasterCard on the check folder. Perhaps he should call Jun or Douggie in New York, borrow a little cash, just as a cushion – in a fortnight, paying for the motel and the rental car would just about wipe him out again.

He tried to think of ways to economize – a smaller car, maybe. There wasn't a cheaper motel in Port Fontaine, but if he drove up the coast a bit . . .

The manager said, "Sir, there seems to be a problem." His barbershop-quartet-style striped shirt was soaked over the front and shoulders, and raindrops beaded on his pale face.

"A problem?"

"I'm afraid your card was declined." He looked Jenner up and down, at the flat wallet on the table in front of him.

Jenner said, "Could you run it again? There shouldn't be anything wrong with it."

"We tried three times, sir. Declined. This card is no good." The managere paused; he wasn't unsympathetic. "We also take Visa, American Express and Discover."

As Jenner fished out another card, his waiter reappeared and handed him a large package.

Jenner had been reunited with his burger, whether he wanted it or not.

In the parking lot he sat in his car and called Jun in New York on his cell phone; he left a message asking to borrow some money. Jun was a prodigy, a geek who'd made a fortune in software design while still at university in Tokyo; Jun could afford the loan.

13

Jenner's route home took him back through the heart of Port Fontaine. The town had been founded in the early 1900s by Ambrose Burmeister, a New York saloon keeper who'd fled Hell's Kitchen after the swill he peddled had blinded several customers. In Florida he promptly came down with malaria in the mangrove swamps along the southwestern coast; legend had it that the idea for Port Fontaine had come to him in a fever dream. Obsessed, Burmeister had refused transfer to a Miami hospital and instead had had his cot moved down to the beach. During his recovery, he would sit in the sand in a big wooden deck chair, his back to the bright blue waters of the Gulf of Mexico, drawing up plans on big sheets of butcher's paper, stopping his sketching only to hold a thumb up to the beachfront to gauge scale, or to shiver violently as the infection boiled in his blood.

With funding from a Chicago meat baron (an exile himself, after being caught canoodling with the mayor's nephew in the back of a brougham) Burmeister aggressively cleared the swamp along a mile-long swath of coast, diverting the brackish water into a series of ornamental canals and ponds. He planted beach grass and palms along the waterfront, where the beaches were covered in sand so white that he marketed it as "diamond dust" in his brochures. His instincts were spot on: the beach and one of the state's first golf courses quickly attracted a wave of affluent home-buyers. Members of the burgeoning middle class who couldn't quite afford Palm Beach swarmed to Port Fontaine. The rush of gold increased further after photographs of Rudolf Valentino and Nita Naldi lounging by the pool at Stella Maris, the Craine family mansion, appeared in *Photoplay* magazine in 1922.

Burmeister's first home, a solemn Beaux Arts box in marble and stone, sat among the pastel pink and green summer houses on the Promenade like a mausoleum in an amusement park. The mansion now housed the Port Fontaine Historical Society: giving Jenner a tour of the downtown historic district, Marty Roburn had joked that, while Port Fontaine didn't have much history, it had plenty of Society. That evening, sitting on the lanai with a cold Heineken in his hand, Marty had told Jenner of his astonishment during the days after 9/11, when waves of Lear jets had arrived at Port Fontaine's tiny airport, each plane belching out another Fortune 500 CEO, mobs of bold-faced names all fleeing to their estates in Douglas county. "They were like pashas, Jenner, each man richer than the next . . ." His voice had died away under the hiss of sprinklers outside the screens.

Jenner drove south on I-55, heading to the Palmetto Court. The highway sliced Port Fontaine in half along class lines, cutting off the Beaches to the west from the Reaches in the east. Burmeister's expansion east into the Everglades had been a constant battle against flooding, and where houses in the Beaches were stately and solid, the Reaches was made up of down-market housing developments built alongside waterways that, the joke went, flooded when the ambient humidity hit sixty-five percent.

Jenner had chosen a cottage away from the motel office, figuring it would be quieter. The motel was pretty torpid during the week, but on weekends it filled up with large groups of farm workers coming into town to blow off a little steam, ten to a room. The first Friday it happened, Jenner gave up on sleep at four a.m. and went to the twenty-four-hour Super Walmart for a break from the noise. He ate a muffin at the Dunkin' Donuts concession, then wandered the dazzling aisles of sporting goods, cut-price clothes and ammo, finally returning to the motel at seven a.m. By that point the revelry had died down, and all was quiet until the late morning; it was a bit like being back in New York.

He parked and climbed out of the car stiffly, ducking his head and cursing himself for not renting a car better suited to his height. After the storm, the air was cooler, soft and wet, sweet with the scent of damp grass. He reached into the car and pulled out his scene kit and the Fontaine Burger Shack leftovers.

Time for bed.

14

Jenner was woken by a loud bang from the lot behind his cottage. It was dark now.

Then another bang, then laughter. Great, he thought. Another night of beers and cheers.

Another bang, and then high yelping, and the laughter grew louder.

He pulled on a T-shirt and shorts, and stepped out onto his porch. He followed the sound around the corner of the walkway. The path led through a handful of rangy slash pines and down a slight slope to a cluster of four derelict honeymoon cottages.

Under the yellow light filtering through the trees from a high street lamp, Jenner took it all in. Three boys, mid-teens, their backs to him. A bottle of cheap whiskey. On the porch of a boarded-up cabin was an open Papa John's pizza box, a couple of slices remaining. Trembling in the shadows behind the porch railings was a squat barrel-shaped dog. Its fur was matted and dirty and its face looked like a funnel stuck on the end of the barrel.

Jenner slipped over the low concrete wall.

The dog began to creep along the porch towards the pizza. One of the boys was waiting for him, a large roofing shingle held ready by his side. When the dog crawled out from behind the railing, the boy wound his arm back and whipped the shingle at the dog with a snap of his wrist, hitting its flank and sending it yelping back to safety. The dog was half-visible in the shadows, shaking with fear and hunger.

Jenner stepped into the light. "Cut it out."

They turned, looking him up and down. The oldest one turned back to the porch.

The dog was hesitating. It started to edge forward, then looked around frantically at the boys, then at the pizza before it slunk back into the dark, whimpering.

The boy picked up another roofing shingle.

Jenner said, "I said: enough."

The boy, a wiry tow-headed kid in a polo shirt with a popped collar, turned, looked him up and down coolly, then said "Who are you? That your dog?" He was maybe seventeen.

Jenner shook his head. "No. I'm someone who doesn't like watching little assholes hurt animals."

"Then don't watch." The other two boys – his brothers, maybe – scurried away. The boy wagged the shingle, gauging its weight and spring, making practice wrist snaps.

The dog started to crawl toward the pizza again.

Jenner said, "Don't do it."

"Or else?"

"Or else I'll show you what it's like when something bigger than you picks on you."

The boy was uncertain now. "You wouldn't. I'd sue."

"I'd deny it." Jenner paused for a second, then said, "Or maybe I wouldn't: what do you think they'd do to me for smacking a – what are you? Five foot ten, a buck seventy-five? – for smacking some overgrown teenager for torturing a puppy? Courthouse in the Beaches, fill that jury with a bunch of nice dog-loving old ladies? They'd probably give me a medal."

The boy's face was sullen as he tried to figure Jenner out.

Jenner glanced at the dog, who was nearing the pizza, snuffling and whining. He didn't hear the footsteps on the soft earth behind him.

The boy's attitude changed. He'd been about to put the shingle down, but instead he straightened and raised it up.

Jenner sighed. "Your parents know you do this sort of shit?"

The boy smirked. "Ask him yourself!" He was looking behind Jenner.

Jenner turned just in time to see the fist flying at his head. The punch connected hard, and Jenner fell backwards, then rolled to scramble to his feet, shaking it off.

The man was in his early forties, in sweatpants and an oversized Nascar T-shirt, pretty far gone on the journey from muscle to flab. The father, his fists floating in front of him as he swayed from side to side. His breath reeked of booze.

"You mess with my boy, you mess with me . . ."

"I wasn't messing with your kid." Jenner rubbed his left cheek and eye gingerly, then gestured at the cabin. "Your boy was beating on that dog over there, and I told him to stop."

The man looked behind Jenner to the porch, where the dog was wolfing down the pizza.

"Dog looks fine to me. Anyways, it's a stray. If the cops came, they'd take it away and kill it – looks like it made out okay." He called to his son. "Don't worry, Mike buddy. You didn't do nothing wrong."

He looked at Jenner. "We clear on this? You got anything to say."

Jenner shrugged. "Not really. But if your kid touches

61

another of those shingles I'm going to bury my boot in his ass."

The man flushed, then started rolling up his sleeves, an angry grin on his face. "You want to get into it over a *dog*?"

Jenner shrugged again, then nodded. "I guess."

The man began to circle the clearing, Jenner following him, their stares locked. The boys moved back into the shadows. In the half-light their expressions were eager; they'd watched their father fight before. And if they looked eager it was because he always won.

The guy was big enough. Contractor? Roofer? Arms like that, had to be some sort of physical labor. But he was big, and he was drunk, and Jenner was counting on him being slow.

Jenner dropped his shoulders and waited for the attack. Six months ago, he would never have done this. But six months ago he'd almost lost his life because he was out of shape and not ready to fight. Things were different now. He ran now, ran most days. At home, he spent an hour a day at an old boxing gym off Canal Street, lifting weights and sparring. He worked the heavy bag and the speed bag until the sweat showered off him. He was strong, and he was fast. He was ready to fight.

No, more than ready: he *wanted* to fight. Marty and Bobbie, the baby-faced sheriff, too broke to pay at the diner – a fucking *diner*, for Christ's sake! And now these little creeps torturing some helpless stray. He wanted the fight. He didn't care if he won or lost, he just wanted to hit someone, to feel his fist smash into a jaw or an eye or a face.

The man lurched at him, arms flailing wildly, Jenner

blocking the glancing blows as he slipped aside, turning in time to get in a good slam to the side of the man's head. The man swayed back onto his heels, dazed for a second, then turned to Jenner, staggering back away from him as he struggled for balance.

Jenner dropped his guard and waited.

The man came at him again in a wobbling gust of acetone and sweat, and again Jenner stepped aside, hooking him hard in his doughy gut as he passed. The man dropped to his knees with an "Ouf!" and Jenner hit him hard in his face. He toppled backwards slowly and hit the ground.

Jenner stepped over him quickly. "Enough? Is that enough?"

The man's head rocked back and forth against the ground, and he held his hands to his face to try to stop the blood pouring freely from his nose.

"I . . . You broke it . . . You broke my nose!"

"We're done, right? This is finished, okay?" Jenner straightened up.

From behind him came the sound of children crying.

The man pulled himself up a bit, nodding. He raised his hand for help, and Jenner grabbed it with his left hand; his right was in agony, fire shooting from his knuckles to his elbow, a numb feeling across the side of his arm. He leaned back to pull the man to his feet, then stepped back, showing both his hands, empty palms forward. Jenner waited for the man's attack, but the guy's aggression was spent.

The oldest boy stepped up and slammed a two-by-four into Jenner's back. The corner caught the back of his head, and suddenly all three boys were on him, holding his arms, punching him, dragging him down, the father swaying on his feet as he watched.

Jenner was on the ground, the smallest boy biting his arm while the other two kicked him. He grabbed the youngest, spun him away, and fought to stand, the middle kid dangling from his shoulders, when there was a loud WHOOP! and the clearing filled with flashing blue and white light.

There was a shriek of electronic feedback, then a disembodied voice crackled, "Get that fucking kid off that man now!"

They all stood frozen, lit up in the glare of the cruiser's spotlight. Then came another siren whoop, and the father lumbered forward to drag his son off Jenner's neck.

"All of you, stay where you are!"

Peering into the dark, Jenner saw the car door swing open. Then the Weeble-like figure of Detective Rudge moved smoothly across the flood of high-beams and descended into the clearing.

Rudge said, "Mike Keener, you old son of a gun! Please behold my astonishment as our paths cross yet again! And Mike Junior? Always good to see you . . ."

He glanced at the other boys. "Hmm. This is a first . . ."

He shook his head, and turned to Jenner. "And Doctor Jenner? I'm surprised at you, disturbing the peace like this! What's the matter? Port Fontaine too quiet for someone from the Big City?"

Rudge turned to the Keeners and said., "You all stay there." Then he took Jenner by the arm and led him out of the light.

"You OK, doc?"

Jenner felt the tender area on the back of his head where the kid had hit him with the two-by-four; his hand came away sticky with blood. His back ached, his left eye felt tight, and the scratches around his neck stung, but the worst pain was in his right hand from where he'd punched Keener; his swollen fist felt like a sack of crushed bone and blood.

Jenner nodded. "I think my hand may be a bit fucked-up."

Rudge laughed and put a hand on his shoulder. "Never scrap with a redneck, doc! They'll beat you every time! Want to go to Port Fontaine General?"

"No." Jenner winced as he felt his hand, then looked over to the clearing. "I was winning until the kids piled on . . ."

Rudge nodded. "Ah, doc, 'I was winning until the kids piled on . . .' If I had a nickel for every time I've heard that. You guys coulda been on *Cops!*"

He looked back at Keener, rubbing his jaw. "But, yes. Yes, you were winning – that right hook? That was a beauty, some *Raging Bull* shit. I was surprised Keener was still awake after that one."

Jenner turned, irritated. "You were watching? How long?"

"I got there just in time to see you two hombres face off."

Jenner shook his head. "Why didn't you do anything?"

Rudge shrugged. "Mike Keener and I go way back, and I liked your chances." He nodded. "Had you as the winner. I didn't want to spoil your fun, but when the boys started whomping on you, well, that just didn't seem sporting . . ."

He looked over at Keener and his sons. The man was still upright, swaying a bit. Behind him, Mike Junior glared at them; his brothers were both quiet and tearful.

"You want to press charges, doctor?"

Jenner shook his head. "No. But maybe Keener needs to go to the hospital."

"Champ! Not that it wasn't a great shot, but he's fine, just fine. What you're seeing there is just the drink. That leaning-over shit? That's his baseline function."

Rudge stepped over toward the Keeners.

"Okay, Mike, this is what's going to happen . . . The doctor, in an impressive display of mercy, has decided he doesn't want me to throw your sorry ass in jail. He's going to let this whole thing slide, both you and your boys. But I want you to hear me on this: you come over here one more time, I hear you've been fucking around here, you're going straight to jail, all of you. And Mike Junior? You're still on probation, right? You don't want me to run you in."

He looked at Keener, leaning against a tree, glowering back at him. "Now you boys get your dad home now; I think he's feeling poorly."

They watched the Keeners head up to the parking lot, Mike Junior propping up his father, the other two following along behind like ducklings.

Rudge turned to Jenner and said, "You sure you're in one piece, doc? Hand still attached?"

Jenner nodded. "What were you doing here?"

"I was going to be neighborly, stop in and say 'Welcome to Port Fontaine.'" Rudge said, "You're on my way home – I live near here, a mile or two down the road in Golden Palms."

He looked over to his car. "I oughta put out the lights before I kill that battery."

Jenner followed him up the slope. Rudge's car was a late-model Taurus with county plates. The detective pulled the mag-mount beacon off the roof and tossed it onto the driver's-side seat, then extinguished the bracket spotlamp on the driver's side.

He looked at his watch.

"Almost eight p.m. I'm looking at you and thinking 'Now there's a man who could use a drink' . . .You up for a drink, doc? "

Jenner shrugged. "Why not? Is there somewhere near?"

Rudge nodded, then gestured for Jenner to follow him. He walked nimbly back down the incline to the clearing where he stooped to pick up the bottle of whiskey. He lifted it to show Jenner: still three-quarters full.

"I grew up poor, doctor. Where I'm from, we don't waste good liquor . . ."

Jenner nodded gravely.

Rudge laughed out loud and slapped Jenner's shoulder. "I'm just messing with you, doc! I grew up just fine!" He paused, his smile wide in the yellow light. "Still don't waste liquor, though." He looked around. "Now, where can we drink this?"

Jenner grinned. "We sit by the pool, we can watch the possums mate. It's all they ever seem to do . . ."

"Not much else to do in Port Fontaine, doc . . ." Rudge took a swig, then capped the bottle; he lifted it and gestured upwards. "Quick, to the pool!"

The dog, having finished the pizza, joined them, trotting in front of Jenner as he walked up the slope, Rudge puffing behind.

"Doc, I think this is the start of a beautiful friendship."

Rudge paused, then added, "*Casablanca*, 1942."

15

The phone was a grinding dentist's drill being jammed through the back of Jenner's head.

He sat up, disoriented in the pitch black; his eyes swam with stars as the drill bit sank deeper into his brain.

He couldn't move his legs. He leaned forward, but they wouldn't move.

He reached out to touch them; he could feel them. He knew that he was still drunk. But he had sensation. Why couldn't he move his legs?

The phone rang again. In the dark he tugged at the sheets over his legs. He was trapped.

Jenner's hands, moving slowly now, touched something big and warm that was lying on him, something warm and wet. With a gasp, he jerked his hand away, rolling away, struggling to free his legs from the body lying on his.

The phone rang again.

He was trapped by the covers, pulling himself desperately slowly towards the floor. Then the dog jumped up, and Jenner slipped off the bed.

The phone rang again.

How much had they drunk? Jenner remembered that Rudge'd had another bottle in his car, remembered them standing bathed in the green luminescence of the swimming-pool light to toast the memory of Marty and Bobbie Roburn. Swearing, he clawed his way to his knees and yanked the phone cord until the phone fell from the bedside table with a bang.

The clock radio read 3:00 a.m.

"What?"

"Doctor Jenner, sorry, it's Jeannie from the service. Sorry to bother you, doctor, but we have a caller who insists it's urgent. Says it's an emergency, but he won't speak to anyone but you."

Jenner turned the light on. The dog heaved itself back up onto the bed with difficulty, wagging its stubby tail. It sat, peering into Jenner's face.

He turned the light back off again, sank his head into his hands as he cradled the phone to his ear. Jeannie's voice seemed unnecessarily shrill.

"An emergency? Tell him to call 911."

"I did, doctor. He says he can't call the police and he will only speak with you. Says he needs to report a death, and only to you."

"Ugh."

He dragged himself back up onto the bed and pushed the dog aside.

"Move."

"Excuse me, doctor?"

"Not you." The dog moved closer, wagging its tail and panting hotly on Jenner as he sat.

"What does this guy want again?"

"To report a death. But doctor? He's calling from a New York City cell phone."

"What? How do you know? What's the number?" If a friend from home was calling, it was important.

"We got Caller ID; it's a cell phone registered to an Adam Weiss."

Jenner shook his head. "Never heard of him."

"He's very persistent, doctor." She paused. "He's actually been quite rude."

"Unh." Jenner struggled to get in gear.

"Shall I tell him to call back during business hours?"

Jenner wiped his eyes, then winced as he felt the tender swelling on his brow.

"No . . . no, I'm awake. Put him through, let's find out what this is about . . ."

He sat up and turned the bedside light back on. The dog was leaning against him. Its fur was wet and smelled of Aveda Cherry and Almond Bark conditioner. In the light, Jenner could see soaked towels around the room.

He remembered Rudge saying that Jenner should wash the dog if he was going to keep it in his room. But why the fuck had he decided to keep it?

"You're on with Doctor Jenner now."

"Doctor? Doctor Jenner, from New York?"

"Yes?"

"Is there anyone else on the line?"

Christ, he didn't need this now.

"No, just me."

"Are you certain?"

"Jeannie, you still there?"

Silence.

"Yeah, I'm certain. What's this about?"

The voice was desperate and nervous. "Okay. Look, I'm sorry, but this is way out of my league. I can't call 911 because these people think the cops are in on it. And I don't want anyone knowing my name and location."

"You're Adam Weiss. From New York City."

"Wh . . . what? *How?*"

"Well, you called on your cell phone, and now you just confirmed it to me a second ago, Einstein. C'mon, this is Florida, not, you know, Biafra or whatever – we have Caller ID. If I wanted, I could even have the police triangulate your location." Jenner wasn't actually sure about that, but this guy had woken him up and deserved a few lumps.

"Oh God!" The voice was young. Late teens, early twenties, Jenner figured.

"Mr. Weiss, either spit it out or let me go back to sleep. I have a bad headache and I don't feel like sitting around bullshitting."

Weiss spoke in an urgent whisper. "Please, Dr. Jenner, you've got to get me out of this. I think my life is in danger . . ."

"Jesus. What is this, a prank call? Couldn't you just have some diapers delivered, or order me a pizza?" Jenner looked around the room, and at the dog. "Either would be good."

"Please, sir. I'm deadly serious. I'm scared."

Jenner paused. Yes, he could hear that. He relented a little. "What's this about?"

There was a sigh, then silence. Then Weiss said, "I'm calling to report several deaths. Murders. I haven't seen the bodies myself, but I have information on where they are. I can't tell you who told me about this, but I believe these people are telling me the truth."

Jenner slumped back against the bed, listening now. The boy kept talking.

"They want you to recover the bodies, sir. They want you to find the people who killed them."

Jenner said nothing.

"Uh, Doctor Jenner? Are you there?"

"Yes. How many bodies? What's wrong with going to the police?"

"At least two bodies – migrant workers. These people say the police may be involved. They're afraid." Weiss paused. "And I am, too."

"What makes you so sure you can trust me?"

"I go to school in New York. I read about you in the paper today and remembered you from that serial killer, the Inquisitor thing. I figured you're new here, so you can't be a part of whatever's going on. I figured you'd be better than the Feds – the people who came to see me also don't trust the government, for reasons I can't say."

The kid was talking a better game, now, pulling himself together.

"Well, I'm assuming they're illegals," Jenner said. "Where are the bodies?"

"In the Everglades outside Bel Arbre. I can give you exact directions – you need to write them down . . ."

"Hold on . . .. Okay, I have a pen. Go."

"Head north out of Port Fontaine on I-55. Turn off on High Lock Road – that's, like twenty-five miles north of town. Follow High Lock Road through the groves until the road ends, about five minutes from the highway. That's as close as you can get by car. Park, then look east. There's a big hammock there – that's kind of an Everglades term for an island of trees. The bodies are in there. The people put a light there so you can see it from the road."

Jenner was writing. "High Lock Road?"

"Yeah. And bring waterproof clothing – you have to walk from the road to the hammock, and it's all sawgrass there."

The line went dead.

Christ. He should call Rudge – at the very least, it'd teach the detective a lesson for getting him so drunk.

But what if they showed up and it was all a hoax?

Jenner stood, a little unsteadily; his stomach felt like it was grinding broken glass. But his thoughts were clear.

No, it was better he handled it himself. See what he found, call Rudge if this was the real deal.

The dog jumped off the bed and followed him, tail wagging, but stopped when he saw Jenner open the bathroom door. He jumped back onto the bed, and when the shower turned on, he burrowed halfway under the sheets and began to gum one of Jenner's pillows.

16

After pushing the dog out of his cabin, Jenner walked through the parking lot; Rudge's Taurus was still there, parked under the slash pines. Rudge had the driver's seat down; in the moonlight, Jenner could make out the round white billow of the detective's shirt as it rose and fell with his breathing. As he got closer, he heard ghastly, throat-ploughing snores, and decided to let the man sleep. He walked on to his own car, feeling vaguely noble, and then sorry for himself and his aching head – and face and hand.

He stopped at the 24-Hour Super Walmart and bought

waders and a heavy flashlight. He gulped down a cup of black coffee at the Dunkin' Donuts counter, and when that kicked in he wandered the gleaming white floors until he found the bug spray. Passing the ammo counter, he realized he'd left his pistol at the motel; too late to go back. He picked up a gallon jug of water from a stand near the cash register.

As Jenner drove up I-55, Port Fontaine faded away gradually. The housing developments, hidden behind tonsured bushes and landscaped terraces, grew farther apart, then the McDonald's and Waffle Houses and Taco Bells died out, and soon he was driving through the night, the gulf somewhere off to his left, the Everglades to his right. The moon, low in a cloud-streaked maroon sky, flooded the low expanse of grass and the scattered islands of gnarled trees choking in undergrowth. In the silver light, the dark trees were sharp-edged and vivid, shapes of cypress and palm punched out of tin and stuck into the marshy ground.

Jenner rolled down the window, felt the air stream against his face, warm and humid. He was sober now. Mostly sober.

He turned on the radio, skipping across evangelical talk radio and Golden Oldies and Latin music until the twanging sitar of Tom Petty's "Don't Come Around Here No More" welled out of the speakers. He sang along for a few lines, even turned it up, but his head throbbed, so he soon turned the radio off and watched the road in silence, feeling the onrushing ribbon of floodlit tarmac disappear under his hood, the trees and bushes whip past.

Half an hour out of Port Fontaine he sailed past High Lock Road, braking too late. The highway was empty, so he reversed slowly along the shoulder and took the turn. For a while he drove through orange groves, the land on either side carved into slabs by drainage canals, each block filled with hundreds of rows of low, dark citrus trees, thousands upon thousands of them. He drove through the groves for about five minutes, then saw high fencing that marked the line where the reclaimed farm land stopped and the marsh began; a Department of Parks and Fisheries sign identified the land beyond as part of the Everglades National Park.

There was a bump, and the road abruptly turned to gravel. Jenner rolled forward slowly, headlights flaring through the rising clouds of dust. On either side scrubby bushes pressed in on the road, and beyond the arc of his high-beams he could see nothing, just an immense darkness.

He ran out of road. The roadway ended in a small turning oval around which a low black-and-white-striped metal retaining barrier protected vehicles from a foot-and-a-half drop down into the River of Grass. Jenner slowed to a stop, heard the crunch of the gravel under his tires.

He peered into the night but couldn't see much beyond the barrier in the glare of reflected light. He turned his headlights off and was plunged into darkness.

The heat soaked Jenner as he climbed out of the car, swallowing him, immediately wet on his air-conditioned skin. He walked to the metal barrier, sat and stared out into the darkness. The moon slipped from behind its wreath of cloud, and light poured across the flooded plain. The Glades had never seemed so vast, the thousands of acres of sawgrass stretching out like an unfurled blanket, bare-trunked cypress and royal palms, thickets of live oak and bustic scattered across them like abandoned toys.

A few years back, Marty Roburn and Jenner had gone out on an airboat to recover three victims from a single-engine plane crash. The park ranger who had led them to the crash site had explained to Jenner that what looked like a grassy prairie was not solid at all but a cloak of pale yellow sedge covering a huge, slow-flowing river; under the grass, the water was always moving, sliding down the infinitely gentle slope to the sea. And Jenner had learned that, if the blades of the sawgrass seemed lush and thick, they were literally blades, their saw-toothed edges capable of cutting clothing and flesh.

As he looked into the marsh, Jenner remembered something else about the crash: while he and Roburn had waded over to the crumpled Cessna, one of the deputies had stayed on the airboat, sitting in the high driver's chair, binoculars hung around his neck, cradling a carbine. With a grin, Marty told Jenner he was looking out for alligators, which, with their thick skin, thrived in the dense mesh of razor-sharp grass.

As he stared out towards the horizon, Jenner tried to remember what the park ranger had said about how to spot an alligator nest.

There was movement out over the water. No, not movement, but a white light in the distance.

It was gone.

Jenner stared, squinting.

And then he saw it blink again. He stood, con-centrating, until his eye found the light. It was a flashing signal, almost invisible in the undergrowth of a large hammock maybe a quarter-mile out into the marsh.

So probably it wasn't a hoax. Probably Weiss wasn't lying about the bodies.

Christ. Why hadn't he woken Rudge?

He checked his cell phone. No signal.

Jenner went back to the car, pulled out the big white Walmart bag and dumped his purchases onto the back seat. He sprayed himself with insecticide until his clothes were sodden. He wasn't sure if the waders went over his clothes or if he was supposed to get rid of his pants to get in the waders.

He decided to keep his pants on, even if that wasn't right. Earlier that week he'd listened to state troopers swapping snake stories. Rattlers, they said, didn't take you by surprise – the sound let you know you were dealing with a rattler – it was the cottonmouths that scared the hell out of them. Cottonmouths would charge you, would come slithering right at you once they got your scent. And they were incredibly fast, and they just kept on coming. And once you got bitten by a cottonmouth, you died slow, the flesh of the bitten limb blistering and oozing, your blood rotting in your veins before the coma took you away.

Jenner looked back out to the hammock. It seemed a long way away.

17

At first Jenner made pretty good time. The sedge was compact and springy; he'd heard that it had been a pretty dry season, and he wondered if the irrigation pumps had lowered the water level near the fields. But as he continued it got wetter, and he slowed, each footstep sinking deeper into the thick mat of grass and mud. Soon he had to lean into his step, the marsh sucking at his feet and ankles as he stumbled forward, struggling to keep his scene bag up out of the damp. The Micosukkee and Seminole had lived in the Glades for centuries, but they had to have known their way, had to have had trails through. And they did it during daylight, without twenty pounds of camera equipment and swabs and tape lifts.

Most of all, Jenner thought glumly, the Micosukkee could tell a clump of bushes from an alligator nest.

He stopped, the sweat streaming down his face, his shirt soaked, the rubber waders keeping in as much moisture as they kept out. The insects caught up with him; despite Jenner's chemical reek, the air around him was furred with tiny gnats. Swatting them away was pointless – more insects gushed back instantly into the bug vacuum he'd just cleared. He gulped down water, the gallon jug seemed heavier with each pace. But ahead, the flashing signal looked brighter.

Then he heard a slow, dry rustling somewhere to his left, the noise of something large moving through undergrowth. He jerked his torch beam round but saw nothing in the dense knot of bushes covering the low mound.

Jenner pushed forward faster now, and behind him he heard the quiet splash of something slipping into the water.

He didn't wait to see what it was, just kept going, heading towards the hammock. The water was deeper now, sometimes reaching his knees; he splashed through it loudly, hoping the commotion would drive away anything that might find him interesting.

Now the hammock loomed over him, a hulking black shadow, a ghost ship at anchor. He shone the torch ahead and saw that the banks rounded up to a solid wall of undergrowth, a dense tangle of vegetation that blocked any sight of the interior, the tree canopy overhead thick and dark. But Jenner could see the signal clearly now, and it was bright.

How had they made their way to the island to set up the signal? Boat, airboat? A swamp buggy seemed unlikely – if Weiss's contacts were in fact illegals, he doubted they'd do anything that flashy. Or expensive. Beyond the bushes, toward the far side of the island, he could make out a slough or a small channel, standing water deep enough for a canoe or an outboard.

Nearing the hammock, Jenner saw small gaps in the thick mesh of plants that surrounded it, areas of exposed mud where some animal had slid off into the water.

He was close enough now to see that the signal was a bicycle safety light, its strap velcro'd to a thin tree trunk. Jenner grabbed the trunk with relief and tried to pull himself up. But he slipped, and struggled for a second on the steep incline, his waders smearing across the slick mud as he fought to drag himself onto the drier land. He rolled up onto the edge of the hammock, swinging the bag across his chest and into the bushes.

He lay there panting, chest heaving, sweaty and filthy.

And then he smelled it, that familiar stench, the nauseatingly sweet fog rolling in under the reek of brackish mud and swamp grass.

No.

They hadn't lied about the bodies.

18

Jenner stood in the mud, peering into the hammock and trying not to slip back down into the sedge. Knotted muscadine and devil's claw pressed all the way to the banks, the entire island packed tight as a bird's nest. In an hour or so the dawn light would help, but he couldn't keep his footing on the bank until then.

From the water behind him he heard soft splashing, and in the gloom he imagined a huge water moccasin writhing through the saw grass, coming at him like a heat-seeking missile.

Time to go in.

There was a tentative spatter of rain, then a thick mist of tiny droplets ticked at the leaves and branches near Jenner. The sound swelled quickly to a rattling roar, the drops striking him hard, flowing down his face, washing the mud from his skin. He held his face up, then his hands, the raindrops pressing into his palms like cold, tiny fingers.

Off to the east, lightning flared the sky purple, each flash illuminating the endless expanse of marsh, the grass garish green-yellow, the naked trunks bleached white, the slate-gray water shirred silver by the driving rain.

Jenner leaned into the undergrowth to get the bicycle light, then thought better of it: fingerprints. He turned slightly, stretched his right leg out into the undergrowth, then wedged himself into the thicket, pushing between two slender trees, the branches poking and scraping as he eased forward, crushing the plants at his feet.

Within a couple of feet the vegetation thinned. A little further and he entered more open space. He wrestled his scene bag through the gap behind him, then shone his flashlight. The narrow beam fell off sharply in the gloom, but he saw that he was surrounded by old-growth mahogany and gumbo-limbo, the trees almost completely hidden by the writhing, choking strangler figs that coiled around them, their wet trunks black and glistening in his light. The ground was damp, slippery with moss, but firm. High overhead the leaf canopy hid the sky but let the rain pass.

Jenner lifted his small Maglite, the thin beam feeble in the black; he cursed himself for not having coughed up the money for a bigger version. The pinpoint of white hovered and bounced across trunks and saplings as he moved forward into the grove, scanning the mud and the moss, searching for the curve of a head, the sharp angle of a bent arm, the contour of a shod foot. Inside the hammock the smell of wet, dark earth competed with the odor of decay.

He reached the center of the hammock; he'd found nothing. Perhaps he should be looking for the turned-earth hillock of a fresh grave, some low pile of dirt covering something rotten. Half-covering, more like – the reek of putrefaction was too strong for a completely buried body. Maybe something had dug up the corpse.

Not too long and it would be dawn. How much light would break through the branches and leaves to reach the hammock floor? It was cooler inside the hammock, almost cold.

A rusty metal chair.

Jenner moved the light. Two rust-pocked metal chairs, folded, leaning against the foot of a big mahogany tree.

He stepped towards the tree, and the Maglite's beam leaped up, jumping over four dangling legs, hanging in the dark.

The bodies were on fire.

They swam before Jenner's eyes, brilliant orange and smoke-black in the flashlight glare. But there was no flame, no smoke, no smell of burning. As he drew close, he saw that the bodies were covered by thousands of small tiger-striped snails, thousands of knobby orange and black shells swarming over the torsos, coating the heads and arms, dripping in clumped orange gouts to the moss beneath the feet. A million eyes staring back at him; a low breeze shifted the body, and the slight sway refracted the flashlight's beam, turning the body into a twisting column of fire.

The bodies hung back to back, so close that they looked like a four-legged creature. Jenner let the beam play over the first body, then up the snail-encrusted rope. Jenner followed its loop around the branch and back down to the second body, where it disappeared under the grotesquely tilted neck.

The two men had been hanged together, the weight of each body used to strangle the other across the fulcrum of the branch.

And they had to have been killed – this wasn't suicide. Jenner had seen one dual-suicide hanging before, a pact where twin brothers had hanged themselves neck-to-neck over a door. But it was vanishingly rare, and if the two people hanging in front of him had killed themselves, who'd folded the chairs and stacked them against the tree afterwards?

Judging from their size, build and clothing, both victims were men. Between the snails and the putrefaction, Jenner couldn't get an impression of age or race, but they looked neither particularly old nor particularly young. The wrists were not tied – how had the killers immobilized the men to string them up? It would have taken more than one attacker, probably several, to corral the two victims, lead them to the site, wrestle them down, tie the rope, loop it around the branch, get the men onto the chairs, then push them off. Even at gunpoint the killers' intentions would've been quickly apparent, and the victims would've fought back.

The two folding chairs were generic; they could have come from any church basement or school auditorium. They were rusty – how long had they been out here?

Jenner looked back at the bodies. The rain had picked up again, spitting through the canopy and down into the dark emerald moss.

Both corpses were pretty decomposed; it had been hot in Douglas county, so they would have rotted quickly. Then again, here they had hung in the shade cast by the interwoven branches of a hundred trees; even at night it was cooler in the heart of the hammock than out on the sedge.

Jenner reckoned that he might have a clearer idea when he saw the bodies up close, in good light, but he figured they'd been there a good week or two.

So why were the chairs rusty?

He walked toward the other end of the hammock, looking for the point where the men had come ashore – there had to be some kind of access point, some place to land a boat where a group of men wouldn't have had to fight through the undergrowth.

As Jenner walked, the clearing narrowed and the trees and undergrowth pressed in again, but he could still make out a muddy path leading through the dense bushes at the edge. He kept going, trying to keep off the path in case there were salvageable footprints.

He stopped, unsure why. He hadn't seen a motion, or a flash of color, hadn't heard a noise, at least not consciously. But something had made him stop.

Jenner turned slowly back to the clearing and began to go over the bushes and trees with his flashlight. Tipping it up, he found two more hanging bodies, these much higher off the ground, the feet drooping down to the level of Jenner's head. These bodies were nearly skeletalized, but they too were covered with snails, a coating of bright orange and black that clung like wax-candle drippings to the clothes sagging from the emerging bones.

There was a low drumming sound above him, and again the roar of rain. The leaves bent and spread, and the water spattered down and flowed through the canopy to collect into slender waterfalls which poured down into the clearing, glittering like silver ropes in his flashlight.

Jenner swung the flashlight up, then back at the other two victims. He walked through the hammock, scanning the branches for more bodies hanging in this orchard of death. Standing in the middle of the clearing, he found that he was afraid to turn off his flashlight.

He spoke out loud, his voice weak and hollow under the spattering of rain in the clearing.

"Christ, Marty. What have you gotten me into?"

19

It was gone eleven a.m. The rain had settled to an intermittent drizzle but the light was still watery and dim. Jenner, in his blue Douglas County rain slicker, sat waiting with Deb Putnam on the largest of the three airboats tethered to the edges of the hammock, peering into the dense vegetation as if he could see into the hive of activity at its center.

The crime-scene techs had processed the landing site and were now deep inside the hammock, photographing the bodies where they hung. They'd managed to get footwear imprints, not sharp enough to nail an individual shoe or boot but probably good enough for brand, model and size.

Jenner glanced at Deb, sitting next to him. The park ranger had been the first responder and had waited with him at his car while the sheriff's department coordinated the airboats. Since Crime Scene had shooed them out of the hollow they'd spent the morning talking and sharing bottles of water from the airboat cooler.

They made small talk. He made her laugh about his trek across the sedge to the hammock. She told him alligator holes were hollows hidden behind mounded-up dirt ramparts; she scanned the area to show him but couldn't spot an obvious gator hole. She pointed out, with a smirk, that the hammock really wasn't all that far from his car. She teased him about his black eye.

But soon the nervous energy faded altogether and Deb grew quiet. Then they watched the hammock, waiting to get back to the clearing. Or for something to happen.

There was rustling as a tech emerged from the bushes to their left. She photographed and bagged the bicycle light, then disappeared back into the trees.

Deb turned to Jenner, hesitated for a second, then said, "Can I tell you something? Those snails? They're Everglades snails – they're endangered, and I've never seen so many before."

Jenner shrugged. "You gotta figure there's easier ways to get more snails."

Deb smiled tentatively, trying to gauge his how serious he was. "Well, things live for a while and then they die – I've made my peace with that. There are plenty more men, but soon these snails will be gone forever."

She realized that Jenner wasn't listening to her. He was crouching at the side of the airboat, hanging on to the rail with one hand as he leaned out to fish something from the water.

He straightened to show her a sodden white bag. He held it by the corners to shake out the damp folds, then placed it carefully on the floor of the airboat, smoothing it down. The red ink had faded in the sun, but they could still read the bleached text: *DELFINE PIGLET FEED, 20lbs.*

"What do you think?" Jenner said. "It's really in the middle of nowhere – doesn't seem likely that it's just some random trash that's floated out here."

Deb nodded in agreement. "Yeah, I doubt it would've."

Jenner said, "We're pretty far from farmland, and something this big isn't going to move very fast. And there's no other garbage around."

He moved the bag onto a seat under the canopy. "We'll hand it over to Crime Scene." He grinned at her. "We'll say you found it – make you look good."

Deb smiled back. She fiddled with a canvas bag beside her, pulled out a thermos, unscrewed the cap, and poured. "Would you like some?"

Jenner nodded gratefully. "God, some hot coffee would really hit the spot."

She made a sorry face, and said, "Chai tea, I'm afraid."

He winced, then grinned wryly. "Well, as long as it's hot . . ."

They took turns sipping from the thermos cap. The tea was milky and sweet-spiced; sitting on the airboat in the middle of the marsh, listening to the rain tapping the canopy, it reminded Jenner bizarrely of Christmas.

Deb watched him sip.

"Can I ask you something?"

He nodded.

"It's not really a question. I was just wondering how you were doing . . . with Marty Roburn."

"You mean how the investigation is going?"

She shook her head, flushing slightly. "No, I meant how you were, y'know, feeling. Tom Nash says you were real close."

He nodded. "Marty was the best forensic pathologist I ever knew. He was kind of like a father to me."

Deb was silent a second, then said, "Well, if you feel like talking with someone about it, you could give me a call."

He turned to her. "That's very kind of you."

"No, no. I'm sort of dealing with the same thing – my dad died a few months back, so I kind of know what you're going through."

"I'm sorry."

"To tell the truth, everything happened so quickly I haven't had time to think about it. The funeral, selling the house, moving my mom up to Sarasota, finding my own place, and all of a sudden it's three months later."

They were both quiet, looking out over the marsh in the drizzle.

She smiled, then stood, stretching. "I love it here – Dad used to bring me hunting out here when I was just a little girl."

"I was wondering why you've been so cool about the bodies."

"Doc, I've been hunting since I was ten years old; nothing phases me."

He said, "Hey, can I ask why you carry a gun?"

"I'm a Law Enforcement Ranger." She grinned. "Don't let the title or the gun fool you – mostly I spend my time making drunk tourists put out their cigarettes."

"So the gun's just for show, is it?"

She shook her head. "The hell it is! I can take the nuts off a gnat at twenty paces!"

"Huh." He grinned. "Isn't that at odds with your sworn mission to protect our precious natural resources?"

Her smile widened. "What can I say, doc? I'm a Florida girl."

She lifted her head suddenly, squinting across the marsh. "We've got company . . ." She pointed with her left hand, and Jenner saw that she wasn't wearing a ring.

A bulky mass was moving toward them across the water and sedge. It was the blocky shape of a swamp buggy heading in their direction.

The rain had stopped, so Deb rolled the tarpaulin back, then sat down next to Jenner. She finished her cup and poured another.

"Want some more?"

Her eyes were bright blue, and her nose was freckled. How old was she – twenty-seven, twenty-eight?

He shook his head. "A little sweet for me."

He stood, balancing himself against the high driver's seat as the airboat swayed slightly.

20

The swamp buggy lumbered towards them, ripping a broad vee of shallow wake in the water behind it, its passengers lofted high above the sawgrass on the jacked-up undercarriage and huge nubby tires.

Deb stood up beside Jenner. As the buggy drew closer, he saw that the banner across the passenger enclosure read *Queeg's Airboat Rides, Everglades City FL*. Under the canopy the sheriff sat next to the driver, like a raja and his mahout riding an elephant into court. Behind them was Port Fontaine's mayor, and, in a bright yellow gas-station convenience-store plastic raincoat, Detective Rudge. Behind Rudge, snapping away on a digital camera, a young man who Jenner guessed was a reporter.

Deb pressed Jenner's arm, motioning him to sit as the buggy slowed, its arriving wake rocking the airboats. They watched Anders climb down the steps, gingerly stretch out a foot, and ease himself onto land. The sheriff turned to watch the mayor descend, then held up a hand to hold back Rudge so that the reporter could slip by. Rudge sat back down heavily, a look of distaste on his face as he surveyed the dense undergrowth of the hammock and the wider landscape of water and marsh grass.

The sheriff lifted an arm to gesture toward the clearing, and held it self-consciously; Jenner realized he was posing. The photographer snapped his shots, then the sheriff turned to a three-quarter profile as he called to Jenner, "What happened, doctor? Fall and hit a doorknob?"

Jenner reflexively reached a hand to his swollen eye.

The sheriff smiled, then looked solemnly at the camera. "They're in there, eh?"

Jenner nodded. Where else would they be? It was an island in the middle of a swamp. He said, "Sheriff, you might want to wait a little. I don't think they're done processing yet."

The sheriff gave a dismissive wave. "Doctor, Port Fontaine may not be New York City but we've handled our share of significant cases. We know what to do." He turned to the mayor and the journalist and added, "Wouldn't you say, Bruce? Jimmy?"

There was firm nodding, and the men disappeared excitedly into the trees. The mayor was wearing a Burberry trench coat over corduroys and dock shoes.

Rudge climbed down the ladder and stood on the hammock, hands on his wide hips, glowering at Jenner, who grinned back broadly.

"Yeah, Jenner, that's right: I brought the A Team! And

we are some *stalwart* motherfuckers . . ."

Then Rudge spied the thermos; his face lit up. "Sweet Jesus! If there's whiskey in there, this sinner shall stray no more!"

Jenner smiled at him and said, "No, sir, Detective Rudge, sir. But you're welcome to enjoy a calming sip of hot chai tea . . ."

"Jesus, Jenner. How you want to play me like that?" Rudge shook his head, aggrieved, then shrugged. "I go now to join my Fearless Leader."

Rudge followed the sheriff through the bushes, his muttered swearing clearly audible through the tangle of green.

21

Adam Weiss pumped the pedals hard, then coasted, lifting up off the bike's seat to slice through the wet air, cutting through every puddle just to fuck up the smooth surfaces.

He'd slept a fitful hour, maybe two, expecting the police to come pounding on his door at any second, demanding to know how he'd known about the bodies. But it was already mid-afternoon, and so far not a sign of the cops. It made him uneasy – the medical examiner had probably called them as soon as he'd hung up, so where were they?

Adam took the short cut through the cemetery, slipping through the back gate and out onto the track. It certainly wasn't what he would've thought of as a cemetery: just a big flat grassy field, ringed with small trees and a low brick wall, falling off into a drainage ditch along one end. With its circular paved track, it looked like a high-school football field, the side-lines dotted with graves, one end-zone dedicated to the bodies of children.

He sped past two sleek young Mexican women, their hair and make-up perfect, one in a teal sweat suit, the other in puce, puffing around the track. There were no parks in the town, so people walked the cemetery for exercise and even picnicked near the graves. Adam had at first been faintly offended, but there were still only a handful of graves – the cemetery had clearly been planned with growth in mind. He'd told Tiff that he thought it was funny that these migrant workers were housed like livestock, six or seven to a tiny little shack, but when they died it was almost a prairie burial. But not, he hastily assured her, like, funny ha-ha.

Tiff – it was strange how everything that had happened had pushed her out of his head.

What was it, twelve hours since he'd made the call? He figured that the Mexicans were finished with him now, that they'd leave him alone. He didn't know them, couldn't recognize them. He didn't remember them from meetings or from farm visits with Ricky. In his heart of hearts, he thought they pretty much all looked the same – small dark men and women with black hair, bundled up against the heat, scattered across the furrowed fields, bent double to scrabble for strawberries or asparagus.

Adam realized that was probably why they'd picked him – Ricky, the True Friend of the Worker, would have known them, would have identified their regional accents or dialects. They'd been smart.

Whatever. Adam had done it, done his job, played his part.

No, more than just played his part: his telling the M.E. had been a masterstroke, he thought – and it had been his own idea. He'd been reading the Port Fontaine paper online, dreaming about buying a motorcycle (just go, get on that fucking thing and go . . .) when he'd read about the murder of the county medical examiner and his wife. He'd recognized Jenner's name and had hatched his plan.

But what if Jenner hadn't gone for it? What if he hadn't gone to check it out? That would explain why the cops hadn't visited. Or what if he'd gone to check it out, and there'd been nothing there?

Adam dismissed the thought immediately. He'd seen the men's faces – no way there was nothing there.

As he coasted into the center of Bel Arbre the shadows lifted and the western sky became bright. The streets were pretty empty; normally on a Monday the place had plenty of traffic, particularly for a town that wasn't much more than a five- or six-block strip of storefront beauty parlors, run-down furniture stores and security-gated check-cashing stores with neon signs advertising money-transmission service. There were a handful of businesses that reflected the town's ethnic make-up – a few taco stands, a piñata shop – but the town's hotspot was the intersection where a Burger King, a Taco Bell and a new Walgreen's faced off across the traffic lights.

The main taco stand was open, but there was no line – and there was never no line at that taco stand. The counterman was watching a portable black-and-white TV.

"*Dos carnitas, por favor. Y una Coca tambien.*"

Wordlessly, the man pressed tortillas onto the grill, then slopped a ladleful of spiced pork next to them. He put a cold Coke on the counter and turned back to the TV.

Adam looked down the street.

"*Señor . . . Adonde estan la gente?*"

The man answered in English. "At the store . . . to watch the TV. To watch the news on the TV."

He folded the warm tortillas into tinfoil, then scooped up the meat, sprinkled it on the tortillas.

"They find dead men. The police. In the Everglades. *Asesinados.*" He mimed stabbing with his ladle, then put it down to pick up the *pica de gallo*.

Adam's throat went dry, and the hair on his arms began to prickle. So, it had happened. And it was already on the news? God, that was quick.

He took his tacos and Coke, and climbed onto his bike. What had they found? What was going on? He needed to know, and he had no TV. Which store did the taco guy mean?

He unfolded the foil and took a bite, then pedaled slowly up the street until he saw a small crowd bulging from the doors of the bodega where everyone bought their lottery tickets. Adam remembered the TV mounted on the cigarette display wall behind the counter.

He chained his bike to the lamp post and approached the store. The dozen or so people crowding the entrance and small floor space were staring at the TV; the proprietor, propped on a plastic stool behind the counter, was haltingly translating the live feed into Spanish.

The onscreen caption read GRISLY EVERGLADES DISCOVERY. A shaky helicopter shot showed a tree-covered hill rising up out of the marsh like an island. There were airboats and a swamp buggy next to the mound.

A man came out of the wood, backing onto the bank near the airboats, and another with him, and then a third right next to them, all struggling to maneuver something bulky and matte black. The camera jerked wide, then zoomed in; there was a murmured buzz as everyone in the bodega recognized the body bag. The buzz grew louder as a second body was hefted out of the bush.

Adam felt like he was waking up from an eight-week nap. Until that body came out of the woods it had all been abstract, some kind of dreamy game he'd been playing by accident. Something that would suddenly end with him back on his couch on West 120th Street, eating Cap'n Crunch and watching *Star Wars* for the thousandth time, waiting for Tiff to go to the movies later – *oh, it was all just a dream!*

But all of this was real, that whole insane chain of events – the drugged-out *campesino*, the Mexicans, him calling the M.E. And now the cops were pulling bodies out of the Everglades. Fuck.

And it was because of *him* that they had found those bodies; he was at the heart of this mystery.

Onscreen the first body was being lifted onto an airboat, and now they were pulling a third body bag out of the trees. Adam wondered how many there were, wondered what the people inside the body bags looked like. Wondered if he'd ever seen them, if he even maybe knew them.

But, of course, that was unlikely. His Spanish was fucking pathetic, and he'd avoided field-work as much as he could. He'd showed up late at the office, skipped most evening meetings, avoided the farm inspections whenever he could. The fact was, Adam hadn't even really tried. He'd gone through the motions, doing the bare minimum to get the credit. Rick probably thought he was a prick, just another overprivileged college kid faking commitment to social service to boost his resumé. He'd supposedly been there to help these people, and his only achievement had been parroting the message of where to find the bodies.

Adam turned toward a sniffling sound to his left, and saw that two of the women were crying. Then the man to his right pulled down the brim of his grubby Britney Spears baseball cap and turned away from Adam. But the bobbing of his head was unmistakable, and soon everyone was sobbing. Under the TV, the owner bowed his head and cried into his hand, and then Adam was the only person in the room who was actually listening to the news anchor's excited speculation about the deaths.

The helicopter dipped down closer to nail a tight shot of the fourth body bag being loaded onto an airboat. The wind from the chopper combed the grass into scudding waves that raced to the island, battering the bushes on the hammock until they threshed wildly. The airboats listed drunkenly back and forth, the water kicking up to spray the cops as they struggled to balance the body. A female park ranger in green and a tall man in a dark blue rain slicker stood on the bank, angrily waving back the helicopter.

Adam looked around him at the people he'd pretended to help for the last six weeks. Saw them huddle and hold each other as they cried, watched their shaking shoulders and clenched fists, their threadbare dusty clothes and their leathery skin.

Now he knew why he was here. He could help them. It was his turn to help, to *really* help, this time. He'd stop being a pussy, he'd go to the cops, tell them what he knew. And then the investigation would begin.

But would it? Rick said that when people got killed in Bel Arbre the cops did the minimum possible. Dealing with a migrant population was hard: many potential witnesses were in the area for a month or two only, most spoke no English, and no one wanted to speak to the police for fear of reprisals or deportation. In Bel Arbre, when someone died violently, everyone who'd seen or known anything about it disappeared within hours.

And the people who paid the police – the citizens of Port Fontaine whose tax money bought the cops their guns and their pensions – those people didn't care what happened in Bel Arbre. It might just as well have been the other side of the world. At some level, even, they expected trouble from the migrant workers, expected the drinking, the drugs, the rapes, the stabbings.

Adam shook his head. No, the cops would do their thing, but this time it would be him who got things done. He had started it, and he would see it through to the end.

22

They brought the bodies by airboat to the Coast Guard substation in the South Reaches Marina. Jenner drove down to meet Flanagan and Calvin Major and the morgue wagon; they waited by the boat ramp, drinking vending machine Cokes and watching the shifts of French and German vacationers climb in and out of the tour boats on the commercial dock, on their way to look at manatees and dolphins.

The afternoon Mangrove Meander tour was almost fully boarded when the airboats came into view, buzzing under the low bridge and swinging wide into the harbor. The tour boat captain shut down his engine, climbed back onto the dock, and stood peering into the south. The tourists chatted obliviously, passing around bottles of water and sunscreen. A handful of Coast Guard crew members ambled out of the base house to watch.

The airboats surged into the marina, the roar of Chevy engines and huge propellers drowning out all other sound. On the tour boat the passengers covered their ears and took photos and videos of the unfamiliar craft, still unaware of the load they carried. Then someone pointed and said something in German, and suddenly all the cameras were aimed at the biggest airboat and the black bags heaped against the first row of seats. The sheriff stood at the very front, next to the body bags, hand on the front railing, looking for all the world like a big-game hunter boasting about his kill. Since Jenner had last seen Anders on the hammock he'd managed to get his hands on a cowboy hat, which he wore tipped back on his head.

Flanagan tapped his shoulder and Jenner turned to see a white TV news van, the insignia of the local Fox affiliate on its side, pulling into the parking lot; the members of the camera crew started bailing out even before the van had come to a full stop.

Jenner scowled. He leaned over to Flanagan and yelled, "I'll see you at the office!"

Flanagan gave him the thumbs-up and shouted back, "OK, doc. We got it here."

As Jenner left, he passed a CNN van pulling into the lot; over at the Fox truck, the mast with the microwave transmission dish was already rising.

This is not a good omen, he thought.

23

It was worse at the office. Driving down the scrub oak *allée* that led to the municipal buildings, Jenner saw a thicket of mobile transmission masts outside the morgue buildings. There were a half-dozen news vans – Port Fontaine, Fort Myers, Miami, even a second CNN van – lined up along the compound's wall. In front of the CNN truck a reporter was gesturing at the County Medical Examiner's Office sign, already broadcasting to the nation.

Jenner drove past them, around to the back entrance where bodies were received. A small cluster of men waited in the shade along the fence; spotting him, they jumped to their feet to record his arrival with shoulder-mounted cameras. Security buzzed him in, the gates pulling back slowly to let him pass. The cameramen set their equipment back down to wait for the real show.

In the loading area everything looked surprisingly ready. After an airplane crash had caused total chaos in the office the previous summer, Roburn had initiated quarterly disaster drills; these clearly had paid off. The technicians had already set up two intake stations by the mortuary entrance; the bodies would be immediately weighed, measured, photographed and X-rayed while still inside the body bags.

Bunny and Bucky Rutledge sat side by side at the morgue entrance, dressed in scrubs, chain-smoking. Next to them Jenner recognized David Carter, a pathologist at Port Fontaine General and the ME office manager's husband, who occasionally helped out with forensic cases. Behind Carter was a short, plump, bald man with a thick black moustache and glasses who Jenner didn't recognize.

The only open parking space had a stenciled black and white sign: *M. Roburn MD, Chief Medical Examiner, District 112*; conscious that they were all watching, Jenner pulled into Marty's spot.

He nodded at the techs, thanked Carter for coming, and was introduced to Dr. El-Bashir, the odontologist. El-Bashir's hand was fleshy and cool; he smelled faintly of rose water. His speech was elegant and precise, with the whispered trace of an English accent.

"A pleasure, Dr. Jenner. I am sorry that we are meeting only now; Dr. Roburn has said many wonderful things about you."

Jenner said he'd heard good things about El-Bashir too; he had a vague feeling they'd met at a forensics meeting, in Denver, maybe.

"I'm delighted to be of service in any way that I can." El-Bashir paused, then said, "I wanted to see you in person to tell you that I have finished the charting and the comparison, and . . ." He tried to find a way to phrase it delicately, but couldn't. "I've confirmed that those are the bodies of Marty and Bobbie." He nodded solemnly, then added, "But I think you already know this."

100

"Believed rather than knew. Thank you, doctor."

They followed Jenner through the entryway and into the autopsy room. He sat on a stainless steel stool and leaned back against the tiled wall with a sigh of relief. They looked at him expectantly.

"Well . . . there's four of them, all look like adult males." His voice rattled in the airy space, bouncing off the stainless steel and tile. "Two are pretty much skeletons, weeks to months, I'm thinking. The other two are pretty putrefied, two, three weeks gone. All four were hanging; at least two were tortured first. All four are unidentified, and there won't be ID on the bodies. Hanging is the likely cause of death in all four; all homicides.

"One thing: this case is already all over the TV, and nationally – CNN sent a chopper out to the Glades to blow our crime scene around. This will be a total media orgy – reporters in front of the building, reporters in the lobby, maybe even reporters coming up to you when you're out walking the dog. They've got cameras by the back entrance so be careful when you're out there, whether you're bringing a body in or just having a smoke. I trust you completely, but please spread the word: if anyone leaks word one of this investigation to anybody, I'll fire them on the spot."

Their faces were grave; they knew that Jenner was serious. "And I do mean to *anybody*, including the cops – I don't want some idiot deputy rushing off to the press with a random juicy tidbit he's overheard. We're going to run a professional murder investigation, not some circus sideshow. I can't stop the sheriff's office from screwing the pooch, but that's not going to be us, okay?"

Jenner glanced around them as they nodded.

101

24

Just after three p.m. they heard the sirens.

Jenner went out onto the loading zone with Carter. Through the mortuary gate they saw a patrol car, turret lights blazing, a deputy leaning out to yell into the entry-point microphone. The gates opened and the patrol car entered, followed closely by the morgue wagon and another patrol car. The lot was too small for all three vehicles and it took several minutes to get the wagon into position. Outside the gates the cameramen jockeyed for position, shoving their cameras through the gate slats to capture the action.

Flanagan wheeled two hospital privacy screens out into the lot, pushing them behind the wagon to block the cameras. Calvin Major and Bucky Rutledge bundled the body bags out of the wagon and onto gurneys; from the ease with which they handled them, Jenner could tell which body bags held the skeletons. He had Calvin process the fresher bodies first, since the autopsies would be longer and more involved than the initial examination of the skeletons. The office didn't have a staff anthropologist, but sent skeletons to the Maples Center up in Tallahassee; Jenner didn't have time – he'd examine the skeletalized remains himself, then consult with anthropologist friends, if necessary.

They moved smoothly. Jenner designated an order: the larger of the two fleshed bodies first, then the smaller one, then the skeletal remains. While Calvin and Bucky did the intake work, Jenner, Carter and Flanagan set up in the autopsy room.

Jenner said, "David, tell you what – rather than

splitting up the cases, why don't you work with me on each case? I'm pretty much toast now, and I could do with an extra set of eyes." In truth, he couldn't trust someone he didn't know.

By the time they'd changed into scrubs, Flanagan had moved the first body onto the table; El-Bashir, wearing a disposable paper smock, had started charting the teeth. He turned to Jenner and said, "Don't worry, Dr. Jenner: I have touched nothing but the lips. I will wait for you before I open the mouth fully."

Jenner nodded. "Let's get him photographed first, Bunny. Then we'll undress him."

He put on gloves and opened the mouth wide; the front teeth were revolting, blackened and broken, skewed in their moorings like tombstones dislodged in a graveyard flood. Behind them, the molars were badly worn. He turned and said, "Dr. El-Bashir, why don't I help you chart the teeth while Bunny gets set up?"

They swapped places, and for five minutes El-Bashir leaned over the body, muttering to himself in Arabic as he moved the stainless steel mirror and dental probe around the mouth, pausing occasionally to adjust the overhead light and call out findings for Jenner to mark on the dental chart.

Jenner said, "I was thinking he's a young guy to have such awful teeth. Could this be methamphetamine?"

"Certainly a good possibility. He's a pretty big fellow – sleep problems with nighttime grinding might cause these problems with the back teeth, but his front teeth are really ugly too, just completely rotted out, bad recession of the gums, which would go along with methamphetamine abuse. Cocaine, too."

El-Bashir put down his instruments and turned to face Jenner. "I think you could be right, doctor. We've seen a lot more meth in Douglas over the last couple of years, and this looks a lot like the meth mouths I've seen when I volunteer at the prison."

Jenner handed him the chart. In the corridor, Calvin was waiting by the second body. Jenner did a cursory examination of the mouth, then gave El-Bashir the okay to continue and went back into the autopsy room where Bunny Rutledge was photographing the larger body with a digital camera.

Under Deb Putnam's watchful eye they'd swept the snails off the bodies at the scene. The clothing was streaked and worn from hanging in weeks of intermittent rain and had been discolored by body fluids. Bucky helped Jenner remove the filthy shirt, covered with thick brown stains on the front but with less bloodstaining on the back. Holding it up to the light to look for defects, Jenner found a hole on the back right panel. He turned to the body, asked Bucky to roll it to the left; there was a surprisingly well-preserved stab wound in the right flank.

Jenner had Bunny photograph the wound, then, as he documented the location, size and shape of the stab wound, Bunny took close-ups of the shirt. The other clothing was unremarkable.

Jenner finished his general external examination, Bunny photographing his findings. The victims's hair was jet black and straight, and the man had a scruffy beard that was beginning to slip off because of the decay. In life he'd been moderately obese, but decomposition had swollen his belly so that it ballooned out, tight and smooth.

104

Jenner could see cuts on the chest, but the shirt had been opened before the man had been carved up. The wounds seemed shallow, just cuts into the skin, enough to cause pain and bleeding and terror, but not fatal by themselves.

Just like Marty.

There were splits in the scalp where the man had been battered repeatedly with something heavy. There were scrapes on the knees and, barely visible amid the putrefaction, bruises on the arms and flanks – probably from being dragged to the chair, from fighting his executioners. There were no injuries other than hanging to explain the death.

They rolled the man over fully and eased his body face down onto the autopsy table. Across his back was a big ugly tattoo of the Virgin Mary, the lines beaded and crude, the ink blue-gray. This was standard jailhouse ink, the clumsily executed design sketched out with a pen or marker, then punctured into the flesh with a pin or sharpened guitar wire. The Virgin of Guadalupe, intended to protect the bearer from gang-rape in the prison showers.

They turned him onto his back, putting the block between his shoulders to prop him up for autopsy. Jenner saw a homemade tattoo of the letter G on the left forearm, faded and uneven; the man had probably done it himself. He imagined the man young, maybe in high school, spiking the glistening black ink into his arm with a safety pin. His initial? His girlfriend's? Probably his, particularly if he'd done it when he was young. Jenner marked the tattoo on the body diagram.

He finished writing his notes, then stepped back and

looked the corpse over one last time before beginning the autopsy.

So, Hispanic, then. First or last name likely beginning with G. Probable prison time. Not much help with Douglas County's largely Latin population of migrant workers. A speed freak, maybe cocaine too. If he'd been busted by the cops here for possession or acts committed under the influence, he'd have been deported, so chances were the U.S. authorities didn't have him on file. Mexican? Dominican? Guatemalan? Christ, he could be from almost anywhere in Latin America.

Jenner nodded at Bucky, and then picked up his scalpel.

A deputy appeared at the door, tapping at the jamb sheepishly.

Jenner looked up, then said, "Come in, deputy."

The deputy hesitated, clearly upset by the smell. Jenner put down his scalpel and walked over.

"Can I help you?"

"Dr. Jenner, the sheriff asked me to tell you he's still talking with the press. He said you are not to perform the autopsy until he is present."

Jenner nodded. The deputy scampered off, obviously relieved.

Jenner, shaking his head, closed the autopsy-room door behind him, turned to Rutledge and said, "Bucky, God protect us from fuckwits."

He picked up his scalpel, scowling, and made his first incision.

25

In the make-up chair Amanda Tucker had been holding still as Gina dusted powder onto her cheeks. Finally her impatience overcame her, and she batted the make-up artist's hands away.

"God, Gina, you're literally suffocating me! I feel like I'm trapped in a dust storm . . . Enough!"

Careful not to spill powder onto her suit, she tugged the bib off her neck and held it out to Gina as gingerly as if it were a loaded diaper. Gina folded a paper towel around her collar, then Amanda freed herself from the chair.

She endured her twenty minutes in make-up twice daily – once before her three p.m. *Update and Preview* spot, and then again before the main event, her one-hour show, *Amanda Tucker's American Crime Prime Time*, broadcast live across the country on the Current Event network and syndicated internationally. At first she'd enjoyed being primped and fussed over, a reflection of her significance. But she'd done the same routine for five years now, and her numbers were big, and she got all the affirmation she needed from the mid-seven-figure salary that followed the big numbers, and the *Saturday Night Live* parodies that followed the big salary.

Amanda left Gina to tidy up, and walked back to her office. She stood in the window, peering out over Madison Square Park, watching the knotted flow of buses and taxis as they trickled down Fifth Avenue, past the Flatiron Building.

Even the view bugged her. A fantastic view, sure, but pretty much the same view she'd had since her show had begun to pull in the numbers and they'd bumped her from an office near the elevators up to one that looked out onto Fifth, and then finally to her big corner office with its views of the park, and Fifth, and her beloved Flatiron.

Shit. Amanda smiled to herself. An office with a 270-degree view over some of the priciest real estate in the world, a hundred grand a week in base salary (not including syndication residuals or royalties from the *American Crime* books and video game), an $8,000,000 duplex on Central Park, and she was feeling restless? How spoiled she'd become!

When Amanda had checked in at the reception desk at her Georgia State Law ten-year reunion in January, the coordinator had playfully refused to give her a name badge, insisting that everyone already knew who she was. And, of course, they had known, particularly since she and Nancy Grace had shared the cover of *People* that October ("New Southern Justice: Amanda and Nancy Lay Down the Law"), and then half of America had been glued to her show through November and December, between her relentless coverage of the Sheldon-cult child abduction in Sedona and the Inquisitor killer in New York.

Her numbers had slipped during the spring – they always did as the days got warmer – but the night before, she'd had to squeeze the juice out of the divorce of a Hollywood producer and his Russian mail-order bride. She'd batted around her usual panel of slimeball divorce attorneys and entertainment reporters like the pro that she was, but her heart hadn't been in it. The producer's name was very Armenian, and the trophy wife's accent incomprehensible, and caller response had been dismal.

Her show just didn't sparkle without some spicy incest/rape trial, or a callous mom/missing tot combo, or even just a contentious appeals trial for some remorseless serial killer.

That's what we need, Amanda thought – another sexy serial killer. Everyone loves a serial killer.

She sat at her desk, pulled out a legal pad, and tried to drum up ideas for the following week. Ray Goldberg, her show runner, coordinated the guests, but Amanda had a lot of input into what topics they'd cover. Tonight they'd revisit the Hollywood divorce, touch briefly on a man suing a fast-food chain because he claimed to have found mouse droppings in his strawberry yogurt parfait, and finish with a canned segment showing Amanda horseback riding with her daughter Holly on her farm in Virginia.

She sat there tapping her pen on the pad for about fifteen minutes, but the page stayed blank. She looked around the room at her trophies from her past. Displayed around the room was a row of photos of the baddest of the bad guys she'd put away – an unbroken record of twenty-four convictions while she'd been a DA with the Fulton County District Attorney's office in Atlanta, and then another straight forty-seven she nailed while prosecuting gang killings in Las Vegas as an Assistant DA for Clark County, where she'd moved with Holly after her marriage had failed. It was in Vegas that she'd been shot, targeted for her participation in the prosecution of a Norteño soldier from the Sacramento wolf pack of El Eme, the Mexican Mafia. The shooting had been a blessing in disguise, bringing her national media attention and ultimately a new career.

With a sigh, Amanda put down her pad and turned on

her TV. She settled on CNN, where the police were recovering bodies from the Everglades. She unmuted the set and listened to the anchor – some kind of multiple-homicide story. Sources were saying four adult males, which wasn't perfect, but the number was good – mass murder always put butts on seats. Probably drugs, she thought.

Ray came rushing into the room, beaming. "Amanda!" He glanced at the TV, and nodded. "Good! CNN! Did you see it?"

She shrugged and gestured at the screen. Helicopter footage of body bags being carried out of woods on an island in the Everglades.

"Multiple homicide, but all grown men. Worth a look, but I don't know if there's really anything for us . . ."

"No, not the victims. Watch this bit, they're showing it again."

She turned back to the set.

On screen, the helicopter moved in very close and the trees and bushes began swaying wildly. Then she saw a tall man in a blue police-type windbreaker and a blonde woman in olive green angrily waving away the chopper.

Amanda sat up in her chair. "Oh my fucking God!"

Ray laughed out loud. "I knew you'd love it!"

"Doctor Edward Jenner, as I live and breathe . . ." She shook her head, grinning from ear to ear. "So that's where you've got to, my precious!"

"It gets better . . . Apparently he's been working down there a couple of weeks now, filling in for the Chief Medical Examiner. Nothing exciting there, but you know who he just autopsied?"

Ray paused dramatically. Amanda muttered impatiently, "Go on!"

"The Chief Medical Examiner! He autopsied his own boss!"

"*No. Fucking. WAY!*"

"Yes! His own boss – murdered!" Ray shook his head. "What the hell is it with this son of a bitch? He runs away, takes a job in Bumfuck, Florida, and the next thing you know everyone's dropping like flies!"

Amanda pounded the table with her fist. "Oh Ray Goldberg, I could just blow you, you old goat . . ."

He pretended to fumble at his belt buckle. She shook her head, grinning. "I can't believe this – it's just too perfect!"

Ray said, "We'll find someone from one of the local stations for tonight, set it up for in-depth on tomorrow's show. We'll have a segment producer and crew down there by morning."

Amanda turned to him. "Screw that! As soon as we wrap tonight, *American Crime* is going on location to . . ." She turned to the TV, couldn't see what she was looking for, then turned back to Ray. "We're going on location to *Bumfuck, Florida!*"

26

In the shadow of the gatehouse eaves Adam Weiss waited for the manager at La Grulla Blanca. It was the first farm on the short-list he'd made using Ricky's notes about the reception he'd received at the different estates. Adam had found four farms where managers had treated Ricky roughly. At two – Pinewhite's and UFL Tomato – Ricky had been threatened with a weapon; Adam had marked those names with a star.

La Grulla Blanca immediately struck Adam as different from the other farms he'd visited. For a start, the central compound, a quarter-mile-wide strip of land that separated the road from the marsh, was unusually heavily fortified, with the free-standing gatehouse where he stood waiting and high fences topped with razor wire. Inside the wire he didn't see anything that looked particularly valuable, just run-of-the-mill farm machinery.

Then there were the bunkhouses. At every other farm he had visited, the laborers lived in and around Bel Arbre and were ferried in shifts to the farms and fields by bus. It was a real racket – the farmers often owned the little shacks, charging outrageous rents which the workers could pay only by sleeping six to a room. But here at La Grulla Blanca there were two long bunkhouses, one with a clothesline out front; the pants and shirts waving gently on the line, he noticed, were all men's clothing. For some reason, then, the men who worked here also lived here.

Adam shrugged – he supposed it saved the cost of running buses. The rent was probably just as obscure.

The most overwhelming thing of all, though, was the smell. He'd recognized that high, greasy, pungent reek instantly from a summer spent on a farm in Pennsylvania: pig shit. It had hit him as he approached the compound; he could feel the corrosive and vile filth settling invisibly to coat his skin, his hair, his clothes.

He wondered how the pigs managed in the heat. A white fence surrounded a sloping field that held perhaps a hundred dirt-covered hogs, many of them rolling in gray mud constantly misted by water spraying from pipes that rose from the earth like saplings. Near the mud pit were a couple of long concrete-block structures, open on the sides, with a corrugated metal roof: shade for the pigs.

Adam shielded his eyes to look back to the pig field. Workers were hosing down the concrete floor. God, he wouldn't want that job.

"What do you want?"

He turned to see a deeply tanned man in khakis and a white polo shirt bearing the blue Grulla Blanca crest, a thick yellow plastic carry-case labeled *Remote Detonator* in his hand.

"Mr. Brodie? My name is Adam Weiss. I'm with the Workers' Solidarity Movement, and I was hoping to speak with some of your workers. During their break, of course."

Brodie looked Adam up and down with disgust. Behind Brodie, a pale man with stringy blond hair bleached acid yellow trotted up, a bulky VHS video camera at his side, a clipboard wedged under his arm.

"Mr. Brodie, want me to videotape this conversation?"

Brodie shook his head.

The man said plaintively, "But you might need documentation!"

Brodie snapped, "I said no."

He turned to Adam. "You can turn around and leave right now. No one here wants to talk to you. No one has anything bad to say about this place." He scowled. "No one's come running to you, saying we treat 'em bad, have they? That's 'cuz everyone here is happy."

The blond man nodded vigorously. "Very happy!"

"Shut up, Tarver." Brodie turned back to Adam. "So you can just turn around and get back on your bicycle and pedal the fuck out of here back to Boston or New York or wherever the fuck you're from. We don't like it when assholes like you come down here to stir shit up. People here work hard, and they get a fair day's pay for a fair day's work."

Behind him, Tarver was again nodding vigorously.

Brodie was turning to leave when Adam suddenly blurted, "I was wondering if you'd heard about the bodies recovered in the Glades today . . ."

Brodie stopped and turned back to him. "What bodies?"

Adam said, "On the news, they said the police have found four bodies out in the Glades. Rumor is they're farm workers."

"Oh, *farm workers*, are they?" Brodie was sneering again. "Well, we aren't missing any *farm workers*, are we, Mr. Tarver?"

"No sir, Mr. Brodie."

"Y'see? All present and accounted for." Brodie glanced at Tarver, who was fiddling with the camcorder lens cap, twisting it and tugging it, obviously dying to pull it off and shoot something. He said, "Tarver, get the dynamite and the det cord – I said that barn would be demolished by the end of the day, and I meant it."

He turned back to Adam.

"Now you can get the fuck out of here. I got a farm to run."

27

Alone in the quiet of the morgue, Jenner sat on a steel stool, filling in the paperwork. He'd finished the two autopsies, done the initial charting and prep-work for the two skeletons, and then sent everyone home. He'd look at the skeletal remains in the morning with fresh eyes, and would give Annie Carr a call; Annie was one of the best forensic anthropologists in the country, and just about the best thing about working in New York.

New York. A thousand million miles away. Home. What the hell was he doing in Florida? Every time Jenner and Douggie Pyke polished off a few single malts at the Temple Bar, Douggie would lean back expansively and say, "New York, New York, Jenner! If you can make it here, who the fuck *cares* if you can make it anywhere else?"

Jenner had done okay in New York – mostly – so anywhere else ought to have been easy. But, Jesus, Florida had been hard.

He was exhausted. He scraped the stool back across the terrazzo floor, stretched and looked at the clock at the end of the room; he had to squint to make out the time – maybe he was just getting old.

9:15 p.m. Fuck.

Jenner undressed in the locker room and climbed into the shower. The medical-examiner facility was still pretty new, and the shower had fantastic pressure. The hot water blasted his skin like a fire hose; he stood there, arms over his head to embrace the torrent, feeling the grime of his day washing off him, draining away. The lack of sleep, the hangover, the slog through the swamp, the bodies, waiting for the cops and crime lab, back into town, the autopsies, all of it, all of it loosening up and sliding off him.

As he scrubbed, he thought about the next day. The skeletons were pretty far gone; to really analyze them properly he'd need to deflesh them completely. He wondered what equipment they had in the office; probably nothing. He'd find a restaurant supply store in the morning, put something together.

As he was drying, his cell phone rang. The sheriff, no doubt.

"Doctor? This is Deb Putnam. From this morning."

He smiled. "Ranger Putnam! It was only a few hours ago – I know who you are. You mocked my fear of gator attacks, then forced chai tea down my throat – after a day like ours, we should probably go out and get matching tattoos."

There was a crackle on the line, and Deb said he sounded like he was in a good mood.

Jenner was surprised. She was right – he felt a bit giddy. He knew the feeling: it was the way exhaustion sometimes came out in him. He said, "Yes. Because I'm finishing up here, and getting the hell out. How can I help you?"

She wanted to talk about what he'd found, and they did, but he soon realized that she had something else in mind. As the initial conversation faded, she paused and then said quickly, "Doctor, I was thinking you're new here, probably don't really know too many people, so I thought maybe, if you'd like, we could get together and I could show you the town a bit. If you feel like it, that is."

Jenner could almost hear her blush. He pressed the phone to his ear with his shoulder and pulled his belt tight. "Well . . ." The leather had gone through the buckle at an odd angle and wedged, and he yanked it to the side to free it, then struggled to pull the leather back a bit.

Deb interrupted his silent battle with a hasty, "Of course, I'm sure you're really busy with these cases. Maybe some other time."

"Oh, no, no – I'd love for you to show me around. I'd really like that."

She sounded pleased. "Well, we could go out tomorrow. Cormo's on the Bay has a swordfish special."

"Ranger Putnam, I'd love to eat swordfish with you, particularly tomorrow, and particularly on the Bay."

Jenner could hear the smile in her voice. "Great! Well . . . how's about I pick you up at five p.m. at your office? They start serving at 5:30 p.m., and we want to get there early so we can get a seat on the dock."

"I'm looking forward to it – I'm sure you have so much more to teach me about gator holes!"

Deb laughed as she hung up; Jenner was grinning again.

Closing his locker door, he thought, *Who the hell eats dinner at 5:30 p.m.?*

28

Jenner dropped the paperwork in the office, then sat at his desk and logged the four men into his casebook.

He was totally wired now – he loved these sorts of cases. Not the sensational side of the deaths – all deaths are sensational at some level or another – but a group of four hanged men? He'd never seen a hanging homicide before. And this wasn't just one homicide, but four. And it wasn't just four hanged men, but four men hung in two separate pairs at different times – an absolute first.

This was murder planned calmly, and executed rigorously and repeatedly. There had to've been more than two killers – two grown men wouldn't have stayed still for a single assailant when it became clear what was happening, even if they were held at gunpoint. The noose would've had to be on one neck first, then up over the branch to be tied to the other man's neck. And then they would have had to get up on the chairs.

And Christ – killing two men, hanging each by the other's weight? Jenner was already imagining the presentation he'd give at the National Association of Medical Examiners annual conference. Where was it next year? Somewhere good, he thought – Chicago?

Someone was crying in the lobby.

Jenner stepped out into the hall. The lights were off – the building had been shut down for hours. How had they got in? He walked down the corridor toward the sound of sobbing. He stepped through the door into Reception, emerging behind the counter to see a girl there, sitting in the dark.

She was a small, undistinguished young woman, maybe twenty-two or twenty-three. She wore jeans and an ill-fitting black top, her glasses dangling from a strap around her neck; she dabbed at her nose with a balled-up Kleenex. There was something familiar about her face.

She jumped when he turned on the light.

Jenner leaned towards her. "Excuse me. Can I help you?"

She stood slowly and walked over to him.

118

"Dr. Jenner? You won't remember, but we've met. I'm Sheree Roburn."

29

Their conversation was brief – there wasn't much to say, and Sheree Roburn didn't have to say anything at all to make Jenner feel the knife twist.

No, the police had no new leads. Yes, there were only five detectives in the county, but they'd all known her mom and dad, and they were really working the case hard.

Yes, it was true that the hanged men were putting extreme pressures on the squad, but that didn't mean the investigation of Sheree's parents' murders had stopped or been put on a back burner.

She just nodded mutely at everything Jenner said.

What did she want him to say? She'd seen the media feeding frenzy over the hanged men, watched her parents' deaths get shoved aside. Her dad had been an M.E. – she had to know the score.

Sheree closed her eyes; Jenner could see her fading in front of him. He said, "You're tired. You should get some rest."

She nodded, then dragged herself sadly to her feet, lifted her bulky black handbag off the seat, and asked him to say something at the memorial service in three days' time.

He promised he'd call as soon as there were any new developments. Again, the silent nod.

He showed her to the door. Her steps were slow and heavy, her head bowed with grief.

Jenner turned off the lights in Reception, but waited by the glass door in the dark, watching Sheree Roburn make her way across the parking lot to her car; he didn't move until the taillights had disappeared into the dark on the other side of the cordon of camera trucks.

He couldn't go home now.

30

Jenner flicked on the lights in the garage. Roburn's car, covered with a weathered green tarpaulin, had been moved to the far side, away from the loading dock. He untied the tarp and dragged it off.

The car was dry now, blotched with fingerprint powder; Crime Scene had found no usable prints.

He opened the front door to pop the trunk; the passenger compartment reeked of mold – the soaked carpeting was furry with splotches of black and gray down.

The trunk was just as moldy. Jenner peered into it, shone his flashlight around, unsure what he might be looking for. He lifted the rotting floor mat; under the carpet there was no wheel well, just patches of settled black sediment. He examined the undersurface of the trunk hood and found nothing.

He opened the side doors to let the passenger compartment air out.

Crime Scene had removed the waterlogged debris from

the floor well and dried it; nothing interesting, just utility bills, some paperwork from an old office budget. There had been several coffee cups, two mugs, a sodden, crumbling cardboard box containing a fishing reel, and a handful of new thriller novels in a Barnes & Noble bag, the receipt dated a couple of days before Marty Roburn had disappeared.

Jenner opened the glove compartment – already emptied by Crime Scene. He lifted the carpeting, jammed his hands down the backs of the seats, felt underneath. Thirty cents' worth of coins, an old brochure from a fishing store.

Nothing. That's what he had found: nothing.

He sat on the old couch that the techs used for cigarette breaks and stared blankly at the car, all its doors open, its trunk gaping wide.

He stood, went back to the car, opened the hood, examined it, looked over the engine.

Nothing.

He sat back down on the couch.

And then he let himself go down a path that he'd been avoiding; once he'd started to consider it, the thoughts wouldn't stop.

Why do people get murdered? Money, love, ego mostly. Random bad luck, not infrequently. Insanity, rarely.

Jenner doubted that the Roburns had been murdered for anything to do with love, or madness, or even ego. They hadn't been killed because they'd showed up in the wrong place at the wrong time. Most likely this was about money. And it wasn't a straightforward home invasion, or a robbery – Marty had been tortured and both of them had been executed.

Marty had been tortured and murdered, just like the men in the swamp. Killed by the same men. Bobbie – not tortured, just bound, thrown into the trunk and allowed to drown when they dumped her husband's body – seemed like an afterthought: this was all about Marty.

So why was Marty Roburn killed?

Jenner sat staring at the car. Five men murdered, tortured, two of the bodies with clear signs of stimulant abuse. He tried to figure out how to connect the deaths, but everything he thought up was absurd and fanciful, the stuff of thriller fiction.

Everything except one. He tried to avoid it, horrified by the implications. But it was inescapable, and no matter what alternative explanation he cooked up he kept coming back to it.

Drugs.

Jenner had seen the bodies of a thousand dead dealers, a thousand dead junkies. Seen men pimp their girlfriends for drug money, seen crack addicts let their children starve to death. Drugs – and drug money – unhinged morality, let the monster out of the man. Most of the cruelty, most of the torture, most of the depravity he'd seen could be traced directly back to drugs.

Drugs . . . But Marty? He couldn't imagine it, couldn't believe it.

He looked down, and saw that his hands were twisting at the fishing catalogue.

Jenner remembered the one place he hadn't looked.

He knelt down by the driver's-side door and reached deep under the dashboard. His fingers stroked down the steering-wheel column until they felt the soft rubber box of a concealed spare-key safe. He tugged at the rubber, slipped a finger into the opening, then touched thinner plastic. He tugged again and it slipped out into his hand.

It was a tightly knotted packet sealed in plastic wrap. He placed the packet on the stainless steel table and carefully opened it, unfurling the outer layer to find a smaller plastic-wrap package inside, still dry. A length of coarse waxed twine – the type used in the autopsy room to sew up the bodies – looped several times around the inner packet.

Jenner fiddled with the twine and the package opened like a flower, several grams of fine white powder sitting in the center of the wrinkled film.

31

The Palmetto Court again. Jenner left the muddy waders in the trunk of his car – God willing, he'd never use them again – and carried the jug of water and the flashlight back to his cabin. The dog lay sprawled across his porch; seeing Jenner, it rolled onto its side to show its belly as it wagged its tail. The dog was unquestionably male.

"Still here, eh?" he muttered. "I thought you'd be off seeing the world, or mating or something."

From behind him, he heard, "Mr. Jenner? Uh, Dr. Jenner?"

He turned to see Mrs. Anderson, the blowsy woman who ran – possibly owned – the Palmetto Court. During daylight hours she had the beery cheer of a Dickensian charwoman, but come dark her scrappy side emerged. On his second night at the motel she'd run half-naked through the parking lot at four a.m., her burgundy house-coat flapping wide as she bellowed, "Ralph??? *Ralph*??? I'll beat the living shit out of you!!!"

Jenner was a little wary of her.

"You're back late!"

He nodded.

"A busy day, right?"

He nodded again. She was clutching a FedEx mailing box tightly to her bosom with both hands.

"I *know*! I saw you on TV!" Her face was flushed and bright. "I saw you with the bodies! And they had your office, too."

Jenner nodded once more, and asked, "Is that for me? The box, I mean . . ."

Mrs. Anderson read the address label and said, "Yeah, sure, sure . . . I brought it right over when I seen you come in." She handed it to him and, as he looked at it, said, "So, I bet they were in pretty bad shape, huh? Those bodies . . .?"

The box was from Jun; too thick for just a check. He looked at her.

"Yes, they were. Very badly decomposed." Jenner paused, then for reasons he couldn't have explained, he decided to make her night: 'They were . . . like . . . soup."

"Like *soup*? Oh my gosh!" She shook her head in exhilarated revulsion, her eyes huge, her mouth slack.

"Yes. Like soup." He nodded solemnly, then added cheerfully, "Goodnight, Mrs. Anderson – time for me to hit the hay!"

She was bursting with excitement; he'd told her nothing she hadn't seen on television, but it was from the doctor himself, and the "soup" detail would be a huge hit in the laundry room where she spent most of her day. She smiled sweetly and said, "Good night, Doctor. I hope you get some good rest – you deserve it! I was saying to Ralph just this afternoon, I just don't know how you do the work you do!". She waddled happily off down the path to the main buildings.

With some difficulty, Jenner squeezed past the dog into the cabin, quickly closing the screen and cabin doors behind him. He dumped his stuff on the kitchenette table and took off his windbreaker. God, how he hated the orange curtains.

There was a creak as the cabin door swung open; the dog was standing outside the screen door, looking up at Jenner expectantly, his tail swishing briskly behind him. Jenner shut the door.

He tore open the FedEx box. Two DVDs, carefully wrapped in pale brown craft paper, spilled out onto the table, with a ball of bubble wrap taped tight. Peering into the box, Jenner found a check for one thousand dollars. One of the DVD packets had a yellow Post-It note that read CALL US!!! in purple Magic Marker, along with a heart with a smiley face drawn in it.

Ignoring the tinny scratching at the screen door, Jenner smoothed the check against the table, then folded it and put it in his wallet. He unpacked the bubble wrap to find eight small brown glass bottles; Jun's girlfriend Kimi had gone through Jenner's collection of essential oils and selected a handful. He sat in a chair, then opened and breathed in the jasmine sambac; he felt the sweet scent soak into his blood, then closed the vial.

He picked up the phone and dialed Jun Saito; Kimi answered.

"Jenner! Good to hear you! How is Florida?" He liked that Kimi never followed the news.

"Busy. I got your present – thanks for the oils. Very sweet of you. What are the DVDs?"

She giggled. "Don't blame me – Jun chose them! I told him to get you the new Miyazaki, but he said you'd like these better. I just wrapped them!"

"Uh-oh . . ." Jenner smiled. "OK, well, is Jun there? I need to talk with him."

A couple of seconds later he heard Jun's voice.

"Hey, Jenner. So, looks like the joint is jumping . . ."

"Yeah, right. Not such a vacation after all."

"At least they're paying you."

"They're not paying me quickly, though. Thanks, I appreciate the check – I'm good for it."

"Jenner! It's kind of offensive you feel you have to say that to me."

Jenner apologized, and Jun said, "No worries, man. It's all right." There was a pause, then Jun said, "So . . .? How did ya like them?"

"What?"

"The DVDs. Kimi picked them out . . ." There was an immediate squeal of protest, and Jenner heard the coarse rub of fabric against the receiver as Kimi struggled with Jun for the phone. In the background she was calling to Jenner that it was all Jun's idea, she'd had nothing to do with it.

He tore off the wrappings, half-knowing what he'd find. No surprises: two Japanese porno DVDs. On the cover of one, an older, voluptuous woman was having sex with various men on an old fishing boat, while the other featured enthusiastic student nurses. Though the nature of the action was unmistakable, in the cover photos the genitals had been altered by a digital mosaic that left an oddly disturbing blur between the legs.

"Jenner, you're really gonna like *Do You Know the Old Woman by the Fishing Port?* – very hot!"

"Yeah, sounds it." Jenner grinned.

"Thanks, Jun." He paused, then added, "And thanks for the money. I'll get you back ASAP."

Jun said, "No worries, mate. Ain't no thang. You hang in there, OK? And let me know if you need more, too." Behind him, Kimi said something in Japanese, then Jun said, "OK, Jenner. Kimi says she needs my sweet lovin', so . . ." There was another squeal and a battle for the receiver that ended when the phone was abruptly hung up.

Jenner spun the DVD box on the table, trying to remember how Jun's tradition of giving him porn had even begun.

He climbed into bed just before midnight. When he turned out the light, the scratching at the door began again, this time furiously. He wrapped the thin pillow around his head but couldn't block out the sound. The scratching died down, only to be replaced by a moaning growl.

Then the scratches came back.

Finally Jenner could take it no more. He got out of bed and opened the door to find the dog sitting there, peering up at him. The dog looked happy.

"Jesus!"

He opened the door a crack, and the dog trotted past him into the kitchen and flopped down on the weathered linoleum.

It turned to look at him expectantly; it wanted food, no doubt. Jenner checked his cupboards. Two cans of beef stew. He opened one, sloshed its contents into his only plate, an old plastic cereal bowl that had probably been in the cabin since the motel opened in 1952. For a second he wondered whether he should microwave it, then just stuck it in front of the dog; the animal didn't seem to mind that the food was cold.

Jenner watched the mutt eat, then climbed into bed, the dog following quickly to curl up on the coverlet. He slept through the night.

32

Jenner lay in bed, talking to Annie Carr on the phone, feeling her distance in the digital distortion of her words.

"So let me get this straight, Jenner: you need to clean the skeletons down to the bone, and they don't have *any* equipment?"

"They usually outsource their anthro stuff."

"Huh. Well, just get the biggest stockpot you can find, and a heating ring. You want the biggest thing you can find, that way you don't have to dismember them . . . that much." Annie was enjoying herself.

"And what do I put the remains in? Water? Meat tenderizer?"

"Yah. You could do it in just water, but that'd take forever. Here's my recipe: detergent to emulsify the fat tissue, meat tenderizer to . . . uh, tenderize the meat, and liquid hand soap, for that meadow-flower freshness."

Jenner jotted done the list, pausing at the hand soap.

He wasn't laughing, so Annie added, "No, really: use liquid hand soap too – it'll help move things along. Macerate the parts at about ninety degrees Centigrade – if the pot comes to a boil the tissues will cook onto the bone, and scraping 'em off will be hell."

He was taking notes on a yellow legal pad; he wrote HELL, and underlined it several times.

Christ.

"OK, Annie, thanks." Jenner scanned his notes. "I got it. How's the missus?"

"She's good, thanks." She was silent for a second. "Jenner? We've been thinking about driving up to Provincetown and making it official. When will you be back? We'd both like it if you could be there."

"That's fantastic! And well past due." He paused. "I don't know when I'll be back. I was just supposed to be here three months, but I don't know what's going to happen now."

She said, "Rats."

"You know I'll make it if I can – I'm all about hot lesbo wedding action!" He scrawled LESBO WEDDING on his pad.

She snorted. "Okay, I gotta go. Remember, Jenner, not above ninety degrees, unless you want to spend the week whittling boiled shoe leather off those bones . . ."

The dog was lying across his bed, snout half-buried in the coverlet. Seeing Jenner looking at him, his tail started up again.

Jenner got up and opened the door, but the dog wouldn't go out. Jenner picked up the cereal bowl, opened the last can of stew and dumped it into the bowl.

He watched the dog wolf it down, then opened the door again so the mutt could leave.

The dog rolled onto its side, peering up at him, tail sweeping slowly back and forth across the floor. Jenner gave up.

33

As soon as Jenner's seat belt clicked shut the dog squeezed forward into the front passenger's side. He draped himself in the open window, paws hanging out. When they were moving, and the baking air in the car had vented, Jenner tried to put the window up. But the dog refused to budge and Jenner left it down.

He drove the few minutes to the Southland Mall, a newish development marked by an Outback Steakhouse at the entrance, anchored by a Super Target at one end and a Publix at the other. He parked under the sparse shade of a small tree, partially closed the passenger window and opened the other windows up a crack to give the dog air, then climbed out.

Jenner studied the mall directory, splashed in aqua and peacock pink; the restaurant supply shop was across the mall, but the Port Fontaine Pet Sanctuary, the no-kill animal shelter that Marie Carter, the office manager, had recommended, was just behind the Super Target. She'd told him to ask for Miss Craine.

He decided to take care of the dog first – he didn't want the thing to melt while he was off buying stockpots.

He found some rope in his scene bag; to his surprise,

the dog offered no resistance as Jenner bent to tie the rope around its neck. It trotted happily with him past the J. Crew, a P.F. Chang's, a Barnes & Noble, an Apple store and a retro-styled shop that sold fudge and ice cream, and then peed vigorously on the gleaming rank of chrome shopping carts gridlocked along the walkway in front of the vast Target. Though the day was not yet particularly hot, Jenner lingered in front of the megastore, enjoying the cool air issuing from the open doors.

The animal shelter looked like it had escaped from an older strip mall. It was cheery enough, with a fresh coat of white paint decorated with poorly executed animal silhouettes in bright colors, but it was at odds with the slick and polish of Southland. The shelter's comfortable ramshackle-ness was offset by a gleaming deep-amethyst-blue Mercedes convertible parked in front, top down, tan leather interior immaculate despite the car being a good twenty-five years old by Jenner's estimate.

The reception smelled of dogs, and Jenner heard the muffled din of yelps and barks from the kennels in the depths of the building.

Behind the glass of the counter sat a blonde girl with glasses, perhaps eleven or twelve years old. She was painfully thin, her skin pale and almost translucent. There was a small bandage on her left wrist, and Jenner noticed small crusted punctures in her lower arm – she'd recently had an IV. Her Hollister backpack spilled colored pencils and notebooks onto the counter top.

She was gravely drawing dinosaurs. She was gifted; she was carefully cross-hatching them, shading the curve of the belly of the brachiosaurus until it had depth. She didn't look up as Jenner and the dog came in; he noticed that she wore small pink ovals of plastic in her ears – some form of hearing aid.

The dog padded forward and she jerked up; behind thick glass lenses her eyes were an astonishing bright blue.

She looked seriously at Jenner and then at the dog, then said, "Hello."

Jenner said, "Hello. Do you work here? I'm looking for a Miss Craine."

She said, "I am Miss Craine."

"Hmm. I was looking for an older Miss Craine. Maybe your sister?"

"Her mother, actually. Can I help you?"

Jenner turned to see a woman watching him from the doorway to the kennels. She was in her late thirties. Underneath her white coat, she wore paint-spattered jeans cut off at mid-calf. Her espadrilles, too, were densely covered with dripped paint – a part-time artist, he thought. Her eyes were green, and she wore her hair back, behind a broad gray velvet band; under the harsh fluorescents, he could see silver strands among the dark blonde. A pit-bull puppy cradled in the crook of her arm chewed on her finger.

"I was hoping you might be able to look after this dog."

Miss Craine looked at Jenner's dog, and frowned. "What, you've had enough of him?"

Jenner shook his head. "He's not mine, he's a stray."

"Oh, okay." She put the puppy on the counter top, and the girl swept it up into her arms. "Lulu, honey – take him to Leo, 'kay?"

The girl slid off her stool and disappeared into the back.

Miss Craine squatted in front of the dog and scratched his head. "Well, you're a podgy fellow, aren't you!"

She looked up at Jenner, studying him. Her eyes were

the color of an ocean in mist; her gaze made him feel adolescent, made him want to stammer.

He said, "I found him near my hotel. A colleague told me to bring him here."

She was looking in the dog's mouth, inspecting its eyes and ears; it was behaving remarkably well.

"Oh, are you the medical examiner?" She stood. "Marie told me you'd be by."

Jenner nodded.

"Nothing wrong with this dog that a good wash won't fix." She jogged the dog's belly with her foot. "And some time on the treadmill, eh? Eh, Podgy?" The dog's hindquarters shook as his tail bounced back and forth.

She put out her hand. "Doctor Jenner, isn't it? Maggie Craine."

He nodded, shaking her hand.

She said, "And now you're supposed to say your first name, Dr. Jenner – that's how people get to know each other, at least down here."

Jenner said, "Most people just call me Jenner."

"Well, I'm not most people! What do your friends call you?"

"My friends call me Jenner."

"OK, Jenner it is." Maggie Craine snorted. "So you're visiting Port Fontaine from New York?" She leaned back against the counter. "Where do they have you? The Arrowhead?"

"Oh, no. Somewhere out in the Reaches, not great, but good enough."

She frowned. "Oh, God. Sorry about that, Jenner." She looked him over. "How did you get the shiner?"

He put a hand quickly to his eye; he'd forgotten.

"I'm sure there's a story there."

"Not a very exciting one. Some kids were hassling the dog, and I got in a fight with their father."

Maggie made a face. "A fight? I hope that's not how you solve all your problems."

Jenner smiled. "If I solved all my problems that way, there wouldn't be much of me left."

"Good. I like your face the way it is; I'd be sad if someone hit it again."

He said, "Me too." The heat of his blush took Jenner by surprise. She ignored his embarrassment.

He said, "Does it help my cause if I point out that he hit me first?"

Maggie was amused. "You have a cause?"

Jenner grinned. The dog walked over to him, sat and leaned heavily against his leg.

She said, "Well, Jenner, looks like you've got a friend there. Maybe you should keep him – no collar, and I couldn't feel any implanted tag, so I doubt we'll find an owner."

Jenner shook his head. "A dog is about the last thing I need right now. Besides, I'll be going home to New York soon, and I have a cat there."

"A cat? You know what they say about men who have cats, don't you?" She leaned over to scratch the dog's head. "Well, I'll have the vet have a look at you when he stops by this afternoon. And then we'll see what we can do about finding you somewhere to live!"

Maggie disappeared through the door with the dog, and then reappeared behind the counter. She scribbled a note in her ledger, then peered up at Jenner.

"Doctor Jenner?" Her eyes were a pale gray-green; he'd

134

seen the ocean that colour once after the storm in the Andaman Sea.

The fifteen year old boy in him had taken over completely.

"Yes?"

"This is a no-kill shelter, which means any pet we take in is properly cared for, fed, watered, all that. We're privately funded, and every little bit helps." She nodded her head to his right, where he saw a small wooden box labeled *Donations*.

Jenner pulled out his wallet hastily. It was empty except for Jun's check, a ten-dollar bill and three singles; she watched as he stuffed all his money into the slot.

"Sorry it's not more – I've been meaning to get to the bank."

Maggie smiled. "Oh, the box will still be here when you come back."

"Here, I need you to fill out this bit here about the dog's history." She slid the ledger across the counter. "I know you don't know anything, so just put that."

She watched him write, then said, "Tell you what. Since I've just sucked you dry, why don't I invite you along to dinner tonight? My father's taking me to dinner at the golf club – we go most nights, and Daddy'll be thrilled to have a guy to talk to, for once."

Jenner was surprised. "Sounds good. What time?"

"Why not come to our house around half past six, seven. You can have a look at the place, we'll have drinks, then we can drive over to the club. Sound like a plan?"

He nodded. "Where's your place?"

"Doctor Jenner! Don't you know you're talking to Port Fontaine royalty?" She smiled again. "Our house is called

Stella Maris; it's the big Italian villa at the uptown end of the Promenade. What are you driving? I'll tell security to expect you."

"Tell them to expect a Chrysler Sebring. A blue Chrysler Sebring." Maggie nodded, her eyes so merry that he blurted, "It's a rental."

She murmured, "Of course," as if no one would ever actually *own* a Sebring.

She got a leash from the office; it took her a second to slip it onto the dog. "So, tonight, Stella Maris, around six-thirty. Sorry, but the Polo Grounds insists on sports coats at dinner, okay?"

Jenner stuck out his hand awkwardly and she shook it, a coolly amused look on her face.

On the way back to his car, he stopped in the ice cream and fudge shop; in one corner of the store, he'd noticed a collection of locally crafted candles and organic perfumes. The young woman behind the counter gave him the encouraging smile given to any man approaching a perfume counter.

He said, "Are any of your essential oils produced locally?"

She brightened. "I have white lotus, pink lotus, ylang ylang, jasmine grandiflorum, wild coffee and tea tree extracts, all sourced in Douglas county. Is this for aromatherapy? Or are you a natural perfumer?"

He shook his head. "I collect essential oils; I've tried blending, but I'm terrible at it."

"It gets easier with practice." Smiling, she looked over her collection. "Which one shall I show you first . . ."

He said, "If you could only show me one, which would it be?"

"The pink lotus absolute – it's just stunning, you really have to have it. But get the ten percent dilution – the absolute is eighty bucks for two ccs."

She unstoppered a small brown glass vial, dipped a paper strip into it and held it to Jenner's nose. The scent was exquisite, floral and ethereal.

"It's fantastic. I'll take two ccs of the diluted." She looked pleased.

As she rang up the sale, he sniffed the lotus again. The scent was deeper than he'd realized, tropical and narcotic. He imagined himself in Sri Lanka again, standing by the lotus pond in the ruined temple.

Only this time, Maggie Craine was there with him.

34

Jenner glanced up at the autopsy room clock. Three p.m. He'd better get moving.

He'd picked up a battered twenty-five-gallon stockpot and a large heating ring from the *Used* section of the Southland Mall restaurant-supply shop. It was now installed at the far end of the morgue, where the ventilation was better. Half-filled with water, meat tenderizer and hand soap, it had been sitting on the heating ring for almost a half-hour, and was now steaming nicely.

Jenner cleaned the skeleton, carefully dissecting off the soft tissue, expertly exposing the underlying ribs and spine. He slowed: scalpel nicks in bone were finer and shallower than the sort of cuts he was expecting to find in the ribs, but he didn't want to give the defense experts any room to claim that he'd created the bone cuts himself.

The reek had eased – his nose was now burned out on it. He leaned over the autopsy table, squinting as he stripped the muscles and ligaments from the junction of ribs and spine.

"Ha! Doc! You should see your face! You look like you just found roaches in your scrambled eggs . . ."

He looked up to see Flanagan grinning at him from the doorway. Rudge was behind him.

"I told the detective maybe he oughta wait until you came up, but he wanted to come down anyway." The morgue supervisor winked at Rudge. "Told ya!"

Jenner nodded at Rudge as he approached the table. "You okay with this, detective?"

Rudge shrugged. "The sweet smell of job security, doc. I've worked Major Crimes in this hot-ass county for five years, and was a deputy for another ten before that; not that I love it, but this shit doesn't throw me."

He grinned at Jenner's black eye. "So, how's your head, Rocky? You okay after yesterday? That shiner makes you look pretty damn hard . . ."

Concentrating on the table, Jenner muttered, "I'm fine. Just give me a second, will you . . ."

He'd severed the spinal column below the ribs, and had cut the ligaments attaching the shoulder girdle to the chest on each side. Rudge watched Jenner open the joint at the top of the spine using short strokes with the tip of his scalpel, then cut around the top vertebrae to separate off the cranium and jaw.

Jenner straightened, placed the skull on the table and put down his scalpel.

"Done!" he said brightly.

He lifted the headless upper-trunk skeleton from the body bag and carefully carried it down to the stockpot. Rudge followed with a look of faint disgust on his face. Jenner checked the thermometer in the pot, turned down the hot plate a little, then lowered the truncated skeleton carefully into the foaming water. The greasy bones slipped under the surface.

"Thanks for coming down." Jenner put the lid on the stockpot, then looked over at Rudge. "Do me a favor – for Christ's sake, spare me the 'let's get ribs' jokes . . ."

"Not me, doc. That's more the kind of crack you'd hear from Detective Bartley, or maybe some of the guys in Highway. I'm more about the subtle puns, the slightly uncomfortable race-based observational humor."

Jenner led Rudge to the dictating room. He pulled open the desk drawer, fished out the small drug packet and put it on the desk.

Rudge said, "No thanks – I just had coffee." He picked up the packet. "So, what's this?"

"I found it in Marty's car – he had one of those boxes where you stash spare keys. It was hidden on the steering column, deep under the dashboard." He hesitated a second. "To tell the truth, I didn't know if I was going to hand it over."

"I feel for you, doc." Rudge nodded. "But you had to – it's the right thing to do. I have to say, I don't figure Roburn for a drug user – I've seen that man at all hours of the day and night, and never once has he been less than a hundred percent with it. Anyone else have access to his car?"

"No clue. As far as I know, it was just him and his wife,

and I doubt Bobbie even knew the hiding place was there – I'm pretty sure this is Marty's. But I have no idea what he was doing with it. I mean, if it was from a case, why didn't he log it into Evidence?"

They stood looking at the packet.

Rudge said, "What do you think?"

"Powder cocaine or meth, probably. Maybe heroin, but it's whiter than most heroin I've seen." Jenner picked up the bag. "I'll take it over to the Evidence Unit now and get it vouchered."

Rudge shook his head slowly. "Y'know, I've been figuring that's what this whole thing is all about – the Roburns, the bodies from the Glades. When people act out like this, it's most always drugs."

Jenner nodded. "The kid who called in the bodies said they were farm workers. You talked to him?"

"Adam Weiss? Bobby Bartley interviewed him. I'd like to speak with him myself, except now he's in the wind. But we'll find him."

"You got people actively looking?"

"We're stretched pretty thin, but we're doing our best."

Rudge stepped out into the autopsy room, looked around, then turned back to Jenner. "Sheriff Anders told me to bring you up to speed on the investigation into Doc Roburn's death." He paused. "Such as it is."

"That doesn't sound good." Jenner slipped the shrink-wrap packet into a clear zip-lock biohazard bag, then tossed his gloves into the garbage. He looked Rudge in the eye. "He's not getting lost in the shuffle here, right?"

Rudge shook his head. "No shuffle. But there's just five of us, and there's a lot of shit to do. We're tracking the

Roburns' whereabouts on the days leading up to their disappearance, we're canvassing the farms for missing field hands, we've put up posters in Bel Arbre with rough descriptions of the clothing – you know that hardly anyone in the Sheriff's Office speaks Spanish? But there's not much news coming out on the hanged men, so now the press is waking up to the Roburns."

He grinned. "I heard Mayor Reynolds tell the sheriff that he doesn't want to see some 'Resort Town of Death' segment on CNN. Anders has authorized maximum overtime, and we got Highway pitching in to look for Weiss."

"You think you'll get something from Weiss Bartley didn't?"

"Maybe – Bartley's okay, I'm better. But maybe there's not much to get. He doesn't know much, I don't think – doesn't know the men who came to him, doesn't know anything about them, says he couldn't pick 'em out of a line-up. He may or may not be lying. He's a city kid, completely lost down on the farm. He's trying to do the right thing, has a bunch of theories, but no definite information."

"Like what?"

"Well, he thinks they were killed by other farm workers. Apparently, yesterday he was going around to the different estates, trying to interview workers – which doesn't go down real well around here. You don't want to piss too many people off up in Bel Arbre: the field hands may be second-class, but those farms are all either part of major agribusiness or vanity projects for the richest citizens of Port Fontaine. Lot of old money up there in those drained swamps, my friend.

141

"Anyway, Bartley told him to calm down and let us do the work. I doubt we'll get very far with the farms – the owners don't want us on their land, the workers know it and won't talk – particularly if they're afraid they'll get killed for talking."

"And what do you think?"

Rudge shrugged. "He could be right. These people . . . they call them migrant workers, which sounds like some romantic Depression-era shit, but they're really just cattle. They pay to get smuggled into the country like animals, work like dogs, make just enough money to cover their bed and their food and their beer, a few leftover bucks to send home . . . Call it what it is: it's slavery shit, Jenner. Pure and simple.

"And do I think farm overseers could be handing out a little intimidation? Sure. It's happened before, I'm sure it's happening now. Even murder. But I figure there's a lot more to it than that, here."

Jenner nodded. "Particularly if Marty Roburn's involved."

Rudge scratched the back of his head. "Shit. You really think he's involved?"

"It's no coincidence that he has the same injuries as one of the hanged men. More than one, I think; we'll see once the ribs are clean."

"The Roburns' house is a wreck – looks like they were packing to leave, but someone's tossed the place. It looked fake, though, like whoever did it was just going through the motions. They pulled the drawers out of the dresser and stacked them on the ground, for instance – every burglar I've seen just yanks the drawers and dumps the stuff out. Sure, any money and jewelry's

142

gone, but they left a laptop untouched on the bedroom dresser."

"Had Marty done any cases from the farms lately?"

"Yeah, I thought of that. I went through the morgue logs with Flanagan – nothing sticks out. This winter we had a stabbing in one of the worker huts in Bel Arbre, and a guy got run over by a backhoe while they were digging a new septic. I'll make it up to the farms in question to check it out, but it doesn't sound promising."

"Had he been on any scenes up there? Maybe he saw something."

Rudge shook his head. "Nope. The stabbing guy died at the clinic in Bel Arbre, and Roburn didn't respond to the backhoe thing."

The door swung open and the sheriff strode in, followed by a thick, hirsute man in a Highway Patrol uniform. Both wore white paper masks and moved gingerly, as if they were worried about being contaminated by touching something unclean.

Over the mask, the sheriff's eyes were piggy little beads. "What're you two gossiping about?"

Rudge shook his head and said, "Just catching the doctor up, sheriff."

Anders grunted. "Well, it's my turn to catch you both up . . ." He looked past Rudge to the stockpot. "What the hell is that?"

Cooper, the Highway Patrol guy, took a paper towel and lifted up the lid, grimacing at the stale reek of the steam. He picked up a ladle from the autopsy table and reached into the pot, pale bone billowing up in the gray water.

"Tommy, check it out – ribs!"

"Jesus! That's disgusting . . ."

He stared at Jenner, then looked back at the stockpot; Cooper was standing next to it pretending to be a chef, waving his hand over the scum as if wafting the scent to his nose. He nodded to Rudge.

"You making gumbo, Fudgie?"

Anders snapped, "Let's talk in the hallway. That's just revolting."

Jenner and Rudge followed him out of the autopsy room, Cooper behind them. Anders pulled off his mask; Jenner noticed the faint sheen of Vicks Vapo Rub on his upper lip before he caught the whiff of menthol.

Anders said, "What are you doing? I never saw Roburn do that."

"I need to see if there's any marks on the bone. This is the safest way to clean them." Jenner shrugged. "I know Dr. Roburn never did it – I had to buy the pot and the heating ring. He didn't do it because they did it for him in Tallahassee."

Hearing those words, the sheriff's face reset, bulging into something unpleasantly smug, lips pursing and cheeks puffed, like a sphinx with a terrible secret.

He began, "Well . . ."

Behind him, Cooper was smirking.

Anders said, "Well, Bobby Bartley just found out something pretty interesting: turns out that no South Florida cruise line has ever heard of Marty Roburn. No reservations, no tickets, nothing. It looks like Marty Roburn was planning to get out of Port Fontaine, all right – just not on a cruise . . ."

35

The shadows of the straggly poplars on the west side of the cemetery were longer now, crawling across the grass to clutch at Adam Weiss's feet. Around him, the white concrete grave markers shone marigold yellow in the slipping sun. When the breeze picked up, the flags at the entrance to the cemetery rippled and snapped, and everywhere he looked Adam saw the scattered fluttering of swaying flowers and brightly colored ribbons gathered and ruched onto board, cheap substitutes for floral arrangements.

Five-thirty, almost. No, gone half past five.

Adam scanned the grounds. No one.

He was alone. Where was the guy?

He was exactly where he was supposed to wait: in the section where they buried the kids.

He looked around him. Here the graves snuggled close together, as if they wanted the children to keep each other warm in the cold ground.

The children's graves seemed so busy to him, so creepily lively. The graves were sealed with concrete, the concrete covered with pebbles, the pebble bed strewn with mildewed statuettes of praying angels and playful kittens and puppies. The sun bleached the pebbles white, and withered the weeds that crept through them. There was a lot of color – vibrant red roses, pots of yellow daisies, bouquets of pink zinnias – all artificial, all enduring as the bodies underneath slipped away. Some headstones bore photos of the children, now faded to washed-out oranges and yellows; on some he noticed toys – rusting metal cars, grubby stuffed animals ravaged by exposure to the elements. When the breeze picked up, dozens of silver Mylar whirligigs spun wildly, splintering back the light as the wind killed the sound.

Adam shivered despite himself.

Where was his informant?

He thought over his day. He'd spent the morning visiting two farms. He'd been unwelcome at both, but the overseer at Endicott had been particularly unpleasant, unpleasant enough for Adam to add the place to his list of suspicious estates.

He cycled back to Bel Arbre, arriving on the main drag hot and sticky – and increasingly uncertain. Of course the farm managers were unpleasant: if Adam ran an agricultural enterprise on this scale, overseeing dozens of workers, draining property, digging ditches, keeping machinery and livestock functioning, wouldn't he be pissed off if some muckraking liberal started poking around in his business?

In the line at the taco stand, he had the eerie impression that the other people there – farmhands, mostly – shrank back from him. He felt like the new, doomed sheriff, arriving at the lawless frontier town at the beginning of the movie, promptly shot so that the *real* hero could emerge. They acted as if to stand next to him meant certain death.

It was his imagination, his own endless font of anxiety. After all, no one actually left the line. But one thing was for sure: no one was talking. And at that shack the chatter had always been so animated that it had bugged him.

Christ, he was going nuts, getting paranoid. How could they know? They couldn't know.

Could they?

The line crawled forward, each second sticking to the last, an age between each step, each order taking a lifetime to utter, an eternity to prepare.

Adam was flooded with thoughts of home – the salty crunch of a hot pretzel with brown mustard eaten on a bench in Central Park, the feel of cool rain on his face as he walked home up Broadway late at night, the smell of rich blonde Columbia girls who dressed like they really cared – it all became overwhelming, heart-breaking. Standing in the taco shack line, he realized he'd had enough. How the fuck had he become all tangled up in this in the first place? It was absurd: trying to impress a girl, he'd ended up as part of an investigation into mass murder . . .

Who was he kidding? Tiff was nothing, really nothing, just some cute chick in his class. One chick in one class in a city full of classes and chicks. And she was fucking Andy Willet, maybe even at that moment, boning the fuck out of him on some futon in Adams-Morgan!

It was time to go home.

Adam pulled out his cell phone. His mom would help with the ticket – she'd called three times since the news broke on TV, leaving pitiful messages about how much she wanted him home. Kuh-fucking-CHING.

The red message light was winking; he played it back. Not his mother, but the detective he'd talked to last night, more questions, blah blah blah. Fuck, he'd given them everything he knew.

Well, on his way home he'd stop in at the sheriff's office substation and talk with them again. One last time.

And then everything changed. He was pedaling down his street, worrying about the tacos leaking through the brown paper bag, when he saw a small white Mitsubishi mini-pickup truck coming towards him.

As they drew closer, the truck slowed. Adam saw the blue insignia on the hood and slowed too, putting his feet down to coast to a stop.

He faced the truck for a few seconds in silence before it began to roll towards him.

He stayed put.

It crept closer, then drew level.

The driver was a small, gaunt Mexican with a graying goatee, his face partly hidden under the stiff bill of his Grulla Blanca baseball cap. He spoke English with a thick accent.

"We can help you. Okay? We tell you, you go to police, okay . . .?"

Adam nodded, his heart suddenly pounding.

"Okay, I go to police. What can you tell me?"

"Not here. Not good place. Meet me at four hours, in the . . . *cementerio*?"

Adam shook his head, uncertain. "Four hours? Or four o'clock?" He pointed at his watch. "*Que hora*?"

The man nodded and said, "*A las cinco.*" Five p.m.

"Okay. *A las cinco. Pero, donde en el cementerio?*"

The man seemed surprised – it was a fairly open space. He thought for a second, then said, "*En la parte de los niños.*"

"Okay. *A las cinco.*"

And with that, the pickup accelerated and disappeared down the end of the street.

Adam went home, showered, ate his cold tacos, the meat like rubber in his mouth. He started to pack, then called the sheriff's office; he would tell the detective what

148

was happening, ask him to meet him at the cemetery at five-thirty – any sooner, and he might spook the informant. But the detective was out, and Adam left a message on his voicemail.

As he hung up, the feeling came back: he shouldn't have meddled. This wasn't his business. The police could take care of it.

But he had no choice. He'd never had a choice – they'd come to him.

He left his house at quarter to five; it took him ten minutes to reach the cemetery. And now the man was nowhere to be seen.

He wasn't going to show. He was already more than a half-hour late.

Adam relaxed, only then realizing how tense he'd been.

He could describe the guy to the detective, tell him to look for an older Mexican man with a gray goatee at La Grulla Blanca, suggest he offer the guy immunity or something so he could testify.

Leaving Adam out of it.

He walked back to his bike. It was cooler now – funny to think of seventy-five degrees as "cool" – and the trees at the far end of the cemetery were now deeply shadowed.

And he was going home.

He climbed on his bike and pedaled towards the exit, picking up speed, faster and faster, and soon his bike was flying across the tarmac, the chain a smooth whir under his pumping feet, heading towards his cottage, then to Miami, then home to New York.

The pickup truck slipped into the cemetery through the western gate – Adam's gate – turning onto the track in front of him with a dry crunch of gravel. It seemed larger;

a trick of the light, he thought. In the setting sun, he couldn't see the interior of the cab well, but it looked like there were two men there now.

Adam coasted to a stop, let his bike down onto the grass and walked over to the pickup, approaching the driver's side.

It was a different man, younger, bigger. Muscular.

Adam said, "Hey, how's it going?"

The driver nodded, grinned widely, and said, "Fine. Everything's fine." He paused, then added, "You?"

Adam nodded, also struggling for casual. "Good, just heading home. Long day."

Beyond the driver, he could see the man in the front passenger seat held a camcorder on his lap.

Grin unchanged, the driver said, "Can I help you with something?"

Adam shrugged. "Nope, I'm good."

The man said, "Oh. Well, you came up to us . . ."

"Oh, no problem, I thought you were someone else."

"Really? Who?"

"Oh, some guy who . . . who was going to tell me the best spot . . ." Adam grinned sheepishly. "He was going to tell me where I could buy some pot round here. You guys don't know, do you?"

"Some pot? As in marijuana? That's pretty pathetic." The man shook his head. "My friend, this is Florida. In Florida, only pussies smoke pot . . ."

The passenger stifled an excited giggle.

"And you don't strike me as a pussy."

The driver cracked the door as Adam backed away.

"Okay, well, I guess I'll have to keep looking."

"Oh, not so much."

Adam was walking back to his bike.

"Kid."

He turned. The man was ten feet from him.

"Kid? You lost."

Adam shook his head, as if not understanding.

"You lost. You lose. You played, but you lost. Time to pay up."

Adam's feet were rooted to the ground. He stammered, "There seems to be some kind of misunderstanding, sir."

"*Sir?* I like that!" The man was grinning now. "That's pussy talk!"

"I think you think I'm someone I'm not."

The man cocked his head. "Really? You're not Adam Weiss?"

Adam stammered, but nothing came out.

"Put the bike in the truck."

Adam was shaking.

"Kid, it's over." The man pulled a black automatic out of his waistband. "Now put the fucking bike in the fucking truck before I fucking gutshoot you and let you bleed shit right here in the cemetery. All we want is to talk with you."

He watched the boy pull the bike up and wheel it to the truck. In the flatbed, several stacked bags of feed and canisters of pesticide peeked out from under a broad weathered tarp.

"Lift it and put it in the fucking truck."

Adam's muscles were liquid, sloshing loosely under his skin. His hands wouldn't grasp, his arms wouldn't lift. Bone, muscles and tendons refused to work together to heft the frame up onto the flatbed.

"Kid, I swear to fucking Christ I will shoot you dead right now if that bike isn't on the truck by the time I count three."

He racked the pistol with a slick, flat click. Adam thought dully: it sounds just like on TV.

The bike's wheels and frame floated up as if buoyed by helium, and the bike tipped up over the side and into the flatbed. The front wheel caught and twisted, the frame tumbling sideways onto the truck, lifting the tarp to expose for a second the bloodied body of a man. Not even for a second, a fraction of a second, just long enough for Adam to see the small gray goatee.

"Okay, kid. Now the three of us are going to go for a little ride, going to have us a little talk . . ."

36

It was just after quarter to seven when Jenner pulled up to the wrought-iron gates of Stella Maris, Maggie Craine's house.

Palace, really, he thought. An old mansion roofed with terra-cotta tiles, the big white house glowed against the overcast evening skies. It had a commanding view straight down the Promenade past all the other big, white houses. The estate was surrounded by high cream stucco walls; tall palm trees peeked over the wall. Behind the black gates, white gravel carriage drive flowed around an oval lawn with a large fountain, where water splashed down through tiered white marble bowls stained with moss.

Jenner pushed the button on the videophone and

waited in the blue glow.

A red light flickered on over the camera, and a voice said, "How may I help you?"

"Doctor Jenner for Ms. Craine."

There was a brief silence; Jenner wondered if they were checking out his Sebring.

"Thank you, doctor. You're expected." There was a buzz, followed by a high grinding sound as the gates swung open. "Please park in the main house lot – that's to the left; if you go right, you'll end up in the pool house lot, so please make sure to take the left."

He followed the drive left, into the house lot, screened from the house by a thick wall of box privet and shade trees. Of the dozen parking spaces, four of the six nearer the house were filled – the household's cars, Jenner assumed. There was a maroon Bentley convertible, a steel-gray Lexus SUV, Maggie's vintage Mercedes convertible and a new navy-blue Volvo station wagon.

Jenner walked along a path through the hedge, discreetly signposted, emerging onto a side garden, the house up ahead to his right. To his left was an immaculately groomed grass tennis court, the chalk lines an eerie gleaming white at dusk.

Floodlights suddenly turned the walls of the house pale gold. Inside, the building was filled with light, every window illuminated, light that spilled out over the grounds, throwing shadows from the tall palms and ornamental shrubs. Xanadu.

Jenner cell phone buzzed.

"Doctor? It's Deb Putnam, from yesterday?"

Christ.

"Deb! God, I'm sorry! I had such a crazy day that I just

came home and crashed. I totally forgot – I'm really sorry."

She chuckled softly. "No problem – I thought it was probably that."

"Where are you now?"

"I'm at Cormo's. I waited at your office for a while, then thought I'd see if you came here directly. I didn't want to disturb you – I thought you might have got held up with something important."

"I'm really sorry." Jenner paused. "I don't think I can do it tonight – I'm completely wiped out. Can I get a rain check?"

"Oh sure! Really, no problem at all – I completely understand."

"Okay, good. I'll call you tomorrow and we can make a plan."

"Sounds good." Deb hung up.

He shook his head. Christ.

"Jenner? Never keep a lady waiting – particularly this one!"

He looked up to see Maggie Craine standing on the terrace at the top of a short flight of stone steps. She was wearing a fitted white silk dress, cut simply to emphasize her shape and her legs; on other women, it would've seemed formal and constricting, but she made it look effortless and light.

"You like?" She smiled at him, and did a half-twirl. "Tonight Miss Craine is wearing James Perse."

Jenner smiled back, and Maggie lifted up her hem and kicked up a heel. "And Prada."

She had a tall glass filled with ice and mint in her hand.

He said, "Sorry about the delay. Call from work."

"If you can drag yourself to the top of these steps, I'll

154

give you a mojito."

"After the day I've had, I'd crawl up those steps for a mojito."

Maggie grinned. "Stop giving me ideas!" She took one step down. "Come on, I'll meet you halfway."

"That's not halfway."

"Well, this is the Craine version of halfway – better get used to it."

Jenner stepped up and took the glass from her.

"Welcome to Stella Maris."

"Thanks." He took a sip; the drink was strong, sweet, the mint stiff, the rum bracing. "It's kind of weird to think people actually live here."

She laughed. "Promise you'll say that to my dad!"

Maggie took him by the arm and walked him along the gravel pathway, past the house; Jenner felt the cool drape of her clunky gold charm bracelet on his wrist.

The house was handsome, with clean lines and a classically Palladian style, but it was the grounds that set it apart. The landscaper had terraced the land into two lawns at slightly different heights, carefully interrupting the formality of the gardens with palms and shade trees.

Jenner said, "This place looks like Versailles would if Louis XIV had built it in the Caribbean."

Maggie giggled. "Oh, tell my father *that*, too!" She plucked the glass from his hand and took a sip. "You've visited Versailles?"

He nodded. "I lived in France for a year before I went to medical school." She raised her eyebrows. "Long story – French girl, love, heartbreak, reunion, rinse, lather, repeat."

Ahead of them a man in a white jacket and black pants was lighting torches along the path.

"And? Still lathering?"

Jenner grinned. "Nope, not for a few years now."

"Good!" she said, squeezing his arm tight.

They turned the corner at the back of the house onto a stone verandah. On the lower terrace, torches flared among white stone columns and arches around a large swimming pool. Underwater lights turned the pool luminescent blue, its surface rippling and chopping as a man swam laps in an urgent freestyle.

"Your father?"

"Yes." Maggie nodded, her eyes mischievous. "I wonder if he's ready for public consumption . . ."

Jenner followed her down to the pool.

She called out, "Daddy! Are you decent? We have company . . ."

Chip Craine glided in to slap the concrete by her foot, then tapped a button on his watch. He tugged his goggles off and looked at his watch. "Forty-two. Good enough!"

He peered up at Jenner. "This the doctor?"

"Yes, daddy. Are you decent?"

"Decent? Maggie, he's a doctor!"

Chip Craine stretched up a hand; Jenner caught it and leaned back as Craine pulled himself up onto the slate flagstones. He was impressively lean, and even more impressively tan. And naked.

"Daddy!" Maggie hid her face behind her hands, giggling. She turned away and said, "Jenner, excuse my father – I'm afraid this is one of his 'eccentricities' . . ."

156

Her father snorted. "The doctor doesn't care, darling. He spends his days looking at half-naked men – isn't that right, doctor? Hand me my towel, will you?"

Jenner said, "Something like that," and handed Craine the towel. "Although they're usually a little paler."

Craine barked a laugh. "Ha! You see, Mags? The doctor doesn't care." He toweled off, grabbed a big white terry-cloth robe and wrapped himself in it. "All right, darling, it's safe to look. Daddy's decent again."

"Don't you believe him, Jenner! My father doesn't have a decent bone in his body . . ."

"What's wrong with the human body? Doctor, perhaps you can help her with her issues – I've spent a fortune on her therapy, and she's gotten nowhere . . ."

Maggie squealed and slapped his shoulder. "Jenner, ignore him. My father's the sort of person who'll greet my date stark naked, and then make us miss our dinner reservation . . ."

"Okay, all right, I'm going!" Craine shook his head stoically. "You two have a drink on the patio while I dress."

He nodded at Jenner, and slipped past Maggie towards the house; there was a squeal as he goosed her.

"*Daddy!*"

They watched him head up the terrace to the house. There was a fresh pitcher on a side table, but Maggie insisted on sharing Jenner's mojito.

Jenner was thinking: "*Date.*"

37

They took Adam out to the fields south of Bel Arbre, Bentas driving, Tarver in the passenger seat, Adam, wedged between them, shaking. It was after dusk when they turned off the highway and started to move through the orange groves, the fruit bright dots, vivid against the dark leaves and overcast sky.

The world flew past Adam in a blur of tangled green under dying light. He saw the trees first as chaotic jungle, but then the mass of vegetation would resolve itself into rows stretching off into the distance before collapsing again into disorder as his perspective shifted.

Tarver and Bentas spoke across him as if he weren't there, a snippy argument about what Tarver should and shouldn't record. Adam barely registered the words. They were now on the empty dirt back roads, the workers long gone.

Bentas flicked the headlights on, and suddenly blinding white flurries of insects engulfed them, spattering against the car. In Adam's eyes they were dazzling showers of radiant particles.

And he wanted them to just keep going because he knew that when the car stopped . . .

It stopped.

Bentas said, "Here's good. He said not too far from the highway."

Tarver was fussing with the battery for the spotlight for his camcorder. Bentas said, "Forget it! Just fucking forget it, you fucking sick freak! *¡Conio!* Why are you even *like* that?"

Tarver started to get all high-pitched and whiny, but Bentas cut him off.

"Let's just do this. You sure you can hold him, you sick fucking freak?"

Bentas climbed out of the car and put on a pair of rubber gloves. He turned back to watch as Tarver started to drag the boy out of the truck. Adam hung on to the headrest, trying desperately to hold on as Tarver grabbed at his flailing legs. He didn't cry out.

Bentas roared with laughter. "Ooh! Ooh! Tarver! *Tarver!* Get his legs! *Get his legs!*"

Stung, Tarver stepped back and pulled out a pistol.

Bentas said, "Oh no you don't! Oh no you fucking don't, bitch!"

He pushed Tarver aside, leaned into the passenger compartment and did something to the boy's head that Tarver couldn't see. There was a yelp, then Bentas slid the boy effortlessly across the seat and out onto the dirt.

"Jesus, Tarver, you fucking dickless bitch! Can't you do anything right?" He looked down at Adam, who was whimpering in the dirt.

"Get up, kid. Get up or I'll do it again." Covering his head with his arms, Adam slowly stood. "Tarver, you take him by the arm now. And try not to let him go, okay? And don't mark him up, either."

As Tarver lead the boy to the edge of the field, Bentas snugged the gloves on his hands, leaned into the pickup, lifted the tarp and pulled out the wine bottle lying by the dead farmhand's legs.

The three stood at the edge of a big field. The furrowed black earth was divided by long straight ridges of arched white plastic film that shone silver in the shadowy moonlight, stretching all the way to dark trees. Beyond the trees, the highway.

Adam stood there sobbing, his cheeks glistening with tears. The occasional sound of a car out on the highway floated across the field; he could see the soft yellow glare of approaching headlights, see the faint red glow of the taillights as they went. Not so far away.

So far away.

The night breeze picked up, and for a second Adam caught the faintest smell of something sweet, something fresh and green. He turned to see that Bentas had torn open one of the row covers and was plucking fruit from a bush.

Strawberries.

Adam was going to die in a strawberry field.

38

The clubhouse at the Port Fontaine Polo Grounds Country Club was a vast white clapboard mansion with green shutters and a gabled slate roof. In the lobby, slowly turning plantation fans stirred the sweetly fetid perfume of bouquets of stargazer lilies around the hall.

They followed Chip Craine through a lounge done up in Plantation Moderne, out onto a wide veranda lit by stylized hurricane lamps and closed at either end with vine-covered trellises. It was a full-on Lilly Pulitzer crowd, dressed in cocktail dresses and blue blazers and sitting at wicker tables, admiring each other as white-jacketed waiters slipped between them with platters of steak and lobster, Planters Punches and Gin Fizzes held aloft.

The moment Craine stepped onto the veranda, a captain rushed to greet him and escort his group to their table. The view from Craine's table was as commanding as that from the portico of his home. To their right, Jenner saw a series of clay tennis courts, grass courts to their left, and between them, shaded by boxprivet hedges a good ten feet high, a flagstone pathway that led to the first tee. Beyond the tee, the golf course stretched out into the dark, small lampposts lighting the pathways through a vast shadowy terrain of compact forests, low, billowing hills and close-clipped putting greens, dotted with ponds black as oil.

A small army of waiters descended upon Craine, snapping his napkin and smoothing it across his lap as a runner arrived with bottles of still and sparkling water. Menus were unfurled and the bartender brought Craine a Negroni unbidden; the sommelier, an attractive young brunette in a clingy knit dress with a surprisingly short hem, dropped to one knee so he could whisper in her ear.

Jenner watched, amused, unaware that Maggie was watching him.

Craine's face was handsome and patrician, his thinning hair swept back, his nose fine, his lips thin. His eyes were as blue as his daughter's were green, his pupils oddly tiny even in the soft light on the patio. He wore an open-necked white Charvet shirt, his initials embroidered in blue on the spread collar, and a well-cut navy blazer, clearly bespoke, no doubt made for him in England.

He was an attentive host, a lively and engaging story-teller who took an obvious delight in pushing his listeners as far as propriety would permit, and pushing his daughter a little further. His stories all started simply enough, but quickly became byzantine and extravagant – a business trip to Belarus to scout locations for a factory turned into a tale of drinking prowess in which Chip faced down a local KGB operative in a vodka duel.

He'd told the stories time and again – Jenner suspected that he could tell them in his sleep – but he was funny, even charming, playing the old rogue to the hilt, easy to listen to, easy to like. Later, Jenner would remember that while Craine spoke his eyes were constantly roving, drawn irresistibly to the younger women on the veranda.

Craine ordered for the table without consulting either of his guests. Grilled Gulf shrimp with a pineapple-and-papaya salsa, then a Surf and Turf with Maine lobster and small filets of Niman Ranch beef, next a cheese plate, and Key lime pie to finish. He spoke briefly with the sommelier, settling upon an '82 Mouton Rothschild, of which he ordered two bottles.

The food was surprisingly good, the best that Jenner had eaten in Port Fontaine; good as it was, the wine far surpassed it. The benefits of being rich, Jenner thought. How sweet Craine's life was – sitting on the veranda at his usual table with his beautiful daughter, enjoying the immaculate grounds, the superb food and wine, surrounded by his other rich friends and *their* beautiful wives and daughters!

As he carved his steak, Craine interrogated Jenner about medical school, about why he'd chosen forensics. Craine had considered med school at one point, he said, but had ended up falling in with his brother to run the family empire. "I was awful at it – never had a head for business! Gabriel runs the company now; I go to New York four times a year to sign papers and attend stock holders meetings, but mostly he's put me out to pasture."

He sloshed some Mouton into their glasses, then leaned back, sipping the wine, musing silently about the path not taken.

He said abruptly, "So, Dr. Jenner – what would you say is the most revolting thing you've ever seen?"

Maggie said, "Oh, *Daddy!*" She shook her head reproachfully. "Jenner, please ignore my father . . ."

Jenner grinned. "It's okay; people are always asking us that. I'd have to say that the most utterly, completely disgusting thing I've ever seen was . . ." He leaned toward Craine conspiratorially. He waited for Craine to lean in too, then said in a low voice, "An instructional film on how luncheon meat is made – I was vegetarian for a week after that."

Maggie giggled, "It serves you right!" as Craine tutted and rolled his eyes.

She stood, then excused herself. They watched her thread her way through the tables, her elegant hips twisting and swiveling as she dodged chair backs and waitstaff. When Jenner turned back to Craine, the man was studying him, eyes narrowed. Jenner flushed.

Craine leaned back and grinned. "She's a very sexy woman, isn't she, doctor?"

He poured out the last of the bottle into his glass, squinting at the lees. He beckoned, and the sommelier appeared at his elbow.

"We're going to need one more bottle . . . what would you suggest?"

He dismissed several suggestions with a curt shake of

his head, then said, "I know – let's have the doctor choose something. Give him the wine list."

The sommelier placed a huge tome with a faux-leather cover and laminated pages in front of Jenner; she stood at Craine's elbow, the two of them watching Jenner turn the stiff pages.

The first thing Jenner noticed was that the 1982 Mouton Rothschild cost $1900 a bottle. The second was that, despite the cheesy leather binder, the wine list had been expertly chosen. He considered the 2004 d'Auvenay, which would stand up well to both the lobster and the filet, but decided that a white Burgundy would be too showy. There was an attractive Soldera Brunello too, but he sensed that Craine might balk at an Italian. He thought about the Côte Rotie, but then closed the book, slid it into the center of the table, and said firmly, "Let's go with the Lynch-Bages, the 1982." He paused, smiled, then added, "Final answer."

The sommelier nodded approvingly. "An excellent choice, sir. Very good indeed, and one of our better-priced, too. It's one of the best wines in this cellar, but I find our clients are sometimes a little . . . resistant to the unfamiliar."

Craine scowled at her as she disappeared to decant the bottle.

"So, you know your wine, doctor."

Jenner shrugged. "I lived in France for a year. When I left, I could speak passable French, and order from a wine list. Not bad for a junior year abroad . . ."

Craine's face lightened. "French women, my God! They're so . . . *reasonable*, compared with Americans, don't you think? In bed, I mean."

Jenner smiled. "I can't say – I fell in love not long after I arrived, and stayed in love the whole year."

"Just the one? Jesus, man! You *wasted* your year abroad!"

Craine was looking across the veranda, where Maggie had reappeared. "A French woman, Jenner, will do *anything* . . . Let you put it *anywhere* . . ."

He stood, and kissed his daughter as she sat.

Maggie asked, "What were you two talking about?"

"Nothing for your delicate ears, darling! Now, come sit closer to Daddy, there's a good girl." She half-stood so he could drag her chair away from Jenner, closer to his own.

As the evening wore on, Craine's charm faded as he became more drunk. He lurched from one story of debauchery to the next, his voice getting louder as his daughter tried to calm him down, pressing his arm with soft fingers, murmuring, "Daddy, please. You're being so loud they can hear you in the kitchen . . ."

Maggie changed too, became more serious, less girlish. She signaled the maitre d', and no more alcohol arrived at the table. It took Craine a little while to notice that the wine had dried up; when he did, he became petulant.

"Some more of your excellent wine, doctor? What was it, the Lynch . . . the Lynch . . .?"

Jenner shook his head. "I think I've had enough to drink."

"Well, that's just as well." Craine picked up the carafe, then paused, holding it in mid-air, shaking it to emphasize its emptiness. "Because, you see, my daughter has cut us off . . ."

He slammed the carafe down onto the table.

They were now the focus of attention in the dining

room, the target of sidelong glances and murmured commentary. The maitre d' sidled over to whisper to Maggie, who replied in an apologetic whisper.

She stood. "I think it's time we headed home, Daddy. Unlike the Craines, Doctor Jenner has to be at work bright and early."

Jenner nodded and got to his feet, with a polite smile. "Sorry to spoil the party, but it really is creeping up on my bedtime."

"Jesus!" Craine glowered at them, muttering, "What kind of man is thinking of bed at 10:30 p.m.?"

He leered up at Jenner. "Unless it's to get a beautiful woman into bed . . . Do you have, uh, *designs* on my daughter, doctor? Can't wait to get her home and unwrap her, that it?"

Maggie stood with head bowed, hand raised to her face. "Daddy, please, don't do this. Please. Not here."

Craine shrugged. "Well, then. Sit back down and let me finish this glass. I'll behave."

She sat, and Jenner followed suit.

Craine sat there, glass in hand. There was something uglier in his silence, his absence of speech like the twitching of an invisible tail, a large cat about to savage a kitten.

"I have to say, it's hilarious that my daughter has appointed herself my moral guardian, particularly with her spectacular past." He looked past Maggie to Jenner, and began to talk about her, distilling her past into a series of bad choices – her abusive boyfriends, her decision to study art history as an undergraduate, and then to go for her Master's, a year intended for studying painting in Italy quickly aborted in favor of spending time in Corfu with friends from New York. His word choice was deft and incisive, their intimacy letting him highlight her most painful moments in the cruelest possible way.

Maggie sat silently looking at her cheese plate, the tears spilling slowly down her cheeks. As he spoke, Craine watched her closely, monitoring her reaction.

"Of course, I bankrolled all this, and never said a thing, even when she flunked out of her program because she managed to get, as they say, 'knocked up' . . ."

Jenner said, "Mr. Craine, I think that's enough. Let's change the subject."

Craine turned slowly to Jenner and said, "So, tell me, doctor: what *has* my daughter told you about her little girl?"

Maggie slipped out of her chair and walked quickly down the broad patio steps, vanishing into the oblivion of the dark golf course.

Craine, flushed and grinning, watched Jenner follow her. He looked around for the bartender; perhaps he could bribe his way to another Negroni.

39

Adam was flying now, pedal to the metal, pedal to the motherfucking metal, howling down his track like a bobsled. And the Hispanic guy, Bentas, put the little canister thingy up to his nose and said, "C'mon, kid. Take another hit. Just one more."

And so Adam snorted it again and felt the top of his head blast wide open. His face was burning, superheated like flames four thousand degrees racing across the

167

surface of the sun. How fast his heartbeat? 10,000 m.p.h. Mach five, no, in miles per hour? *Go, Speed Racer, go!*

There was the roar of an infinite snare-drum roll, no, not the sound, it was inside him, in his chest, his heart, 10,000 per hour.

Overhead the sky was black and a thousand stars points of light in the black, turning to streaks as Adam made the jump to light speed. At this speed how long would it take to reach a star? He could make the Kessel Run in less than twelve parsecs.

In front of him, the crop covers were bright rays, sunbursting out from his feet to connect the darkness where he stood to the gilded rim of the highway.

Now Tarver was snorting from the little canister too, throwing his head back and laughing, and it sounded like the squeal of horses when they fall, like the whistle of a screaming rabbit.

There was a WHOMP! in Adam's chest and he staggered he'd been shot no not that no it was a skip of his snare-drum-roll heart. WHOMP! again.

He moved forward now, stumbling a bit, falling in between the humps of two rows. And then it went backwards and he was standing upright again, Bentas yanking him up by the back of his shirt as if he were a yo-yo.

Bentas said, "Hey, here, drink this," and held up a bottle of wine. Wine. He wanted him to drink the wine so Adam thought yes okay I'll drink that.

Then the top was off the bottle and Tarver was behind him, clutching him around his chest in a bear hug, locking him down in case his heart went WHOMP again and Tarver had a nose bleed, and Bentas had the purple gloves with the wine bottle. The label on the bottle said the wine came from California, smooth green glass and wine. 2002. No, 2007. No, 2002, 2002, 2002. He giggled. Red red wine.

Tarver was pulling Adam's forehead back, and Bentas's purple fingers wrapped around the label 2002, tipping the bottle up, the red spilling onto Adam's chest, and gushing into his mouth and he glugged it down as fast as he could, but Bentas was pouring it too much and it – WHOMP! – was horrible, tasted like acid rustwater peed out of a radiator, it was black and battery acid in his mouth on fire, the spit pouring out.

"Let him go," said Bentas and Tarver let him go and Adam staggered forward into the field.

retching and spitting red

red red wine

"Follow him. He's almost done now."

And Adam stumble-shuffled between the strawberries, his dark horizon ahead, the dark screw-toothed line of trees bouncing as he fell forward onto his legs as they rose to meet him.

He began to trot, a teetering, wide gait, a toddler's stambling run.

Bentas and Tarver sauntered behind, Tarver pressing a paper napkin to his bleeding nose. Tarver was saying they should just shoot Adam, and Bentas was saying that Brodie wanted it to look like the kid was tweaking and had died from doing too much speed, and Brodie had also said that if he didn't fall out pretty quick they could let him have a swig of the insecticide to get him over.

And to not mess him up. They'd leave him where he fell, they'd find him when everyone came back, and by then he'd be rotted. But still don't mess him up.

Tarver stopped and threw his head back to stare up at the night, pressing the napkin hard to his nose.

"Vucking theng won't stob bleeding."

"Press it harder, asshole." Bentas snorted. "Ever occur to you maybe you shouldn't do so much meth?"

Bentas looked back to the truck, and was surprised at how far they'd come. His head snapped back and he stared at the boy making his hurried, waddling way across the field.

"Christ – that fucker's going to make the highway . . . Come on!"

He began to run.

Adam tottered out from the rows of strawberry plants, staggered across the rind of bare earth at the edge, then into the surrounding drainage ditch, squishing forward through the black ooze to clamber up the other side. Shrubs whipped at his skin as he moved past, but he reached the low wire fence and leaned over, the top sagging as he toppled over and fell onto the grass by the shoulder of the road.

He heard the splash as Bentas went into the water, and dragged himself forward onto the blacktop, crawling now.

Adam was on the road.

Behind him he saw Bentas at the fence, hesitating.

Then Adam began to vomit.

Bentas was slipping over the fence and walking towards him hesitantly, glancing left and right for traffic.

Adam watched him moving closer slowly; Bentas was being so careful that it was funny now, like he was making that tinkling piano noise when Sylvester tiptoes across the living room to get Tweety.

Adam snorted (blood now): Bentas was standing on

170

the shoulder of the road, staring at him as if Adam were levitating, floating up toward the sky in some blinding white tractor beam, abducted by aliens. Lying on the highway, the blood streaming from his nose, Adam started to laugh.

But the sound didn't come. Now he couldn't move – his breathing was ragged – fast and shallow – his chest tight as if a house had fallen on it. He vomited again, and felt the sweat pouring from his burning face.

Bentas had stopped on the grass verge. This had to be it: the kid was dying now.

Adam's scalded mouth filled with spit, the rattling scrape of his breathing harsh in his ears.

Then there was light on the highway, and he saw Bentas turn to shadow as he raced quickly back to the cover of the fence and the bushes behind. Adam laid his head back on the tarmac, then turned his face to look at the bright monster light bombing towards him and suddenly thousands of diamonds glittered on the blacktop around him, and Adam breathed rubies into the diamonds, and then he closed his eyes, and then the impact.

40

The black Mercedes SUV skidded, the rear wheels fishtailing wide across the centerline, heading into a spin. There was a screeching lurch and the car swung back into its lane, swaying for a few seconds as the driver over-corrected right and left.

Finally, the vehicle rolled to a halt.

A minute or so later, the SUV reversed, the taillights illuminating the road as it pulled slowly back towards Bentas's hiding place. When Adam's body broke the edge of the light field, the car stopped sharply.

The driver's-side door swung open, and the sound of a girl screaming repeatedly filled the air.

The driver was young, a dark-haired kid maybe Adam's age, driving – what? His dad's car? Bentas looked for the plate: a Palm Beach county plate surrounded by a loop of pulsing blue lights: it read GTARGOD. A rich kid's car, then.

The boy climbed out and ran to Adam's body. He kneeled and looked at him for a second, then started pacing, hands pressing the top of his head as if holding his skull together, muttering "*Ohmigod! Ohmigod!*"

He paused, then glanced up and down the highway.

Bentas knew what the driver was doing: math. The kid was figuring out if he could get away with it.

The boy began to back away, looking shakily in the direction of his car where the girl was still screaming. She'd undone her seat belt, and her shrieking was punctuated by the rhythmic chime of a door alarm.

From where he crouched, Tarver now squatting close behind him, Bentas could see that Weiss's body was really fucked up. One of his arms was impossibly twisted, and his right leg was bent out at an unnatural angle. His head lolled to the left in a dark gleaming puddle of blood.

The boy was hesitating, standing there with his cell phone out, looking down at Adam's body, looking back at the car containing the screaming girlfriend. Bentas thought: *Leave, you little fuck. Just leave. No one will find out. No one will ever know . . .*

And then Adam moaned.

The boy stiffened.

It seemed impossible. Enough methamphetamine to kill a circus elephant, washed down by an insecticide chaser and then smashed by that tank of a car, and Weiss was still alive? *Impossible . . .*

The sound galvanized the driver, who started dialing his cell.

Tarver touched Bentas's shoulder, then held up his pistol, tapped it silently, then pointed first at the driver on his phone, then at the screaming girlfriend.

Bentas shook his head quickly, and jabbed his finger in the direction of the field. They crept down the slope, moved quietly across the drainage ditch and out onto the strawberry field.

Bentas muttered to Tarver to put the gun away. "No need: kid was already ninety-nine percent dead. This way is perfect – they ran him over while he was alive, lying on the road, fucked up on crystal meth. Just one more dead stupid fucking tweaker."

Tarver moaned as his nose began to bleed again. "Shit!"

Bentas snickered at him. "Yeah, one more dead stupid fucking tweaker." He paused. "Hey, Tarver – you thirsty? I got some wine . . ."

By the time they reached their truck, they could hear the distant siren.

41

The maitre d' escorted Chip Craine through the lobby and out onto the drive. They waited together for the Bentley.

"Dean!" Craine fumbled in the pocket of his blazer and pulled out a thick wad of cash. He began to peel off hundred-dollar bills like a game-show host. "Dean, okay, I want you to give this to the black waiter, this to the blonde . . . The two guys who were clearing the plates can share a hundred. Here's two hundred for the sommelier, and a hundred for the bartender."

The maitre d' nodded, looking expectantly at the pile of cash on his flat palm. Craine continued, "And for you . . . one, two, three hundred." He paused. "Is that acceptable?"

"Well, Mr. Craine, you're very generous, as always. But there's the small problem of complaints. I told the Walters, who were sitting behind your table, that we'd take care of their dinner check . . ."

"You did?" Craine thought for a second. "Good thinking. Put it on my tab. And here's another hundred."

He tucked the rest of the money back into his blazer. "We're good now?"

The host folded the thick stack of bills into his pocket and nodded. "Yes, sir. We're very good."

The lights of the Bentley flooded the steps. The valet stopped at the *porte cochère* but the maitre d' waved him on, past the main entrance to the club: kickbacks or not, Mr. Craine had caused enough trouble for one night.

He walked Craine to the car, and said, "Sir, Mr. Canning has instructed us that the car keys are to be delivered to your daughter. He's asked me to make sure you're comfortable in the car until she returns."

Craine grunted. He stood impassive as the valet swung the heavy door open for him, then asked him to move the passenger seat forward: he would sit in the back seat.

Once he was installed, the valet closed the door, hovering by the vehicle until Craine groggily pulled a fifty from his pocket and handed it to him. Then the maitre d' and the valet left him to his own devices.

Craine sprawled back in the middle of the seat, arms outstretched wide, idly caressing the tan leather of the broad seat back.

Overhead, the sky was deep indigo, filled with bright, distant stars.

He wondered how long his daughter would take to get over her little tantrum. He snorted: it was absurd how easily she worked herself into a mood.

His fingers began to drum the seat back. He was bored.

Craine pulled out his phone to check for messages. Nothing.

A peaceful look settled across his face as he began to dial.

She answered on the second ring, her voice sweetly excited and expectant. She always answered on the second ring – he'd learned that they always did, at that age.

42

Jenner walked out beyond the barrier of the box-privet hedge and onto the dark realm of the golf course. He couldn't see her. The hedges funneled walkers down the golf-cart road, and she was wearing heels, so she'd probably followed the paved surface.

He walked along the road, down a small slope and around to the right. His way was lit by black ornamental lampposts, glowing like fireflies on either side. Seen from the bright haloes of the path, the greens were gloomy and dark, the color of poison yew.

Jenner walked for about five minutes before he spotted Maggie. She was on a bench by the first water trap, her dress floating around her like a luminous cloud, pale blue in the moonlight.

She glanced up, then back out over the still black water.

"Hey." He sat on the bench right next to her.

She ignored him.

"You okay?"

She turned to face him and snapped, "Really? That's really what you're going to ask me?" She snorted. "What do you think, Jenner? How do you *think* I am?"

"I'm sorry."

"You know, you're as bad as he is. You did nothing, Jenner! Nothing!" She looked down at her hands, her fingers working at some invisible knot. "My father has . . . problems. He was drunk, he couldn't help himself. But you . . . ?" She paused before continuing.

"What, you couldn't think of anything to say?" Maggie shook her head angrily. "How could you just sit there and listen to him say those things, and not say a word yourself?"

Jenner, stunned, stayed silent.

"You have no idea how hard all of this is – dealing with him, trying to raise Lucy, keeping the shelter going . . . I have no one! No one supporting me, no one to see the things I have to do, no one to help me."

She was crying now, and he lifted a hand to touch her shoulder.

"*Don't!*" She brushed it off. "And don't say the nanny – she doesn't count, she's a paid attendant. I need someone to be a part of this, to really help me."

Maggie settled back, spent.

Jenner said softly, "I'm sorry. It must be very hard for you."

"Wrong answer!" She was quiet for a moment, staring at the water. "I don't want your pity."

He took her hand gently but she pulled it back. He said, "I'm sorry. I had . . . I didn't know he'd behave like that. I'm so sorry . . ."

She breathed out, then turned to him. "Pass me my purse. I need a cigarette."

Jenner picked the black patent-leather purse up off the grass and handed it to her. It was surprisingly heavy, and when she snapped it open he saw a small pistol. It didn't surprise him – in Miami, he'd known several women whose clutch purses held a shiny little .25 semiautomatic.

Maggie stuck a cigarette between her lips and opened the matchbook. As the match lit up in her hand, he saw that her eyes were clear, her cheeks dry again. She took a deep drag, shook the match out, then slowly exhaled the smoke, her eyes shut.

She looked at Jenner, weary and expectant. "So. I know you're just dying to share your impressions about how messed up we are. The Craine family."

"Actually, I'm not really excited about saying anything right now."

177

"I know, I know! Poor Jenner!"

Another quick drag; she blew the smoke out harshly.

"I know how it must seem. I'd tell you that my father was a decent man, that he and my uncle were the best guys on earth, just really misunderstood, but that'd be a lie. Daddy's a son of a bitch – he keeps me utterly dependent on him, gives me just enough to cover my expenses, and Lucy's, but not a penny more. And, if anything, my uncle is worse."

"Your uncle?"

"Oh, Gabriel Craine, another magnificent branch of the glorious Craine family tree, Jenner. He runs Craine Brothers Medical now – he took control in the early 1980s; each month he shits out a measly little allowance for Daddy. He's a ruthless bastard – he doesn't approve of my father or me, not one bit."

"Well," Jenner said, "it can't be all *that* measly . . ."

Maggie shrugged. "Daddy's clever with money. But it's a pretty tiny stipend, considering how huge Craine Brothers is – you know, when *People* magazine profiled us in 2004 they said we make one in four of the items in your medicine cabinet. Do you have any idea how rich my uncle is?"

"Anyway." She inhaled again, more slowly now, and let the smoke seep deep into her lungs. "So, what else can I tell you about the Craine Curse? Well, you're a doctor – I'm sure you know that Lucy's anorexic."

When Jenner didn't answer, she glanced at him and saw that he knew. "Yeah, thought as much. Guess I can't hide anything from you." Another drag.

She looked him in the eye. "So, well, sorry, Jenner. Sorry I'm a disaster. Nothing I can do about it . . ."

She let out the smoke slowly, then stood and flicked the cigarette into the water.

Maggie smoothed her hair, then turned to him, studied his face. "You see how I am now, right? So now what do you think – still interested?"

"Maggie, wait. Just . . . slow down."

"This is how it always works – it's because of you, you know?" She smiled sadly. "I find someone I like, my father fucks it up. He's not like that when it's just him and me at dinner, or with his friends."

"He clearly has problems."

"Problems? Christ, Jenner, you don't know the half of it!" She laughed, the sound sharp and thin. She was quiet for a second, then said softly, "But who am I to judge? I'm no better. Besides, he's my dad."

Maggie glanced at him, standing there uncertainly, and smiled. "It's okay, Jenner. I'm okay now."

When he didn't answer, her smile widened. "Really, no, I'm okay. I'm sorry I kind of lost it there – I ruined our date more than he did."

"You didn't ruin it. But . . . it *was* a date, then?"

She laughed. "Of course it was – I'm damaged, not dead! You're the most interesting thing to wash up in Port Fontaine since Ambrose fucking Burmeister!"

Jenner raised an eyebrow.

She stood, and looked at him critically. "After all, you're okay-looking. You're tall. You have a job. You're straight."

Maggie paused. "You *are* straight, right?"

She turned to him as he grinned, and caught his arm. "Because, you know, if you tried to kiss me, I doubt I'd fight it . . ."

Jenner leaned into her, and her lips met his; pressing against her skin was like going under, body-surfing in the warmest sea, soft and hot, a feeling of continued motion when both of them were still, the heat melting slowly across his skin and through his body.

Her lips lingered, and when she gently pushed him back, her hand over his heart, he breathed out, as astonished as if he'd witnessed a miracle.

Maggie smiled. "We should get back there before he molests the coat-check girl or something."

43

Jenner drove the Bentley back to Stella Maris, taking it slow more to prolong the drive than out of fear of damaging the quarter-million-dollar car. Maggie rode in the passenger seat, Craine, subdued and quiet, in the back.

Maggie asked Jenner to wait while she took her father inside. He watched her support Craine as they walked up the path to the side door. He waited by the fountain, sitting at the wheel of the beautiful car in front of the beautiful house, looking at the beautiful grounds.

After a while, he walked down to the house parking lot; he'd just opened his car door when Maggie appeared again at the gap in the hedge. She'd let her hair down, and had a pale blue wrap around her shoulders.

"Thanks again, Jenner." She shook her head. "I'm really sorry you had to see us like that."

She walked down the steps and this time didn't stop at

the Craine halfway point. She stepped quickly up to him, and he held her head and kissed her mouth as she pulled him close. He wrapped her in his arms, stroking her back through the thin cashmere.

Jenner pulled back and kissed her lips, then her cheek, then her forehead. Her eyes were soft and dreamy, and her body felt small against his.

"You must think I'm crazy. I was upset – you understand, don't you, Jenner?"

He shook his head. "You're not crazy. You're just in a tough spot."

"Oh, I'm crazy, all right." Maggie gave a wan smile. "Jenner? Promise me we won't fall in love? It'll hurt too much when it ends."

He hushed her, but she pushed him back, her eyes dark and serious. "I mean it."

So he promised, smiling. She kissed him again, and he felt the press of her lower lip between his teeth as she ground her hips against him.

There was the quiet clearing of a throat, and Jenner looked over her shoulder to see a member of the Craine house staff standing on the walkway, hands folded in front of him. "Excuse me, Miss Craine? Your father wants you to stop by his study for a quick word."

Maggie nodded; the person disappeared. She pulled away from Jenner, kissed the palm of her hand and stroked her kiss onto his cheek.

He climbed into his car; as he reversed he looked for her on the steps, but she was already gone.

44

Jenner listened, suddenly awake.

The cabin was quiet.

The battered clock radio on the bedside table read 2:05 a.m.

Then the tapping came again. The front door.

He put on a T-shirt and sweats, and opened the door to find Maggie, her eyes rimmed with blurred mascara, shivering despite the wrap clutched tightly around her. Behind her he saw the Bentley, straddling two parking spaces.

"You okay?"

She shook her head as he opened the door, and she slipped into his arms as she kissed him over and over.

"What is it?"

Maggie shook her head again, and the wrap slipped off her shoulders, and she guided Jenner hand back, helping him pop the catch at the top of her zipper. His hand smoothed the zip down her back, and her dress fell away, and then she was naked and smooth against him, tearing off his T-shirt.

Jenner pulled her down onto the bed, she kissed his face and his hair and then moved up to straddle him, pushing him down and leaning back so he could admire the swell of her breasts.

"Am I pretty, Jenner?"

He grinned and reached up for her, but she slapped his hand away. "Tell me."

He smiled and said, "You're beautiful," and he meant it.

Maggie reached down, traced the width of Jenner's

shoulders, touched along the scar on his arm. She leaned up over him so he could kiss her stomach, and as his lips kissed and licked she stroked his hair and he rolled her so he was on top.

She slid her wrists above her head, and he knew she wanted to be pinned down, and when he did her hips lifted to him. He pressed her down, and her breath was hot on his neck as she whispered he should do whatever he wanted to her, that anything he wanted to do, she'd do it . . . Anything, anything, *anything* . . . She would be his slut, be his little bitch, be anything he wanted, if he would just . . . if he would just . . .

Afterwards, when they'd both finished, Maggie let him sleep, and lay there and watched him for a long while. She pressed closer to him, kissed his shoulder and whispered, "I'm sorry, Jenner," because she already knew how things would go between them.

A little later, she went to the sink, filled a glass of water, and put it on his bedside table. It was hot in the room, and he might get thirsty.

45

Jenner woke at seven a.m. Maggie was dressed, the white dress wrinkled, her face scrubbed, putting her hair up in the dresser mirror.

She seemed slightly vexed that he was awake. "I have to go see Lucy off to school – don't get up."

He walked her to the front door anyway. He held her hand, but her mood had turned cool; she was already thinking about the day ahead, and the previous night was now history.

On the porch she gave him a peck on the cheek, then walked to the Bentley without the slightest trace of self-consciousness or shame. Her indifference was particularly impressive because Mrs. Anderson was gawking two feet from the car in a Marshmallow Peep-yellow housecoat and matching slippers, her curler-knotted hair secured under a fuchsia kerchief.

They watched the Bentley pull out of the lot. Mrs. Anderson looked at Jenner, shook her head slowly, then steamed off towards the laundry room.

He sat at the table with his bowl of Weetabix, thinking not so much about Maggie as about the context of her life, her father in particular.

Lying in bed talking in the small hours, she'd told him that Craine had bought her and Lucy their own house ten minutes' drive from Stella Maris. She made a point about how important it was to be independent, but her assertion seemed hollow; Jenner figured her independence had a fairly clear dollar value, a value shaped largely by her daughter's needs. Without a job, Maggie had no medical coverage other than what her father provided – and she needed that coverage for Lucy.

Lucy was thirteen, and had been anorexic for a year as far as Maggie knew. She'd just got out of a rehab center near Fort Myers that specialized in eating disorders – she'd collapsed at school, dehydrated from an exclusive diet of dry toast in the morning and laxative tablets the rest of the day. In the E.R., at five foot six inches tall, she'd weighed in at barely one hundred pounds. But the doctors were optimistic – she'd done well at the clinic, and Lucy, her mother and grandfather met weekly with Dr. Vargas at Stella Maris for an hour of discussion, visualization exercises and creative role play. Lucy was already up twelve pounds.

Jenner changed into his running clothes, then called the morgue. There were two bodies, the first an elderly woman with a long history of heart disease who'd died after cardiac bypass surgery; she was Jewish, and the family had a religious objection to autopsy, so he'd perform a quick external examination, then photograph and release the body without a single incision, certifying her death based on the available medical history.

The other case would need an autopsy, but was straightforward, an unidentified white man hit by a car on I-55 south of Bel Arbre, probably a migrant worker, one of the new urban poor who now competed for jobs that had always gone to illegals. The driver was young, but he hadn't left the scene and had passed roadside sobriety tests. Here the challenge wouldn't be the cause of death, but identifying the corpse.

An easy day, then. Jenner was relieved – he needed time to work on his eulogy for the memorial service the next day.

Plus, he thought, I didn't get much sleep.

He stretched in the sunlit kitchen, and, thinking about the night before, he allowed himself a grin.

46

Clay Martin tapped the desk in front of Arlene Soto and said, "God, Arlene, how much longer will he be?"

"Oh, okay, Clay – why don't I just go in there and tell Sheriff Anders that Clay Martin and Gordie Cooper from Highway are sick of waiting for him to finish preparing for his national TV interview with Amanda Tucker on *American Crime*? That what you want?"

Martin snorted and said, "No, no, you know I don't want that. But jeez! Feels like we've been out here an hour!"

"Nuh-uh. You been here twenty-four minutes."

Martin walked back to the bench where Cooper sat reading *Guns & Ammo*; Cooper didn't look up. He was about to sit when the door to Anders's office opened, and there was Anders, in full Class A uniform, flushed, his brush-cut hair shiny with Brylcreem. Martin nudged Cooper, who got slowly to his feet.

"Hey, sheriff."

"Boys." Anders adjusted his tie, checking his reflection in a shiny black commemorative wall plaque. He turned to them. "So, how do I look?"

Cooper said, "Sharp, Tommy. Real sharp." From the way he said it, Martin knew that Cooper was enjoying himself; his words always got tight when he was having fun.

"Thanks, Coop." Anders nodded at his reflection in the plaque, brushing the epaulets flat on his shoulders, then gestured into his office and said, "What can I do yer for?"

They followed him in and Cooper motioned for Martin to shut the door. The stacks of paper in Anders's office had been spruced up, his shooting trophy and the medal he'd received for bravery during a traffic stop shuffled to a prominent place on his desk, next to a framed photo of

Anders as a boy standing next to his father, Sheriff Richard "Big Rick" Anders.

Tommy Anders sat behind his desk, and tried placing his pen set first on the right side, then on the left. He looked up. "Sorry. What you got, Gordie?"

Cooper shook his head, a reluctant expression on his face. "I'm not one for stirring things up that don't need to be stirred up, but I thought you should know this . . ."

"Okay." Anders leaned back, his eyes narrowing. He knew Cooper well enough to be wary of him even when sharing a beer at a cookout in his own backyard. "What should I know?"

Cooper shook his head again, looking pained. "This morning when Clay and I were heading over to Denny's in Golden Palms, we passed by the Palmetto Court – where the doctor is staying?"

"And . . .?"

"Well, we saw a Bentley in the lot."

"Huh."

"Well, so, there's more. On the way back . . ." Cooper glanced at Martin, as if for moral support. "On the way back, we took another look, and we saw Maggie Craine come out of the doctor's cabin, then get in the Bentley."

Anders was silent for a second, his expression blank.

"Was the girl with her?"

"Nope. But Maggie looked like she'd spent the night with him." Cooper shifted in his chair as if his clothes were sticking to his skin.

Anders shook his head, then shrugged. "Not my concern, Gordie."

"Looked like she was dressed up from the night before."

"I get it."

"Sure, Chief." Cooper stood. "Just figured you'd want to know."

Anders looked at him bleakly. "That it?"

"Pretty much."

"Okay – see you guys around."

As they left, Cooper turned back and grinned. Anders was still moving the pen set around on his desk; only now the sheriff's right foot was tapping urgently.

47

As Cooper and Martin left the office, a small mob headed toward it: Arlene the receptionist and Diane from Public Affairs were escorting Amanda Tucker and her entourage down the hall.

The sheriff opened his door, framing himself carefully in his doorway for a second, before approaching, hand outstretched, broad smile on his face.

"Miss Tucker, a real pleasure to meet you, ma'am."

Amanda grasped his hand and said, "Me too, Sheriff." He enjoyed her grip, cool and confident, yet soft and feminine; the country needed more women like Amanda Tucker.

The segment producer suggested that the two should chat casually as they toured the building, so the camera people could get some interesting background shots, then sit down in Anders's office for an hour or so for a formal interview. The sound man clipped a small microphone to the upper part of the sheriff's shirt, where the straining buttons yielded to a puckered ruff of white T-shirt, then had him slip the slender cable all the way down under his shirt. He threaded the cable out between two buttons, plugged it into a black box smaller than a pack of cigarettes, then placed the box in the sheriff's pocket.

The sound engineer listened to his headphones, then gave a thumbs-up to the camera operator. The cameraman said, "A quick white balance, then we're a go . . ."

Amanda waited, head down, for the signal. She knew her hair was good, but her face felt too made-up. Whatever: it'd probably play well in the South.

The producer nodded at the cameraman, who said, "Rolling . . . Speed."

"Okay, Amanda, whenever you're ready."

Close-up on Amanda: "This is Amanda Tucker. We're on location today at the Douglas County Sheriff's Office in Port Fontaine, Florida. This wealthy, picturesque resort town was rocked last week by the discovery of the decomposed bodies of the county medical examiner and his wife in a sunken car. Both of them had been tortured and murdered.

"Then, two days ago, the bodies of another four as yet unidentified men were found out in the Everglades. They had all been killed by hanging.

"At the center of the investigation of these six homicides is a man who'll be very familiar to regular viewers of *American Crime Prime Time* – disgraced former New York City medical examiner Edward Jenner. Doctor Jenner is . . . Sorry, can we cut it there, Rob? I want to go again – I don't think my energy was right."

"Okay, Amanda. I thought you were fine, but we need

189

to adjust the mike levels – you're pinning the needle in the red."

"Okay. Plus I think I want to go with putrefied, instead of decomposed. What do you think?"

"Yeah, nice. Putrefied's better."

The sheriff leaned over and said, "Very interesting. Uh, Ms. Tucker? What do you mean 'disgraced'? What you were saying about Dr. Jenner . . ."

"Please, sheriff – Amanda." She pressed her hand to his arm conspiratorially, smiling, her eyes gleaming. "You don't know his story? I'm surprised. My team in New York is putting together a bio reel for Dr. Jenner – watch *Update* this afternoon. I think you'll find it quite an eye-opener."

Christ, Anders thought. What now? He'd let Roburn sort out his vacation coverage, and the M.E. had said he was bringing in one of the best. Jenner's name had sounded familiar, but . . .

"Sheriff, can we get you and Amanda over by the statue and the flags?"

The producer moved them into position, the sheriff suddenly stiff and self-conscious beneath the flags and the bulky bronze bust of his father. Amanda said, "Let's not talk about Dr. Jenner's past right now – I'd prefer your unbiased opinion . . ."

Anders shook his head. "You know, Amanda, I have to admit I've developed some concerns about the doctor."

She appraised him coolly. "You and me both, sheriff. Let's chat about this later – I think we can help each other out."

The white light flared up again. Anders felt the flush of

his face; he could almost hear his sweat as it began to trickle.

"This is Amanda Tucker with Sheriff Tom Anders at the Douglas County Sheriff's Office, here in Port Fontaine, Florida. This picturesque, wealthy resort town was rocked last week by the discovery of the putrefied bodies of the county medical examiner and his wife . . ."

The segment producer watched with admiration. Amanda could be an utter, screaming bitch, but he had to give it to her: she was a pro. He savored the way she gently pushed "putrefied" without making it vulgarly obvious, like a con man forcing a card on some rube.

48

The Highway Patrol lieutenant had suggested that the road-accident victim might be a migrant worker but to Jenner he didn't look like he was from Bel Arbre.

Jenner stepped back to survey the body. A young white man, maybe twenty-two, twenty-three. Black hair shaggy, but cut fashionably, like a British pop star's. Clean-shaven. Good general hygiene. Circumcised.

A migrant worker? The arms were feebly tan, but the hands were soft, no calluses, no scars – they'd never held anything more serious than a pen. Most migrants were Latin American, Catholic, and uncircumcised.

In recent years, though, marginalized young people who called themselves "travelers" had joined the migrant workers, following the harvests from state to state. But travelers wore their disenfranchisement like a uniform –

hair in matted dreadlocks, skin tanned deep brown, facial piercings, anarchist tattoos. Their bodies were lean and hardened, often scarred with needle tracks and wrist scars.

This kid was pale, a little doughy, and his teeth were perfect.

Well, almost. Lifting the upper lip, Jenner noticed a slight color difference between two of the premolars, a single tooth subtly paler than the others.

He had Bunny wheel over the X-ray machine and do a full mouth X-ray; he was pretty sure that tooth was an implant. All the fillings were carefully tone-matched ceramic, high-end work, not mercury amalgam packed in on some side-street butcher shop in Juarez or wherever. This was Park Avenue dentistry – no way was this kid a field hand.

They cleared the room for Bunny to zap the film, then Jenner waited by the viewing box.

"Hey, Jenner! What's up?"

Rudge was at the entry to the main body cooler. Next to him was a middle-aged black man in a dark suit, standing next to a collapsible gurney topped with a maroon velour cover. A funeral director.

"Morning, Detective Rudge. How's it going?" Judging from Rudge's breath, it'd been going pretty well the night before.

"Doc, I want you to meet my cousin, Reggie Jones. He's making a pickup, so I rode down with him."

Jenner shook hands. "Good to meet you." Reggie had the same next-day booze smell. "Rode down – you guys live together?"

Jones said, "Just for the moment, doc. My brother

192

Jimmy and I had a place, but he moved to Atlanta so I'm staying with Dave until my new house is ready."

Rudge clapped his hands on Reggie's shoulder and said, "See that, Jenner? This is what we should be doing! There's money in dead folk! Reggie's building a house near the golf course, acre of land, partial canal view, three-car garage . . ."

"Four now," Jones said, nodding solemnly. "Four-car garage."

"Hear that? That's what I'm talking about! A *four*-car garage! And Jimmy's house in Atlanta is even bigger!" He clapped Reggie on the shoulder again, and said, "I tell you what we do, Jenner: we quit the hell that is law enforcement, we go to funeral home school, we rent ourselves a place.

"Because I'm naturally good-looking and have a winning way, I put on a suit, run the front of the house, take care of the customers, all that. Because you're a naturally tall-ass white guy who'd scare grieving relatives, we'll put you in the basement, give you your own slab and some formaldehyde, let you loose on the bodies . . . We work a few years, then we franchise the shit out of the operation, and retire young, rich, and good-looking . . ."

Jenner thought for a second. "Whose name first?"

"Say what?"

"Mine or yours? Rudge & Jenner, or Jenner & Rudge? It makes a difference."

"The idea man always goes first."

Bunny poked her head into the hallway. "Doc, I'm done."

She slapped the film up onto the viewing box, and Rudge, his cousin and Jenner gathered in front of it.

Jenner tapped the image of the upper premolar; the tight white shadow of a small screw spiked into the bone of the jaw. "There we go."

"What you got, Jenner?"

"This pedestrian from up near Bel Arbre."

"So what's his mouth saying?"

"He's telling us that he's not just any pedestrian from Bel Arbre. And that his dental work is much too good for a migrant worker."

Rudge said, "Highway's going to love that!"

Reggie said, "So he's not ID'd yet, doc?"

Jenner shook his head. "No. He will be, though – this is the kind of guy that people look for . . ."

49

Bunny was closing the body when Highway Patrol showed up. She led the two officers to the back area, where Jenner was laying out the victim's clothes to be photographed. He recognized Cooper and Martin from the hallways; Cooper was the stocky fireplug, Martin blond and etiolated. They were unhappy he'd summoned them to the morgue.

They shook hands.

Jenner said, "Thanks for coming down – I have a couple of questions about the investigation, and there's something you need to see."

Cooper looked at Jenner with a concerned expression and said, "You okay, doc? You look kind of tired."

Jenner shook his head, slightly confused. "No, I feel fine."

"Late night? Because you look kind of pale."

"Not really."

He walked towards the body; behind Jenner's back, Cooper winked at Martin. "Oh, okay, good. So what do you think? Intoxed? Unlucky? Both?"

Jenner shrugged. "There's a few strange things. First off, this guy is no migrant worker. High-quality dental work, hands that have never seen a day's work, no tan, no foreskin – I'm wondering if he's even from around here."

Martin looked up from his notebook and said, "Any tattoos or identifying marks?"

Jenner shook his head. "His head's in pretty good shape, so once we have a tentative it'll be an easy photo ID. There's a scalp laceration, but the skull isn't fractured, and there's no brain trauma or bleeding inside the head. In fact, the rest of him isn't too bad, either. The impact busted his arm and leg, but from his injuries I'd say he wasn't so much hit as run over . . ."

Cooper said, "Well, the kid driving the SUV swears he didn't see him – said they felt a bump, then the car suddenly skidded. I guess that makes sense."

"Did the driver touch the victim? Approach him, stand over him or anything? Was the driver injured?"

"He says he didn't. He went over to the body, but says he didn't touch it. And nope, no injuries on the driver – they basically just skidded to a stop, they didn't hit anything else." Cooper glanced at Martin writing away. "Why do you ask?"

"Did the victim say anything? Was he moving?"

Cooper shook his head. "Nope. Didn't say anything,

wasn't really moving. He was making noise – moaning – though."

"Well, if he was alive after the impact, he was alive before it." Jenner shook his head.

He looked at the body on the table again. "Did they notice anything else while they were waiting for EMS?"

Cooper said, "Not really. Just moaning. And drooling – they said he was lying there moaning and drooling."

"Drooling?" Jenner shrugged. "I don't know what that's about." Probably some weird effect of the head injury.

He glanced over at the dental X-ray again, at the immaculate fillings and the perfectly executed implant.

"This isn't adding up, sergeant. You've got a guy who's lying on the road, alive, hit by a car. He's badly injured enough to eventually die, I suppose, but I can't understand why he died so quickly – according to EMS, he died in the ambulance minutes after being hit. I've seen people die from shock and pain from tissue damage, but he's young and healthy, so . . . It's . . . weird."

Jenner looked at the clothing on the table in front of him. The shirt, cut open by the paramedics during resuscitation, lay roughly reassembled, the cut margins stuck together with tape.

"Okay." Jenner shrugged. "There's something important here I need to show you."

He lifted the shirt and turned it to the cops. "The front of his shirt is soaked in what looks and smells a lot like red wine. And that's fine – maybe he *is* just some poor bastard who had too much to drink and passed out on the road. But . . ."

He turned the shirt around to show them the back,

holding the arms wide open, as if the boy had been flying.

"You've got smeared blood here at the top of the left shoulder; this stain lines up pretty nicely with the cut in his scalp. Big deal. Now look all the way down here . . ." He gestured to the back of the shirt. "Down here in the low back, near the tail of the shirt, you have droplet spatter, little droplets of blood, some of which are quite fine."

Martin said, "So, what does that mean?"

"The blood pattern doesn't fit with his wounds." Jenner laid the shirt carefully down onto the photo stand, and plugged in the cord to the stand lamps.

He turned to face the officers.

"Basically, I don't think this is his blood down here."

He smoothed away the ridges of the shirt on the photo stand, picked up the camera, and turned on the tungsten lights. "And we know it's not the driver's blood. It looks like it was dripped onto him, with these tiny droplets here, maybe coughed onto him."

He paused, then looked the Highway Patrol cops in the eye.

"Let me spell it out for you: there's someone else out there you need to find. Another victim, possibly. But maybe also an assailant . . ."

50

Jenner shut the autopsy room door with relief.

Martin and Cooper had quickly turned surly: Jenner was spoiling an open-and-shut case with forensic straw-clutching. No way could Jenner know how the body had rolled when the SUV hit it; maybe blood from the scalp wound landed on the body as it turned, or spattered off the vehicle undercarriage onto the victim's back.

Jenner listened, nodded patiently, and stuck calmly to his guns – the pattern was what the pattern was, and he couldn't explain it by the victim having been run over.

The shirt was now lying face-down on the photo stand. He took a wide photograph, then shot close-ups of the blood spatter on the shirt back. He tore open a package of sterile scissors and cut a two-inch square of bloodstain from the shirt. He placed the stained fabric in a coin envelope, and labeled the envelope with the case number and the location on the shirt. Then he cut another square of fabric from high on the shirt, from an area that he thought held the victim's blood, then finally a square of unstained fabric for comparison.

Jenner turned on the radio; mellow soft rock – Air Supply or Toto, he couldn't tell which, didn't care which – oozed out of the speakers into the quiet of the autopsy room. He spun the radio dial – anything but that. Down at the bottom end there was religious broadcasting and country, then Latin music floating across the Glades from Miami. As he moved up on the dial, a popping bass line filled the air, quickly plastered over with vamping 1980s synthesizers – Ready for the World's "Oh, Sheila!"

He turned it up with a grin and went back to work.

He turned the shirt over. The maroon blotches on the front were definitely wine – he could smell it rising from the shirt as the stand lights heated the cloth.

Oh, baby, love me right, let me love you till I get it right

He adjusted the shirt, pressing it flat so that the spill pattern was unruffled. Sweating under the bright light, in the heat of the bulbs, he felt a little dizzy. He wiped his forehead, took a hand lens, and bent close to the fabric, searching for droplet spatter.

On the radio, the sound of "Oh, Sheila!" began to blur, the popping base notes falling flat into the room, smeared and loose.

The cloth swam before his eyes, and then his face was flushing, tears streaming down his cheeks, watery fluid pouring from his nose as his mouth filled with saliva. He staggered back retching, his stomach vaulting and twisting.

He pulled himself unsteadily to the wall, dragged over a stool and slumped down, easing back until his shoulders and head pressed the cool tile. The spit in his mouth was acrid and thin, and he let it dribble out onto the floor in front of him. He wiped his eyes, but the tears came faster; he began to wheeze.

His breathing was harder now. He pulled himself to his feet. Time to go, time to go quick.

Jenner turned to the sink, rinsed his face – he could barely see through the tears. He splashed water on his scrub top until it was soaked, then pulled it up to cover his nose and mouth. Gasping and heaving, he went back near the photo stand, hugging the wall as he made his way to the lighting power cord; he yanked the cord out of the wall socket, sending the expensive stand crashing to the floor in an explosion of sparks and popping bulbs.

The shirt was on the floor now, half-covered by the wrecked photo stand. He tossed a disposable plastic shroud over the shirt and stand, then moved back to the far wall. He found the high-powered accessory ventilation switch and turned it on; there was a low hum, and then he felt cooled air moving against his skin.

He pushed through the swing doors into the corridor, stepped quickly into the breezeway and slumped onto a bench, breathing the warm, humid air.

The wheezing eased, but Jenner was still breathless. It took a minute or so for the heaving to stop; he was spitting less, but tears were still pouring from his eyes.

It took another five minutes before he felt normal. He walked back into the morgue wing and peered through the autopsy room viewing window, staring at the red-stained shirt, still visible under the splintered photo stand plinth.

Now he knew exactly what had happened.

51

With the entire mortuary staff standing in the sheriff's office parking lot, the Emergency Evacuation was festive. Someone opened a case of cold Coke, and Calvin had the door of his Hyundai open, pumping dancehall reggae loud into the lot. A splinter group gathered over near the loading bay to smoke, until the safety officer, a, thin angry-looking woman who drove a Volvo station wagon the color of a freshly stubbed toe, chased them away, warning of the exposure risk.

She monitored their sheepish departure, then returned to Jenner.

He said, "Look, the fumes only developed because I heated the shirt with really hot photo lights – I'd had it out all day, and nothing happened! The lights are off now, I bagged and sealed the shirt, I turned on the room exhaust, the autopsy room air has been exchanged many times. There was no need to evacuate the entire building – or even just the autopsy wing."

The woman wouldn't budge.

"Doctor, this constitutes an Airborne Toxic Exposure Event, and until the Hazmat team says it's okay the Forensic Sciences wing will stay shut. On your say-so, I've let staff law-enforcement personnel return to the main municipal building, but the forensic labs, including the morgue, are closed . . ."

Jenner shrugged irritably. "Well, whatever. Your call. But it's a complete waste of time. And I need to get back in there as soon as possible so I can test my samples and find out exactly what we're dealing with."

The safety officer shook her head decisively. "Out of the question. The morgue stays shut. The lab stays shut. Those specimens will keep until Hazmat gives the all-clear."

"No, they won't! If I want meaningful test results I need to centrifuge the blood as soon as possible!" Jenner ran a hand through his hair. "When the hell will Hazmat get here?"

"They're coming down from Fort Myers. I'd say we'll be up and running again in about three hours." She scribbled something on her clipboard, then peered at him over her glasses.

"Do we need to worry about the body? Is that contaminated?"

Jenner thought for a second, then grudgingly decided that the question was fair. "It's okay; he's been sutured closed, and is in a body bag now. Actually, I remember feeling a bit light-headed a couple of times during the autopsy; I just chalked it up to lack of sleep last night. In fact, I think I felt a bit woozy when I collected the stomach contents, which makes complete sense now."

The woman's eyes were sharp. She said, "So, doctor, tell me again, in your opinion: what are we dealing with?"

"I think someone fed him an organophosphate poison. You'll find organophosphates on every damn farm in Douglas county – insecticides, mostly. But they also exist in weaponized form – Sarin, Tabun . . ."

It was the wrong thing to say: now she was leaning forward intently, pen hovering over God only knew what disastrous checkbox. Terrorist threats were porn for safety officers – they lived for the stuff. If Jenner didn't talk her down, she'd shut down the whole county and call in Homeland Security.

He said, "This is pretty clearly an insecticide poisoning. Someone spiked his wine with some kind of bug juice."

She seemed disappointed that they'd moved on from poison gas. "But if it was insecticide, wouldn't he . . . wouldn't he have been able to taste it in the wine?"

"Yes, I think so. They probably held him down and poured the stuff into his mouth – the splash pattern on his shirt looks more like, well, splashes, than if he'd puked it up."

The woman put a hand to her throat. "So you think . . ."

"He was murdered." Jenner paused, then looked at her intently. "They got him drunk, poisoned him with insecticide, then somehow he escaped and made it onto the road where he was hit. Or maybe they pushed him in front of the car. The accident is just a distraction – he'd have died sooner rather than later."

She said, "Oh my gosh! How horrible!"

She jotted on the clipboard, then said, "Now, coming back to the poison gas for a second . . ."

Jenner watched her write. "The sooner we get into the lab and run those specimens, the sooner I can tell you if there's anything more serious going on . . ."

The safety officer pulled out her cell phone, hit the walkie-talkie button and asked where the hell the Biohazard Containment team was.

52

Three hours: enough time to get up to Bel Arbre and see the accident site. In his gut, Jenner knew there was no way this killing wasn't tied in to the hanged men from the farms and, most importantly, to Marty.

But where was the scene? The EMS report, all the records, were in the barred autopsy room. But the EMS dispatch log wasn't – he could ask Rudge to dig up the ambulance call location.

He set out for the sheriff's office, heading for Major Crimes. As he walked down the hall, the sheriff was walking toward him, half hidden by a TV news crew. And walking alongside the sheriff . . .

Jenner stopped.

Amanda Tucker.

He was instantly back in his loft, Ana climbing into his bed crying, kissing him through her tears, saying, "Jenner, the things she said about you . . ." – weeping, pressing her hands against his chest like a treadling cat. "Why are they doing this, Jenner? All you've been is good to me. Why can't they leave us alone?"

And then, later, waking to find her by the bed with her little bag, whispering that she couldn't stay with him anymore, couldn't watch what they were doing to him, she couldn't take it anymore, she had to leave him, and it was better for him, and she hated what this was doing to them . . .

Jenner stared at Amanda Tucker, watched her smiling approach, her cameraman scooting around to get the two of them in frame together, the sound man swinging the boom mike his way.

She nodded, almost did a little curtsy. "Doctor Jenner!"

Anders stormed into the shot, blustering, "What the hell, Doctor Jenner? You shut my entire facility down?" The camera swung towards him.

Jenner spoke in a low mutter, through gritted teeth, too quiet for the sound recording. "I did nothing of the sort. I was the only person exposed, the only person at risk. I contained the hazard, then informed your safety officer. *She* closed you down – take it up with her."

He gestured at Amanda Tucker, and said to Anders, "Be careful, Sheriff – this bitch would sell her mother if it got her a bump in the ratings." He slapped the boom out of his face, then shoved past the sound man and the producer, and stalked off to Major Crimes.

There was a peal of delighted laughter from behind

him, and he heard Amanda Tucker call, "Doctor Jenner! How did you get the black eye?"

The last thing Jenner heard before pushing through the door into Major Crimes was her saying, "Gene darling, tell me you got him saying 'bitch'!"

53

Rudge found Jenner in the loading dock, standing over a folding table onto which he'd spilled the cleaned ribs of the hanging victims. From a distance of ten paces, he watched Jenner arrange the ribs by side and by size, smallest at the top, recreating the chest wall with the now spotless bones.

Jenner bent close to the table, scanned the ribs with a moving finger, pausing every couple of seconds to adjust the bone positioning. Finally satisfied, he straightened, and scrawled notes on a diagram on his clipboard.

Rudge said, "We can rebuild him . . . Steve Austin, right, doc? *The Six Million Dollar Man?*"

Jenner looked up, nodded. "Hey, Rudge. Thanks for coming down."

"I hear you had a close encounter with Amanda Tucker."

Ignoring the comment, Jenner gestured to the sealed mortuary access. "I'm still locked out of the morgue. Thank God I'd put this stockpot out here."

"Oh, you know it! When I'm on my knees by my bed tonight, I'll be thanking sweet baby Jesus that Doctor

Jenner put his corpse soup out to cook in the garage today . . ."

"Well, don't mock the soup, detective – it's given us answers . . ." Jenner beckoned Rudge over and gestured at the bones. "It's what I was expecting – there are bilateral fine score marks down the anterior aspects of the ribs in the midclavicular line."

"And again in English?"

"They cut him on the front of his chest, both sides, deep enough to cut the ribs." Jenner paused. "Just like they did with Marty."

Rudge nodded. "I see."

"I think that kid from Bel Arbre is connected to all this. He doesn't have cut marks, but . . ."

"Any drugs on him?"

"Nothing in his pockets. Tox'll take a couple weeks."

Rudge stepped back. "I like him for a connection. And I like him for a homicide, too. Look, we're a two-homicides-a-year county, so when you get two messed-up murders, then another four even more messed-up murders, and then another really, *really* fucked-up death, the dots pretty much connect themselves."

"Good." Jenner smiled. "So, I don't suppose you want to talk to Cooper and Martin in Highway Patrol."

"Nope – I start talking to them, I want to hit something." Rudge raised an eyebrow. "That something ideally being Gordy Cooper . . ."

"They want it to be a simple accident; I'm worried they're going to shitcan the investigation. Any chance you want to take a little road trip?"

"Where to?"

"Bel Arbre, see where they found the kid."

"Can we stop at the Arby's out by Mitre Road?"

"Sure."

The detective gestured grandly out beyond the open garage shutters to the parking lot. "Through these gates, doctor, the path to untold knowledge . . ."

Jenner slung his scene kit over his shoulder, then followed Rudge.

54

Jenner tossed his bag into the back seat, shaking his head. Rudge's Taurus was filthy, the side panels streaked with road grime.

He fastened his seat belt, and squinted through a windshield starred with pale insect debris. "I'm hoping it rains soon; I figure that's the only time this car ever gets a wash."

"This fine layer of dust protects my paint finish." Rudge turned to him. "Well, she may not look like much, but she's got it where it counts, kid."

He waited for Jenner's response. "*Star Wars*, Harrison Ford as Han Solo talking about the *Millennium Falcon*."

He paused again. "The ship, Jenner. The *Millennium Falcon* is Han's spaceship."

Jenner said, "I know, Rudge. Just drive!"

"Did you really know, or are you just saying that?"

"*Drive!*"

55

They drove north on I-55 into a darkening sky. Rudge had pulled the highway mile marker location from the call sheet, but the actual accident site was harder to identify. The SUV driver had been traveling northbound, so they parked the car a tenth of a mile before the marker and walked the highway. They rounded a slight turn, and then the road dipped slightly downwards.

The shoulders of the highway were well-tended; Jenner had seen convict labor from the county jail mowing the roadsides, black and Hispanic men in cartoonish white and black striped uniforms watched over by equally cartoonish mirror-shade-wearing Corrections Officers with pump-action shotguns. Beyond the shoulders was a six-foot-wide border of cleared grassland, beyond which a continuous fence, generally overgrown by bushes and shrubs, separated the highway from the fields a couple of feet below.

Jenner peered over the fence. An irrigation ditch separated the fields from the highway. Long rows of pale green bushes stretched off into the distance, those to his left hidden by covers. Shimmering in the heat before his eyes, a dozen or so workers were scattered across the field, their heads wrapped in clothing to protect them from the sun. They were pulling up metal hoops and plastic sheeting, leaving the plants open to the sky. He squinted: strawberry plants.

He pulled out his cell phone; Maggie hadn't called.

Back on the road, Rudge was about twenty feet ahead of him.

"Doc, got some EMS stuff here . . ."

He was pointing to a purple glove discarded on the roadside.

A few feet further on, there were more gloves and paper detritus; the wrapper from a disposable defibrillator electrode flapped listlessly against the fence.

"This looks like it." Jenner glanced back down the road. "They'd have been coming this way, hit him, maybe shunted him twenty feet up toward us as they ran him over. And look, up there – tire marks from a skid."

They walked toward the fence, scanning the grass, reaching it without finding anything.

Jenner looked out over the field. There was nothing out that way, just the strawberry fields stretching out under the dark sky. Beyond the field was an access road, beyond that the grid of orange groves resumed, and then beyond the orange trees the Everglades. But they were thirty miles north of Port Fontaine, and a good ten south of Bel Arbre; it was more likely the victim had come from the fields than walked along the road.

Unless he'd hitchhiked.

"So, what do you think, Jenner?"

"I don't know. I doubt he was walking along the highway. Did he come from the fields? Why would he be out here late at night?"

Jenner scanned the field, then the road beyond it. "Doesn't look like he's left a vehicle behind."

He leaned over the fence.

"We should have a look on the other side."

Rudge tugged uneasily on the wire at the top of the fence, then turned to Jenner. "Doc, you get on over and have a look around. I'll see what I can find up on the shoulder here, on this side of the wire."

Jenner found an area relatively free of vegetation, pressed the fence down, straddled it and climbed over.

He looked up and down the bank, then felt himself starting to slip and took a couple of quick steps down, his foot squishing into the soggy loam of the drainage ditch before he hastily stepped up onto the field.

Cursing, he shook the water off his foot, then straightened, and walked on the edge of the field, adjusting to the squelch of water in his shoes. He looked back up at the fence and stopped: the area where he'd climbed over was bordered on both sides by pretty dense shrubs and grass, but the greenery toward the right side had been trampled and crushed.

Someone had been there, had stood there.

Jenner moved along the field until he was level with it.

There was no question, this was the area where . . . where what? Where the victim had been . . . forced to drink insecticide-laced wine? The whole idea suddenly seemed pretty sketchy. Who would do that in an attempt to kill?

Maybe this was not some big mystery after all. Maybe this was just a suicide: some poor bastard, sitting by the fence, grabs the insecticide, can't face the taste straight so he mixes it with wine, chugs it down, staggers out onto the road, passes out, bang, that's all she wrote. Maybe Jenner was overreaching with the blood spatter. Maybe Cooper and Martin were right.

So where was the bottle?

He looked up the slope. Nothing up there.

Maybe the bottle was out here in the field. Jenner looked over to the workers – perhaps one of them had found it. After all, they'd been stripping up the row covers and had already processed this part of the field, so if there was a bottle they'd have come across it.

Unless the young guy had drunk it out in his car, out on the road.

But again, no car.

Chances were that he'd have originally come from the feeder road, walked across the field and up onto the highway.

Jenner scowled – any footprint evidence would've been tamped into the ground during the day as the labourers worked their way along the rows.

He turned to look at the slope again, and froze.

In front of him, he could see visible blood-spatter on the crushed leaves and vines at the bottom of the slope up to the fence.

"Rudge!" Jenner took out his camera and bent forward. There was a single clot of dark purple-brown blood, perhaps an inch across, gumming several leaves together; as he stared at it, a halo pattern of sparse, irregular droplet-spatter resolved before his eyes on the stems and leaves around it.

He knew that, in the two-dimensional reduction of the digital image, the pattern would be too spread out and uneven to be readily apparent, but he was sure it was real.

And at the very least, the DNA analysts would have a field day with that little puddled clot.

A raindrop hit his cheek, and he looked up in surprise.

Within seconds, the rain was pelting down from a suddenly black sky, thick, cool drops spraying down, spattering and ricocheting off the leaves and the grass; it was as if Jenner could hear the strike of each separate drop as it crashed down and destroyed his evidence.

Before he could even react, the central blood droplet was soaked, the matted leaves springing apart, the blood dissolved and washed off.

Out in the field, the workers looked up at the sky, then back down to the earth, and went on with their toil, pulling up the row-cover hoops and bundling the plastic.

56

Rudge was calling Jenner from the roadside, his jacket held tented over his head.

Jenner scrambled up the slope and climbed back over the fence. The detective was waiting, his cell phone in his hand.

"I found blood-spatter down the side of the trench there. I lost it when it started to rain, but . . ." Jenner said.

Rudge interrupted him with a wave.

"They ID'd the crash victim. It's Adam Weiss."

Jenner stopped. "The kid who called in the bodies?"

Rudge nodded.

"Fuck!"

Rudge nodded again. "You got that right." They started towards the car together.

"Christ." Jenner stared at him. "So it *is* connected . . ."

"Looks that way." Rudge shook his head. "The sheriff's shitting a brick – we don't like it too much round here when the white folks start dying."

"How'd they ID him?"

"The kid didn't call for his dad's birthday yesterday, so they called him up but he didn't answer. Then today they saw the news . . . NYPD emailed us his driver's license photo; it's him. Mom and dad are coming down to sign the papers, but Bobby Bartley took a look at him – he took the kid's statement the other day. He says no two ways, it's Weiss."

They climbed into the car, silent in the drumming rain; both had seen too many parents identify too many children.

Rudge popped the glove compartment, handed Jenner a fistful of McDonald's napkins, then took a fistful to mop his own face.

"So what now?"

Rudge shrugged. "Now you'll get to see Florida's finest in action . . ."

"What are you going to do?"

"Po-lice work, Doctor Jenner. Sheriff wants me to go to the kid's home, see what I can see."

57

Maggie looked at the dog that Jenner had brought in.

Even to a dog lover, he was a ridiculous, stumpy-looking thing. There might have been a splash of corgi, or perhaps of one of the uglier terriers, but not enough to nudge him into any category that was either familiar or desirable. With his stubby legs and a conical head that sprouted from a body the shape of a pot roast, he looked more like a root vegetable than a dog.

She smiled at him, ruffled his floppy ears and gave him a treat. The treat disappeared in a snap, the truncated tail waggling as if he were a coin-operated mechanical toy.

Maggie shook her head. The dog was washed and fed, dewormed, brushed, as polished as he'd ever be. But he was also full-grown, with an unwieldy bulk and strikingly lacking in appealing features; in a word, he was likely unadoptable.

Except.

Her eyes gleamed.

The dog would be the perfect pet for a bachelor.

58

Rudge and Jenner ate in the parking lot next to the taco stand in the pouring rain. They sat in the Taurus with the motor running, the A/C blasting icy gusts of mold-scented air into the greasy fug of carnitas and refried beans.

Their visit to Weiss's little shack had been uneventful. The cops at the Bel Arbre substation met them at the cottage with the landlord, an excitable little man who peppered them with questions about selling off the boy's things to cover the rent.

The door had been locked and there was no evidence of forced entry through the door or windows. The place was no messier than any other apartment inhabited by a twenty-two-year-old male college student. Nothing broken or obviously out of place. A good-quality wrist-watch sat on the bathroom sink, and there was a laptop out in the open on the table.

There was nothing to see, but the case was high-profile so they called in Crime Scene. They left the uniforms at the cottage to calm down the landlord, who was convinced the criminalists would tear up carpet and cut out sections of wall.

Before opening his dinner, Rudge set Weiss's notebook on the dashboard, open to a list of eight names. Six of the names were ticked off and, of those, four had been marked with a star – UFL Tomato, La Grulla Blanca, Pinewhite's, Endicott.

They ate in silence, listening to the rain on the car roof, occasionally glancing at the list.

After a few minutes, Rudge maneuvered the rest of his last taco into his mouth, cupping his hands around the tinfoil to stop the juices spilling down his shirt. He wiped the corners of his mouth, then blotted his goatee.

"So, Jenner. Anything you want to share with me?"

Jenner looked at him blankly. "Such as . . .?"

"I see." Rudge, nodding gravely, squeezed his damp napkin into a ball and pushed it into the paper bag. "Well, I think we need to have a little talk."

"A talk?"

"Yeah. Time I straightened you out on a couple of things."

They pulled out of the parking lot and headed toward the highway.

Jenner leaned back expectantly. "Okay. This oughta be good."

"So, you lived in the city most of your life?"

"Pretty much."

"Port Fontaine is different. Don't let the Armani and

215

Chanel boutiques on the Promenade fool you – this is still small-town Florida, and everyone knows everyone else's business."

"Uh-huh." Jenner grinned. "I've seen stuff like that on TV."

"I'm serious. The whole of Port Fontaine – me, everyone at the municipal building, that fucker we just bought our tacos from – we all know all about your business." Rudge turned onto the feeder road to the highway. "And don't think I'm kidding."

Jenner was becoming wary. "Go on. This is interesting . . ."

"Jenner, everyone knows you got with Chip Craine's daughter."

Jenner froze. "But . . . but that was only . . ."

"Last night? Sure, why not, whatever. But everyone already knows. Including the sheriff."

Jenner was puzzled. "So what if the sheriff knows? What, he's going to enforce some weird sex law they still only have down south?"

"Weird sex thing?" Rudge pursed his lips. "What exactly did you do last night, Jenner?" He grinned, then said, "Y'see, this is what happens when you go poking little Jenner around without knowing what you're getting into." He shook his head. "Maggie Craine is a fine-ass woman." Rudge paused, relishing the information he was about to impart. "But . . . she's also Tommy Anders's ex-wife."

"What?" Jenner couldn't imagine Maggie and the sheriff in the same decade, let alone the same bed.

"Oh, relax, player – this is years ago. She went away to college, grad school or something in New York, came

216

back pregnant and single. She knew Tommy from the Polo Grounds – his daddy was a big man back then. Tommy saw his chance, she said yes, and they got hitched. She dumped him a couple months after the baby arrived."

"Wow." Jenner looked at the detective. "So why are you telling me this now?"

"I figure it's good to know when the guy you're working for probably doesn't like you too much."

"Are you warning me?"

Rudge threw back his head and laughed. "No, doc, you're on your own . . . She's a fine-looking lady, no doubt. You know Charlotte Rampling, the actress? That's who she reminds me of. Just be careful with her, you know what I'm saying? She's been with a number of men here, and the landings are never smooth – once I had to arrest her at that motel out by the Miccosukee reservation, had to take her out of there in handcuffs."

"Well, thanks for the heads-up." Jenner looked at Rudge. "I don't know what's going to happen next. I thought she'd have called me by now."

"You call her?"

"No."

Rudge shrugged. "Well . . ."

He grinned, then gestured to the road ahead. "It's getting late – let's hit the list. UFL first, then La Grulla Blanca on the way home."

"Why them?"

"Weiss might have visited those farms on Workers' Solidarity business, but we know he'd been doing his own investigation and these are the last names he wrote down."

Jenner looked at the list. "I'm betting he's ticked off farms he's visited, then . . . what, put asterisks next to the ones which made him suspicious?"

"Maybe." Rudge settled back against the headrest and laid his arm across his belly. "This is where it gets sticky. These are some big properties – big money here, know what I'm saying?"

He swore, spotting a bright orange spatter of annatto-colored oil on his belly. He spat onto a napkin and began dabbing the shirt. "UFL Tomato has been in the news all year. Workers want a nickel more a bushel, the company and the fast-food chains they supply say no way. Last November, the WSM held a meeting to organize the workers. Maybe twenty showed up; when they were all inside the WSM building someone blocked the door with a chair and tossed in a Molotov cocktail."

"Jesus."

"Yeah, we figured it was UFL Tomato, but no one saw anything, no one said anything, and the fire marshal finally shitcanned it. We tossed it to ATF, but they had nothing to go on and buried it a couple months later."

"So UFL is high on the list?"

Rudge shrugged. "Eh. Maybe. But you gotta figure it'd be a pretty risky play for a company already under the microscope."

"And the other three?"

"Well, we'll see."

They drove on.

59

The UFL visit could've gone better. The farm manager mistook Jenner and Rudge for a state inspection team due that day; he greeted them extravagantly at first, then, when the true purpose of their visit became clear, shunted them into an outbuilding, where they waited for twenty minutes until a foreman arrived with a pale, harried-looking lawyer, sweating through his gray worsted wool suit.

It was a painful process. Every question Rudge asked was run past the lawyer before the foreman could answer; the lawyer had no understanding of the day-to-day workings of the farm, and the foreman's English was terrible. The lawyer kept leaping in to assure them that there were regular visits from an agricultural consulting group which numbered many ex-union men on their board, all with the aim of ensuring good working conditions for the field hands. UFL Tomato was justly proud of their labor relations, and the transparency of their operation, he repeated, mopping his brow with a white handkerchief.

They were getting nowhere.

Jenner stood under the eaves of the grain house and looked out over the fields, watching the farm machines move slowly through the drizzle. Near the central farm buildings, most of the land was freshly tilled, dark and rich, and narrow red vehicles with insect-like limbs crawled across the soil, small groups of farm workers following like drones.

Rudge called his name, and they moved on, the lawyer, foreman and detective all hugely relieved. There was one odd thing, though: Jenner had the distinct impression that two of the Mexican farm hands had been watching them. The impression deepened when they got back into Rudge's car; one of the men pulled out a cell phone, and made a call as he watched them drive away.

North of Bel Arbre they crossed a low bridge over a river through mangrove swamp, the twisted branches and trees knotted dense and thick, the water grey as old tin. The late-afternoon sun appeared in a fissure in the clouds; the rain-washed tarmac was sleek and black as a new tuxedo, the fields and trees streaming by on either side a vibrant pale green, as if they'd just burst from the earth.

La Grulla Blanca was a large mixed-use estate about five miles north of Bel Arbre, wedged between I-55 and the Everglades. They were waved past the gatehouse, under a high white arch painted with the farm's name in block letters. They followed the long drive to the main farmhouse, a white clapboard affair with green shingle roofs and shutters, a deliberate echo of the Polo Grounds club house.

The drive divided the property into a big upper field and a smaller lower one. The property sloped gently down to the waterfront, hemmed in by the dense press of mangroves stretching off to the west, toward the Gulf of Mexico. Next to the farmhouse, at the top of the low rise, were two white clapboard bunkhouses and the remains of a demolished barn. The lower field tilted down to the river, where there was a boat shed and dock.

On the upper slope there were two open structures with corrugated tin roofs over poured-concrete floors; metal slop troughs lined the single full wall in each building. A smaller enclosed building nearby had the same white clapboard walls and green-shingled peaked roof as the farmhouse, and a miniature of the main house's rooster weather vane. There was a white picket pen around the building; as Jenner watched, a flap door opened and three small pigs trotted out. Everywhere, hoses sprayed mist for the pigs, which tromped the water into the earth and lolled in the cooled mud.

They were met at the farmhouse by the manager, Mr. Brodie, a dour man wearing a blue and white La Grulla Blanca-logo polo shirt and cap, and the farm overseer, Mr. Bentas.

They introduced themselves, but before Brodie could even begin to speak Rudge turned to Bentas and said, "Sir, I have to enquire if that pistol you're carrying is registered, and if you have a concealed-carry permit."

Brodie flicked the back of his hand towards Rudge, as if he were waving away a card at a blackjack table. "Detective, of course Mr. Bentas's weapon is licensed. We have a problem with snakes here, copperheads and rattlers, especially in the cleared land, and last year we lost a pig to gators."

"Mr. Brodie, I support the right of our agricultural workers to superior firepower, I surely do. But the concealed-carry permit? You're telling me that Mr. Bentas needs to get the drop on a gator?"

"Glad to see you have time to joke, detective. You find this funny?" Brodie tipped his head to one side and spat, the white ball landing two feet from Rudge's foot.

Rudge stiffened and grew still, his eyes small and black in his wide face. His head dipped slightly and he peered up at Brodie from under a heavy brow.

Brodie continued, "Mr. Bentas accompanies the payroll deliveries to the farm every Friday. He needs the weapon – Bel Arbre can be a dangerous town, particularly 'round pay day. As you know."

He spat again.

Jenner said quickly, "So, we're here . . ."

Brodie said wearily, "Yeah, about the missing farm workers. Well, we ain't missing any farm workers. We told that to the deputy who called a couple days ago. Told that to the guy who came yesterday."

Rudge said, "What guy came yesterday?"

Brodie put his hands on his hips and leaned back. "Oh, some kid, asking questions about missing farm hands, and were people happy with working here." He worked his lip a bit, then spat again. "I'm telling you the same thing: all our workers are present and accounted for, all of 'em happy to have a job here with us. And we pay well, and they're happy. And The End."

Rudge shook his head and, with a wide smile, took a step back. "Well, Brodie, I figure you'd have to pay them extra because of the goddam smell. Tell the truth – you use that gun to keep the vultures away, right?"

Brodie's eyes had narrowed to slits. "Detective, we don't take to cursing around here. I gotta ask you to speak to me civil, or not at all."

"Sorry, Mr. Brodie. I figured you'd be used to the question by now." Rudge spat.

Jenner looked down the field, where two Mexican farmhands were herding pigs down to another mud bath. "So, Mr. Brodie . . . Why pigs? Not too hot for them down here?"

"The sprayers keep 'em cool." Brodie lifted his shoulders in an infinitely long shrug; it was like watching a snake slowly raise and uncoil before striking. "The owner wants pigs, he gets pigs."

Behind Brodie, Bentas stood, face somber, hands on his hips. When he turned, Jenner saw the blocky shape of a pistol grip under the man's shirt, wedged inside his waist band at the back; he had no idea how Rudge had spotted it. It occurred to Jenner that they were out in the middle of nowhere and Rudge was antagonizing a man who had an armed bodyguard. What was it Douggie Pyke always said? *Don't poke a skunk.*

He was about to suggest that they move on when Brodie tipped his head back, took off his cap, spat again, then said to Rudge, "You got anything else, boy? Because we got work to do."

Hearing the word "boy", the stiffness instantly slipped away from the detective's body. His smile grew wider. "Nothing for now, Mr. Brodie. But we'll be back with a warrant, get a good look around here without having to disturb you."

He turned to Jenner, nodded at the car.

Brodie said, "You're welcome to look around all you want! But hell, yeah, you go get yourself a warrant! Let's keep it nice and legal."

Now Brodie was smiling too. "Y'know, we got lawyers, too. We know that game. This is a working farm, we got shit to do, can't be giving tours of the property all the time. So, you go ahead, you just show your probable cause to the State Attorney. Tell you something, though: when you do, he'll tell you you can kiss his fat white ass with your warrant."

223

The smile stopped. "Now get the fuck out of here, boy."

Rudge's own smile didn't falter. "Well, Mr. Brodie . . . I guess we'll come on back tomorrow, y'all! Y'hear?"

As they walked back to the car, Rudge called out, "I'll need to see registration for the handgun, and your associate's carry permit and state or federal ID."

As Brodie and Bentas watched, they climbed into the car.

Jenner said, "Well, that went well!"

Rudge's smile had gone. It didn't return.

They drove in silence, looping down the driveway between the fields. As they passed the miniature barn on the way back down the drive the door opened, and Jenner glimpsed a farmhand standing in a room filled with piglets, surrounded by wall-mounted shelves stacked high with red and white feed bags. The piglets poured around the man's legs like bubbles, charging out to lose themselves in the mud.

"Why did you ask about the carry permit?"

"I didn't like that guy; if he's got a record – any felony, domestic violence, whatever – he shouldn't have a permit."

Jenner looked out over the farm. Near the mangrove swamp he saw a large airboat by the dock, and next to it a shallow-draft swamp boat. The Everglades stretched beyond the fields in an infinite green swath, shot through with glimmering gold threads in the setting sun.

As they reached the gate, their path was blocked by a large white box truck. Rudge steered the Taurus onto the grass shoulder so the truck could pass; the truck had a logo Jenner couldn't quite place, a pale blue globe with the letters CBM.

He glanced back toward the main buildings. In front of the farmhouse another man had joined Brodie and Bentas. He was tall and skinny, wearing a black cap. Bentas and the new man went to meet the truck but Brodie stayed on the porch, staring at the Taurus, talking on his cell phone. Even after they'd passed out of sight, even after they'd reached the highway, Jenner felt Brodie's stare still on them.

60

It was past seven p.m. when Rudge dropped Jenner at the M.E. Office. The main municipal building was brightly lit, but the lab wing was dark.

Jenner reached for the door handle, then turned to Rudge and said, "Hey, did you get the feeling we were being watched at the farms? Not by the management, by the workers, I mean. I could swear one of the field hands made a phone call about us as we were leaving UFL."

Rudge nodded and grinned. "Actually, Jenner, I think the first call was made by the guy at the taqueria in Bel Arbre. No two ways about it: we're being watched."

"The farm owners, you think?"

"Since it was the guy who made the tacos who called, unless they also own the taco stand, I'd say no. I think it's the Mexican."

"The same people who approached Adam Weiss?"

"Maybe them, maybe bad guys – no way to know." Rudge stretched. "Okay, Jenner, I gotta go write up my notes. See you tomorrow."

Jenner crossed the shadowy lobby and went down the hall into his office. The red voicemail light blinked aggressively on his phone. He scanned his desk, didn't see what he wanted and stepped back into the hallway to check the mailboxes.

Still no paycheck.

He sat behind his desk, punched in his code and listened to his messages. There was a message from Anders's secretary Arlene, asking him to see the sheriff as soon as possible. She stressed that no matter what time he got back the sheriff would be in, and that he wanted to see Jenner urgently.

The last message was from Deb Putnam. She spoke softly and with an unforced warmth. She was following up – they'd talked about maybe getting dinner tonight. She'd called during the day but he'd been out. She hadn't left a message because she knew how busy he must be. She figured he'd probably be too tired, but if he felt like it he could give her a call when he got the message; she wasn't doing much anyway, so if he wanted to hit Outback they could do that, or maybe one of the fancier places down on the Promenade, although, she figured, he'd probably be too tired.

Jenner added her number to the call list, then hung up the phone.

He pulled out his cell. He hesitated for a second, then dialed Maggie Craine's number.

It was her voicemail. He had an instant of indecision, then spoke.

"Hey, Maggie. It's Jenner. It's about 7:30 p.m. and I'm about to get off work. Wondered if you felt like getting a drink or something. I'll catch up with you . . . Take care."

He hung up, feeling like a high-school boy – he regretted calling, regretted the message more.

He left the gloom of the lab wing and crossed the glass-block passage into the main building. The walkway was brightly lit from outside; the glowing corridor of white light reminded him of near-death experiences, and then of death. He grinned – he'd never been good at thinking about his own mortality.

The door to Major Crimes was open, and on seeing Rudge, Jenner stuck his head in.

"Hey."

Rudge nodded grimly. There was another detective, a young man, sitting on his desk; he glanced at Jenner when he entered but said nothing. The two were looking at the TV.

Jenner turned to see what they were watching so intently. He recognized the show instantly – the lurid red, white and blue graphics (truth, justice and the American Way) would have been enough, even without the tawdry *American Crime* logo in the corner.

Jenner was on TV.

Of course. That was why Amanda Tucker had come herself, rather than sending one of her winged monkeys. The horrible deaths of four men couldn't have dragged her down to this godforsaken swamp. Marty Roburn and his wife, rotting gently in a drowned car for weeks? Also not enough.

She'd come for Jenner.

She'd come to play with him, come to carve him up again, pop out his limbs like some gluttonous king tearing apart a chicken, come to open him up and serve him to her public.

Jenner pulled up a desk chair and sat.

American Crime had put together a biographical video; they'd done their homework. Over the caption INQUISITOR PATHOLOGIST IN FL, the camera panned slowly across a photo of him in medical school, his mother and father applauding as he received the prize in physical diagnosis. Then a montage from the ensuing years – on Miami Beach, Jenner next to the body of a drowned swimmer. Video of Jenner in court, gesturing emphatically as he testified in a child-abuse case. A *Miami Herald* photo of him standing next to a bullet-riddled car in Liberty City, the bloody body of a man dangling through the driver-side window.

He watched it all, almost unable to hear. There was a skyline shot of Manhattan, sliding down the West Side from the Empire State to the World Trade Center. Then the familiar 9/11 video – the planes hitting, the towers collapsing, the thousands of dust-covered workers fleeing in horror. Then Jenner's photo from his New York M.E. ID card, the word QUIT in red block letters materializing across his face. His face was then replaced by that of Robert Farrar, the Inquisitor killer, head shots of his victims punching into the screen with a rat-a-tat rhythm. When they showed Joey Roggetti's funeral, the detective's flag-draped coffin surrounded by a welling ocean of blue serge dress uniforms lining the streets of Queens, up the steps of the church. Jenner's chest tightened and he struggled to breathe.

And then Ana de Jong. Ana. The *New York Post* telephoto shots of them on the sidewalk in front of his building, Jenner fully dressed, Ana in one of his sweat-shirts, bare-legged in sneakers, up on tiptoe to kiss him.

Then Jenner with his arm around her shoulder, lifting his coat to shield her from the photographer. Then grainy ambush video, slowed to a crawl, the two of them running down Crosby, fleeing the paparazzi. Jenner hadn't seen that one before; it was from after he'd killed Farrar, from when he'd brought Ana home from the hospital.

He watched the flow in silence, the images gushing through him. Amanda Tucker now, the return of the "*creepy, creepy sexual opportunist*" clip. Then Jenner, his New York State Physician Identification, the words LICENSE SUSPENDED forming onscreen. A map graphic showing southern Florida in orange, with Douglas county highlighted and a yellow star for Port Fontaine. The camera zoomed towards the star, then cut to standard tourist footage of the town – beaches, high-end boutiques along the Promenade, a waterfront seafood restaurant.

Then Marty and Bobbie Roburn, and an artist's rendering of four men hanged in a jungle, then a photo of Adam Weiss, the images stacking into a neat pyramid on the screen, Weiss at the top.

Amanda Tucker in front of the municipal building, shaking hands with Tom Anders, walking the marble hallways to Anders's office. Anders in front of the huge bronze bust of his dad at the entrance to his office, talking about the investigations. Then in the sheriff's office, Anders's sweaty sheen an uncomfortable contrast to Amanda Tucker, cool and dry in her cream pants suit.

Jenner stood. He didn't need to see this.

But he didn't leave.

Onscreen, Amanda was showing Anders their video

biography of Jenner. She then asked the sheriff if he'd known that Jenner had lost his license in New York. Anders stressed that, though he was vaguely aware of Jenner's involvement in the Inquisitor case, today was the first he'd learned of the suspension. The late medical examiner, Dr. Roburn, had recruited Jenner and had spoken extremely highly of Jenner's skills.

Amanda pushed it. "And now that you're aware of these issues, will you be looking into Dr. Jenner's qualifications? Have there been any problems with his performance?"

Anders pursed his lips, then nodded, saying, "I would say that some of Dr. Jenner's decisions have seemed questionable to me."

"And, Sheriff Anders, do you now feel that Dr. Jenner is . . . the ideal person to be investigating these killings? Particularly given that one of the victims is his former mentor, Dr. Roburn."

"Well, I'll tell you this, Amanda. My office will review his credentials, and if there's anything that doesn't meet Douglas County's standards, appropriate action will be taken."

"And what would you mean by 'appropriate action'?"

"Well, today I've spoken with the Dade County Medical Examiner's Office in Miami; they've agreed to provide forensic pathology coverage, should the need arise."

Amanda Tucker nodded, a look of firm approval on her face, said, "I see."

The outro clip was the slow-motion video of Jenner and Ana running to the safety of his loft.

And then they were in a commercial break, an earnest Vanessa Redgrave-lookalike urging American investors to consider gold in a time of crisis.

Rudge, with a long whistle, leaned back, then looked at him. "Hey, Jenner – maybe if you're really extra good this year, Santa will bring you the DVD . . ."

Jenner, unsmiling, shook his head.

"That all true?"

Jenner stood. "What do you mean, 'true'? Yeah, that was me. Yes, I did those things. Yes, I was with the girl, and yes, she was an Inquisitor victim. But it wasn't like I . . . you know, *planned* it or anything – it just happened. I was having a hard time, she was having a hard time, and it happened. And it's all right now, she's gone."

"And the cop? The detective? Roggetti, was it?"

"What about him?"

"What *really* happened?"

"Just like it said in all the papers: Farrar got the drop on us. He beat the crap out of me, killed Joey Roggetti and cut up another detective real bad."

Rudge thought for a second, nodding.

"You're lucky to be alive."

"Well, I'm luckier than Joey," Jenner said, forcing a fake grin.

Rudge raised his hands in irritation. "Jesus, you gotta let that shit go. Roggetti was a cop, one of New York's Finest. He knew the risks – we all know the risks, but we know the odds are in our favor, know what I'm saying? And sometimes it don't work out, and we lose. But we do what we do because we believe in it. Roggetti died doing what he believed in. He protected and served, right? He's a hero. And you killed Farrar, right? You tracked down

231

that muthafucka and flat-out killed him dead. You did what had to be done for Roggetti, so in my book you're a hero too."

Rudge shook his head. "You can't go around carrying this shit, Jenner – I saw you tense up when the funeral came on. Sooner or later you have to tell yourself 'it's not my fault' . . ."

Jenner said, "Look, I watched Joey die in front of me, watched him bleed out maybe four feet from where I was lying. Farrar beat me down, beat me enough that I couldn't move, that all I could do was watch my friend die. Joey died in my building, trying to help my girlfriend. So don't tell me whose fault it is or . . ."

"Doctor Jenner?" He turned to see Anders right behind him. "You and I need to have a little talk. Please come with me."

61

Deb Putnam sat on Jenner's porch, her stomach growling. This is a terrible idea, she thought, but what the hell – she'd always felt worse for not having tried than for failing.

She wouldn't normally give someone this much slack. He'd blown her off twice now, and usually for her it was a case of one strike and a guy was out; she could afford to be picky. But Jenner was different. The night their date fell through, she'd seen the TV coverage at Billy's on the Sands; she knew the pressure he was facing, the stress he was under.

For her, their moment in the limelight had been exciting. She'd liked watching herself and Jenner running and waving away the helicopter, liked seeing herself on the hammock in the middle of the Glades from overhead. Everyone at Billy's treated her like a celebrity, and she drank for free, and Dwayne Kretcher tried to take her home, but she hadn't been that drunk, thank God! She'd been disappointed that Jenner had canceled, but it wasn't like she'd gone to Billy's to get trashed and pick up some guy to take the edge off.

Deb grinned as she thought of Jenner describing his trek through the Glades in the dark, a hundred percent sure he was being hunted by gators. Her father would've liked Jenner. And, she figured, Jenner would've liked the old man, too.

The sadness came back quietly. It had been horrible to watch her dad waste away; throughout it all he'd never complained, but in the end, he'd clearly welcomed his death. She remembered how the quiet had descended on her life like a fog, how the emptiness had trickled into the little home they'd shared. Some days it felt like she'd tracked that emptiness into her new place, as if the old furniture she'd brought with her came with the sadness still attached.

She liked that Jenner was new. For him, her loss was something already in the past; he'd offered no pity, no rote condolences, he'd just been friendly to her.

And had listened to her talk about snails.

She smiled. If something happened, it happened. If not, Jenner was a nice guy, and there was no shame in trying for something more.

She looked at Jenner's weird dog again, its belly flat on

the floor, its pointy snout resting on her foot by the food and water bowls. The handwriting on the envelope tacked to Jenner's door was delicate and feminine. Deb was curious about the note, but too polite to look.

So she'd learned something new: she quite possibly had competition. To her surprise, the thought pleased her: an opponent added a little spice to the game. Let them bring it – she liked her chances. She was smart, she was well-read, she was pretty.

And she could cook. She glanced at her watch: almost eighty-thirty p.m. She was ravenous – she hadn't eaten since breakfast, just after six a.m. And there she was, sitting on his porch with two thick roast beef sandwiches on homemade bread, a bottle of pinot noir tucked into her book bag. Showing up with dinner and wine was completely transparent, but it wasn't as if he'd be astonished to discover she was interested.

Besides, she was happy on the porch. The air had cooled with the seeping dark, and the mosquitoes weren't too bad tonight.

Deb stood, walked casually to the door. She turned on her cell phone and peered at the envelope in its glow. The fat looping "J" and the billowy letters weren't just feminine, they were girly. She smirked.

She shielded her eyes from the glare as high beams flooded the porch. It was an SUV; Jenner had a rental Sebring. The SUV pulled up in front of his cabin, and a young couple with matching sunburns and FIU windbreakers climbed out. They said good evening, and went into the cabin next door.

She paced the porch for a while, her activity arousing no interest whatsoever on the part of the dog.

It was closing in on nine p.m. – what if Jenner had been called out?

Maybe she should just grab her sandwiches and go. She smiled, imagining herself in her Miata, tearing open the wax paper to finally take a huge bite of sandwich; she could almost taste the rare roast beef, the Swiss cheese, the bite of horseradish mayonnaise . . .

Headlights tipped over the low ridge from the street and Jenner's car settled slowly towards the cabin. Deb watched him park and climb out. He stretched stiffly, then reached inside to pull out a bag of clothes. He headed toward her.

The dog shuffled to the porch step, and Deb followed. From the shadows, she could see Jenner's face clearly in the pathway light – his surprise at the dog, then his grin as he saw her silhouette moving forward.

But when she stepped into the light, his expression turned guarded – the smile stayed, but he was disappointed. He'd thought she was someone else, and, when he saw it was just her, he was disappointed.

He said, "Hey, Deb." He looked exhausted.

"Hey, Jenner." She hid her own dismay. "You look beat."

"Huh. Maybe I should've used more concealer under my eyes – they're a real problem area." He smiled wearily. "It was a rough day."

"Yeah, well, I know." She smiled and raised her eyebrows. "I guess you heard about *American Crime*?"

"Heard about it? Oh, yeah." He paused, then shrugged. "The sheriff just fired me."

"I'm sorry to hear that. Is there anything you can do?"

"Nope. I'm just a temp here, and the man who hired

235

me is dead. On Monday, pathologists from Miami are taking over until the county finds a replacement. I've got a week to finish up my paperwork and get the hell out of Dodge."

"I'm so sorry."

"Yeah, well." Jenner produced an envelope from his pocket and waved it. "On the bright side, I got paid."

"Well, good." Deb held up her book bag. "I figured you could do with some company tonight, so I brought you a bite to eat. Just sandwiches, but . . ."

"Y'know, I'm so hungry I could slaughter a cow and eat its bloody flesh right here." He glanced at the dog. "How come you brought him back?"

"Nothing to do with me – he was snoring on the porch when I got here. There's a note." She nodded towards the door; she couldn't stop herself. "A girl, I think."

Jenner walked to the door a little quickly, plucked down the envelope and read it in the porch light; she noted his expression didn't change.

He folded it into his pocket, and turned back to her. "It's a bit of a dump inside. Want to eat out here?"

"That'd be nice."

He disappeared into the cabin, and she unwrapped the sandwiches on the small table and pulled out the bottle. She called out, "Got a corkscrew, Jenner?"

"There's wine?" He appeared at the doorway with a box of mosquito coils. "I've got a knife with a corkscrew."

She sat. "Hey, if you want to have a shower or something first, I'm in no hurry."

"Really?" He hesitated, grinning. "To be honest, I'd love a shower. If you can hang on, that would be great."

She smiled back. "Wouldn't have said it if I didn't mean it."

Smelling the food, the dog waddled up and pressed his paws on her leg. Deb hoped that Jenner hadn't heard the grumbling from her stomach.

62

Daylight. Jenner had left the curtains open, and the cabin was bright in the early-morning light. He picked up his phone from the side table: no messages.

He dragged himself out of bed, opened the door for the dog. He stood on the porch in his T-shirt and boxers, watching the thing snuffle and root around under the cabin. Standing there, dressed in his underwear, watching his mutt crapping on a bush, it occurred to him that he'd never felt more at home at the Palmetto Court.

He let the dog inside and lay back down on the bed.

He was surprised he wasn't hungover; after they'd split Deb's wine, he'd opened one of his own bottles. They hadn't finished the second, but he'd definitely been feeling the alcohol by the time he'd said goodnight.

Deb Putnam was adorable. Bright, incredibly kind, funny. That she was the youngest of five and the only girl was no surprise – she understood him in a way many women didn't. Dealing with four brothers had left her with keen insights into how men work.

Not that she was a tomboy – far from it. Off duty, her clothes were simple and not expensive, chosen carefully to emphasize her athletic shape and long legs. She was impressively well put-together, her hair bleached from the sun, her skin dark, her eyes all the bluer for it.

She liked him, too, and didn't care that he knew. And she was different – at least, different from New York women; her interest was relaxed, patient, artless. There'd been no look of recrimination when he'd rejected her with a goodnight peck on the cheek, like she was his baby sister. They hadn't talked about it, but Deb understood there was Someone Else.

He wondered if she'd read Maggie's note.

He opened it again.

> *Jenner: Take him back, we got plenty!*
> *Use him to pick up chicks, or something.*
> *Maggie Craine*

He looked at his watch. 7:30 a.m. Too early to call.

"Maggie Craine". Formal, distant – maybe the "pick up chicks" suggestion wasn't a joke. Maybe he should get a clue.

There was a lolloping sound from the floor, and he leaned over to see the dog licking clean the sandwich plate. He lay back.

The memorial service was at eleven a.m.

Jenner got up and sat at the breakfast table, reading over his notes. He knew what he needed to say: that they'd all been better for knowing Marty and Bobbie, that Marty had made him a better pathologist, and in doing so, a better man. He hoped when he spoke at the church he'd stay clear and focused, not get too emotional. But if he wept it wouldn't be the end of the world.

He needed a black jacket for the service. He showered

and dressed, and headed to the New Promenade mall. He deposited his check at the ATM next to Nordstrom, then spent a few minutes sorting out his money. After paying off American Express and the minimum on his main Visa card, he realized the check money wouldn't go much further. The bank wanted the full balance, nearly $3000, before they'd reactivate his frozen MasterCard; it would have to stay frozen. When all his money had been allocated between his various accounts and debts, he had barely enough to take out $300 in cash.

His cell phone rang. The tox lab director, confirming that Adam Weiss had been poisoned with Malathion, an organophosphate insecticide – the Safety Director would be happy.

Jenner folded the money into his wallet and went into Nordstrom. It was just after opening, and the store was still quiet, the air slightly stuffy and humid with the faintest hint of mold. The salespeople were chatting dully, polishing counters and setting up. By the escalator next to the menswear department there was a baby grand piano, its gleaming black lid open; a man in a dark suit and a bow tie was tapping keys one by one, listening to each note critically.

The jackets were handsome, and good-quality, but the prices were New York prices. He paid with his Visa, but the $460 charge broke his limit, and the machine rejected his card. The salesman sent the sale through twice more, until the card was accepted with a $290 charge and $170 in cash.

Jenner refused the suit bag, had the salesman cut off the tags and slipped the jacket on in the store. He smoothed his shirt and straightened his tie in a mirror, noticing that, somewhere along the way, his face had become tan.

He splurged on a coffee at Starbucks, and read his notes. They were good, his words heartfelt and true.

Jenner was ready to say his goodbye.

63

At 10:30 a.m. Jenner was dictating his description of the rib injuries when he looked up to see David and Marie Carter and Richard Flanagan in his doorway; he'd never seen Flanagan in a tie before.

"Time to go?" He put down the microphone, and turned to slip his new jacket off the hanger on which he'd carefully hung it.

They filed into his office somberly, and Flanagan shut the door.

They'd designated David Carter to do the talking. Carter knew what he had to say, but clearly found it hard.

"Dr. Jenner . . ."

Jenner nodded. "What's going on, David?"

"When I was driving here to pick Marie up, I passed the chapel. It's a . . . a mob scene out there – reporters, news vans, at least twenty TV cameras. And Amanda Tucker is outside right now . . ." He shook his head.

Jenner said, "Go on."

Marie Carter broke in. "Dr. Jenner, *Eye on Port Fontaine* showed the report about you from the Amanda Tucker show this morning, and then they had Diane Sales from the Sheriff's Department saying that you're leaving next week. They said you had problems in New York, and there are problems with your work here."

David Carter said, "We understand that's all wrong – we've worked with you, and we've seen the great work that you've done here." He hesitated. "But if you go to the memorial service, it'll be all about you – they'll ask Sheree about you, they'll talk to the sheriff about you. And when you show up, they'll bombard you with all sorts of questions. Let's face it: they're going to persecute you – I think you know that, don't you? They're making you the fall guy for everything that's gone wrong."

He paused, then said, "And if you go, Marty and Bobbie will get lost in the shuffle."

Jenner put the jacket down on the desk. "You don't want me to go."

The three nodded, and Flanagan said, "Doc, we hate to ask you. We know you were closer to him than any of us were. And we know you're getting a bum rap here. But you show up, it'll be like Clown Day at the circus."

Jenner looked up at them for a while, then down at his notes. Then he nodded, and said, "You're right. Of course I don't want to get in the way."

He didn't look up as they left.

He picked up his speech, folded it in half, in quarters, then across into eighths, and let it drop into the bin.

64

If there was anything that stank worse than pig shit, Brodie had yet to encounter it.

He stood at the top of the gentle slope, looking out over the outbuildings and pastures. Down toward the road, two of his field rats were herding a cluster of sows, leading them back up to the slop troughs.

He scowled: for some reason, he found their white and blue La Grulla Blanca baseball caps particularly irritating today. He loathed the way the fucking wetbacks swanned around in them, as if the farm were a fucking yacht club and they were all commodores.

Brodie had never liked the hats. He agreed they gave the estate a respectable look, but when the men went into town the hats marked them, set them apart, and that was bad. The crew from La Grulla Blanca scrapped with farmhands from other farms, bare-knuckled fights after dark, out in the cemetery or near the weighing stations, stripped to the waist, punching, kicking, beating until the other was unconscious, surrounded by drunk, jeering men snapping photos on their cell phones.

It wasn't the fighting that worried Brodie – the men he hired could take care of themselves. His men were some of the toughest fuckers around, hardened by years on the streets of the District or in Tijuana, and most had done long bits in the big Mexie prisons.

No, the men could take care of themselves; just not their mouths. They drank, they fought, they won, they drank more, they bragged, they flashed their cash. And that was the problem.

Most growers paid pickers about fifty cents for a thirty-two pound basket of tomatoes. A hard worker – and most of the Mexies were hard workers – would get up at four a.m. to get a prime position at the bus hub for the foremen's six a.m. visit to choose day laborers. He'd work the fields all day, home at five or six p.m., now richer by sixty bucks.

Brodie turned and walked back over the slope, past the foundation of the barn they'd demolished, back to the bunkhouses. Inspection time.

Yeah, the money. Always the money. Depending on their position, the fifteen or so workers at La Grulla Blanca made a lot more than average. Each of them – and they were all men – would get about $500 in cash at the end of each week, with Brodie holding another $500. Twice a month, Brodie sent a $1000 wire transfer to their home country via telegram for each worker.

The system had evolved by trial and error; at first he'd paid cash, but things quickly got out of hand, his men all showy in town, blowing their money gambling and drinking and whoring. People were starting to talk about the La Grulla crew having more money.

So Brodie shut down the pump, paid them enough so they had cash but didn't stand out. And he started sending their money back home to their families. The system had paid off big time; gratitude from their *abuelas* and *mamacitas* created a work ethic that neither money nor the threat of violence ever could. And of course, there was always the threat of violence; the men understood that Brodie knew where their families lived, and had seen his ruthlessness firsthand.

Tony was leaning by the door to Bunkhouse A, the cookhouse; he nodded at Brodie. The wind picked up and the smell of pig filth sharpened abruptly; Tony's white *guayabera* billowed, and Brodie glimpsed the dark handle of his .45. Just under the lip of the house, hidden by tall grass, there were two Tec-9 machine pistols.

Tony stayed silent as Brodie passed; Brodie was grateful not to have small talk.

Brodie cracked open the door and peered in. It was cold in the long room, four industrial air conditioners keeping the temperature in the low sixties. But it was never the cold that struck him so much as the smell, the cloyingly sweet smell of the acetone they used to extract the pseudoephedrine from the cold medicine, the sour citrus smell of the product.

They were nearing the middle of the forty-eight-hour cook cycle. At the far end of the room, three men in hooded white Tyvek jumpsuits and painters' masks gathered around a globe-shaped glass flask the size of a beach ball that was wrapped in a steel heating mantle. As Brodie watched, they slowly trickled red phosphorus onto the pseudoephedrine they'd extracted that morning. There were three other triple-necked twenty-two-liter flasks, each half filled with a bubbling slurry the color of caking blood; corrugated orange hoses crooked off the flask tops, pumping waste gas into tall plastic canisters packed with cat litter to hide the reek. This was a back-up – they kept pigs on La Grulla Blanca to mask the smell of methamphetamine cooking.

Brodie didn't speak – the phosphorus was lethally poisonous and could ignite from friction, and the hydroiodic acid in the flasks could burn a man's eyeballs out. The greatest danger was fucking up the mixture and making phosphine gas, which would kill them all within seconds. This was why all his cooks came from Michoacan State, from Apatzingan or Tepalcatepec, where all the best meth cooks came from – Lord knows he didn't want a roomful of dead Mexies on his hands.

He watched them tip the last of the phosphorus into the funnel, then carefully ease the canister down to the ground. They stepped back, relieved; one capped the open necks while another checked the heating-coil settings.

Brodie closed the door and looked out over the land. The farmhands had reached the feed pens now, and were smoking in the shade as they watched the sows crowd the trough. The average profit on a pig raised and slaughtered was less than twenty dollars; a two-day cook cycle produced thirty pounds of methamphetamine with a street value of roughly $800,000. Always the money.

He thought of his daughter back in Mendocino, begging him to give his idiot son-in-law a job but to keep him out of the meth business – Tarver already had a strike against him in California. But Tarver wanted money, and factory or warehouse work wouldn't cut it. Besides, Brodie had decided that he could use a man with Tarver's special gifts: the psycho would do things that most men wouldn't. It had been Tarver who'd come up with the idea of showing the other men what happened when you broke one of Brodie's commandments.

Tarver had videotaped Tony as he'd worked on them, and after the interrogations he'd videoed the executions. Later, all of the men had been gathered together to watch the tape of their colleagues being killed. Brodie had shown the first video at the monthly barbecue; the men had mostly been pretty drunk when Tarver had rolled out the TV.

When the video finished, the men stood in stunned silence. Bentas explained that the mistake of one man destroys the lives of all, and that the weakness of one can overcome the strength of many. He said that the hanged men had been stealing meth, using it and dealing in Bel Arbre, and had risked exposing them all. And, of course, some of the workers had known it – or at least suspected it. Then Brodie announced that the pig they'd slaughtered that morning was just ready, and the Corona and tequila flowed again, and everyone gathered around the pit to eat.

Later, Brodie asked for their attention again: he said he was grateful for all their hard work, and they'd each be getting a five-hundred-dollar bonus. Then he clapped his hands and pointed to the main farmhouse. Headlights turned on and a minivan trundled slowly to the barbecue area, the van full of whores from Bel Arbre, big fat *mamacitas* probably ecstatic not to be still fucking donkeys in TJ. And while Brodie usually brought in just two or three women, that night there were six.

When the owner came to a barbecue, Brodie would have to supply young ones; he'd been surprised how easy it was to find a fourteen-year-old – for the right money everything was possible. He didn't like it, though – not from a moral point of view, but because he felt it was an unnecessary exposure. People talked about a fourteen-year-old whore in ways they didn't when the girl was seventeen.

So Brodie took precautions. He sent out a different man to meet the procurer each time, used a rental car, blindfolded the girls immediately and didn't take the blindfolds off until they were inside the main farmhouse. Afterwards, the weeping girl (and they were always crying by the time the boss finished with them) was soothed with money and tequila, then blindfolded again and taken on a circuitous route back to the town. The challenge of procuring girls for the boss had become harder as the man's tastes had evolved; it was now difficult to find girls young enough and thin enough to make him happy.

Brodie spat and adjusted his cap. Fuck it – depending on the supply of ingredients, the farm did do two forty-eight-hour cook cycles a week, pushing the gross to near two million dollars. He could overlook a little risk.

65

Leila, the head of Craine's household staff, was waiting for Maggie at the steps.

"Your dad's on the terrace; he's expecting you." Maggie had given up trying to read her father's mood from Leila's expression; that Chip had summoned her to Stella Maris at all was never a good sign.

Her father kept the house glacially cold; when she'd been a kid, the tiles in the ridiculously formal entry hall had always felt like ice under her bare feet. Hugging herself against the chill, she crossed the living room. The view was as gorgeous as ever – the green sweep of perfect lawn, beyond it the Gulf of Mexico, the water now blurred in silver haze.

Maggie pushed through the big glass doors and out onto the terrace, down the steps to the pool. Her father sat at the table in his robe, eating scrambled eggs and toast as he read the *New York Times*. He was wearing a pair of handmade Italian sunglasses that cost over three thousand dollars.

He accepted her dutiful kiss, and gestured to the other chair.

"Coffee? Juice? I can have Rosalba make up some eggs if you'd like . . ."

Maggie shook her head. "I had coffee at home." She sat.

"I've been going over the bills from Palm Haven." Chip Craine tapped a leather folio on the table. "Lucy's stay is going to cost over $32,000."

"My God!" The number was astonishing. "But they did really well with her – I think she's doing really well."

Craine nodded. "And of course, that's the most important thing – that Lucy keeps making progress and getting better. It's what we all want."

Where was he going with this?

He slid the folio aside and leaned back. "So, have you seen any more of the doctor?"

Maggie didn't like this. "I was going to call him yesterday, but I had a charity planning thing at the club, and after that it was too late to make plans."

"You spent the other night with him."

She flushed. How could he know that? She didn't answer.

"Of course, your affairs are none of my business." He shrugged. "But I have to say that I don't like him."

"You never like them."

"What?"

"You never like anyone I date."

Craine chuckled. "That's just silly – I liked Charlie Endicott."

"He was a prick – you only liked Charlie because his dad hated that he was dating me."

"Ah! I am a bad man indeed, comforted by the discomfort of my enemies!" Craine said. "But, anyway. I disapprove of the doctor – I mean, the man cuts up dead bodies, for crying out loud!"

Maggie was silent for a second.

She said quietly, "I like him. He's kind to me, patient with me."

"Well, I think we've all been very patient with you." Craine took a sip of grapefruit juice. "But I've seen you do this a thousand times. You always think you've fallen in love and fling yourself at a man. Then, a few days later, a week later, you realize they were wrong all along.

"You make bad decisions, we both know it. Most adults are independent, work for a living – but not you. I buy you a house, I give you an allowance, I even fund your damn shelter so you can pretend you've actually done something with your life! And in the end I have to jump in and clean up after you. It's like dealing with a six-year-old."

She was teary now. "Daddy, please. You're being unfair."

"I watch you throw yourself at this doctor, and it's just one more Maggie Craine disaster in the making. I've had just about enough. I need you to assume more responsibility."

Craine opened the folio and tapped his finger firmly on the Palm Haven bill. "Lucy gives me enough to worry about without you disappearing with strange men all the time – you should be home looking after her! How on earth did you let her starve herself like that? Where were you, exactly, when she was making herself throw up?"

He watched his daughter cry.

"$32,000 dollars! You act like the money grows on trees!" He pulled another invoice from the folio and pushed it across the table. "And the family therapy? You think that's free? Three hundred dollars an hour. How would *you* like to pay for it?

"Really, Maggie, if you're independent enough to run out and sleep with every man who catches your eye, you can also be responsible enough to take on the financial burden of the medical care that Lucy needs because of your neglect."

Maggie leaped to her feet, grabbed his juice glass and threw it at him. It hit the robe silently, spattering juice onto his neck and chest and lap; Craine caught the glass before it fell to the floor.

He called after her, "Wonderful, Maggie! I completely take back what I said about you being immature!"

She kept going, and didn't turn when he shouted, "It's up to you – let me know what you want to do . . ."

66

In the embalming room, Smith watched Reggie Jones open Mrs. Rosenblum. He thought it hilarious that Tony refused to watch them pack the meth into the bodies; Tony was a stone-cold bastard when it came to cutting on a live man, but he quailed like a bitch when it came to fucking with the dead.

Reggie popped the staples that the doctors had used to close the woman's chest after the bypass, then extended the incision down to her pelvis; he would staple it back up later, and the few who saw her naked body would assume it was the handiwork of the surgeons.

He placed a sternal retractor into the chest incision and cranked it wide open, then quickly and methodically removed the lungs and the heart, and opened the flat sheet of muscle that separated chest cavity from abdomen. Then Smith held the abdominal retractor while Reggie cleared out the liver, intestines and other abdominal organs.

Reggie looked at the clock; in less than fifteen minutes, he had hollowed out Mrs. Rosenblum's carcass. He rinsed the cavities with a sprayer, then turned the valve and sucked all the water back up. He pressed absorbent material into the empty thorax and abdomen to dry it out.

He looked over to the table, where Smith and Tony had stacked a dozen bricks of methamphetamine, each a kilo in weight. "You bring the leg tubes?"

Smith nodded. He spread open his gym bag and showed Reggie the blue PVC pipes, roughly the diameter of a baseball bat, cut down to twelve-inch segments. This had been Reggie's masterstroke: with a scalpel and bone saw, he would remove the femurs and other leg bones from the bodies, along with their muscle. Then he'd wedge the tubes back in, each packed with a kilo of meth, and sew the tissue and skin shut over them. This increased the payload of each transported body by six kilos – they could usually jam two into each thigh, and a kilo into each calf.

They couldn't pack the legs on every case, but when

Mrs. Rosenblum had had surgery the surgeons had cut into the thighs to harvest veins for her bypass; it was a piece of cake for Reggie to enlarge the incisions, tear out the flabby muscle and soft tissue and refill her before closing her up.

Reggie surveyed the hollowed-out body. With a bit of effort, he'd cram fifteen keys of methamphetamine into the corpse; by the time she hit Chicago, the old bitch would have a street value of five hundred thousand dollars.

67

Jenner needed to get out of Port Fontaine. Head up beyond Fort Myers, maybe, find an empty beach. Feed the gulls, drink cold beer and eat fried fish. Or go east, into the Glades, take that weird turn out by the Miccosukee reservation, follow the arrow on the battered hand-painted sign that said *Mudding, Fishing, Gator Burgers*.

But the sign was ancient – who knew if the place still even existed? Jenner imagined it as a tumbledown shack in the woods, the trees choked with Spanish moss, the windows long gone, the roof sagging, the parking lot now a jungle, everything buried in the irresistible creep of grasses and bushes and saplings.

He could stop by the shelter, see if Maggie was there. But why would he do that? She hadn't called, hadn't answered his messages. Her feelings were pretty obvious – why couldn't he just acknowledge it, and let her go? Anyway, it would mean driving past the chapel, and he didn't have that in him.

Out on I-55, he rolled the windows down and didn't care when the air blasted in and shuffled the junk on the back seat. And though the wind killed the sound and warmed the car and sent paper skidding into the front compartment, it wasn't enough to block the image of Marty, bloated and blotched green like a toad, lying glistening on the shroud beside the drowned car, arms uplifted and face so badly swollen that even his close friend couldn't recognize him.

Twenty minutes north of town, Jenner's cell phone rang. The office, needing a signature on an out-of-state transport approval for Mrs. Rosenblum. She'd already been removed by the funeral home – if Jenner could stop by and sign the form, Mr. Jones, the funeral director, would pick it up later.

Jenner asked where the funeral parlor was, then said, "If you fax it to Mr. Jones, I'll head back into town and sign it there, save him some trouble."

68

At lunchtime, her mother still wasn't back from the memorial service, so Lucy took the sandwich up to her room. Rosa was supposed to watch her eat it, but she'd been fighting with her boyfriend recently and spending a lot of time crying on the phone to her sister in Ocala; Lucy's eating had been good lately, so after she'd taken a couple of bites Rosa let her finish it in her room.

Lucy hooked her iPod into the speaker system and put

on the Jonas Brothers, turning it up loud enough so that Rosa wouldn't hear her. Then she went into her bathroom, tore up her sandwich and tossed the pieces into the toilet. Then she made herself bring up the half sandwich she'd eaten, and flushed the toilet.

It felt good. It hurt, and sometimes when she was sick she'd wipe her mouth and see a little blood, but it felt good to feel the ache of her empty stomach grinding away on nothing.

In her closet she found her old Blue's Clues sleeping bag and slipped the scale out of it.

She placed it carefully on the wooden floor so that it was even, and climbed on. She watched the red needle bounce and sway, then dip below one hundred and ten. *Yes!*

She put the scale away, opened her Mac Book and read her affirmations in her husky whisper:

> *every time you say no thanks to food you say yes please to thin*
> *hunger hurts but starving works*
> *i want to be thin more than anything, even food*
> *this is forever*
> *i will do whatever it takes*

69

At the funeral home, a steady stream of mourners filed in and out of the viewing of James Prescott, a much-admired school principle. The parking lot was overflowing so

Jenner parked behind the Dairy Queen next door. He slipped through a gap in the ragged hedge that separated the two establishments, and found himself across from the access bay in back.

Rather than barging into the viewing, he took the short cut; there'd be someone in the embalming room or preparation area who'd help him. As he made his way past two white Cadillac funeral coaches and a waiting white Lincoln hearse he wished he'd brought his new jacket.

It was quiet in the lower level. Reggie Jones ran a tight ship – a prosperous one, too, apparently. The two hearses in the garage were also late-model Cadillacs, one white, one black. The walls were a pristine white and the air had only the faintest whiff of formaldehyde.

Jenner rapped on the door frame. "Hello?"
Silence.

He walked inside, and around the corner found a large embalming room. The body of an older black man was on one of the two tables, formalin pumping into the body via a cannula in the right side of the neck, waste fluid draining from the left thigh. The embalmer, a young black woman, was massaging the fluid into the left arm, bending it at the elbow, straightening it again, and squeezing the fluid down towards the hand.

Jenner said, "Hi there."

Holding the arm lifted in front of her, the young woman looked over to him, surprised. "I'm sorry, sir, but I'm afraid no one's allowed down here."

Jenner said, "I'm the medical examiner – I'm here to sign an out-of-state transport permit letter for Mrs. Rosenblum."

"Oh, sorry, doctor – I thought you'd wandered down

255

from the viewing." She smiled, and placed the arm back down by the side of the body. "I don't know anything about the permit, but Mrs. Rosenblum's in the prep room across the hall. I just finished making up her face; Mr. Jones embalmed her earlier."

She lead Jenner to the second prep room but the door was locked. "Huh. This should be open." She shrugged. "Anyway, that's her."

Jenner peered through the viewing window. Mrs. Rosenblum lay on the nearer table, her limbs wrapped in thick plastic bags, her trunk covered in translucent plastic sheeting.

There was something odd about her; Jenner was trying to figure out just what when Reggie Jones appeared. He wore black dress slacks and a white shirt and black tie. He came towards Jenner hastily, rolling his shirt sleeves down; Jenner caught a glimpse of his arms, which had scattered amateur-looking tattoos. Jailhouse ink.

"Doctor! We were expecting you upstairs. Thanks for stopping by." He shook Jenner's hand warmly and tugged him towards the hallway. "I have the permit letter just around the corner, in the office."

The hallway was wide and well-lit, and the basement office bordered on sumptuous, with two large computers and a big plasma TV mounted on the wall. There was a grid of six black-and-white monitors, CCTV cameras showing views of the funeral home entrances and the embalming and prep areas.

Jenner gestured at the security array. "Problems with body snatchers, Reggie?"

Jones grinned and said, "Ever hear of 'wet', doc? Kids down here steal formaldehyde and sprinkle it on their pot.

We even have some kids trying to huff the stuff, if you can believe it."

Jenner made a face. "God, I can't imagine that."

Reggie said, "So what do you think of my place? How do you like my hearses? Brand new!"

"Impressive. I'm giving more thought to Jenner & Rudge." He glanced over the letter, than scrawled his signature. "There. Where's she heading – Chicago, was it?"

"Yes. She'll go out tonight – the viewing's this afternoon, then she'll be on her way."

"And you transport her all the way there?"

"Yes. She'll be received by a funeral home up there; they'll take care of the interment."

Jenner said, "I'm surprised they let you embalm her – was that because of the long journey?"

Jones shook his head. "She's not embalmed, doc, just wrapped. By the time she reaches Illinois she's going to have lost her looks a bit. Still, she'll be fine for her friends and family down in Port Fontaine this afternoon, and that's what matters."

"You do a lot of transporting?"

"Quite a bit, actually. There are so many folks from the Northeast and the Midwest who winter down here with us, not to mention all the retirees. Lots of them have plots up there – last year we shipped over two hundred. We work very closely with the JBFS."

"The JBFS?"

"The Jewish Benevolent Funeral Service. It's an organization that helps out getting the bodies of Jews back up north. And not just Jews nowadays."

"I see." Jenner felt ill at ease but couldn't say why.

"Okay, Reggie. Good seeing you – if you see Rudge, say hi."

Reggie gestured to the stairs, but Jenner said, "I'll just cut through the parking lot here."

With Reggie following, he walked back down the hall. He stopped by the door of the second embalming room and stopped to peer in again at Mrs. Rosenblum.

"What is it, doc?"

"I don't know. She looks . . . different."

"Different light, maybe," Jones mused. "And Tonya's done her make-up – could be that's it."

What was it that was different? Reggie was probably right, Jenner thought – the cosmeticians had all kinds of tricks, like using brown eye shadow to add extra depth to the eyes when they were viewed in the casket from above. It was probably something like that.

He turned. Reggie was looking at him – no, not looking at him, watching him. Smiling.

Jenner tried to shake off the nagging feeling. "See you, Reggie."

"Doc."

Jenner walked outside, still battling the vague suspicion that something wasn't quite right. The sweltering humidity had turned into a steady drizzle. He ran through the lot, and, as he was about to step through the hedge into the Dairy Queen premises, glanced back at the lower-level entrance. He was surprised to see Reggie standing under the overhang, watching him, unsmiling now, and talking on his cell phone.

70

The Medical Examiner's Office was still deserted. Bucky and Calvin were in the break room, sharing a two-liter bottle of Pibb and a party-size bag of Cheetos. They nodded at Jenner.

"Memorial over, doc?"

Jenner shook his head. "Don't know – something came up, so I couldn't go."

He left before Bucky could ask any questions.

In his office Jenner opened the VeriPic photo-storage software and sifted through the month's cases until he found the external shots of Mrs. Rosenblum.

He pulled all four photos up onto the screen and pored over them, cursing that they hadn't photographed her back too.

They were unremarkable. An elderly woman with a stapled incision over her breast bone, a couple of sutured incisions on her trunk where drains had been placed, pacing wires passing into her solar plexus to fix her heartbeat. There were small incisions in her thighs where they'd harvested leg veins.

And that was it.

So what had he seen?

Jesus, *had* he seen anything? They'd taken her to the funeral home, worked on her, touched her up to get her ready for viewing that afternoon. Jones was probably right – just a trick of the eye, a little blush, a little eye shadow.

But the cosmetician had said the body had been embalmed, and Jones said it hadn't. And if he hadn't embalmed her, why was the body wrapped? Usually they wrapped the body to keep fluid from leaking – but why would Mrs. Rosemblum's corpse leak? Her sternotomy incision was tightly sutured, as were the chest-tube and drain sites. A small amount of gauze packing would've kept her dry.

And then it came to him: the abdominal incision.

At the funeral home, blurred by layers of plastic, Jenner had seen an abdominal incision, a dark line under the plastic, stretching down to the pubis. And there'd been none when he'd examined her.

As Jenner thought about it, he realized she'd seemed larger now, too, her belly almost bloated. Which made no sense at all – why would she swell? She wasn't decomposing.

He checked the photos again: the chest incision stopped just below the breastbone, and her belly was intact.

Maybe the embalmer had started to work on her before Jones had stopped him. Embalming an observant Jew would mean a major lawsuit, a big enough risk for Jones to lie about.

But embalmers didn't open the belly. Jenner had once watched a funeral director use a trochar, a tool like a thick knitting needle, to treat the abdomen: she had pushed the trochar through the skin into the belly, and then violently jammed it around inside in all directions to puncture the organs. Then she'd pulled out the trochar and instilled embalming fluid into the cavity, finally sealing the trochar hole with a button-like plug and some stitching.

No, the embalmer wouldn't have done an abdominal incision.

What *had* they done?

71

When the staff began to filter back into the office in the early afternoon, Jenner slipped out through the morgue and crossed into the municipal building. He found Rudge working the phone in Major Crimes; the detective held up a hand and gestured for him to sit.

Rudge thanked the caller and hung up. "Hey, Jenner. Missed you at the memorial."

He nodded at the phone. "That was Azure Oceanic. Interesting development: I spoke with Sheree Roburn after the service, she told me she'd booked her parents' cruise tickets personally. Azure just confirmed it. Bartley screwed up first time around."

When Jenner didn't react, he said, "What brings you over here? A little early for dinner . . ."

Jenner shook his head. He hesitated, then said, "Something weird."

Rudge leaned back. "And that would be . . ."

"Your cousin . . ."

"Reggie?"

"Yes – he ever had any problems?"

Rudge stood. "C'mon, let's get some air."

They walked downstairs and out into the breezeway, and joined the administrative staff members smoking in the shade.

Rudge turned to Jenner. "So, what's this about?"

"Probably nothing. I noticed something strange that's really picking at me."

"What?"

"Your cousin is transporting a Jewish body up to Chicago. Family objected to autopsy; they'd have objected to embalming too, and Reggie said she hadn't been embalmed. But the cosmetician said she had, and when I looked at her body, I'm pretty sure she'd been opened up and sewn shut. Also, she was . . . bigger."

"Bigger?"

"Yeah. She looked kind of . . . stuffed."

"What are you saying?"

"I don't know." Jenner sighed. "I'm just spinning my wheels."

Rudge nodded. "Well, look, Reggie's had some problems in the past, but he's been doing real good down here. He's put his past behind him, built up a great business, doing things right this time. I'm sure this is nothing – later, we can go by the place, get you another look at her, ease your mind, okay?"

"I'm sure there's a reasonable explanation." Jenner paused. "So what was Reggie in for?"

Rudge shot him a look. "How did you know?"

"He had his shirt sleeves rolled up and I saw his ink."

Rudge shook his head, sighing. "Doc, it was some stupid shit – he got mixed up with some people slinging meth in De Kalb County, Georgia. Did a five-year bit at Phillips State. But he was just a kid then. He's really got his act together – you've seen the funeral parlor."

"I'm sure it's nothing. But can you give him a call, ask him if we can stop by later?"

"No problem. I'll set it up."

72

Smith was pissy. It was a cash month – every fourth month they made a payment in cash, instead of routing the money into laundered external investments or offshore accounts. For the deliveries he had to babysit the money with Brodie, which meant hours of painful silence waiting in the truck with a man who scared him like no one else did.

He leaned against the pickup, smoking American Spirits and watching the cookers come out of Bunkhouse A. Their long shift finally over, they stretched and blinked like moles in an afternoon sun newly bright after midday showers. There were smiles and laughter as they headed towards Bunkhouse B for a shower and some sleep.

At a desk in Bunkhouse A, Brodie and Bentas were monitoring the money count, watching a worker run bills through a pair of whirring mechanical counters, packing them into rubber-band-bound two-hundred-bill wads with a practiced flip of the wrist. The standing order was simple: one million dollars, used, unmarked, in two duffle bags, split five hundred thousand in fifties in the larger, five hundred thousand in hundreds in the smaller. Brodie would then hand count the packets into the bags, and the bags would be reweighed. Every weight was noted and cross-checked.

The door opened, and Brodie emerged with the bags. Both were navy-blue canvas, stenciled *Tina Mayweather* in block capitals, standard laundry bags; together, the two weighed less than fifty pounds.

Smith tossed away his cigarette and climbed in the driver's side, then leaned over to help Brodie slide the duffle bags into the middle of the seat. Brodie climbed in after them and shut the door.

Brodie put on his sunglasses and spat outside the window, then rolled it up and turned to Smith. "What are you waiting for?"

As Smith turned the car, Bentas came out of the bunkhouse and waved, grinning. He had a stick of dynamite in his right hand and was clutching a fistful of roofing nails in the left. Smith turned to Brodie and said, "What's that about?"

Brodie said, "Turn up the AC." He exhaled slowly, tipped his head back onto the headrest and said, "That pathologist is getting too nosy."

Smith nodded: so that was how it was going to be.

He cranked up the air conditioning and kept his eyes on the road. Maybe Brodie would sleep.

73

Jenner decided to try Maggie Craine one last time. The phone rang five times; when she didn't answer, it defaulted to voicemail.

That was it, then. Enough – she was done with him. That night at the Palmetto Court was it, the beginning and the end of their relationship. She'd warned him; he hated that he still wanted more.

Rudge had arranged for Jenner and him to visit the funeral home at half past seven; they met for dinner at Red Lobster.

The meal passed in almost complete silence. Rudge

was quiet and guarded, as if bracing for the fallout from a predictable disaster. Jenner felt guilty for his suspicions. When the check arrived, he moved to treat, but Rudge pinned it to the table and insisted on paying his share.

They drove to the funeral home in the Taurus, parking under shade trees hoary with Spanish moss; except for a gray Acura, the lot was empty.

Rudge rang the bell and they waited on the porch in silence. The scrub oak lining the street formed a gloomy canopy in the gathering dusk; the only sound was the flutter of insect wings in the buzzing overhead light.

Rudge rang again, then walked the length of the porch, peering in the side windows; all the ground-floor rooms were lit, but there was no activity inside.

The detective nodded towards the parking lot. "We can go in the entrance to the embalming area."

The loading-bay doors were shut, but the side door was unlocked. Inside, light from the prep-area hallway spilled into the bay; in the garage, the hearses were lined up neatly in place.

They found Reggie in the office. A clock radio on a shelf was shrilling Motown hits; he didn't seem to notice Jenner and Rudge as they came in.

Rudge said, "Hey, Reggie. We're here."

Reggie stood up hurriedly, "Dave, doctor, sorry! I didn't hear you – time got away from me."

He shook hands with Rudge, then slipped on his jacket. "Look, I'm sorry, but we got a problem . . ."

Rudge was suddenly grim. "What problem, Reggie?"

His cousin shifted uneasily, looking at the floor.

"There was a mix-up, and . . ."

"And what? Now no body?"

"I'm sorry. They were rushing to get her up to Chicago; her son was going to ride with her body and wanted to get moving. There was nothing I could've done without offending them." Reggie looked at Jenner and added, "And you know how people are when they're mourning, doc."

Rudge was shaking his head. "You should've at least called, Reggie."

"Dave, what was I going to do? Make the family sit and wait, knowing their mom was rotting in the van? I made a judgment call, and I made it on behalf of the family."

Reggie looked back at Jenner. "Doctor, what's this all about? I don't understand."

Jenner said, "I don't even know if it's about anything." He turned to Rudge. "Give me a ride back to the morgue?"

Rudge said, "Okay. But, seriously, Reggie . . . you fucked up."

Jones said, "C'mon, Dave! There's only so much I can do."

Jenner said, "Actually, mind if I have a look in the embalming room?"

"No problem, doc. Go ahead. We got nothing to hide."

Rudge and Reggie watched from the doorway as Jenner looked at the table, the cabinets and the shelves. The lights were harsh in the tiled room, and Jenner could smell the same subtle sour-sharp chemical aroma of formaldehyde, and the waxy smell of make-up. But there was nothing to find, and Jenner found nothing.

He wasn't even sure what he was looking for.

But now he had an idea.

74

After the memorial service, the news cameras around the medical examiner's office had disappeared. Some of the crews were out shooting B roll on the Promenade or in the Glades, but now that the cases had stabilized, and there were few fresh leads with live, interviewable witnesses, most of them had been called back to the mothership.

But not all.

Smiling, Amanda Tucker watched Jenner climb out of the Taurus. It was her last night in Port Fontaine, and she wanted it to count. She tossed the remains of her frappucino into the bin and called to her producer. They wouldn't catch Jenner before he made it into his building, but perhaps when he left . . .

As she watched him make his way across the lot, alone in the dark, something much better occurred to her: apparently, Jenner was staying in a sleazy motel in the Reaches, the run-down part of Port Fontaine. Footage of Jenner in his new habitat might be good TV, she thought – Amanda confronts the ethically contaminated doctor in his moldering pile of a hotel. It'd been a while since she'd done any real attack journalism out in the field, and that sort of thing always played well.

"Billy, let's get some dinner now, then we'll head over to the doctor's motel. You got the address?"

"Yep, I got it. Great idea, Amanda!"

She smiled. Yes. Yes, it was.

75

The office was deserted; the staff had gone home early after coming back from the chapel, and the investigators took calls from home.

Someone had left a program from the memorial on Jenner's desk. It was tasteful, printed on heavy cream stock, edged in black, a sober typeface for a somber event. Jenner's name was listed among those giving eulogies.

Down in the mortuary, the lights were now switched to the Energy Saver circuit; every quarter of an hour, they'd turn off, and Jenner then had to walk to the other end of the autopsy suite to punch the button for another fifteen minutes of light.

In the office, he pulled the body logbook. He unfolded his copy of the timetable that Rudge had developed for Roburn's whereabouts on his last day, and smoothed it flat on the desktop.

The day before he was due to leave for his cruise, Roburn had said goodbye to Jenner in the morning, booting him out of the office, telling him to relax and enjoy the town until eight p.m., when he'd officially become Acting County Medical Examiner. Jenner had wished Roburn a good trip, and spent the day at the beach.

Roburn did an autopsy and an external exam in the morning. He ate lunch with Flanagan and Marie Carter in the break room. He'd used his cell phone a couple of times during the day, both calls to his wife, one shortly before he left the office in the late afternoon. His last call had been to Jenner a little before 6:30 p.m., but hadn't connected.

Jenner opened the log and ran his finger down the date column. Roburn's last cases were unremarkable – a man in his fifties who'd had a heart attack while jogging, and an elderly woman with a history of metastatic lung cancer. The man had been handled by a funeral home in Port Fontaine, the woman by a Fort Myers funeral director.

He checked the day before; that day, Jenner himself had autopsied two motor vehicle accident victims, and had done one external exam.

And then he found what he'd been looking for: his external case had been removed by Jones Brothers, Reggie's funeral home. The deceased had a Jewish surname, Gottlieb, and the entry on the register indicated that the removal of the remains had been authorized to "Jones & Carmen/JBFS" – the Jewish Benevolent Funeral Service. An uptown Manhattan address was listed for Mr. Gottlieb's home.

Jenner paged back in the log a month, looking for similar entries; he found sixteen cases where bodies had been released to Jones & Carmen. Some were external exam only, but most had been autopsied, and a dozen had been co-signed to the JBFS despite having gentile-sounding names. All those cases in which the JBFS had been involved had home addresses in northeastern states.

Jenner sat back. He had it now.

Time to tell Rudge.

He walked into the autopsy room to stretch, then sat in the dictation room. He called the detective and asked if he'd heard from Toxicology about the packet from Marty's car.

Rudge said, "Jenner? It's nine p.m. Let it rest a night, eh?"

"I was just wondering if you'd heard."

There was the sound of rummaging for a couple of seconds, then Rudge said, "Actually, yeah. Message on my desk. Let's see . . ."

There was a low whistle.

Jenner said, "Let me guess: methamphetamine."

"Yep. About ninety-five percent pure."

"Impressive . . ."

"That's dealer purity." Rudge paused, then said, "Jenner, I think we're both thinking the same thing . . . I mean, what regular citizen gets tortured, then killed? What regular guy has a stash of uncut methamphetamine? I'm sorry, but Marty *has* to have been dirty. He was up to his neck in this."

No. Jenner walked into the dictating room and sat, leaning back on his chair. "I don't know."

But Rudge was right – all the fingers pointed toward Marty. And, after all, it had been a decade since they'd last worked together. People change.

Just not Marty Roburn.

Barely two weeks ago, Jenner had sat with Marty on the lanai, talking late into the night about Marty's plans for retirement – staying in Port Fontaine in the same modest house, and going fishing with Bobbie every day. Nothing extravagant, nothing fancy.

Jenner couldn't believe Marty was dirty. Wouldn't believe it.

Finally, he said, "There has to be something else."

"Well, you find it, you show me. Because I'm really going to need to see it for myself."

"I think I have an idea what this is all about."

"Oh?"

270

There was a faint sound in the autopsy room; Jenner had thought he was alone.

Jenner said, "I have to call you back," and hung up. He stared into the autopsy room through the large glass window; he could see nothing.

Everything suddenly went black – the timed circuit had kicked in. Jenner cursed and got to his feet. He could barely see five feet; he stood in the faint moonlight that trickled through the clerestory windows, waiting for his eyes to adapt.

There was a clanging crash from the shadows at the far end of the long room, the unmistakable sound of the metal pan from an autopsy scale being knocked to the floor.

Jenner said, "Hello?"

No answer.

"Hello?"

He took another step into the dark, straining to see.

Against the pale far wall, he caught the barely perceptible shifting of shadow on shadow, the form of a man, moving silently toward him across the tiled floor.

"Who's there?"

The figure stopped. Or was it a trick of the dark? Jenner wasn't certain that anyone was even there.

He wasn't taking any chances. He moved sideways, edging towards the organ cutting board by the sink, facing the gloom. The small skylight over the sink let in faint gray light. On the cutting board, he could make out the outlines of his tools, laid out ready for work.

The shadow stayed still, watching him.

Jenner reached over to the cutting board, felt across it.

His hand nudged the handle of his autopsy knife, a Wusthof slicer with a ten-inch blade. He held it up.

He went forward again, into blackness so intense that it felt as if not just light, but also sound had been extinguished.

Another step, and now he was sure there was someone there, crouched in a half-squat not fifteen feet from him.

Jenner took one more step, and the shadow sprang up and ran for the exit. Jenner hesitated for a couple of seconds, then ran after the shape, knife clutched in his right hand. He heard the autopsy room door swing open, then the sound of a man sprinting down the corridor.

He pounded the light switch at the doorway, and the autopsy room lit up brilliantly, dazzling white and stainless.

He pushed out into the hall and hit the corridor switch; the hallway lights flared on in time for him to see a man run around the corner at the far end. It was barely a glimpse, but he'd seen enough to recognize the light brown of a standard Douglas County uniform.

Jenner stood there in the hallway, wondering if he should confront Anders about his spy right away.

He jumped at the buzzing on his thigh.

He flipped open his cell, and read *DavidSpenceMD* – the senior coroner's pathologist in New Orleans. Spence was a good forensic pathologist working in a tough system. Whenever they were at a forensic meeting together, they'd make the time to have dinner, or at least a drink.

"David?"

"Hey, Jenner. You OK? You sound out of breath."

Jenner leaned against the wall. "Yeah, I'm fine. The ringer took me by surprise."

His heart still pounding, he looked at the knife in his hand, then stared down the corridor to the door to the municipal building through which the cop had disappeared.

Spence said, "I was calling to see how you were holding up, son. I'm real sorry about Marty and Bobbie – he was one of the good guys. I know you were close."

"Thanks, David. It's been rough here. The case is barely crawling forward, and I can't take a step without someone shoving a TV camera in my face."

Spence chuckled. "It was a bit like that here after Katrina . . ." He paused. "How was the memorial? I bet there were a lot of folks there."

Jenner hesitated, then said, "Yes, a lot of people came out for that."

He made his way back to the dictation room to sit. There was something going on – Spence wouldn't call just to console him.

Spence said, "Well, there's something else." He paused. "You probably figured that."

"What's up, David?"

"You know I'm on the Board of the National Association of Medical Examiners, right? I tell you, that thing is a damn spear in my side . . . Well, this week the jungle drums have been pounding."

"Oh?" It didn't surprise him – of course they'd be talking about him again; he'd been too busy to think about professional politics.

"There's eleven of us – I think you know most of us. Jerry Carson from Nevada, Blake from Rhode Island. A bunch of guys. Barbie Koppel from Houston."

"Yep. Some good people there."

"Sure. Some real old-timers, too."

Jenner grinned. "I wasn't going to say anything."

"Probably a good plan, Jenner – there's trouble afoot."

"I figured." He leaned back in the chair. "What have I done now?"

"It's the same old stuff. Steve Whittaker has a few pals on the Board. He's got them convinced that what you did this winter was cowboy stuff, bordering on criminally negligent. Breaking and entering at the morgue, getting a cop killed, another cop on the critical list. It's no secret he wants you out of NAME."

"No news there."

"You seen that *American Crime* stuff?"

Jenner felt his skin start to crawl.

"Yes."

"Okay, well, you know, then. That woman has some kind of major hard-on for you, boy. It's not going away. You see that latest thing? Not your finest hour."

"Which latest thing?"

"You calling her a bitch."

So that was out, then.

"Haven't seen that one yet. It's true, though."

"Of course it's true – we all saw it. Now there's a whole e-mail clusterfuck going on. Next week we're going to vote on whether or not to revoke your membership."

"Huh."

"It's not looking good. Whittaker's crew want to take you down, and they may have the votes. On your side, you got me, your little buddy in San Diego – the blonde with the . . . uh, curves?"

"Candy Webster."

274

"Yeah. Me, her, a couple others. But the numbers don't look good."

Jenner was silent.

"Your biggest hope is people abstaining because they don't have the facts yet, so now would be a good time for you to stay out of trouble, you hear? Keep your nose clean, and for God's sake steer clear of Amanda Tucker."

76

"Hold still just a sec, Amanda. I'm going to tape the mike inside the shirt; when he's talking, don't move – the fabric noise will drown him out."

She stood in front of the mirror, hands on hips, while Gene, her sound man, busied himself with her shirt. Sitting on her bed, George, the segment producer, was still on the phone, arguing with Travel about their flight home the next morning.

Gene leaned back. "Yep, you can't see it. Turn to your left?"

She turned, and the two of them looked at her ass in the mirror.

"I think it looks bulky. I shouldn't wear a pencil skirt."

He shook his head. "Nuh-uh! It's flat! That's one flat, beautiful ass you've got there, Amanda. Besides, I don't believe you even *own* anything that isn't a pencil skirt."

Watching her reflection, Amanda bent, straightened, then pushed her butt out. Then she jiggled from side to side a little.

The transmitter was the size of a pack of cigarettes:

even if Gene couldn't see the transmitter, she could.

Still, her ass *was* looking pretty good. And her jacket would cover the bulge.

"Okay. Thanks, Gene."

"'Okay?' I'm a fucking miracle worker! I just used a micro shotgun mike to convert a wireless assembly into a bug! I'm a fuckin' genius! This is FBI shit!"

"Okay, Special Agent Cooper. Let's test it."

Gene slipped his headphones on, and plugged them into his digital minidisc recorder. He plugged the mike receiver into the recorder, checked the levels, nodded at Amanda, and stepped out into the hall.

There was some scraping of cloth, then Amanda's voice saying, "Hi, Doctor Jenner, you handsome ratings star, you . . ."

Then George's voice, surprisingly clear: "Amanda, I'm on the phone – keep interrupting me and you'll be flying Coach."

Gene walked back into the room. "Perfect. Stick close to him, and keep your chest pointed in his direction; this ought to work perfectly. Turn on the recorder before you go into his room – check that the red light is lit up. There's a couple hours of recording time at this speed. You got new batteries, a new blank minidisc. Just stay within twenty feet of your handbag, or the signal won't reach the recorder. Turn for me?"

Amanda turned. She yelped as he slipped two fingers down the back of her waistband and fiddled with the transmitter box.

"George! Gene is molesting me!"

The producer, still on his cell, rolled his eyes and moved into the bathroom.

Gene stepped back, nodded with satisfaction.

"Yep. I really am just that good . . ."

"Well, thanks, Einstein. We'll share credit when I get my Emmy."

He looked at her. "Hey, has the Current Event network ever won an Emmy?"

There was a brief silence. Then they laughed together.

77

Jenner didn't see Maggie's text at first. It wasn't until he pulled out his iPhone to call Rudge back that he saw the notification.

> PLEASE STOP CALLING. I TOLD YOU NOT TO
> GET ATTACHED. THIS ISN'T WORKING FOR
> ME.

He read it twice, then deleted it.

He'd call Rudge in the morning.

78

Rudge checked the clock on his kitchen wall: he'd made it home with minutes to spare.

He was exhausted. He hung his jacket up on the hook, then slipped off his shoulder holster and laid it on the counter top.

He rolled the foot-long Chicken & Bacon Ranch sandwich out of the Subway wrapper and put it on a plate, then opened the bag of Lay's potato chips and spilled them out alongside it. He took the pickle jar and a can of Budweiser from the fridge, and then set his dinner on the table next to his chair.

Tonight he would limit himself. He'd started the day hungover and it had been rough.

So he'd limit himself: beer only.

But the thought of just beer by itself was a sorry thought indeed; he'd had a rough day, and reckoned he deserved something with a little more heat.

Rudge's sink was filled with plates and glasses; he selected three Dolly Parton shot glasses (a campy gift from Mikey after a Dollywood trip) and lined them up on the side table. He splashed an ounce or so of Jack Daniels into each, then screwed the top tight and shut the bottle back in the cabinet.

He lined up the remotes on the table next to the plates, then kicked off his shoes, unbuttoned and dropped his pants. The velcro fasteners on his ankle holster opened with a satisfying rip; he let the holster and the little silver .32 revolver slide onto the carpet. He checked that the chair was pointing directly at the TV, then pulled the lever, easing the recliner back into position. Finally, he calibrated the rise of the footrest.

Rudge sat down, sighing heavily, and hoisted his sock-clad feet up onto the rest.

He lifted six inches' worth of cold cuts and feathery bread, tore off a giant bite and chewed contentedly. He swallowed, then picked up the first shot and downed it, chasing it with a huge gulp of cold beer. He put the can back down, sighed again, and chomped into his sandwich.

The overloaded sandwich needed support, so he used the remotes one by one with his free hand. The Warner Brothers shield logo in black and white silently filled the screen, then the sound kicked in, a tinny shrill of brass and strings over rolling tom-toms as a map of Africa appeared. Then the star credits – Bogart, Bergman, Henreid – and finally, splashed across the whole continent, *Casablanca* . . .

Rudge wriggled his butt deeper into the recliner, pressed back, and sighed again.

79

Amanda Tucker was waiting for Jenner at his cabin, standing on the porch by herself, shielding her eyes from his headlights as he parked.

He got out of his car and looked around angrily. There was no camera crew, no network van filled with technicians hunched over broadcasting components and screens.

He stood by the car. Amanda gave him a little wave.

"What do you want?"

"Good evening, Doctor Jenner." She smiled warmly.

"What do you want?" he asked again

Amanda shook her head, still smiling. "A truce, doctor. I want to call a truce."

"No, thanks. You want to get off my porch now?"

Jenner stepped up onto the deck. She took a polite step back so that he could open the door.

"It's time we buried the hatchet. We might be able to help each other here."

He jiggled the key in the lock, then turned to her. "I'm not interested in helping you, and I don't believe you give a rat's ass about helping me. What's the matter, ratings slipping? Your viewers bored of watching you gnaw away at me?"

Amanda threw back her head and laughed. "Doctor Jenner! *Gnaw* – how poetic!" She shook her head merrily. "No, no, they still love hearing all about you. But I've been thinking that we've only presented one side of you. I'm sure you have some . . . opinions about how we've covered your story; I just thought you might like a chance to set the record straight."

She was still smiling, but she seemed serious enough.

"I don't believe you."

Amanda shrugged. "Doctor, I can promise you that my audience would be fascinated to hear your side."

"You do know I'm out of the picture now, right? You got me fired."

"That's unfair, and we both know it. The segment producer put together a bio clip of things that you'd done – that was you in all of it, wasn't it?"

"Your coverage has been impossibly skewed. It forced Anders to fire me."

"Well, then, you've nothing to lose, have you? You can come on my show and say that!" Amanda pursed her lips, then looked Jenner in the eye. "Also . . . I think the sheriff finds me very . . . appealing. If you'd talk with us, I'd be willing to speak with him for you."

Shaking his head, Jenner opened the cabin door. The dog wheezed out of the cabin and began to sniff him.

When Jenner pushed him back down, he trotted over to Amanda Tucker and poked her with his nose.

She laughed and pushed him away, then exclaimed, "Oh my gosh! He's filthy!"

Jenner saw dark streaks across the front of Amanda's skirt. The dog sat at her feet like a happy keg of beer, looking up at her, tail thumping the floorboards.

"I'm sorry. He must have got into something."

He peered in through the door and saw dark paw prints smeared across the linoleum; in the center of the floor lay a chewed plastic squeeze bottle of chocolate syrup.

"It's chocolate syrup."

"Doctor, this is an Eileen Fisher linen suit. I need to get the fabric damp before it stains."

Jenner nodded, and held the door open for her. He set the catch on the screen door so it stayed open, turned to the dog and said, "You! Out!"

Placidly, the dog trooped back out of the cabin, tail still bobbing.

Amanda was standing by the shallow sink, splashing water on her dress.

Sweet Jesus, Jenner thought. Amanda Tucker, here in my living room . . .

80

Onscreen, Dooley Wilson was at the piano in Rick's bar, singing "Knock on Wood". Rudge poured out three more shots and popped the tab on a fresh Bud.

The scene made him uncomfortable – the happy Negro

and his orchestra entertaining the well-dressed European sophisticates with jazz, all smiles and natural rhythms. Was it straight-up racist, simple and plain, or a fair representation of life back then? Both, maybe. Black jazz musicians probably played to similar crowds in Europe today – one of Mikey's old boyfriends had moved to Paris, where he played in a Josephine Baker show that had been running for more than two years.

Basically, Rudge figured, Europeans liked black music.

He slammed down the shot and chased it with the Bud.

Humphrey Bogart was about to slip the letters of transit into Dooley's piano when the screen suddenly froze. The buffer held the frame for about three seconds, and then the screen went black: green neon letters at the top read *Searching for signal.*

Fuck!

Rudge knew what it was – when they'd set up his system, the installer had spliced cables together to connect the rooftop satellite dish to the TV; sometimes a brisk breeze would separate the splice near the front door.

It'd take him a second to fix it. He cursed. It was late enough and dark enough – and he was drunk enough – not to put on pants. He heaved himself out of the chair and went to the door. He flicked the porch-light switch several times; nothing happened.

Weird. That bulb was pretty new. An electrical fault? But the lights were still on in his living room, and his house was small enough that there weren't many separate electrical zones.

Rudge stepped out onto the porch and looked up, curious. The white wire from the rooftop cable feed dangled freely; the cable tacked along the porch ceiling had been torn out and now lay across the floorboards.

God, he was stupid. For a second, he wondered if he would've made the same mistake had he been sober.

81

Amanda stood at the sink, holding up the hem of her soiled skirt.

"Do you have any club soda?"

Jenner shook his head. "Sorry."

"Any spot remover?"

"I have some detergent."

He poured some Tide into a cup, and added water.

As they fussed with the skirt, the dog waddled back in through the door and heaved himself up onto the couch. He rested his paws up on the back of the sofa to watch what was going on on the other side of the counter; he was tracking chocolate everywhere again.

Jenner said, "I'm going to shut the dog out. I'll be right back."

There was a crash of breaking glass, and something compact and heavy skidded across the floor. Amanda gasped.

It was a length of metal pipe about eight inches long. The dog bumped down from the couch and began to amble toward it, sniffing.

Christ.

Jenner threw open the refrigerator, yanked Amanda against him and pivoted in behind the door. She was about to speak when the explosion roared into them, the pain instant and intense, the door slamming into him, smashing him on top of her.

When he opened his eyes, there was no sound. The curtains were on fire, the horrible orange drapes consumed by listless flames. His arms were stinging, a twisting, pinching burn, like thousands of rubber bands wrenching and pulling against the hair of his arms. There was no sound, but there was smoke.

He wasn't on top of Amanda. He turned; she was sitting up against a floor cabinet, shouting at him silently. He turned and looked at the fridge; the battered door canted off its top hinge, orange juice and milk drizzling to the floor from punctured cartons. The door swung toward him, bristling with nails, the white enameled surface pocked by bolts and nuts.

Jenner looked at Amanda again. She was crying now. Her legs were bloody, but he couldn't see any injury.

The pinching sting of his singed arms. He pushed himself up against the interior of the fridge, half-slipping on the juice-slick floor, knocking a head of lettuce off the shelf into his lap. He sat up and looked at himself. He was okay, he thought. His legs were working, arms working.

He looked down at his legs. He was bleeding into the juice from somewhere, a faint rim of red diffusing into the orange. He was hit. He saw nails sticking out of his left calf, but his thighs and trunk were mostly okay. His back hurt; there had to be some shrapnel wounds, but the fridge door had taken the brunt of the bomb.

It will hurt more if I wait until the adrenalin fades, Jenner thought. He stretched down and plucked the nails out.

Something tugged at his wrist. Amanda was standing

over him, mouthing, pulling on his arm. He nodded, struggled to his feet.

The bomb had destroyed half of the cabin. Small hunks of shrapnel had blasted through the outside wall, and the cheap chipboard of the kitchen counter had been blown apart, scattering pots and pans across the living room.

The dog.

Jenner could only see his front half; he wasn't moving, buried under the kitchen table and couch pieces. The table, its thin metal legs torn off, had tipped over on top of him, hiding his hindquarters. His muzzle was covered in blood, the fur of his chest matted.

Amanda was leading Jenner toward the door but he pulled away and went to the dog. She watched him drop to his knees, slide aside the linoleum table top and its bent aluminum frame, and lift the debris off the animal.

The dog's eye turned toward him; it tried to raise its head as its tail twitched.

Jenner stroked the animal's back, feeling for nails. Deep in the fur of the chest, he could feel small punctures, the size of buckshot. Shrapnel injuries through the fur. His hands came away bloody.

People were coming in through the doorway now; he recognized the two stocky college guys who'd been tossing a Frisbee around by the pool the day before. They held their jerseys up to cover their noses and mouths, but most of the smoke was venting through the blown-out windows or the holes in the wall.

The taller one took Amanda out, the other grabbed at Jenner's arm.

Jenner shook him off.

Now sound was starting to come back; Jenner could

hear a quiet roar, dulled and flat, as if he were standing knee-deep in it. The jock grabbed his arm again. Jenner pushed him away angrily.

He got up onto his knees and gently slipped his arms under the dog's body. He struggled to stand; then the guy saw what he was doing and helped him from behind as he got to his feet.

Jenner had the dog. He moved toward the door, behind the jock.

The burning drapes had set the breakfast-nook paneling on fire, and the pale wood finish now burned sluggishly, darkening and peeling as if some effect was slowly being applied from a spray can.

Walking was hard – Jenner's injured leg threatened to buckle with each step.

The jock went out the front door, and a fireman with an ax came in, followed by another fireman.

The second one went to help Jenner, but Jenner shrugged him off and kept going. The fireman tried to take the dog, but Jenner held tight, shaking his head fast until the fireman backed off. The fireman put a hand on Jenner's shoulder and pressed him firmly from behind, steering him to the door.

The parking lot was gridlocked, residents scrambling to move their cars away from Jenner's burning cabin. An ambulance was in front of the cabin, another at the lot entrance, and two large fire engines were jockeying for position, their lights illuminating the Palmetto Court residents like escaped convicts in a prison spotlight as they milled around in sweatpants and bathrobes.

Amanda Tucker was slumped on the step at the back of the ambulance, breathing oxygen while the paramedic felt her pulse; Jenner could see the condensation in her plastic mask. She looked at Jenner coolly. She was completely calm; she could have been sitting by a fountain in the atrium of a mall, sipping an Orange Julius.

The dog twitched in Jenner's arms. He had to get him into the car.

One of the firemen – apparently the chief, certainly high up – stood in front of him, talking and gesturing at him; Jenner couldn't hear what he was saying.

He looked over to Amanda. Her jacket was gone, her shirt torn open, her skirt bloodied. She had yanked the mask off and was speaking into a cell phone. She turned to the paramedic, and Jenner saw the black transmitter box tucked into the back of her skirt, saw the wires disappearing under her shirt, and he knew.

The chief was still talking at him. Jenner shook his head. Carefully, he formed the words, "I have to get my dog to the vet." He knew it came out too loud.

The chief stopped talking, and just jabbed his finger toward the EMS truck.

Jenner shook his head. Again. "I have to get my dog to the vet."

A fireman came and pulled the chief away, and Jenner sagged against the roof of the Sebring. The door was unlocked, his keys still in his pocket; he'd been home less than five minutes.

He tugged the door open, slid the dog onto the passenger seat, felt the tail slide wetly over his arm.

The engine started immediately; the right front light had shattered in the blast. It hurt Jenner to turn – he definitely had shrapnel embedded in his back. He pumped his horn twice; there was a flurry of cluttered movement behind him as sightseers stepped away. He reversed slowly. A fireman was waving at him to stop. Jenner saw no one behind him, so he kept pulling back.

He made a tight, painful three-point turn in the lot; now there were two firemen waving him down.

Jenner edged forward. A sheriff's-department car was at the entrance now that the fire trucks were in the lot.

He had to tell Rudge. Rudge should know. Rudge would help.

The fire trucks. Jenner turned his head and leaned back; the hoses were spraying into his cabin. Now white steam was rising from the windows. It wasn't a big fire, wasn't a big loss.

He felt the dog's tail flick against his arm. He looked down; in the pale green light of the dashboard the blood glistened dark brown. Jenner reached out to stroke the dog's flank, felt the hurt muscle fibrillating under the short fur; his hand came back sticky and red.

He edged the car forward slowly, but the crowds were too thick.

He turned the wheel, lurched up onto the sidewalk. There were angry shouts as the firewatchers scattered, and then he was going down the shallow grass slope towards the honeymoon cottages. The car shook and bumped, and then he was on the dirt ramp. He turned left and drove up the slope alongside the main parking lot. At the barrier he got out and took down the chain, then drove through into the back lot.

It was quieter here. A few of the motel guests were already making their way back to their rooms; the firemen had things under control, and the spectacle had become less appealing. Or maybe a bombing and a cabin fire just couldn't compete with *American Idol*.

Jenner nosed the car out onto the road. His hearing was getting better; now there was sound, but it felt distant, a dull low roar, like he was on a plane, like he was over the ocean at 34,000 feet. He passed another sheriff's-department car heading toward the motel.

Then the damp road was empty, the world quieter. The light on the streets seemed yellower.

He pulled out his cell, found Maggie's number.

He watched the bright little screen; he couldn't hear the receiver. He worked his jaw and swallowed, trying to pop his ears as if he was on a plane approaching the final descent. The animation showed the call had connected, and he said, "I'm sorry to bother you Maggie, it's Jenner. I . . . I need your help. If you're talking, I can't hear you. There's been a bomb. My dog is hurt – I'm on my way to the shelter. I need your help . . . I don't know if you can hear me . . . I'll be there in about fifteen minutes."

Jenner didn't know if he was speaking to her or her voicemail.

82

Jenner parked the Sebring in front of the Super Target. The mall lot was almost empty; there was no sign of Maggie's Mercedes.

He took a towel from the trunk, wrapped the dog in it, and carried him to the shelter entrance. There were lights on inside. Jenner leaned against the buzzer. The dull sound sharpened abruptly as his higher-pitch hearing returned.

A young black woman in blue surgical scrubs and short dreadlocks opened the door for him. He heard most of what she said – enough to tell that she had a faint African accent – and guessed the rest from the movement of her lips.

"Doctor Jenner? Ms. Craine said you'd be coming. Let's get him into the exam room so I can have a look at him."

She seemed young. Her scrubs had the logo of an animal hospital in Miami, and her name tag read Dr. Gubi Ade; she was a first-year veterinary resident.

She saw him looking at her tag and grinned. "Don't worry, doctor. I'm volunteer labor here, but I'm good at what I do."

Jenner nodded and said nothing. He laid the dog down on the metal table; the animal's eyes were closed, and he wasn't moving.

"What happened?"

"Someone threw a bomb into my cabin, a pipe bomb, packed with nails and screws. He was on the ground when it went off."

Dr. Ade palpated the dog's chest, her bare hands feeling through the bloody fur. She said, "When did this happen?"

"Fifteen minutes ago, maybe twenty."

She was going too slowly. He asked, "Do you have X-ray or fluoroscopy here?"

"X-rays." She turned to him; her expression grave but gentle. "Doctor, he's got multiple defects in his anterior chest; some might be penetrating the chest cavity. His

290

pulse is fast and thready – I think he's lost a good bit of blood. Was there a lot of external bleeding at your cabin?"

"A bit. Not a lot." Jenner wiped his eyes blearily. "But, I don't know – I'm used to humans, and I don't know if that was a lot for a dog. There was a cup of blood, maybe two."

"That's a lot for a dog."

The door opened and a tan man with sandy blond hair came into the examining room. He wore green scrubs, *S. Reed DVM* over the breast pocket. He nodded at them both and said, "What have we got?"

"Older male dog, multiple penetrating injuries of the thorax, possible barotrauma – a pipe bomb filled with nails. He's going into shock."

Reed glanced at Jenner. "You're the owner?"

Jenner nodded, then said, "I'm a physician – I understand the situation."

Reed turned to Dr. Ade and said, "Let's get some oxygen and fluids going."

He looked at Jenner. "He's in critical condition; I'm sure you realize his chances aren't good. We'll shave his chest, get a better look. Take an X-ray, check for projectiles."

On the stainless steel table the dog's legs were twitching, but his eyes remained shut, his tongue lolling from his mouth onto the bare metal surface. Dr. Ade placed a funnel-shaped mask on the dog's snout, and Jenner heard the hiss of oxygen.

Reed put a hand on Jenner's shoulder. "Okay, doctor: think you can carry him into surgery? We'll take it from there."

Jenner nodded and hefted the dog up in his arms. Reed led the way into the operating room, Dr. Ade following closely behind Jenner with the oxygen cannister.

83

No answer from Rudge.

Jenner shut his cell phone and continued pacing the waiting room.

Maybe he should go in? He was medical, they'd let him stay.

But they wouldn't want him there, either. He'd done autopsies with family members present, and it was something he was in no hurry ever to do again.

Family members! He hadn't even given the dog a name. Anyway, he didn't know if he wanted to see that.

He sat. There were stacked copies of *Dog Fancier* and *Show Dog World* on the side table, but nothing . . . normal.

"Jenner."

Maggie Craine stood in the doorway, dressed in black and gray. Her tawny hair was loose, spilling onto her shoulders; it looked contrived to him, like she'd taken the time to style it just so, rather than the result of hurrying from her home to the shelter.

She looked down at Jenner, then took the cigarette from her mouth and exhaled through pursed lips. She said, "You look like shit. Have you seen yourself?"

He shook his head. "You didn't have to come, Maggie."

She stuck the cigarette back between her lips and sat

next to him. She rummaged through her big orange Kate Spade beach bag, then pulled out a packet of wipes. She murmured through the clenched cigarette, "Sit up."

He sat straight, and looked into her face.

Maggie dabbed the damp tissue around his forehead and temples, around his eyes, washing him down like a cat grooming a kitten. There was a faint smell of rubbing alcohol.

"Chin up."

Jenner tilted his head back and she wiped his neck. She leaned back and looked at him critically. "Better."

Not once had she made eye contact.

"Oh, God, your arms! I can't do those – that's too much." She stood. "Come on – go into the bathroom and wash yourself down, Jenner. You can't sit around bloody like that."

He stood, a little dazed. "I'll be back in a minute."

"Okay. I should finish this outside anyway." He was exhausted. He watched her sweep out of the waiting room, then walked slowly to the bathroom. His adrenalin was settling and now he felt every step – and every step hurt. He didn't understand her.

In the tiled quiet of the bathroom Jenner looked himself over. He looked like that cartoon where the black cat gets dipped in flour; his hair was black with soot, but Maggie had left his face glowing white.

His arms weren't funny, though, torn up and smeared red and brown; no wonder she'd complained.

Jenner washed his arms gingerly. His shirt was soaked in blood; it stuck to him, clung to his face and neck as he fought through the pain to lift it over his head. As the garment peeled off his back, it snagged and caught; he kept pulling at it, then winced as something popped out of the skin and the cloth tore free. He heard dry gravel sounds as shrapnel fragments hit the floor.

And then the shirt was off. Jenner turned slowly; the left side of his back was leopard-spotted with shrapnel punctures and scratches, many now freshly bleeding, some with torn tags of metal still embedded. Staring at his back in the mirror, he tried to stretch back to reach them. But the pain got worse and blood began to leak out, so he stopped.

His hands were bloody again; he was leaning against the sink, trying to decide what to do when there was a tap at the door. Maggie, he thought.

"Come in." He didn't turn.

He heard a gasp and straightened. In the mirror he saw Deb Putnam peeking around the door. She froze, and her eyes filled with tears. She stepped inside and closed the door shut behind her.

"Oh, Jenner, my God! I'm so sorry . . ."

He kept rinsing.

"I'm okay, Deb. It could've been worse – they're just cuts."

"Jenner, they're worse than that. Wait here."

She disappeared, came back a couple of minutes later with some towels, a spray bottle of Bactine, a kidney-shaped steel bowl and a scrub-suit top. She was wearing a flannel shirt and jeans; she took off the shirt and tied it around her waist. She was wearing a ribbed white cotton tank top underneath and when she stood next to him it felt intimate.

"Bend over the sink. I'm going to clean you up."

"How did you find me?"

"Saw it on the news, went by the motel. Bobby Gentry from P.F. Fire and Rescue told me you'd run away with the dog; I figured this was where you'd bring him. How's he doing?"

"They're looking at him now."

Deb tore open a paper envelope and removed a sterile forceps. She soaked one of the towels in warm water, and Jenner did his best to stay still as she wiped his back softly, and then went over it slowly, plucking out small chunks of metal, dropping them in the bowl, then wiping the skin clean.

He tried to say something, but she shushed him. "Let me finish."

After about ten minutes, Jenner needed to sit, so she dragged in a chair from the waiting room, turned it so the back pressed against the sink, and had him straddle it facing the sink; she talked to him while watching his reflection in the mirror.

Deb smiled. "My dad once got peppered on a turkey shoot. My Mom picked the birdshot out of his back in our garage, then hosed him down with the garden hose before she let him inside."

He flinched as she pulled out one of the larger pieces.

"I'm sorry, Jenner, but the tape I have isn't very sticky – it's not gonna hold that well. Give me a call tomorrow – I'll redo the dressings. It'll give us some time to chat about Maggie Caine – I have to say, I didn't see *that* coming. How long have you been seeing her?"

"I don't think 'seeing' is the right word. Are you almost finished?"

"As a matter of fact . . ." There was a quiet click as Deb dropped a fragment into the bowl. "That's the last of it."

She washed down Jenner's back, ignoring his wincing as she patted him dry. She stepped back to look at his wounds and whistled quietly. "I hope you like scars – you're going to have some nice ones."

Her voice was thick, and when he looked in the mirror, Jenner was surprised to see that Deb was crying again. She saw him watching her and looked away.

She grabbed the Bactine. "Okay, Romeo. This is going to hurt you more than it hurts me."

84

Doctor Reed and Dr. Ade were in the waiting room, talking with Maggie Craine. She looked over at Jenner and Deb as they came out of the bathroom, then turned to the vets.

Doctor Ade said, "He's pretty lucky he's a fat, hairy beast – the extra padding saved his life. He's stable at the moment. One of the projectiles breached the chest cavity – there was some subcutaneous emphysema and a small hemopneumothorax. We've put in a chest tube, drained a little blood, and the lung seems to have expanded nicely."

Doctor Reed jumped in. "We don't know how extensive the injuries in the thorax are, but we want to avoid opening the chest unless we absolutely have to; the shrapnel injuries are probably shallow, but any lung damage from the shock wave could be worsened if we do a thoracotomy. We've packed the chest, sealed the wounds. We're going to see how he does like that."

He looked Jenner in the eye. "Your dog's not out of the

woods yet – he's lost a lot of blood, and he's not a puppy anymore – but Doctor Ade and I are hopeful."

Jenner shook their hands and said, "Thanks, I understand. I really appreciate it." He turned to Maggie and said, "Thanks, Maggie."

She nodded, then stood, and draped her wrap around her shoulders. "I should get home. Lucy's with Rosa; I don't like to leave her alone for too long."

Maggie barely glanced at Deb as she swept out, but her glance lasted long enough for her to appraise and judge.

85

Jenner needed to see Rudge, talk it out, figure out how everything was connected.

He tried to spot Deb's dark blue Miata among the shifting arrays of red taillights floating in front of him on the dark highway; he was regretting having agreed to her "short cut" back. She was an aggressive driver, and, in the night and on unfamiliar roads, he'd quickly lost her.

When he caught up to her she was sitting in her car opposite the Palmetto Court, the hood down. Jenner pulled in and stared at what was left of his place. The crowds and fire trucks had departed, and the ragged paving of the parking lot had almost dried. His cabin was now an exposed half-charred shell of a building and a ribbon of yellow crime-scene tape had been strung limply across the porch.

Deb tapped on his window. "You want to go in and get your stuff?"

Jenner shook his head. "It'll wait. I need to talk to Rudge first."

"You shouldn't leave your things in there – this isn't the best neighborhood."

"I don't have anything left that's worth much. My laptop was in the car, and that's about it."

Deb headed back to the Miata, and he leaned out to call after her, "Hey, try not to lose me this time."

86

It was gone eleven p.m. when they reached Rudge's place, a brown ranch house on a half-acre of land, roughly separated from the neighboring houses by stands of slash pine. The Taurus was in the driveway, and Jenner saw the light of a TV flickering in the living room.

Deb leaned against her car.

"You need me, Jenner?"

He shook his head and smiled. "I'm okay. Thanks for getting me here."

"Where are you staying tonight?"

Jenner rubbed his face wearily. "I guess I'll find a hotel."

"You can stay with me if you want. I have an empty room – take me a second to air it out, put out some towels and such for you."

"You feel like rescuing someone?"

Deb shrugged. "You seem like a guy who could do with a little rescuing."

He grinned. "I think the hotel's a better idea. And the county can pay."

She hooted. "Yeah, boy – good luck with that!"

Jenner stepped over to her and pecked her on the cheek, smiling. "Fuck 'em – I think I'm now officially sicker of Douglas County than it is of me."

"Awww . . ." Deb made a sad face and hugged him gently, her hands on his waist to avoid his injuries. "I'll call you tomorrow, check in on you. Say hi to Rudge from me, eh?"

He walked up the driveway and stepped onto the path. She called over to him, "Hey, Jenner! The Gulf Breeze over on the bay has a government rate."

"Thanks."

He was nearing the porch when she called out to him again. "Jenner? My offer still stands, okay?"

He waved, then stepped up onto Rudge's front deck. He watched Deb climb back into her Miata, pull a tight three-point turn, then roar off down the road.

Jenner pushed the doorbell, heard the buzzer inside, and waited.

There was a pair of dark wicker rocking chairs on the porch; it seemed like a nice place to sit and do whatever people did around there when sitting on their porches. Drink ice tea, he imagined. Lemonade.

After a little while he grew impatient; he pressed the button again and stepped back. The blinds were drawn; the living-room lights were on low, and the TV was flashing dry white and blue-gray shadows onto the blinds.

He opened the screen door and rapped on the frame.

"Rudge! It's Jenner."

He could hear the TV, but there was no sound of movement inside. No scurrying from the kitchen, no hurried flush of a toilet. Not even the quiet rush of a shower.

Jenner noticed a light switch and flicked it. Nothing happened. He flicked it up and down again; looking up, he saw that the socket of the porch light was empty.

Then he saw a bulb resting neatly on the wooden deck railing. He picked up the bulb and, curious, shook it; the bulb was good.

He reached up, screwed it into the slot; the bulb flickered and came on brightly, dazzling him slightly.

He walked along the deck and tapped at the big living-room window. He pressed his ear to the glass; he heard nothing beyond the TV set.

Something wasn't right.

Jenner moved quickly now, back to the door, and tapped again. He waited a second, reached down to the doorknob, turned it and pushed gently; the door swung open.

The air inside was thick and stale, smelling of smoke and dry metal. And, swimming beneath that, Jenner caught the copper whiff of blood.

He pushed the door wide open.

"Rudge." He realized that he wasn't even raising his voice; he already knew.

He stepped inside the house.

The living room was to his right, much of the space taken up by a bulky rear-projection TV set, a good eight or nine years old. Henry Fonda was onscreen: *The Grapes of Wrath*.

There was an ugly dark wicker sofa with cushions upholstered in a bright tropical pattern, and a pair of matching ugly armchairs similar to the ones on the porch. The floors were bare white tile, except where the blood had pooled.

In a recliner directly opposite the TV set, Rudge lay sprawled, tilted back, legs comfortably supported by the leg rest. The bullet had entered his temple by the orbit of his right eye; it had gone through his head, exited the back and embedded itself in the wall, a gray hole surrounded by an ugly red sunburst of blood and blown-out tissue.

Rudge's body had slumped to the right; heavy bleeding from the entrance wound had caked the right side of his face, the drying blood puddling in his lap around his right hand, which still held the revolver, and dripping onto the floor to flow across the tile to his feet. The steady dripping had spattered tiny droplets over the TV remote, which lay by the base of the chair.

On the table beside the chair was a line of empty Budweiser cans, a near-empty bottle of Jack Daniels and a neat row of shot glasses; one of the shot glasses had five unfired cartridges pushed into it, bullet tips down, submerged in amber liquid.

Jenner glanced around the room. It was pretty much what he'd have expected. One wall was taken up by bookshelves filled with several hundred DVDs and a small library of film books. Jenner wondered why the detective didn't have a better TV.

As he walked over to the bookshelves, he saw there were trophies, too, plaques and certificates for valorous service, stacked rather than displayed. There was even a presentation box holding a large bronze medal on a wide blue ribbon.

Jenner tucked the ribbon back into the box and flicked it shut. What was he doing?

In the kitchen there were more empties stacked by the sink – mostly beer, but liquor too.

Jenner saw the phone on a coffee table in front of one of the ugly chairs. He sat down and dialed 911. He identified himself, reported the death, indicated that the deceased was a police officer. He didn't know the address, just that he was in Golden Palms, but the dispatcher said it was fine, they had 911 call-location software, and officers would be responding immediately; he should just wait with the body.

Jenner hung up the phone and wept.

87

Jenner had been fired, for all intents and purposes, but it would be two days before the Miami pathologists took over, so he had to document the scene. And he would do Rudge's autopsy.

Major Crimes still wanted to interview him about the Palmetto Court bombing; Alcohol, Tobacco and Firearms had sent an agent over from Miami, and he arrived at Rudge's house with Bobby Bartley and another detective to conduct a joint interview.

While Crime Scene processed the living room, Jenner sat in a metal patio chair at Rudge's kitchen table, answering questions about how he'd found Rudge's body – no, Rudge hadn't been expecting him, yes, the door had been unlocked, yes, he'd just walked right in, no, he didn't think he'd touched anything, other than putting the porch light bulb back in – for an hour.

They paused while Bartley caught up with his notes. Bartley's partner Halvorsen, a ruddy faced, white-blond detective originally from Minneapolis, announced, "I count eight empties of Jack, twenty-two empty cans of Bud. Four full bottles of Jack, four cans of Bud." No one said anything.

Then Halvorsen said, "Doc, you were with Rudge yesterday afternoon, weren't you? What were you doing?"

"We were visiting farms around Bel Arbre, trying to retrace Adam Weiss's steps."

"Where did you go?"

"UFL Tomato and La Grulla Blanca."

"That's Chip Craine's place, isn't it?"

Jenner said, "What?"

One of the uniforms said, "Yes, sir, that's Mr. Craine's farm. La Grulla Blanca, that's Spanish for the white crane – you know, the crane bird?"

"Half the members at the Polo Grounds have estates up there. La Grulla Blanca is Chip Craine's place," Bartley muttered. "Now can we focus on today? I don't want Dave Rudge lying here any longer than he has to."

They talked about Rudge and what Jenner had found, then went back to their time at Bel Arbre. Jenner told them about the tension between Rudge and the farm overseer at La Grulla Blanca. Then it was the ATF agent's turn, another twenty minutes of what Jenner had seen, what he'd done, if he'd seen anyone when the bomb was thrown, noticed anything.

The agent questioned him again about UFL Tomato, but Jenner had nothing to add. Then Richard Flanagan arrived with the morgue wagon, and the Crime Scene lieutenant let Jenner back into the living room.

They were all watching him – the uniformed officers,

Bartley, Halvorsen, the ATF agent, Flanagan and Bucky Rutledge. They watched him pace the room, watched him photograph the dead detective, watched him take Rudge's temperature, bend his arms to check for rigor mortis. Jenner knew they'd all seen or heard about the *American Crime* thing, and guessed they were all thinking the same thing: *This man gets cops killed.*

But Jenner did his work right. He ignored them, had Flanagan and Buddy move Rudge so he was sitting upright in the chair, and measured the height of the wound again. Then he squeezed behind the chair to the wall, and measured the height of the bullet impact mark on the wall, the yellow tape measure finicky clean in the center of the vivid halo of blood spatter.

Jenner photographed the bullets that had been shoved into the shot glass. The table around the glass was dry, apart from the blood droplets.

He took close-ups of Rudge's wounds, Flanagan holding the head so that Jenner could see the injuries clearly. A uniformed officer shone a flashlight on Rudge's face, trying to be helpful; Jenner waved him away – the camera flash would be enough, and the flashlight could wash the image out.

He photographed the wound from different angles, bracketing each exposure. Then he went into the kitchen, tore off a sheet of Bounty, moistened it in the sink and wiped the blood gently from Rudge's face.

Jenner looked at the damp towel – there was gray smudging amid the blood; he couldn't be sure whether it was gunshot residue or just grime. He preserved the towel in case Ballistics wanted to test it.

It was a close-range shot: that much was certain. Not a

contact wound, but close-range, a cloud of little scratches, gray gunpowder residue in the skin, spreading around the hole in a three-inch circle. The pattern was neatly circular on the skin behind the wound, but in front the scratches scattered out over the cheek and the right side of the nose.

Jenner looked at the revolver, a .32 caliber Smith & Wesson snubby, a typical cop back-up piece; automatics jam, revolvers don't. The short barrel meant that the spray of gunpowder particles that caused the scratches would've spread out rapidly; Jenner estimated that the muzzle had been about six inches from Rudge's face when the trigger had been pulled.

Jenner saw that Halvorsen was holding Rudge's revolver, examining the barrel. He said, "That hasn't been fingerprinted yet." Halvorsen glanced at Bartley, then said, "Sorry, doc. You're right." Bartley disappeared into Rudge's bedroom.

Halvorsen placed the gun down on the coffee table and said, "Crime Scene can rule me out – they got my prints back in the lab."

He paused, looked around the room and then continued, "But I think we're all thinking the same thing here, aren't we?"

Jenner turned to him. "What am I thinking?"

Halvorsen said, "Doc, I don't mean to be, like . . . disrespectful . . . But you don't know Dave Rudge like we do. He's a great cop, and we love him like a brother, but the fact is, the Job isn't easy, and Rudge took it serious. He had some problems – and we all do – but the fact is, he drank pretty hard."

"So what? He drank pretty hard – lots of cops do."

Bartley returned with a gray plastic gun case in his hand. He opened the case, set it on the coffee table, took the cleaning rod and the cloth and laid them on the end nearest to Rudge. The ATF agent stood up and walked wordlessly out of the room.

"Okay, doc, this looks like an accident to me. Rudge is here, he's cleaning his weapon. He's had a bit to drink. He thinks he's emptied the cylinder; he's checking the barrel, he slips, and that's it."

Bartley looked around the room. "And I think that's what we're all thinking, right?"

Halvorsen nodded, the uniforms nodded, Flanagan hesitated, then nodded slowly.

Jenner said, "Then you don't understand what's going on here."

"Doctor, those first pictures you took when you entered? It's so easy to screw up and accidentally delete an image file." Bartley paused. "I think you missed the cleaning equipment in your first photos; you should probably go right ahead and take some new ones. I think the cleaning equipment set out like this, right in front of him, is a pretty big clue to just what happened, wouldn't you say?"

Jenner shook his head. "You have *got* to be kidding me. This is how you protect his reputation?"

Halvorsen piped up, "You've been here not even three weeks, doc. We've known Rudge for a decade, the sheriff has known him since they were kids. Rudge was a great cop, one of the best. We've all got our personal demons, and if one night, in the dark of night, Rudge's demons took him over, and he . . . made a bad mistake, well . . . he shouldn't have to pay for that."

Then Bartley said, "I think this is open and shut. He's a bit messed-up, he's had one too many . . . He's watching TV, drinking . . . He picks up his gun, fooling around with it . . . He empties the cylinder, thinks he's emptied it completely, and it's a complete accident. Or maybe he decides to see what it'd be like to, y'know, tempt fate, and leaves one round in. He spins the cylinder, points it at himself, pulls the trigger . . ."

Halvorsen leaned in to interrupt. "We don't want him to go out as a suicide, doc. That isn't right. It doesn't have to be that way."

They were all looking at him now.

"Listen," Jenner said, "It's not a suicide: it's a *murder*."

Halvorsen said, "What?"

"Someone shot him in the head and set it up to look like a suicide or a Russian-roulette death."

Bartley said, "How you figure that?"

"A few things. First of all, the range of fire: I put the muzzle of the gun at three to nine inches from Rudge's face. Suicides need a guarantee, they want to be sure they're buying a one-way ticket. They press the muzzle against their temple, or stick the barrel in their mouth. They don't want any mistakes – try holding a heavy revolver eight inches from your face, see how confident you feel about your aim."

Bartley was looking unsure.

"Another thing: he gets shot in this chair, obviously. The bullet goes into the right side of his head, exits the back on the left side, and lodges in the wall behind him."

"Yeah . . ."

"The bullet goes in a straight line; from the height of

the wounds and the bullet impact mark on the wall, he was obviously shot while sitting up.

"When people shoot themselves, typically they hold the gun to the temple, pull the trigger. Most times, the path is from right to left, a bit backwards and a bit upwards. But here the exit wound is lower than the entry one.

"I measured the height of the entry wound above the floor with him sitting vertical, the height of the exit wound, and the height of the bullet's impact site in the wall, and it lines up neatly . . ."

"And?"

"He was shot by someone standing above him, shooting down."

Halvorsen looked at Bartley. "Bobby?"

Bartley shrugged. "I guess . . ."

Jenner said, "Okay, all right, wait. Something else. See that glass with the live rounds? You see it's got blood droplets on it?"

"Yes. And there's blood drops all around it, too – it was there when he shot himself."

"You sure, Halvorsen? Pick it up."

The detective pincered two fingers and lifted up the shot glass by its rim; on the table underneath where it had sat there were several smudged droplets of blood.

Jenner said, "This glass was on the table when he was shot, but was moved into this position afterwards, I assume when they put the bullets into it while dressing the scene."

Halvorsen said to Bartley, "What do you think?"

Bartley picked up the gun case. "I think I should put the cleaning equipment away."

88

It was late, but he knew her mother was out.

"Hello?"

"Lucy? It's your Papaw."

She was silent; he imagined her little face, stricken at the sound of his voice – this was just why he hadn't given her a cell phone with caller ID. Besides, it wasn't as if she could complain – her mom would be upset if she knew that Lucy had her own phone, hysterical if she knew who had given it to her.

"Hello, Papaw."

"What are you up to, sweetie? You're up late."

"I'm going to bed. I just washed my face and brushed my teeth. I did my homework."

"Good girl." He paused. They both knew what he'd say next.

"So, Lucy . . . You were a little piggy today, weren't you? I bet you stuffed your little piggy face at the trough."

Her voice was so soft that he could barely hear her. "No, Papaw. I was good."

"Speak up when I speak to you, Lucy!" He smiled. "So, were you really good? Did you weigh yourself?"

She was quiet. "Doctor Vargas says I can't weigh myself anymore. She says it's making me sick when I do that. She said I could only leave the hospital if I promise not to weigh myself."

"That fat sow? Of course she'd say that!"

"Mommy found the scale tonight and took it away."

"I bet there's one at school, though."

She was quiet.

"There is, isn't there, darling? Lucy, I want you to weigh yourself at school tomorrow, okay?"

Silence.

"Sweetie, when I saw you at the shelter the other day I could tell you'd been stuffing your little piggy face again. Your thighs look like cottage cheese!" He paused, waiting. He heard the snuffles begin, smiled and said, "Aw, sweetie. You know Mommy and I will always love you, no matter how fat you are."

He let the sobs get wetter. "But I won't always be here, and Mommy won't always be here, and no one will love you if you're a fat little sow. You know that, don't you, darling?"

There was silence, and then, in her sweet little voice, "Yes . . ."

"Good." He listened to her sob a little. "Now, things are very bad between Mommy and Papaw right now. We had a fight just this morning, and Mommy ran away. And I don't know if I want her to come back. You know how she is, Lucy? Your mommy sometimes just can't manage to do the right thing . . ."

The girl was crying freely now.

"Aw, sweetie, don't worry – even if Mommy doesn't come back, Papaw will look after you! Papaw loves you. Papaw will never leave you, okay, Lucy?"

He smiled as she wept.

"You know what? You're the only reason Papaw looks after Mommy. Sometimes she's so difficult that even I can barely stand it, but I love you so much that I look after her because that's the only way I can look after *you*. But if she's really bad, I'll have to send you both away; I shouldn't have to deal with that. And if I have to kick you out, that would be difficult for you. Because your mommy isn't good at very much, you know that, don't you? She'd have to get a job as a waitress or a maid at a motel."

He listened to her sob. "And you know what else? If I let you go, I wouldn't pay the bills at the shelter any more, and Mommy can't afford it. And you know what that means?"

She snuffled, "*What?*"

"Well, they'll have to kill all the dogs. Put them all to sleep. Even the little puppies . . ."

She began to wail. Craine realized he might have pushed it too far: if she kept it up, the nanny would check and find out who she was talking with, and there'd be problems.

Time to calm her down.

"Aw, baby, don't worry. I'll keep looking after Mommy. But you're going to have to be a very good girl for me. Okay? Don't worry, my darling. Everything's fine. Mommy will come back in a little while. Okay?"

She sobbed yes.

"Good. I just need you to be a good girl. That's not so hard, is it? Just behave yourself, and don't eat like a little piggy.

"Now I want you to call me or text me with your weight tomorrow."

Now to finish.

"Do you remember your Motivations, Lucy?"

"Yes, Papaw."

"Let's say them together now, okay?"

And they began, Craine murmuring softly so that he could hear her voice say the words:

*every time you say no thanks to food you say yes please to
thin*

*hunger hurts but starving works
i want to be thin . . .*

89

Jenner stood in front of his burned-out cabin, a big
garbage bag for his belongings in his hand. It was almost
two a.m. and the air had cooled; there were no insects,
maybe because of the smoke.

A drowsy attendant answered on the second ring, and
told him his dog was sleeping – sedated, but he looked
okay.

Jenner sat on the lip of his porch. He looked at the
parking lot, breathing in the wet burned-wood smell and
acrid chemical aroma of scorched plastic and fire-
retardant foam.

Home.

His phone was half-charged. He dialed Jun in New
York; Kimi answered.

"Jenner! It's good to hear your voice. We were worried
about you . . ."

"I'm okay, thanks."

"When are you coming home?"

"Soon, I hope."

"Good. You need to be where you belong. What's that
song – 'where everybody knows your name' . . .?"

"The theme from *Cheers*."

"Yes! That's where you need to be! With your friends,

back in New York – we miss you!"

Jun took the phone. "Hey, Jenner. You okay?"

"Yeah. Just about. It's been rough . . ."

"We know. We've been watching it on TV. Fucking Amanda Tucker, right? She's all over your jimmy."

"She's been on TV *tonight*?"

"Yah. It was actually pretty great – they had her in the hospital ER, all bandaged-up and shit, broadcasting live."

"What did she say about me?"

"She said you saved her life, man! It was great!"

"Huh."

"But then she said other stuff, not so great."

"I bet." He smiled.

"When you coming back?"

"Soon. They're throwing me out."

"Well, maybe that's a good thing. You need money, bro? Just say the word, I'll wire some down tonight."

"I don't know. I'm almost out. I have to do one more autopsy, then I'm gone." Jenner checked for soot, then leaned against the porch post.

"I just don't know if I can let go – Marty Roburn was like a dad to me, and I don't trust the cops here to do right by him. I think they're crooked, at least, some of them – they've been following me."

"Jenner, the cops are *always* crooked! Fuck, man, let it go! I respect your friendship, but you've done enough. They tried to kill you! Just get in that fucking car and *drive*, man! Florida's not the place for you."

"What, and New York is?" He thought about it. "Maybe you're right."

Jun said, "You know it. Also, Amanda said you'd hooked up with a billionaire's daughter – that true?"

313

Jenner was silent a second. "Sort of."

"Whoa! Nice work!"

Now everyone in the world knew. He flashed on Bartley saying that Chip Craine owned La Grulla Blanca.

"It's over. It was just a one-night stand."

"They had a photo."

Christ. "It's over."

"Dude, if I was you, I'd rethink that – seriously, she was *hot* . . ."

"Yes, she's very hot. But it was a one-night stand. Her choice, not mine."

"Well, that's harsh . . ."

There was a quiet sound behind him, inside the cabin, from deep in the shadows.

"Jun, I gotta go."

"You gotta go? *You gotta go call her,* dude! That's where you gotta go . . ."

Jenner hung up.

Jenner stood on the deck and looked into the darkness beyond the yellow tape.

There was the flare of a match, and he saw Maggie's face for a second as she lit the cigarette.

"Hi, Jenner. Who's hot?"

"You are."

She shook out the match, but it continued to glow. She shrugged and, with a dry laugh, threw it on the floor. "Not like it can do much damage now . . ."

She was on the couch in the unburned half of the room, a blanket spread beneath her. In the black velvet shadow, in the smell of burned wood and plastic, dappled by the light that fell through the charred timber frame, she was immaculate and whole, her hair glowing faintly, her bare

314

shoulders elegant and pure; he'd never seen her more beautiful.

Maggie held something in her lap, a flat rectangular box. With the ghost of a smile, she lifted it up and said, "*The Old Woman by the Fishing Port*, Jenner? I'm not sure I'm flattered you think I'm hot."

He shrugged. "You've been there all this time?"

She looked at her watch. "Since about 12:30 a.m., one. I figured you'd come back for your stuff."

"You could've called."

"I thought I'd surprise you." She took a drag. "*Surprise!*"

"What do you want?"

Maggie smiled brightly. "*Blood*! I've come back for *blood . . .*"

Jenner sat, and looked at her silently.

"Not in a joking mood, eh?" She exhaled. "Where's your little woodland friend?"

"Ranger Putnam?" He didn't know why he said it that way, so formally.

"Ah, yes . . . *Ranger Putnam* . . . Where is Ranger Putnam? Putting out forest fires?" She smiled mirthlessly.

"There's something I need to ask you."

"What?"

"Your father's farm . . ."

"La Grulla Blanca?" Maggie wrinkled her brow. "What's there to know? Daddy keeps prize pigs, and they grow vegetables, I think. What about it?"

"Does he go there a lot?"

"No. Pretty much the only reason he owns it is for the Fourth of July party – we have a big thing each year at Stella, and they dig a barbecue pit and roast a couple of

315

his hogs. He probably goes up there one night a month, maybe two – the manager comes down to Stella from time to time. Why? What's this about?"

"He stays the night?"

"Yes, usually." Maggie's eyes narrowed. "Why? What's so weird about that?"

"It's not a long drive back to town. Why does he stay there?"

"Because he *owns* the place?" She rolled her eyes. "Jesus, Jenner, I don't know, ask him – maybe he likes to get up early to run naked with the pigs!"

He didn't laugh. "Do you know what happened here?"

"Yes!" She motioned with her cigarette at the wreckage. "Someone threw a bomb into your cabin! Is it because of the hanged men?"

"I think so." Jenner paused. "Did you hear anything else?"

"Nope. Well, I know Amanda Tucker was with you when it happened – what's up with *that*, Jenner? A little taste of forbidden fruit? After the hatchet job she did on you . . ."

"Did you know Rudge – Detective David Rudge?"

Maggie shook her head. "The name sounds familiar, but I don't think I've met him. Is he from Port Fontaine? Should I know him?"

"I don't know. He was assigned to that case. He was murdered tonight."

She was silent.

"Here's the thing, Maggie: someone killed him, and someone tried to kill me. And they did it after we went to your father's farm."

She was confused. "But . . . why would you go to Daddy's farm?"

"It was part of the investigation. When we were there Rudge made some threats; a few hours later someone shot him in the head, and someone threw a pipe bomb into my cabin."

There was a quiet rustling in the trees, and it began to drizzle. Maggie drew her wrap tighter around her and moved closer to him, under the remaining deck canopy. "You think Daddy's involved, Jenner?"

He shrugged. "I don't know what I think. But they've killed a cop – now they've really crossed a line."

She was close to him, shivering. He fought the urge to put an arm around her.

"Why are you here, Maggie?"

"I'm not sure. I felt . . . bad." She smiled softly, raised her cigarette and gestured dramatically. "Yes, I felt *bad*, Jenner! I wanted to say I was sorry. I didn't want it to go like this. I didn't think it *would* go like this . . ."

Jenner said nothing.

"It's not all about me. You know I have . . . problems. You came along and fell into them. I didn't want to hurt you. I'm just . . . you know, fucked up."

"Yes, you're fucked up, it's not your fault, nothing you can do." He shrugged again. "I understand now that you only have so much you can offer to another person. I'm not the first, and I won't be the last – people like you keep moving from person to person, never finding what they need."

"Whoa!" She whistled, smiling. "Been waiting to say *that* for a while, haven't we, doctor?"

"Why me, Maggie?"

She shrugged and inhaled, then breathed out, and said, "You're smart. You're not bad-looking. You were new. Fuck, I don't know – *you liked dogs*! I don't care – take your pick . . ."

"I think it's sad."

Maggie scowled. "Sad? Yeah, well, Jenner, that's the nature of a 'one-night stand', right?"

She flicked the cigarette off the deck.

"Where's the Bentley?"

"At Stella. I took the Volvo."

She turned to him. "I came to ask you out. On a date. I thought things over a bit. But I see now you wouldn't have said yes."

Jenner paused, then said, "No, I wouldn't."

"Is it because of whats-her-name, Woodsy Owl?" Maggie sneered.

"Maybe, a bit, I don't know – I like her." He shrugged. "But it's mostly because of you."

Maggie flinched slightly, then gathered her wrap around her as if it were just the cool air that had made her wince.

"I earned that," she said. "And I own it."

She opened her clutch purse and pulled out her cigarettes. She slipped one between her lips and dug for her matches; she'd used the last.

"Fuck." She looked at him. "I suppose it would be pretty poor form for me to ask you for a match . . ."

"I couldn't help you."

90

In an airy room with light streaming through sheer curtains that swayed slowly with the breeze, Jenner woke to the sound of gulls.

He blinked and sat up, momentarily disoriented. The walls were pale robin's-egg blue, and there were framed prints of seashells and coral. He was lying on a feather bed, the cotton sheets stiff and almost luminously white. The room smelled of fresh paint, clean and fresh. He lay back and stared at the ceiling.

The gulls screeched right outside his window and behind them he could hear the quiet rush of surf.

The Gulf Breeze Hotel.

Jenner climbed out of the brass bed and went to the window, holding up a hand to shield his eyes against brilliant sunshine. Guests were having breakfast on the patio below him – eggs Benedict and mimosas, Gucci sunglasses on folded copies of the *New York Times*. No doubt everyone was saying what a beautiful day it was, and talking about how to spend the day.

Beyond the patio flagstones a grass croquet lawn led down to a jungle of sea-grape trees and bushes, the undergrowth thick with beach saw grass; a boardwalk path led through the trees to the beach beyond, smooth and white as a fur cape.

For a minute or two Jenner let himself imagine that he was on vacation, staying in an old resort hotel. It was a beautiful day; he'd have breakfast in his room and then decide what to do with himself. Perhaps he'd carry one of the hotel deck chairs down the boardwalk path and out onto the sand; he'd plant it at the high-tide mark and spend the entire day on the beach. And Jenner wouldn't repeat Ambrose Burmeister's mistake: he'd keep his eyes on the sparkling green water, watch it stroke and hiss through the diamond-powder sand, his back turned firmly against Port Fontaine.

He could do that, if he wanted. All he had to do was admit it: Time up. Game over.

Rudge, shot in the head. Marty tortured, his throat cut, gulping down his own blood as he died. Bobbie drowning, writhing and twisting as the water rose in the coffin of the family sedan.

Adam Weiss poisoned, then mangled by a car. The hanged men rotting in the cave-like hollow out on the island in the Everglades.

They were his responsibility, each and every one of them. He'd had the opportunity to see it right. And he'd failed.

All this stuff, all these deaths, connected; all these deaths now spinning away from him, the links stretching and snapping like worn elastic. They'd bring in new eyes, new people, and those people would figure it out. And once again he'd been booted out, once again disgraced. And he'd lost the only friend and ally he had left in Port Fontaine, had probably got him killed.

Jenner smiled bitterly. There it was! The guilt! Always lurking in the background, always ready to leap out of the shadows . . .

Anyway, it was bullshit: he had another ally – Debby Putnam.

Woodsy Owl. He shook his head. Christ!

There was a printed menu on the wicker secretary. He sat in the matching chair, pored over the menu, then called room service and ordered scrambled eggs and sausages, and coffee and orange juice. He did the math – twenty-eight dollars, plus a three-dollar delivery fee on top of a twenty percent service charge. Twenty-eight dollars – he could eat breakfast at Denny's for a week on what this one breakfast would cost! But for once he was in a decent hotel, and he was hungry, and he wanted breakfast. And the room-service attendant had addressed him by name when she'd answered the phone – he would've felt foolish just ordering a pot of coffee.

He phoned Deb Putnam; the call went straight to voicemail. He left a brief message, then showered quickly. He'd eat breakfast, get dressed, then do the autopsy.

The autopsy: it would be even harder than those he'd done on Marty and Bobbie. Rudge wasn't decomposed; on the autopsy table he would be still, as if he were just lying there for a little while, just resting for a tick. It wasn't like on TV where you could tell the dead by the unearthly pallor of their skin and their frigid blue lips: in the real world, dead people looked like live people. And Rudge would look like Rudge.

But Jenner would do it. He didn't believe in a soul that stayed with the body; when you died, you died. If there was a soul, it was the energy roaring in the billions of cells; when you died, all the chemicals fell off their little conveyor belts, and the warmth inside you went away. And when the energy stopped, and the warmth went, that was it – there was no soul to leap anywhere. Your body was dead. You were gone.

And Rudge was gone.

After the autopsy he'd finish his interview with Halvorsen and Bartley and the ATF guy. Then he'd

321

walk back to the M.E. office, mutter a few awkward goodbyes, and hand in his Douglas County Medical Examiner shield. He'd drive back to the motel, pick up the rest of his stuff, and get the hell out of Dodge, just leave Port Fontaine, leave Douglas County. Go back to New York, to his own world, to people who understood him.

Where everybody knew his name.

91

When Anders called, Jenner was sitting at the wicker desk in a fresh T-shirt and clean jeans, polishing off his eggs and drinking coffee. The conversation was brief and to the point.

The situation had moved on to the next level and the county managers had become involved. Sandy Hart from Miami would arrive later that morning; she would do Rudge's autopsy. That was good, Jenner thought – she was an excellent pathologist. They were expecting Jenner at Major Crimes around noon, after the autopsy; he was not after all to attend Rudge's autopsy, and the pathologist and investigators had been instructed not to discuss their findings with him.

Once he'd handed in his report from Rudge's death scene and given his statement in Major Crimes, Jenner would be free to go. The County Comptroller himself had cut Jenner a check for the salary balance he was owed. Down the road, the medical examiners who were replacing him might have questions about his cases; the sheriff trusted that Jenner would assist them out of a sense of ethical responsibility. The questions, if any, would be few and Jenner should expect no further remuneration from Douglas County.

Jenner hung up. He'd lasted less than a month in Port Fontaine.

He sat at the desk, staring at the half-eaten toast and the little pots of imported jam. Outside, the tourists were dispersing, some to the beach, most on a mangroves-and-Everglades tour, where they'd peer at manatees through glass-bottomed boats as the manatees did their best to get out of the damn way.

The phone rang – Dr. Ade from the shelter letting him know that the dog was fine, just about a hundred percent better and eating like a horse.

So now he had a dog again. Would the dog like New York? He should leave it with Maggie, make it her problem. And he'd have to pay for the dog's medical care somehow.

Jenner opened the window and leaned into the breezy sunshine. Beyond the emerald wall of sea-grape trees the beach was still almost empty; the first tentative sun worshippers were now creeping out onto the sand like wary crabs.

He could go to the beach. Why not? They didn't need him until noon. He could lie on the beach, get some sun.

Or he could run, he could get back to running, hit the trails, feel his legs pounding, his breath tearing up his lungs, feel his body work. He could run the path along the canal, where he'd been running when . . .

He didn't want to think about Marty now.

He rifled through his bathroom kit. There was a minitube of toothpaste next to the box of CBM Daytime Cold tablets.

Jenner froze.

He picked up the white box, looked at the Craine Brothers Medical logo and pale blue globe, the *No. 1 in Cold Medicine* slogan. Turned the box to read the ingredient list.

And then he understood.

Cold medicine. The white van with the blue globe CBM logo. The farmhouse. The well-paid field workers. It all fell into place.

It was all about the box van entering as they'd left Craine's farm, the van with the Craine Brothers Medical logo on its side. It wasn't stocked with shampoo and baby powder – there were twenty men, tops, working there, they'd just buy locally in bulk.

No, that Craine Brothers van was bringing something more specialized: cold medicine. Tens of thousands of tablets filled with phenylpropanolamine or pseudo-ephedrine. In the farmhouse or in one of the bunkhouses there would be men breaking down the capsules and tablets and then, through the magic of modern chemistry, converting the active ingredients into methamphetamine.

That was why the bodies in the forest had had such fucked-up teeth – Christ, this was probably why Craine kept pigs! An M.E. in Iowa had told Jenner about meth labs set up on pig farms because the pig shit hid the smell of the meth chemicals.

With a well-run lab the meth would be exceptionally pure. What was it Rudge had said? The packet he'd taken from Marty's car was approaching one hundred percent purity.

How did that fit into the picture? How did Marty come to have their product?

And it was obvious to Jenner now. The original packet in Marty's car had been tied with the waxed twine they used to suture the bodies in the autopsy room – Jenner had assumed that was where Marty had got it. But funeral directors used identical twine to sew up their bodies, and Marty had been at Jones & Carmen the day he went missing.

Where was the connection between the farm and Jones?

Reggie had previous convictions for methamphetamine dealing on his sheet. Maybe he had connections with someone at the farm, with one of the overseers, maybe with Brodie. They were probably doing two or three batches a week at the farm, making as much as fifty or sixty pounds of product, maybe twice that, maybe even more.

Moving that weight would be a challenge. The D.E.A., local police, Highway Patrol and the Florida Department of Law Enforcement were all over the state, combing the highways and the back roads for meth and cocaine. But they'd be less likely to stop a hearse. Christ, Jones could even ship the bodies by air – did they even check luggage on domestic flights with drug-trained dogs? These days it was all about bombs. And even if they checked luggage, Jenner doubted that they'd open the coffins to check a cadaver.

This was a professional operation – there was no way Chip Craine was masterminding it. Craine was hungry, he was corrupt, he was a risk taker. He would be the perfect silent partner for a Mexican syndicate, less for his farm than for his cold-medication connections. And if his "allowance" from his brother was as miserly as Maggie had suggested, a steady flow of cash would certainly help. And the money would be huge.

Everything was streamlined for Craine's benefit, the pigs and crops providing him with cover, the cookers in the bunk houses providing him with money. There was minimal risk – his biggest problem would be handling all the cash; there was no way to launder the sort of money he would be raking in. Of course, *that* was why he tipped so extravagantly, *that* was why he paid his house staff in cash – he had more money than he could dispose of.

Jesus. He must be making a *fortune*. Hundreds of thousands, no, millions every month.

Jenner was pacing now. He thought about Craine's house, his cars. His swimming pool with its view out over the sea. The servants. Everything, everything, every fucking luxurious thing. What must it be like to live like that, knowing that each month, or every two months or every six months or whatever, a big glob of cash would fall into your lap?

Jenner remembered sitting in the diner, the fat manager standing over him, telling him that his card was no good, that Visa wouldn't cover him for the miserable fifteen bucks. Thought about having to pay for the jacket for Marty's funeral with a combination of the end of his credit and the last of his cash. He flushed at the unfairness of it all; just a single month of Craine's profits would've left Jenner set for life.

He imagined what it must be like to have money

like that, imagined having so much money that it would be impossible to spend it all, no matter how hard he tried.

Christ, the money.

Jenner sat on the bed for a while, dizzy with the sense of the money that swirled invisibly around him, never touching him.

He got up and began to pack. It didn't take long – all he had to do was fold the few shirts he had left, a pair of pants and some underclothes into big black plastic garbage bags. In the bathroom he brushed his teeth, then carefully packed the complimentary toothbrush and mini-toothpaste and helped himself to the wrapped soaps and unused bottles of Crabtree and Evelyn shampoo and conditioner; he'd need them at the forty-dollar-a-night fleapits where he'd be sleeping on his drive home.

There was a tap at the door. Jenner peered through the peephole, then opened the door.

"Good morning, Mister Craine."

92

Craine was wearing sunglasses, an open-necked white shirt and a cream linen suit. At his feet was a brown leather Ghurka overnight bag.

He set the sunglasses on the table and glanced around the room, unimpressed.

"The Ritz is better – you should've stayed there."

"I like this place. Besides, it's half the price."

Craine shrugged.

"So, doctor, I hear you've reached a crossroads in your time here."

"By which you mean . . ."

"By which I mean I hear they're throwing you out, bringing in some hotshot from Miami to clean up your mess."

"Ah. Is that what you hear?"

Another shrug. "I don't really blame you for this. You were up against individuals and entities that are stronger, smarter and better equipped than you are. It was always a lose-lose situation."

Jenner grinned. "The story of my life!"

Craine looked at Jenner's garbage-bag luggage.

"You'll be leaving soon, I imagine."

Jenner nodded.

"I had breakfast with my daughter this morning, and she told me something curious: she says you think I'm somehow mixed up in everything that's happened here. Is that true?"

"True that's what she told you, or true that I think you're involved in it?" Jenner grinned at Craine's irritation. "Yeah, that's what I think. I think you're in it up to your neck. I know what you're doing, I know how you're doing it, I think I even know *why* you're doing it."

Craine's expression darkened briefly, and his lips tightened. Then he relaxed and smiled warmly.

"Doctor, you know nothing – and can prove even less."

"Perhaps. But in an hour or so I'll be sitting down with the nice detectives in Major Crimes and explaining to them why you killed a brother cop, and why you tried to kill me. And how your men killed Marty and Bobbie

Roburn. And the hanging men. And that kid from New York. And I'll lay the facts out very neatly, and at the end they'll be itching to string you up themselves. Trust me – I can be quite persuasive."

"I'm sure you can, doctor! I'm sure you can . . ." Chip laughed. "But again, you can prove nothing. And if you tried to, I've got enough influence here to make your evidence disappear and you disappear along with it. Come at me with anything and I'll destroy it, destroy you. It really is that simple."

Craine watched Jenner pick up a piece of cold toast, twist open the little pot of Seville orange marmalade, and scoop some onto the bread.

Craine relaxed a little. He held his hands up, palms open, with an expression of genial helplessness. "Doctor, I have no personal vendetta against you – you're a helluva lot better than some of the assholes my daughter has dragged home.

"May I sit? I think it's cards on the table time." He sat without waiting for a reply. "You have to understand: my associates are not the live-and-let-live types. You screw them, they screw you, then they kill you. Then they screw your family, and they kill them, and they find your dog and they screw it, and they kill it, too. And then they burn your house down, for completeness's sake. You piss them off, they wipe every trace of your DNA from the surface of the earth. And they do it in a very public way so that others can learn from your example. It's never personal, it's just their way."

Jenner took a bite of toast, then said, "So, does your brother know what you're up to? I'm guessing he doesn't, does he? He's doing quite nicely with his huge corporation, and he wouldn't want to get sucked into your nasty little side business . . ."

"What Gabriel does or doesn't know isn't your concern, but you'd be surprised at just how protective of me he can be." Craine raised a hand impatiently. "But wait, doctor, please! This conversation is going in entirely the wrong direction – this needn't be so . . . confrontational."

Jenner was silent.

"I came to make you a proposition. And I think it's more than generous. I've made some enquiries into your . . . situation, and it seems that you're not quite as comfortable as one might expect a well-qualified senior pathologist to be." Again, he glanced at the three garbage bags holding Jenner's clothes.

Jenner's gaze strayed to the overnight bag next to Craine.

Craine nodded. "Yes, doctor – a bribe! You should know that, if you tell the police about your theories, some of them will not believe you, because they are sympathetic to my cause. But if they were in some way induced to act on your speculation they'd have to go in front of a judge. And you know they'll have a very hard time indeed persuading any judge in this county to issue a warrant to search my land. And I assure you that when and if they finally got a warrant the police who searched the property would find nothing but pigs and feed and fertilizer."

He picked up the bag and put it on the bed.

"Now have a look, doctor."

Jenner shook his head, so Craine unzipped the bag and turned it upside down. Cash bucketed out, tightly wrapped packets of used hundreds and fifties, Craine shaking until no more money fell out. There was a heap, easily a foot in height, of bricks of cash on the bed.

"I brought this for you, doctor. I'm not sure exactly how much is left in this one, but it's at least $820,000. That's more than three quarters of a million dollars in cash, laundered and untraceable, for you to do whatever you want with." Craine paused, and made his eyes twinkle. "Although I would suggest not mentioning it to the IRS!"

Jenner looked at the money.

There was a lot of it. Even as a loose pile the cash had the compact density of stacked cement blocks. He wanted to touch it, to muss it up even more, to send a $5,000 packet of fifties flying across the bedspread with a flick of his wrist. To see what money felt like as a material, rather than as a token for something else.

"You brought this for me . . ."

"Yes. I thought it might smooth things over between us, help you to leave Port Fontaine with at least *some* fond memories." Craine smiled widely, his eyebrows raised expectantly, his teeth immaculately white in the tan of his face. Jenner remembered his body at the pool, tan, glistening, bronzed.

"And in exchange . . ."

Craine sat at the table and gestured to the money. "Here's my offer: take this little farewell present from me. You tuck it away in the trunk of your car, hide it under those garbage bags there. You talk to the detectives. You tell them whatever you want about yesterday, about your visit to my farm; you just avoid any speculation as to what might or might not have happened later as a result of your visit, and you note that there was nothing out of the ordinary at La Grulla Blanca as compared with any of the other farms you visited.

"In your discussion with the detectives, there would also be no need for you to spin yarns about what Mr. Jones does at his funeral home; your speculation is surely inaccurate, and, could cause tremendous suffering and grief for the relatives of the deceased. If you decide to have bodies exhumed, they'll only have to dig up a couple of empty husks – none of which will contain anything the least bit illicit – before public outcry destroys the career of any law enforcement officer involved in the witch hunt. The investigation will be dropped faster than a dirty Band-Aid picked up off the floor of an Ebola ward."

"Go on."

"Well, actually, that's about the size of it."

"That's not enough. People died here, people who were my friends. And you can't just go on doing this."

"I told them you might be this way." Craine sighed. "Very well. We're prepared to go further: if you can be discreet, I guarantee I'll close down any clandestine activity at my estate and get back to just raising pigs and strawberries again. Maybe tomatoes, just to piss off Bob Gonzalez at UFL Tomato." The twinkle again; he was smooth, Jenner had to give him that.

"I've done very well with this project, but it's also been very stressful, particularly recently. I was told that everything would be run smoothly and efficiently, and I'd have to say that lately it's been anything but."

Jenner said, "Well, I'm sorry if this has caused you some angst. But I lost friends, people I cared about."

"I was coming to that. So, all narcotrafficking operations at La Grulla Blanca will stop, and the people whose actions resulted in the loss of your friends will be dealt with. Severely."

"What do you mean by 'severely'?"

"Neither you nor I want to think about that, I promise you. Let's just say: *very* severely." Craine said it as casually as if discussing an aphid problem with his gardener.

"If your associates are such bastards, what guarantee of safety would I have? Why would they just give me money and let me walk?"

Craine's brow furrowed. "Well, doctor, you're a celebrity now, on TV day and night. If we'd lost you last night – and I had nothing to do with that attack – your part of the story would be over, and things would settle down. But you survived an attempt on your life, and now you are even more newsworthy; my associates feel this whole fuss would be much better handled if the authorities question you but nothing untoward comes to light. You placate them, you reassure them. Then you disappear from the area and the investigation, and life gets back to normal.

"As far as the cash goes, well, that's the price of doing business." Craine winked. "It's my own money, but I wouldn't suggest asking for more – my partners would see that as an act of extremely poor faith.

"This whole affair will be wrapped up quietly and quickly. I'm leaving town this afternoon, to spend a month or two in Europe and Asia with my daughter."

Craine gestured toward the stack of money. "I'd suggest that, once you've spoken with the authorities, you do something similar."

Jenner was silent. The money was almost ten years'

take-home pay for a medical examiner. With eight hundred thousand in cash, if he lived frugally, Jenner would never need to work again. He could set himself up somewhere quiet – an island in the South China Sea, maybe, or a small cottage in the Alps. Spend a year reading, running. Doing yoga. Getting better. He could go to Grasse in the south of France, study perfumery; it was almost lavender season.

And he would be able to do good with the money, too; he'd be free to donate his time, his expertise. He could evaluate victims of torture for one of the international human rights organizations, or lend his expertise to the excavation of mass graves in Eastern Europe, or in Cambodia.

There was a *lot* of good he could do with the money.

Craine was right: even if the cops took Jenner's theories seriously, there'd be nothing at the farm by the time they could get in. And if they found something it would be almost impossible to implicate Craine. The code of silence enforced by the Mexican cartels meant that no one would cooperate, no one would rat out Marty's killers.

Jenner looked at Craine. "I want to know why Marty and Bobbie Roburn were murdered."

"I wasn't involved in that." Craine shook his head. "But if it's any consolation, my understanding is that the two men responsible for what happened to Dr. and Mrs. Roburn were . . . severely punished. And the punishment was administered in a public way as a warning about what happens to those who interfere with civilians in this county."

"The hangings."

Craine inclined his head very slightly.

"What about the other two?"

Craine looked weary. "I don't really know, Dr. Jenner. I feel that there's been some kind of . . . moral slide in the management of the farm. They did something – most likely took drugs, or blabbed about what happened on the farm. And they were punished. I don't know what that university student did – I *own* the farm, I don't run it – but he probably said the wrong thing to the wrong person. He was perceived as a threat, with minimal visible downside to his elimination.

"I think the people running this business have been so successful for so long that they feel invincible. It's very sad – this has been a stable, non-violent operation for some time. I'm not going to claim this is a victimless enterprise, but after business school I worked in our construction company, building large condominium complexes in Miami, and each year we had two or three deaths; one accepts there is a human cost to any industry."

Craine grinned weakly. "But I've had enough. I'm out. I want to close up shop. I just want to take my daughter and go, spend some time in Cannes, or in Cap Ferrat, put this behind me. Drink too much red wine, get fat on foie gras . . ."

"And if I take the money . . ."

"If you take the money, you could do the same. Get a tan, drink wine, get fat eating whatever you want! Although, no offense, I don't think either of us want to look up from our glass of house red and see the other across the restaurant."

"How will you know if I live up to my end of the bargain? How will you know I didn't just walk into Major Crimes and lay it all out for them?"

Craine shook his head in feigned disappointment. "Doctor Jenner, I'll know what your statement says before you walk out of the interrogation room. Trust me on that."

He stood and put on his sunglasses. "I don't mean to be melodramatic, but it's an easy choice, doctor: you can walk away rich, or die poor."

Jenner looked at the heap of money on the bed.

"Oh, for Christ's sake – just say yes!" Craine leaned against the back of the door, smiling. "I don't want to pack that fucking bag again!"

Jenner turned to him.

"Yes."

93

A faint, coppery smell of sweat and paper and coin rose from the cash. Jenner selected packets of bills, riffled them to see they were all real, not just real hundreds disguising stacks of white paper. He pulled notes out at random, squinted at them looking for forgeries; he didn't really know how to spot a good forgery, but these looked real, and when he held them to the bedside lamp, a ghostly gray watermark appeared in every one.

They were real.

He grabbed the overnight bag and scrutinized it. How large were electronic trackers? On TV they were tiny, but what about in real life?

Jenner opened his jackknife and cut into the lining of the bag, tearing it up with a coarse rip as the blade sawed along the thick green fabric. It took several cuts to free the lining completely; underneath, Jenner saw nothing that wasn't leather or some structural element from the world of luxury luggage.

He shoveled the cash back into the bag, zipped it, then carried it into the bathroom. He was surprised at the weight – a good fifty pounds, he figured. He wedged the bag under the vanity, then draped a towel over the portion that stuck out and slid the stool in front of it for additional cover. He reached into the shower stall and turned the tap.

With the water roaring, Jenner went back into the main room, pulling the bathroom door shut behind him. He grabbed his car keys and sunglasses and stepped out into the hallway, turning to drape the DO NOT DISTURB sign over the doorknob.

94

Twenty minutes later, Jenner returned to his room carrying two Winn-Dixie shopping bags. The sign was still on the doorknob, the roar of rushing water still coming from the shower. Under the vanity, the bag was untouched. And he was pretty sure that no one had followed him.

He tossed the bag of rubber bands onto the bed, then a box of contractor-weight heavy-duty garbage bags. He set one of the empty Winn-Dixie paper bags on the floor between his feet, and went through the packets one by one. Some were professionally wrapped with paper binding ribbon, while others were held together by rubber bands; Jenner tore off the wrappers and the rubber bands, discarding them into the paper bag at his feet, and replacing them with fresh rubber bands.

The packets were mostly in hundreds, the bills non-consecutively numbered. Some of the notes were pristine, and a smaller number were ready for shredding, but generally the cash was in fair to good condition.

It took Jenner an hour to go through the money; when he finished, he had a heap of $835,000 in used currency, apparently unmarked and untraceable. He took a laundry bag from the closet and shoved $100,000 into it. He divided the remaining packets between two heavy-duty garbage bags and then jammed the gutted overnight bag and its torn-out lining into a third.

It was 10:30 a.m. Everything was packed. Bartley was expecting him at noon; he had no intention of leaving close to a million dollars in cash in his car any longer than he had to, even in the Municipal Building parking lot.

He decided to swim for a few minutes. He pushed the garbage bags back under the vanity; they fitted better than the leather overnight bag had, but enough plastic poked out that Jenner again covered them with towels.

He dug through his clothes bags until he found his swimsuit. He changed, then put on a white terry-cloth hotel robe. He turned on the shower again, then went out into the hall in bare feet, checking that the DO NOT DISTURB sign was still on the knob before he headed to the elevator.

The elevator came to rest on the garden level, between the pool and the patio restaurant. Jenner walked between them, staying on the warm, soft grass of the croquet lawn, and then stepped onto the boardwalk.

The hotel owned a small stretch of beach, cordoned off from the common sand by a series of hip-height partition shades emblazoned with the hotel's tasteful logo. A grid of old-fashioned wooden deck chairs, sparsely occupied, filled the space; a barman in a white shirt and black slacks waited patiently under the large parasol that covered the wet bar back near the wall of sea-grape trees.

Jenner tossed his robe onto a deck chair, then walked to the water's edge, feeling the wet sand slip and then compact between his toes, watching the clear water wash over his feet. It was surprisingly cool. He stepped quickly into the surf, gasping as the water rushed around him, feeling the goose bumps rise on his legs and flanks.

He swam out a ways, and floated on his back, feeling the water's gentle shove toward shore; the cuts on his back prickled and stung with the pressure of the waves. He felt himself sliding in too quickly, so he straightened to tread water. He looked out over the sea; seen from the water, the Gulf of Mexico was a deep indigo, a slowly shifting dark mass that raced out to the horizon to meet the pale sky.

Jenner looked back at the hotel, trying to pick out his room. He was swimming back to the beach when he finally spotted it – the window was open. He'd left it that way, not on purpose, but it helped him locate it.

He walked back to the deck chair enclosure, shaking off the sand that clumped on his feet. He turned his deck chair to face the hotel; the towel boy rushed to help him, then positioned the chair's back so that Jenner would be comfortable. Jenner ordered a Cuba Libre, then spread the white towel on the seat, and sat.

The drink appeared almost instantly. Jenner set it on

the broad chair arm; although he hadn't noticed it because of the breeze, the day was humid; a mist of condensation formed quickly on the glass and trickled down the sides in dark rivulets. From this part of the enclosure Jenner could see his room clearly, even while seated. He relaxed.

Behind him, the surge of the sea softened and fell away.

95

Jenner couldn't let go, not with all that money in his room.

After a few minutes, he settled his tab, put his T-shirt back on, and walked back up the boardwalk ramp to the hotel grounds. As he was about to cut across the croquet lawn, he noticed a young woman talking to two friends in front of the elevator; he hadn't seen her in her glasses before, but Jenner knew her immediately: Sheree Roburn.

Jenner hung back, waiting in the shadows of the seagrape trees. When Sheree's group had got on the elevator he slipped quickly across the lawn before she reached her room, looked out and saw him down there.

96

As Jenner looked for a spot at the parking lot of the Municipal Building, creeping past cop cars and uniformed officers who were on foot, he could almost *feel* the money in the trunk, feel it expanding, breathing, sending out signals . . . The three bags of cash were jammed right at the bottom of the luggage compartment, flattened against the carpet, hidden by a layer of loose clothes, the clothes covered in turn with the garbage bags filled with his belongings.

Bartley was out front having a smoke as Jenner walked up to the building entrance.

"Hey, doc. Good timing. Mind if I finish this one? It's been a hell of a night."

Jenner nodded. "I bet."

A converted school bus drew up to the curb in front of them, its windows covered by grids of thick metal. It had been repainted white, and bore the county-jail insignia. A half-dozen men in bright orange jumpsuits sat quietly inside, with three guards lounging up front. The door opened and one of the guards climbed out.

The corrections officer nodded at Bartley. "Morning, Barts." He shot Jenner a quick glance and added, "Sir."

"Yo, Crispo! Taking your mutts out for a walk?"

Crispo stopped and shook his head wearily; he spat, bummed a cigarette from Bartley and fired it up.

"They got me on Polo Club detail today. It's supposed to hit ninety-five degrees later, and they want my boys to pick up trash, rake, then edge the drive, the carriage circle and the entire goddam length of the property along Lakewood East!"

Bartley puffed his cigarette, and said, "Sounds about right – it'll give 'em a chance to say hi to the crooked State Attorneys who put them away, the scumbag lawyers who failed to defend them, and the corrupt judges who sentenced them . . ."

Jenner looked at the bus, then over to his car. He imagined an inmate slipping out of a window, sprinting the forty feet or so, and tearing off in the Sebring.

Crispo wouldn't let it go. "Seriously, Bartley – don't you think it's bullshit? Why not the hospital grounds? Why not Burmeister Park? These country-club fuckers can afford to pay for their own help. Shee-it!" He spat again; he had a rectangular gap in his upper teeth.

The detective snorted. "Jesus, Crispo – didn't you grow up here? The only thing I can't believe is how you can't believe this."

Two uniformed cops came out of the building and marched to the flagpole near where Jenner, Bartley and Crispo stood. The younger cop busied himself somewhat self-consciously with the halyard on the pole, the older one – a sergeant – moving back a few paces to watch the flags. Everyone in the plaza in front of the building stopped; the civilians stood still, some with heads bowed, others with hands over their hearts. The cops stood at attention. The two other C.O.'s got out of the bus and stood stiffly by the doorway.

They lowered the Florida flag first, a big red X on a white background. The young guy worked the rope, the sergeant monitoring the height. When the flag was at half-mast the officer tethered it to the cleat and then lowered the Stars and Stripes. They stepped back from the flagpole and snapped to a salute, and then every law enforcement officer on the plaza was saluting, and the aqua-tinted windows behind them were filled with cops, all saluting the flag, all saluting Rudge.

They stood that way for a minute, at full attention. It was midday, and the magnesium-hot sun was high

342

overhead, Jenner's shadow a stunted puddle at his feet. From the new development beyond the small wood behind them, he heard floating snatches of ice-cream-van music.

The sergeant released his salute, then turned smartly and marched back into the building, followed by the rookie. The cops and civilians in the plaza thawed, and the day went on.

Bartley nodded at Crispo, turned to Jenner and said, "Come on, doc. I know you want to get out of here, and we've got things to do – I don't think we need to keep you long."

97

The interrogation room smelled of stale sweat. As the video technician set up the camera, Jenner tried to figure out which of the detectives was the bent one, Bartley or his partner; maybe they both were.

He was surprised that they were videotaping it – probably Craine's idea, locking Jenner down into his false statement.

The tech gave the thumbs up, and Bartley kicked off with a summary of the date, time and location, and identified the law enforcement personnel present. Then he had Jenner say that he'd come to the Major Crimes department out of his own volition, that his statement would honestly and accurately reflect his observations, and that it had not been coerced in any way.

Their questioning was perfunctory, mostly a repeat of

the stuff Bartley had covered during the night at Rudge's house. The ATF agent got all woody again about UFL Tomato, even though Jenner said nothing remarkable had happened there, other than feeble attempts at spin control. The ATF agent also raised the possibility of Amanda Tucker being the intended target of the bombing, but no one took that very seriously, including the agent himself.

Jenner was neutral about La Grulla Blanca – he implied that they'd been greeted politely, if not warmly, and said the foreman had answered their questions brusquely but without real incident. He couldn't recall a point in their investigation when they'd come across clear animosity, and, while he hadn't been with Rudge every second of every day, he had personally received no threats. In short, he had no idea why he and Rudge had been targeted.

Then Bartley asked if he had a weapon, and Jenner said, "Nope. They don't look kindly on guns up in New York." No need to mention the 9mm under his front seat.

The specter of Northeastern liberalism set Bartley off. "Doc, seriously, screw that! If you're staying in Florida, we'll fix you up with a carry permit. Can you shoot?"

Jenner nodded. "Yeah. But don't sweat it, detective – I'm heading back to New York this afternoon. I'll come back down for Rudge's funeral next week."

"Well, you'll have to wait a little, doc. His cousin Reggie said the Jewish Burial folks are going to fly him up to Chicago for free – that's where his brother is. We'll have a memorial service in a month or so, when things have calmed down a bit."

"Ah."

"Well, OK, then, doc." Bartley shuffled his papers.

"This is still a mystery and a tragedy – we really have nothing to go on. Forensics didn't find anything useful at Rudge's house, the bomb-disposal people did the usual song and dance about how the testing will take a while, but basically said it looks like a big pipe bomb, probably dynamite. We got no leads on the Roburns, and the dead men from the hammock . . . well, they're still dead."

He stood and looked down at Jenner. "You heading out today?"

Jenner nodded. Bartley shook his hand, leaned in and said, "Good luck!"

For a second Jenner thought he might not be crooked after all.

But only for a second.

98

Jenner made his goodbyes at the morgue quick; it was awkward as hell for all of them.

Flanagan walked him out to the car. Clapped a hand on his shoulder, shook his hand and wished him well. He watched Jenner drive through the electric gates for the last time.

And then Jenner was free.

His spirits lifted as he drove under the scrub oaks on Municipal Drive for the last time.

He made good time to the Southland Mall. He parked in front of the Outback Steakhouse; before he picked up the dog, he had business to take care of. He left the air conditioner on and unplugged his cell from the charger.

Garcia picked up on the second ring. "Lieutenant Garcia, Manhattan South Homicide."

"Rad, it's Jenner."

"Jenner! Jesus! I'm glad to hear your voice." Jenner smiled. "You okay? We saw your motel on the news last night, and Dulcie says it's time for you to come home, get the fuck outta that fuckin' swamp."

"I'm almost finished up down here." Jenner paused. "This a safe line, Rad?"

"This is my direct line. Doesn't even go through the switchboard." He was serious now. "What's up?"

"I need a solid contact in the South Florida D.E.A. office."

"What you got?"

"This whole thing is all about methamphetamine. And I'm talking Mexican cartel connections, major distribution through the East Coast corridor, tens of millions a year."

Garcia whistled. "Mexican speed?"

"No, they're cooking it up right here," Jenner said. "It gets worse. You know Craine Brothers Medical?"

"Of course – '*Craine – when purity and excellence count.*' Dulcie won't buy any other baby powder."

"Well, Chip Craine is a major player in this. He owns the farm where they're making it, and they use his connections to get the precursor chemicals for the crystal."

"So this is what the killings are all about?"

"Yeah. It's all tied in, this whole place is one giant cesspool. And there's something else – there are bad cops down here. I don't trust anyone."

"Fuck." Garcia was silent for a while. Then he said,

"Okay. Let me make some enquiries – I doubt the D.E.A. has an office in Douglas, so it'll probably be Dade County or Broward. I'll find someone good and get back to you. Where you at now? You going to get out of town?"

"I'm almost gone already. Just got to pick something up and then I'll be on my way."

"Good. Just get the fuck outta there. What do you have as far as proof goes?"

Jenner thought for a second. "Not much, really."

"They're going to need something, Jenner."

"They'll find it at Craine's farm. Rudge – the detective who was killed last night – had a run-in with them yesterday afternoon, and that's what set them off. There was a delivery of precursor chemicals in a Craine Brothers truck the day before yesterday – those chemicals are controlled substances, so if they poke the CBM distribution records things will unravel pretty quickly." He breathed out slowly, then sighed, and said, "Also . . . Chip Craine paid me off."

"He gave you *cash*? Can you tie it to him?"

"Well, he'll be on the hotel surveillance video, but he gave me the money in my room. I broke it up into different bags to hide it, but I kept the original carry bag."

"Okay, keep that bag, maybe they can use that."

"Of course." Jenner could hear the detective scribbling. "Craine's going to skip the country today."

"Shit. Well, they won't have time to get the necessary warrants, but they can certainly start tracking him." More writing. "Shit! Okay, I'll move quickly."

Jenner heard the sound of a sheet of paper being torn off a pad. "Wait, Jenner. How much did he pay you?"

"A lot."

"Don't be a bitch, Jenner! Just how much are you worth?"

"One hundred thousand dollars."

"Whew!" Garcia whistled again. "It's going to sting to give that up, my friend!"

"Rad, you don't know the half of it . . ."

Garcia snorted. "Okay, Jenner – now, you promise me you'll get the fuck outta there right now. It's not safe there for you. You got a gun?"

"Everyone keeps asking me that today – yeah, I have a gun."

"Keep it cocked and locked, just in case, eh, buddy?"

"Okay."

"And Jenner? You sure you know where the safety is? Because last time . . ."

"Fuck you, Rad. Call me when you have a contact for me."

"Ha-ha. Okay, Jenner. You just get yourself the hell out of there ASAP; I promise you, by the time you hit fucking Disney World the drug boys will be breaking down fucking doors and knocking fucking heads."

Jenner grinned. "Team America!"

Rad said, "*Fuck yeah!*" and hung up.

99

Jenner called Deb Putnam. She was in the field, on the way to Bel Arbre; someone had reported kids riding four-wheelers in park grounds.

He said, "Hey. I wanted to see you to say goodbye."

She was quiet for a second, so he said, "Deb?"

"I heard you."

"Oh. I thought I lost the connection."

"Nah. I'm still here, at least until I really do lose the signal – service is terrible out here."

"Well, anyway."

"I shouldn't be too long up here. When are you leaving?"

"A few minutes. Just have to pick up the dog, and then I'll hit the road."

"Which way you going?"

"I was thinking I'd head across to Miami on Pelican Alley, then straight up I-95."

"Come up this way; you can go up via Tampa and across. Much better. Plus you can stop off here for a goodbye taco."

Jenner smiled. "Sounds like a plan."

Deb paused a second, then said, "No way you'd hang around a little? You could stay at my place, rest up, get some sun."

He was silent. She said, "I guess you just want to shake our dust from your feet . . ."

"I want to go home."

She was quiet again, so he said, "Maybe you should come up sometime – we have swordfish in New York, too, you know."

"Sure. But it's different when you're eating swordfish on a dock, looking out over the Gulf of Mexico at sunset."

Jenner said, "Yeah, well, it's also different eating swordfish on the fifth floor of a beautiful modern skyscraper looking over Central Park in fall through floor-to-ceiling windows. So, there's that."

"Well, I also read that swordfish has been overfished, so I'm cutting down on eating it." He could hear her smiling. "So there's that."

100

Jenner was relieved that the Mercedes wasn't at the shelter.

He rang the bell a couple of times before Dr. Ade appeared, slipping on her white coat.

"Oh, doctor, I'm so glad it's you."

He grinned at her. "So, how's the patient?"

Her face was serious. "He's fine – he's acting almost as if nothing ever happened. But there's something else, and it's urgent: Ms. Craine has been calling. She's lost your number." She scribbled the address on a yellow Post-It note and handed it to him. "She wants you to go to her house right away. I'll let her know you're on your way."

"What's this about?"

"She didn't say. But she's been calling every five minutes, so I think it's really important. Do you know where she lives?"

Jenner looked at the Post-It. "No. Is it far?"

"Five minutes. It's right next to the golf course, in a small gated community called the Polo Course. It's a white house with a blue gate. She'll buzz you in through the main gate – her house is the last one on the street."

She called to him as he was about to head out through the door. "And doctor?"

He turned.

Dr. Ade hesitated for a second, then said gravely, "I think she might be . . . drunk."

101

The Polo Course was a luxury development – seven or eight big houses on large plots, each one widely separated from its neighbors. The architectural styles were a potluck, from modernist glass and concrete to faux Mediterranean, but the group was united by immaculate lawns and shrubs, all meticulously trimmed to the regulation lengths laid out in the community bylaws.

Maggie Craine's was at the end, where Polo Course Lane curled into a cul-de-sac. It was the largest, a white clapboard house with a wraparound porch, carefully designed to evoke Old Florida. The borders of Maggie's lot were demarcated by handsome tall trees, already old before they'd been transplanted from their original location.

A Hispanic maid in a gray uniform and white pinafore let Jenner into the house. It was dark and cool, with glossy ebony floors and tall white sheers covering the windows. The maid gestured wordlessly to the gloom of the back of the house; she looked like she'd been crying.

He walked through the huge kitchen and out onto the back veranda. The veranda was screened in; it held a half-dozen empty outdoor sofas and chairs, and smelled of cigarettes.

The back garden was beautiful, an extravagant

outburst of tropical plants – clusters of big white Amazon lilies, spikes of red and orange heliconia, elephant-ear leaves the size of platters, still glistening from the previous night's rain; the air was sweet with the perfume of thick vines of shining jasmine dripping from an old mahogany tree. Jenner walked down the steps and made his way to a glassed-in cabin at the bottom of the garden, where a sentinel mynah bird tethered to a black metal stand hopped silently from foot to foot.

The cabin seemed to be built of glass casement windows, and as Jenner approached he saw that it was Maggie's studio. A big easel supporting a half-finished, brilliantly colored self-portrait in oils stood in one corner, the easel supports and the floor underneath thickly encrusted with dripped paint. More self-portraits leaned against the walls of the studio; most were portraits of Maggie's face, others were nudes, her body painted so that the breasts were lush and full, but her belly, flanks and hips were gaunt. To Jenner's eye, they owed a debt to the more luridly expressive painters, Schiele and Kokoschka, and perhaps Munch; also to Jenner's eye, they were adolescent and awful.

Maggie coughed and he turned to find her behind him. She was dressed in a paint-flecked man's shirt tied at the waist, and similarly spattered rolled jeans and espadrilles. Her hair was up in a ponytail, and her eyes were red.

"You hate them."

Jenner shook his head. "No, not at all. They're very striking, very . . . expressive."

She dismissed his comment with a wave of her hand. "I've been calling you at the shelter all afternoon."

"Why didn't you call my cell?"

She shrugged. "I deleted you."

He didn't react. She said, "She's gone, Jenner."

"Who?"

"Lucy." She fumbled for her cigarettes in her jeans pocket. "I think Daddy took her."

"Oh." He was confused. "Well, call his cell."

"He's not answering."

"When is your flight?"

"What flight?"

"He said you were going to France today."

"*What?*" She began to cry. "No! *No*, we're not going to France! Why would you think that?"

"That's what he said. I thought . . ."

"What did he say?"

"I think his words were something like 'I'm going to take my daughter to Cannes this afternoon.'"

Maggie was crying hard now. Jenner put a hand on her shoulder but she shook it off, weeping as she tried to put a cigarette in her mouth. He said, "I don't understand."

"He's taking *Lucy* to France!"

"Oh. I'm sorry, I misheard him."

She turned and raced across the garden to disappear into the house. He followed her, winding through the kitchen into the den. She was opening a small wall safe tucked into a bookcase; the door swung open to reveal several large envelopes, a jewelry box and stacked bundles of cash. Weeping, she held up a passport – hers.

"*He took her passport!*"

Then she sagged into a chair, put her face in her hands, and shook with sobs.

Jenner stood next to the chair, put a hand on her shoulder.

"Do you not want her to go?"

She sobbed, "Jenner! You never understand *anything*!"

"Listen – you're her mother. You're her legal next of kin; she's in your custody, and it's up to you whether she goes or not. Maybe you should call the police . . ."

"I *can't*! You *know* I can't!" Maggie's hair had come out of her ponytail, and she was mopping it across her face into her tears. "He *told* me he told you! You know! You *know*!"

He sat next to her. "Look, he doesn't have the right to take her. It's that simple. How would he get to France? Has he gone before?"

"We go at least four times a year." She sat up, face flushed. "There's a JetBlue flight at 7:30 p.m. from Fort Myers to Atlanta, and that connects with the 11:30 p.m. Delta flight to Charles de Gaulle."

"Okay, well, let's find them, then. It's almost two p.m. now, and it's, what, an hour's drive to Fort Myers? We've got almost four hours to find them. Have you been to Stella?"

Maggie snuffled. "I was there a little while ago – he's not there. He's closing it up. The staff have been moving valuables into storage and putting everything under covers since yesterday; he told them he's opening up the Connecticut house before the summer gets too bad here."

"Okay, well, where else could he be?"

"He doesn't go anywhere else. We have a boat, but it's in dry dock for a new keel. And that's it."

Jenner said, "Except the farm."

"Well, yes, I guess." Maggie nodded slowly. "Except the farm."

She was silent for a second; when she turned to Jenner,

354

her eyes were desperate and pleading.

He knew what she wanted, and he couldn't say no. He told her to stay at home in case Lucy came home, or her dad called, and said he'd call when he'd found them.

He entered his number into Maggie's cell phone again, then got into his car. He told her not to worry, and set off. She stood in the driveway and watched him leave.

102

Deb Putnam steadied the clipboard on the hood of her jeep to write the citations. The four boys sat on their ATVs, watching her with amusement. She didn't know these boys, but she knew their type – she'd been dealing with their sort for the last five years now. And their family names were immediately familiar.

She thought about how funny it was that, for all that America was the Land of the Free and the Home of the Brave, dynasties were just as central in the New World now as they'd ever been in the Old. She didn't know if she knew their surnames from busting their brothers doing the same thing, but in Douglas County it was just as likely that their father owned the bank that held her mortgage, or the dealership where she bought her Miata, or the company that made her birth-control pills.

The thing was, if Deb recognized their names, chances were they were rich, and the fine would be meaningless, and there was no reason for them not to go tearing through the sawgrass and bogs, trashing the terrain and filling the air with blue smoke and engine din.

She laid out their driver's licenses on the hood in a neat row and sighed; all four lived in the Beaches. Big surprise.

She glanced back at them, and immediately one of the little fuckers looked away, his face flushing deep red; he'd been checking out her ass! Great! Horny little environment-destroying cretin! What was he, sixteen years old, seventeen tops?

Deb supposed the boy was at *that* age. She decided to take it as a compliment, but mostly it was just irritating. And it was hot and sweaty out here, and Jenner hadn't called to say when they'd meet.

Two of Captain Bashful's friends were yakking on their cell phones, not at all worried or concerned – at their age she'd have been petrified. The fourth had taken off his shirt and was stretched out on his four-wheeler working on his tan, the long bill of his Polo Grounds cap tilted coolly over his face.

She liked writing the citations out longhand – once she'd started, she could show the perp the pressure copy underneath, so they'd know there was no way she could tear it up. By that point they'd usually gotten over their astonishment that a park ranger could write a traffic ticket and were embracing the anger, in their outrage implying that she'd somehow sandbagged them.

Deb had just finished the fourth citation when she saw Jenner's blue Sebring drive by – he was moving fast. She cursed under her breath and pulled out her cell; the display showed a couple of bars, but immediately dropped them. He'd probably been trying to reach her but hadn't got through because of the shitty reception in the Glades.

A couple of minutes later, an unmarked county car, a cream Taurus, flew by, heading north after Jenner toward Bel Arbre; to Deb's surprise, she recognized Tom Nash at the wheel. Even odder, he was in plainclothes. She wondered if there'd been a killing in Bel Arbre, then remembered that Jenner was finished as the M.E. now.

She turned to the boys and handed out the paperwork. "There you go, gentlemen. I'll be calling your parents, just to make sure the word doesn't slip through the cracks."

The tall, tan kid smirked and said, "Thanks, officer. And our parents will be calling your boss, just to make sure their gratitude for you not shooting us doesn't slip through the cracks."

His boys snorted as Deb rolled her eyes and tapped the Glock at her hip.

"If we didn't have to fill out so much paperwork for shooting someone, things might've gone differently." She smiled sweetly. "Now, please remember to think twice the next time you decide to ruin a beautiful ecosystem!"

She started the jeep. She didn't have turret lights, but if she hurried she might be able to catch Jenner. The boys were peering dully at the citations; she was sure the tickets would be in the trash in under fifteen minutes. Or, far more likely, blowing across the beautiful ecosystem.

As she pulled out onto the road, turning towards Bel Arbre, Suntan Boy followed her, grinning. He called out, "Yo, Ranger! Thanks for this! This is the start of the best 'How I Spent My Summer Vacation' essay *ever*!" His toadies all fell about laughing on their ATVs, way overplaying their parts.

Deb headed north, half an eye on the rearview mirror,

wanting to see what they'd do. They didn't disappoint her: Suntan Boy climbed onto his four-wheeler, stood high off his saddle and, when she was at a safe distance, dropped his pants and pointed his ass in her direction.

She laughed out loud – now *that* was something she'd have done at their age!

103

Jenner was a few miles south of Bel Arbre when he saw the blue light flashing behind him.

This is it, he thought.

As he pulled over, he felt under his seat for his Beretta; during the drive the gun had slid further back. His fingers touched the diamond grid of the grip, felt the cool metal, solid and inert. He tried to coax it forward with his fingertips while sitting upright, but the weapon was too heavy to budge easily.

In the rearview mirror Jenner saw a late-model Taurus with a blue dashboard light; he couldn't see – or count – the occupants. Could they see him? Would they see him if he bent to extricate the pistol from under the seat?

He decided not to risk it. He put both his hands up on the dashboard; he wasn't going to give any motherfucker an excuse to "accidentally" shoot him. He imagined the cop shooting him in the head while he sat in his car, the whole thing caught on dashboard camera. Imagined Robin Meade playing the video on *Headline News* the next morning, warning viewers that the footage they were about to see might be disturbing to some. Imagined the blocky white numbers of the date/time stamp ticking away in the lower part of the video as the cop approached Jenner's car and shot him dead.

Then it occurred to him that an unmarked car wouldn't have a dashboard cam. He smiled grimly – his murder would go unwitnessed on national television.

The cop had parked ten yards behind him on the shoulder. The area was remote – traffic between Port Fontaine and Bel Arbre was light, and at this time of day there'd be a good ten minutes between vehicles.

Jenner rolled down the windows, then killed the engine. The heat flowed into the car, with it the chatter of birds. The fields that stretched out to the swamp were like the ones that Adam Weiss had staggered out of: long rows of plants. But the harvest was over now, and these plants were bare, just straggly green stalks wilting in the heat.

Behind him, in the Taurus, he could make out the driver – a single male, he was pretty sure now – talking on his cell or radio. The cop had shut the dashboard light off; he probably didn't want to attract attention.

Finally, the man opened his door and climbed out to stand between the door and frame, looking Jenner's car over slowly.

There was the blast of a horn; a truck loaded with vegetables covered in white plastic sheeting was behind the cop car, the road too narrow for it to pass without the cop shutting his door. As the cop waved to the driver and began to climb back inside, Jenner quickly bent forward and scrambled for his pistol, sweeping his fingers desperately between the underseat metal struts. It was hopeless – he must've adjusted the seat since stashing the

359

handgun, because there was barely an inch gap. He straightened as the truck passed, four Latino workers peering at him over the backboard.

He put his hands back on the dash.

In the mirror, the man got out of the car again. He wore jeans and a T-shirt, but Jenner could see the weapon at his hip.

Jenner recognized Nash, the deputy who'd helped recover Marty Roburn's body. He saw Nash's hand dip to his waist, pop the back strap on the holster. As he came closer, Jenner could almost hear the quiet creak and click as the open strap flapped against the holster tab.

Nash approached from the driver's side, pistol in hand; he was careful to stay slightly behind the driver's compartment. Clever – Jenner couldn't see Nash properly, and if he tried to pull a weapon on Nash he'd have to make such an awkward turn that the deputy could drop him before Jenner could even face him. It was slick, probably some standard cop trick. Or maybe just something he'd learned on TV.

"Hey, doc."

"Nash."

The deputy gave an awkward grin. "Sorry it has to be like this."

"Me too. I thought you were a decent guy."

Nash flushed, then the grin came back and he said, "Well, doc, I thought you were, too. And yet, here we are . . ."

They were both silent, then Jenner said, "So what happens now? Are you here to kill me?"

Nash shook his head quickly. "Oh gosh, *no*, doc! I'm a low man, you're talking to a low man here – I do minor shit, and they pay me minor money. I still sleep at night."

"So you're not going to kill me."

"Hell, no. Word has come down that too many dead people are bringing too much heat. You're good to go – unless you decide to make trouble up in New York. *Then* they'll do something – but it won't be me. And they say that's all up to you. Mister Craine says they've already got your statement on video, so it'll be a lot harder for you to change directions now."

"So what's this about?"

"Come on, doc! You know why I'm here: you have something that belongs to my employer, and he wants it back."

"I do?"

He rolled his eyes. "The money, doc! Mr. Craine wants his money back – sorry, but you don't get to keep it."

"Oh, the *money*." Jenner said. "It's in the trunk."

"I'm going to need you to get out of the car, open the trunk, get the cash, and stick it in the Taurus, okay?"

"I could just pop the trunk for you, if you'd like."

"You're a funny guy, doc! 'Pop the trunk' – I like that!" Nash grinned thinly. "I don't care what they say about you – you're all right!"

Nash wiped his forehead with the back of the fist that held the Glock. Jenner wondered if he was sweating as much as Nash.

Nash said, "Well, let's keep our friendship going. You move the bags, and I watch you move them. And then you head back to New York, and I head wherever I have to with the money. Okay?"

Jenner opened the door. Nash stepped back; he was smiling but wary.

"Okay, doc. Go easy now – they say you don't have a gun, but if *I* had a million in cash, I'd sure as shit be packing a goddam cannon . . ."

Jenner said, "I don't have a gun."

"Well, doc, I do. Now nice and easy, and in three minutes you're on your way, dreaming of bagels and Yankee Stadium . . ."

"We're on the same page."

He opened the trunk.

"Hold it!" Nash said, "Let me look first."

Jenner stood on the grass while Nash, half-turned towards him, quickly searched the trunk, lifting the garbage bags, feeling their weight, patting down the carpet.

"Okay, doc. Go for it."

Nash pointed his key fob at the Taurus; there was a quiet clunk, and the trunk opened slightly.

Jenner needed the laundry bag with at least some of the money, needed the leather overnight bag. He *had* to hang on to some kind of proof.

He scooped his clothes aside; quickly tipping his cell phone into the trunk, he hit redial. Leaning in to block Nash's view, he shoved the hotel laundry bag into one of the bags that held his clothes, then made a show of yanking the two bags of cash together; the original leather carry bag, now thoroughly dissected, he left underneath.

"Hey, a coupla things. First, I dumped the carrier bag Craine gave me and divided the money into different bags – I didn't know if the original had some kind of tracker device on it."

"A tracker device? Smart move, doc! I like that – don't think I woulda thought of that. What else?"

"I don't know how much money they told you they

gave me but I only counted $735,000. It was never a million."

Nash's eyes narrowed. "You sure about that? You don't want to fuck around with these people. These are very bad people . . ."

"Look, I don't know if Craine is playing some kind of game here, but that's all the money he gave me. You can ask him."

Nash relaxed and shrugged. "Okay – your funeral. You realize you're almost out, right? Almost home? You don't want to fuck this up now."

Jenner looked at Nash's Glock; Nash glanced down, and said, "Yeah, sorry, but I gotta be careful with you – I read what you did to that guy in New York. Trust me, I don't want to use it."

He grinned, then gestured with the Glock towards the Taurus. "Okay, let's do this. Let's get you back home quick, okay?"

There was the cheery toot of a horn, and they turned to see Deb Putnam's jeep pulling in behind Nash's Taurus.

She leaned out of the window beaming, and called out, "Hey, Jenner! Hey, Tom! Is this Boys Only, or can girls play too?"

104

As Deb got out of the car, Nash murmured, "Doc, don't make me shoot her; I like her more than I like you. And if I shoot her, I have to shoot you, too – please don't pull anything stupid."

"I won't."

She walked over to them, smiling; Jenner saw she was wearing her weapon.

"Hi, guys. What's up?"

Nash was standing close in behind the Sebring, right arm held straight down so that Deb couldn't see his pistol.

"Hey there, Deb. Not much."

Jenner nodded at her. "Hi. Sorry I didn't get through to you."

She smiled. "It's okay, Jenner – I've been out on the mud all morning, busting rich little pricks from the Beaches riding their four-wheelers in protected wetlands."

She glanced in the open trunk, at Jenner's bags of clothes. "You two look like you're up to no good!"

Nash looked blankly at Jenner.

Jenner said, "The ATF wants to send some of my stuff from the bombing to the federal lab in DC, test it for explosives residue and whatnot; Deputy Nash was kind enough to meet me halfway to pick it up."

Deb frowned. "Why didn't you do it in Port Fontaine? That would've been a lot simpler."

"Timing. I wanted to get on my way, and I was going to meet you in Bel Arbre, and Nash was heading up here anyway, so we just figured we'd meet up here."

"You shoulda waited and done it at the substation in Bel Arbre – air conditioning!" She was cheery. "Okay, well, let's get that stuff moved, then get some lunch."

Deb looked over at Nash. She hesitated a second, then said, "Hey, Tom, want to join us for a farewell taco?" Her tone was measured and completely uninviting.

Nash shook his head. "Nah, thanks, Deb. I gotta get

this stuff back to the lab pretty quick; they want it up in D.C. right away."

Jenner picked up a bag; before he could stop her, Deb reached in and grabbed one of his clothes bags. It slipped open and the laundry bag fell out, spilling packets of hundreds across the trunk's carpet.

"Whoa."

She stepped back and turned to stare at Jenner, then turned back to the car.

"Deb, don't."

But she leaned in, grabbed one of the knotted garbage bags, pushed a finger into the thick plastic. The dark plastic film stretched pale gray, then tore raggedly and she jammed her other hand in and pulled her fingers apart to rip a big gape into the side of the bag.

The bag looked like it was filled with kryptonite, all the money glowing pale green in the black plastic shell.

As she stepped back, Deb saw Nash's Glock in his hand. She looked him in the eye, then went for her own pistol – and Nash shot her.

105

Brodie stood on the farmhouse porch, looking at the bunkhouses. The blenders in Bunkhouse A had been grinding all day, crushing cold medications into the powder that was the raw material for making methamphetamine.

But they didn't have enough time. This fucking thing was blown, and there wasn't enough time, and Brodie knew it.

The cook cycle still needed a good thirty-six hours, and he didn't think they had it any more. But he'd received his orders and he had no choice. The pseudoephedrine had been processed, and the cooks were in the kitchen. In thirty-six hours, they'd have another forty pounds of pure meth, with a street value – once the middlemen had cut down the purity – of well over a million; that wasn't chicken feed.

How much time before the bust? It had to come, and come soon. Brodie had learned in California that it didn't matter how many cops you had on your team: if one died, they all came after you. Craine was connected, sure, but not connected enough to stop that vengeance wave when it came. Their best hope was that the locals wouldn't get their act together – it would take the Feds a couple of days at least to pull their thumbs out of their asses and greenlight a strike team on some rich guy's property.

Of course, it was cake for some guy sitting at a desk in a shabby office in Tepalcatepec to tell them to risk everything to finish that last batch – he, after all, risked nothing. But that was the nature of the business.

That morning, when word had come to close up shop after this cycle, Brodie had taken it as a sign. This would be a good time to retire. Two more days – finish the production and the distribution – then he'd fly down to Costa Rica, take a cab to his beautiful villa on the mountainside in Playa Hermosa, and unpack for the last time. He'd shower off the filth of the last three years, scrub himself until his skin was pink and stinging, then walk naked through his palatial home and climb into that beautiful pool, cantilevered out over the mountainside, the pool's invisible edge fusing with the horizon so that it

366

looked like he could swim forever. And he'd float in the warm water and look at the stars and think about the millions in cash buried in the grounds and buildings in insulated steel cases, and it would be the last time he would ever let himself think of the things he'd done to get that pool.

The western sky had grown dark and heavy, the clouds sinking onto the horizon; it'd rain soon. Down the slope, a farmhand chased a loose piglet across the field, laughing, driving it back toward the feeding pen.

The pathologist was pretty much buttoned up now, Brodie figured – too compromised to be a threat. It had cost Craine a little cash, but nothing compared to what that rich fucker had raked in over the last couple of years.

Brodie hated the way the cartel handled Craine, all white gloves and finger sandwiches. One time in Sinaloa, he'd watched them cut the ears off every member of some poor bastard's family when they thought he'd shorted them – cut the ears off the grandmother, the father, the wife, the daughter, the baby. It made him sick that they pulled shit like that while they massaged Craine like a prize cow – filled his offshore accounts to overflowing, gave him cash by the bucket load, fed his hunger for skinny little girls.

Brodie spat. The fucker made him puke. Craine was staying at the farm that night, and Brodie would have to listen to him prance around like some kind of criminal mastermind. The man was totally in awe of himself, his supposed ability to straddle two worlds: one foot on the top rung of Port Fontaine society, the other in narco-trafficking. And that was the word Craine used – *narcotrafficking.*

Fucker.

In front of Bunkhouse A, Tarver and Bentas were bickering like an old couple; Tony sat on a chair, watching in mute disgust.

Brodie's lip curled. God, Tarver was a loathsome fuck. Tomorrow, when everything wound down, they'd do a clean-up operation and then they'd clear out. Brodie had decided that, son-in-law or not, Tarver was one of the things that needed cleaning up.

The thought cheered him, and as he felt the first drops of rain strike his face he looked up and grinned. His daughter would never know exactly what happened – this was a high-risk business and bad things happened all the time. When she got out, her life would be all the better for being rid of that psycho.

Besides, it would leave the world a better place.

106

"Jenner! Get her gun! Get her pistol. *Now!*"

Nash was near-hysterical. Deb lay there, eyes shut tight from the pain, arm pressed across her belly.

Jenner tried to keep Nash calm as he leaned over Deb's body, moving and speaking slowly. "Okay . . . I'm going to take her pistol out now."

"*Don't move!*"

Jenner didn't move. He squatted next to Deb, his reaching hand frozen in mid-air, the muzzle of Nash's gun now floating in front of his face.

As he stared at the pistol, the black hole of the muzzle

wavered and bobbed; Nash was losing it.

"Okay, Nash. I need you to listen to me."

"*What?*"

"I need to look at her . . . Just let me see if she's badly hurt, okay?"

Nash squinted down at them, his eyes filling with tears.

"I want you to move her gun first!" It came out as a squeak, a plea from a frightened boy. "I'm going to stand behind you – my weapon will be pointed right at your head, man."

Jenner said, "I only want to help her. I don't care about you, or the shooting – I know it was an accident. I know you didn't mean to do it. I just want to look after her, make sure she's okay."

He looked up at Nash. The cop's face was wet with tears, watery snot trickling from his nose as he sobbed.

"Come on, Tom. Let me help her. I'm a doctor, just let me help her."

Nash nodded. "I didn't want it to be like this – you gotta understand."

"I know. I saw it – it was an accident. You were looking at her and the gun just . . . went off."

Jenner was surprised by the first drops of cool rain. He leaned over Deb to keep her dry, then wondered why. Across her belly, her khaki shirt was already soaked with blood.

He did what Nash wanted.

"Okay, Tom, you see? I've snapped open her holster . . . I'm going to take the butt of the gun between just my thumb and finger, see?"

Nash nodded again. "Jenner, please, you gotta believe me. Mr. Craine just told me to get his money back. He

369

told me there wouldn't be a problem. Why did Deb have to come along?"

The gun was wobbling in Nash's hand. Christ – Jenner didn't even want to think about what would happen if a car passed them.

Jenner said, "Keep it together, Tom. I need you to keep breathing, just be steady now, okay? Pull it together. I think she's going to be fine, okay? Just hang in there . . ."

He showed Nash her gun, dangling from his fingers.

"Okay – I have her weapon. Where do you want it?"

"Throw it over toward my car."

Jenner tossed the pistol, but with the gun's weight and the two-fingered throw from his weaker arm, the pistol landed less than six feet from him. Nash circled round to the weapon, kicked it further away, and kept his Glock on Jenner as he squatted to pick Deb's gun up. He jammed it into the back of his waistband.

"Now get me her cell phone. And I want yours, too."

Jenner unclipped Deb's phone from her utility belt. He made a show of searching his pockets, then looked up at Nash. "I don't have mine. Must be in the car."

"Find it."

Jenner stood reluctantly. "I should look at her first."

"No. Find your phone first, then you can look at her."

Jenner walked to the car and leaned into the open trunk. He moved the money, glanced at his phone. The screen was dark now; either the cell had lost the connection or the battery had died. But at what point? Had Rad heard the shot? He made a show of looking around a little longer, then shut the phone and announced, "Here it is."

370

He handed it to Nash, who said, "Okay. You can go ahead."

Jenner knelt to examine Deb. He tugged her shirt up, untucked the tank top underneath and yanked it up, too. His hands were quickly slick with blood.

He pulled the tank top down and wiped her belly with it.

There was a dark hole the size of a penny below her rib cage on the left. Jenner pressed it gently; blood welled out freely.

Deb flinched, her eyes open.

"Jenner . . ."

"Deb, I need to turn you on your side, okay?"

"He shot me."

"I'm sorry – this is going to hurt a bit . . ."

She grimaced as he rolled her to the right, but she brought up her knee to brace herself and moved silently into the turn.

"Why did he shoot me?"

"Shhh . . . Let me have a look at you, then we can talk."

Deb's back was smeared with blood, too; there was a ragged little slit in her left flank where the bullet had exited.

"Can you breathe okay?"

"Why is all that money in your car?"

Jenner rolled her back flat; again, she flinched, then lay still, breathing fast.

"We'll talk in a second."

He pulled her shirt higher, above her bra, then leaned over to press his ear against her chest.

"Take a deep breath."

Deb put a hand on Jenner's head and tried feebly to

push him away, then gave up and let her arm down. Close to her skin, he could smell the blood now, feel his ear sticking to her skin. She coughed, then inhaled sharply; he heard her breath sliding clearly in and out of her lungs. He listened on the other side of her chest, also okay. He laid his left hand flat on her chest, then tapped it firmly with his right hand; the sound was hollow. Her chest was not filled with blood; the bullet had passed lower.

Jenner sat up. The drizzle swelled to a roar, the rain pelting down on them. He watched blankly the blood on her belly turned pink and thin, and washed off into the grass.

The wound site below her rib cage meant possible injuries of her spleen, liver, stomach, pancreas, left kidney. Intestine. A thousand arteries and veins. But the hole was far enough to the side that her liver and stomach had probably been spared; he was more worried about her kidney and spleen, because they could really bleed. And all the fucking arteries and veins.

Jenner leaned over Deb, staring at her injury, shielding her from the rain with his back. She was looking up at him. He took her wrist, felt her pulse. Fast, but strong; a good baseline. Maybe it was just soft tissue and muscle . . .

"Jenner? Where did you get that money?" Deb pulled her wrist from his grip. "Did you kill Rudge?"

Her hand floated down to lie across her chest. Her eyelids blinked weakly; her voice was quiet. "Did you kill . . . *Dr. Roburn?*"

107

Nash motioned down the highway, tapped the barrel of his gun against the Taurus's windshield and said, "Drive faster, Jenner."

Jenner glanced back at Deb, stretched out on the garbage bags that Nash had taken from his car.

Nash was sharper now that the initial shock of actually having shot someone was subsiding. He'd taken their cell phones and thrown them out on the highway.

"Faster – I want to get off the street."

They passed the combination piñata shop and Haitian hair salon, a former gas station painted an electric blue on the Mexican side and bright pink on the Haitian. They'd reached Bel Arbre.

Nash lowered the gun to his lap, keeping it trained on Jenner. He was being careful to stay as far from Jenner as he could, pressing himself against the door, waiting for Jenner to try something reckless.

"Okay, now, be cool. We're about to pass the sheriff's substation, on the left."

They'd entered downtown Bel Arbre – all six or so blocks of it. The streets were dark in the downpour, the backlit signs and streaks of neon blurring brightly in the windshield. Taco Bell, furniture stores, check cashing, a 7-11. Cars on the street, people on the sidewalk hurrying through the steady rain.

Nash said, "Slow down, drive careful. No stopping."

The rain eased to a drizzle. Jenner did as he was told, listening half to Nash, half to Deb's shallow breathing. He needed to get her to a hospital; it seemed more than just a perforating soft-tissue injury.

"Fuck! *Fuck fuck fuck* . . ." Nash's voice had turned desperate again, and Jenner saw why: up ahead, idling in the middle of the road, two police cruisers had pulled level with each other, one facing north, the other south. Periodically, a tan arm poked out of the cop car in their lane to gesture emphatically.

Several cars ahead of them slowed to a halt behind the cruiser; no one in this town would give the cops grief. They were in no hurry.

"What do you want me to do?"

Nash shook his head. "I don't know! Let me think . . ."

Jenner said, "I can turn here, go a block east, then a few blocks north before cutting back onto the highway."

Nash nodded. "Okay, do that. But slow."

Jenner steered the car onto the shoulder, then took the right.

They moved through the back streets of Bel Arbre. Half the houses were ramshackle and overgrown, with grubby children and chained pit bulls sheltering from the storm on porches behind the junk-clotted yards. But the other half was new – clean modern homes, freshly painted, with small, neat lawns and stainless mesh fencing still silvery bright.

Beyond a new low-income development of town-houses, Jenner saw a sign that read *Bel Arbre QuickMed Drop-In Clinic*; it was brightly lit, although the parking lot was empty.

Feeling Jenner slow the car, Nash said, "What are you doing? Keep going!"

Jenner said, "Look, if she doesn't get real medical help soon she could die."

"It's her fault! She was going to draw on me." Nash's

voice was shrill. "I'm sorry, but she . . . she brought this on herself."

"We could just slow down, drop her in the parking lot and go."

"Are you insane? This county is Oxycontin Central – every clinic has CCTV security. We can't go in there! Besides . . ." Nash's voice trailed off.

Jenner knew what he was thinking. *Besides . . . if she goes in there and they patch her up, she'll say who shot her, and that'll be that.*

But Jenner knew that it really *was* already all over, for Deb and for him. When Nash shot Deb, he'd signed their death warrants. There was no getting past that now – Nash couldn't take the bullet back. But the cop didn't have the stones to shoot Jenner in cold blood, to put another bullet in Deb. No, when they got to the farm, someone else would take Jenner and Deb out back and shoot them, dump their bodies in the Glades.

The Taurus bumped over disused railway tracks; in the back seat, Deb moaned. Jenner and Nash turned. Her shirt was open, the tank top underneath soaked with blood, blood puddling along her hip and flank as she lay there. But Jenner was surprised that there wasn't more blood – the bleeding was slowing. A good sign.

Unless, he thought. Unless she's bleeding internally. Or out of her back wound. Or going into shock.

There was another jolt as they dropped back onto the main road out of Bel Arbre.

And then there was open highway in front of them. To the sides of the highway the fields fell away, replaced by sawgrass marsh, and the marsh got wetter and wetter, and soon there were small stunted trees, all intertwining branches and twisted, knotted roots plunging into cloudy gray water, and they were over the mangrove forest.

And ahead was the bridge over the river through the forest and, beyond that, the road to Chip Craine's farm.

108

Smith and Bentas watched the Taurus approach up the main drive.

Bentas called out to Brodie, "It's Nash – and he's brought the coroner."

The Taurus pulled to a halt in front of the farmhouse. Nash leaned over, turned off the ignition, took out the key. He got out, walked up the slope toward Brodie and said, "There's a problem."

Brodie said, "Is it my problem?"

Nash looked befuddled, so Brodie said, "Have you jammed me or my operation up with some bullshit?"

Nash shook his head, then stammered, "I . . . No, I don't think so."

Brodie said, "Well, okay then. Go sob on Craine's shoulder."

"I shot a cop."

"Really?" Brodie grinned at Bentas and Smith. "Well, *that* ain't right!"

Bentas smirked. "Particularly what with you being a cop yourself and all, too, right?"

Brodie said, "So let me guess – you're here because you want our help with the body?"

Nash shook his head. "No. She's not dead." He turned

and gestured to the car. "Just wounded."

Brodie bounded off the porch and grabbed Nash by the scruff of his collar, shaking him like a rat. "You stupid fuck! You shoot a *cop*, and you bring her *here*?"

He stared at the car. Jenner was watching impassively from the driver's seat; Brodie could almost *feel* the man figuring his next step.

He turned to Bentas and snapped, "You and Tony get rid of the cop and the M.E. Strip the bodies, burn the clothes. Fuck up their faces, tell Tony to get cut off the hands. Then take the airboat and dump them out there – I don't give a fuck where, somewhere far out enough where they'll stay gone for a long while, though."

Bentas was walking to the car when Brodie said, "No, wait. Hold it."

He turned to Nash. "I want to get this straight: you shoot a cop, then you bring her here with another witness? What are you, some kind of fucking retard? This can only end one way – they both die."

Nash nodded slowly.

Brodie spat, then said, "You started this, *you* finish it. Take them down to the water and get rid of them."

He started back to the cook house, leaving Nash standing there, pale and trembling.

Bentas clapped Nash on the shoulder. "Hey, nut up, buddy! It's your chance to show us what kind of man you are!"

Smith called out, "Yo, Brodie! It's a *chick*! She's pretty fucked up – there's blood everywhere . . ." He was leaning against the car, peering into the back. He straightened. "She's not a regular cop, she's wearing a green uniform . . . I think maybe she's a park ranger or something."

Bentas said, "Maybe she's a fucking leprechaun!"

Brodie walked back to the car and stared down at Deb Putnam. He turned to Nash and said, "Take care of them in the boat shed. If you don't, I'll let Mr. Bentas do it. Either way, both of them will be dead an hour from now."

He paused, and looked Nash in the eye. "And if you can't handle it, Mister Bentas will take care of you, too."

109

Nash was jittery and pale, talking a mile a minute. He made Jenner drive down the unpaved road through the lower field to the dock, then held the gun on him while he helped Deb into the boat shed. Nash put a tarpaulin on the ground beneath her; the room wasn't cold, and the tarpaulin served no practical purpose other than to keep the surface beneath Deb clean, but it was a gesture.

They laid her on the floor, and then Nash hovered, watching Jenner. He was struggling to appear in control; Jenner realized that the man was too frightened to go back outside.

He eased Deb flat onto her back, her knees bent. Nash edged away from them, absorbed in his own anguish. He stood at the waterfront window, peering through the security grille out over the mangrove swamp.

Deb seemed to be okay. The bleeding had slowed, and her breathing seemed normal. Jenner took her wrist and slipped his fingers over her pulse; it was fast but not weak.

There was a creak at the door as Nash stepped outside. He closed the door behind him; Jenner heard the latch fall into place, then the quiet click of a padlock bolting the latch shut.

He whispered to her, "How do you feel?"

She whispered back. "Like someone shot me."

"Wow!" He smiled. "Screw park-ranger school – you shoulda gone to medical school!"

She didn't smile back. "Am I going to be okay?"

Her hand was cool in his. He said, a little too brightly, "You're fine. The bullet went all the way through. You've lost some blood, but you look pretty good to me."

"Jenner, don't bullshit me, okay?" Deb pulled her hand back. "I don't want you to fucking kumbayah me – if I'm going to die, I want to know."

He smiled. "You're going to be fine. If the bullet hit anything important inside you, you'd be a whole lot quieter by now."

Deb's expression was dubious, so Jenner said, "Really. I'm telling the truth."

"And what about the money? Tell me the truth about that. Why did Nash shoot me?"

Jenner told Deb about the meth, about the lab on Craine's farm. He told her that Craine had offered him money to walk away, that the money was the only proof he had that Craine was fully involved in the drugs. That he'd called in the DEA, and that they should be there soon. As he talked, her hand crept into his.

Jenner looked around their cell. The shed was maybe fifteen feet by twenty. One window faced northeast toward the farmhouse, the other to the southwest, over the swamp. The room was lit by a dim yellow bulb, and smelled of pine pitch and gasoline. Orange plastic jerry-cans were lined up along one wall, next to a pair of canoe paddles and a double-tipped kayak paddle; there was no kayak or canoe in the shed.

A rough wooden table held a couple of fishing-tackle boxes and a large wicker-and-canvas catch basket. Next to the bench, several tall old-fashioned fishing rods leaned against the wall. Jenner knew nothing about fishing, but these implements were beautiful, each apparently fashioned from a single long stick of flexible bamboo, with circular wire guide-loops tied neatly to the rod with black thread and varnished into place. Handmade, expensive.

There was a low, heavy bench against the opposite wall. O-rings had been bolted to the scuffed legs, and the floor in front of it was scraped and battered. There were brown stains spattered on the floor and on the wall behind; Jenner doubted that they were fish blood.

There was a scraping sound and the door opened again.

Brodie nodded at Jenner, then at Deb. He glanced around the shed as if he were a prospective renter, then turned to the two of them again.

"Kind of too bad, isn't it?"

Jenner shrugged. "I'd have liked it better if it had gone differently."

"You think Nash has the balls to kill you?" Brodie grinned. "I'm not so sure."

Jenner was silent.

"Tony does." Brodie motioned towards the bench with the bloodstains.

"Who's Tony?"

"The tall guy with black hair up there on the porch, the one with the big fucking knife." Brodie paused, then his grin got a little wider. "I figure he'll end up being the one who takes care of you – after all, he took care of the last M.E."

Jenner stiffened. "Ah."

" '*Ah*'? That's *it*? What are you, some kind of tough guy? I tell you we killed your buddy, and all you say is '*Ah*'?" Brodie shook his head. "If it's any consolation, because of Coburn, I had to get rid of a couple of my men."

"What happened?"

Brodie hesitated for a second, then shrugged. "I sent two guys to Port Fontaine to transport a body. The body wasn't ready so the funeral director sent them away for a couple hours. Those fucking idiots went and smoked some meth. They got really high, and then they went back for the body way late.

"Because they were out there dicking around, the body was still there when Coburn showed up at the funeral home to sign a death certificate. Later, Reggie Jones noticed the body had been fucked with – someone had opened it and snagged a sample from one of the bricks.

"Reggie put two plus two together, and realized it had to be the medical examiner. So I sent Tony to visit the guy . . . and the rest you know."

He shook his head. "Your pal figured we had cops working for us, so he didn't know who to turn to. He was probably trying to figure out his next step when Tony showed up on his doorstep – he didn't see that one coming. He thought he had time – you know how that is, right, doc? When you think you have time, but then it turns out you don't?"

Jenner didn't reply.

Brodie grinned.

"He was a tough old fuck – didn't say a word, no matter how Tony carved him up. We tore that place apart but never did find what he took." He chuckled. "All this over a couple bucks' worth of product!"

Brodie glanced at his watch.

"Anyway, just came down to see if that cocksucker had stepped up." He looked down at them both, then said, "I guess not. But, whatever – things will get taken care of down here pretty soon, either by Nash or by Tony."

Brodie slipped through the door. Jenner heard him call to Nash, then his voice faded.

Jenner waited a couple of minutes, then went to the window. Nash was alone on the dock, talking on his cell phone. In the drizzle, the river looked gray and cold, cast in dirty lead. Jenner glanced at his watch; it was just a question of time before Nash would be dumping their dead bodies into the dark water. He imagined his body hitting the water, sliding under, being swallowed by the black.

Deb was looking up at him. He caught her eye and smiled, then walked over to look out the back window. Brodie was walking up the slope to the farmhouse, where several men sat on the porch, smoking and talking. The door to the first bunkhouse swung open and three men filed out into the rain. They peeled off hairnets and surgical face masks with obvious relief, and stood in the drizzle in their white jumpsuits, relieved to be in the cool, wet, fresh air.

Someone pointed, and all heads turned to the road, where a dark Volvo station wagon was approaching.

110

Brodie watched Craine drive up to the farmhouse. He sat in the porch rocking chair as Craine got out of the station wagon, spoke to his granddaughter in the back, then approached him.

Brodie said, "Not the Bentley today, Mr. Craine?"

Craine ignored the jab and asked pointless questions about the cook cycle. The fake conversation didn't fool Brodie – there'd be a couple more questions before Craine asked what he *really* wanted to know. Brodie always knew when Craine was about to ask it – the man's speech grew faster, pitched up as he got ready to spit it out.

And then he did.

"And, uh, Brodie . . . you have something waiting for me downstairs?"

It was always the same question, the same words spoken in the same way. It creeped Brodie out, made him feel implicated in Craine's filth.

He nodded, disgust edging his expression.

Craine stood back, flushed. He glanced at Brodie's men watching them from the porch, at the meth cooks smoking under the eaves of Bunkhouse B, then back at the Volvo.

"I'm going to bring my granddaughter inside; she can stay in one of the upstairs rooms. Read a book, or something."

Brodie nodded, said nothing.

"Okay, then. I'll go get her." Craine hurried toward the car, then turned to add, "She won't get in your way. Though I think it'd probably be best to lock her in – so she doesn't go wandering."

Brodie spat. Yeah, it would be best to lock the girl in – she should never see the things her grandfather did in the basement. He gestured at his men; they left the porch and trooped toward the bunkhouses.

He shifted. "Actually, Mr. Craine, there's a matter which needs your attention."

"Later, Brodie. One thing at a time."

Brodie grinned. "Yes, sir." Fine by him – Craine would freak the fuck out later when Brodie told him about the bodies waiting for him in the boathouse.

Craine led his granddaughter into the farmhouse. She was a pretty little girl – very skinny and watery pale, but pretty. Brodie stood as she stepped up onto the porch; when he lifted his cap, she looked away quickly.

The child didn't like him. Or maybe Brodie frightened her.

The thought stung a little – he wasn't so bad. There were worse men than him.

Brodie listened to the door close behind him. He didn't turn; what happened in the farmhouse wasn't his business.

He walked over to Craine's station wagon. The rear compartment was filled with fancy suitcases; apparently Mr. Craine was off on a little trip.

Brodie walked back up to the porch and sat in his rocking chair. But soon the sounds from the basement bothered him, and he walked over to Bunkhouse B to find Tony.

It was time.

111

Deb was sleeping. Good.

Jenner went to the other window and looked out over the mangrove swamp. Nash still stood forlornly on the dock; Jenner wondered if he'd make a break for it, just grab a boat and go.

But that wouldn't work, and Nash would know it. They'd know where Nash lived, and if he tried to make a break for it they'd cut his family down before he set foot on dry land. Besides, Nash didn't have the guts to do that.

When it came down to it, really, Nash had no choice – if he didn't, they'd kill him, too.

So, okay, yeah. No two ways: Nash was going to kill them.

As Jenner watched, Nash pulled out his pistol and stared at it. He racked it, checked to see that there was a round in the chamber, then turned and looked back toward the shed.

The shed window was empty.

112

As he walked, Nash felt his rain-soaked shirt cling to the gun stuck inside his waistband. He was still scared, but something had turned inside him and he was ready now.

Bartley would've handled it the right way from the beginning. They'd been partners until Bartley got the nod, and moved over to SWAT as a sergeant, and then got bumped up to detective. Nash had always felt short-changed, been sure he was every bit as good as Bartley, but now he recognized that wasn't true: Bartley had always been willing to take that one step further, to do whatever it took to get the job done. And even now, he was the one calling the shots.

The cell phone still felt warm in his pocket. Nash knew that Bartley was right: he *had* to kill Deb and Dr. Jenner – they were witnesses.

Bartley had been putting together his assault team since Nash had first called, but he still needed another half-hour to set things up. A half hour gave Brodie too much time to get antsy about Deb and Jenner still being alive. So Nash had to get rid of them, get rid of any link between them and him.

And in the meantime, Bartley had been thinking much bigger, and Bartley's plan would solve *all* their problems. All the evidence, all the threat, any witness who could tie them to the drugs would be gone.

And they'd be rich.

Because he and Bartley were going to take all the money in the farmhouse.

Just the money – that there'd be drugs, too, and SWAT would need something to show for the raid. An assault team in full gear, posing with H&K MP5s and Baker batshields in front of seized assault rifles and stacked bricks of white powder would make for great TV. Bartley and Nash would make sure that none of Brodie's crew made it out alive. Then they'd find and stash the money, and they'd be free and clear, sitting on . . . well, who knew just how many millions the operation had at the farm?

Everything had to go smoothly, starting with Nash's

own part in the script. All he had to do was get past that first step.

And it was a big one.

Nash didn't want them to suffer; he'd known Deb since kindergarten. He tried to think of a way to kill them separately, without the other having any clue: he couldn't think of a method. Maybe if he took Jenner outside first, took him down near the water . . .

As Nash walked along the dock, he began to cry. He tried to stop it but he couldn't – it was all just too much. How had it ever come to this?

He squatted on the dock, to think, to get his head together. He told himself, *after this, it's all finished. Just one more hour and I'm out, done with this forever. Rich.*

The rain was cold on Nash's face and skin, on his scalp.

His arm shook as he reached back to check that the shirt tail still covered the gun; when he pressed the Glock against his clammy skin it felt solid and real again, a promise, a guarantee that he could get through this. And he told himself it was them or him, and he breathed more comfortably.

Because it wasn't going to be him.

There was a creak, and he looked up to see one of Brodie's men, Tony, standing on the dock in front of him.

"Hey, officer. Brodie wants to know have you taken care of it yet?"

Nash walked towards him, saying, "I'm just going in to do it, right now."

Tony shrugged, and said, "Well, Mr. Brodie was very clear in his instructions."

"I know. I just needed to get myself . . . to get ready to do it."

"I meant his instructions to me." Tony lifted the Tec-9 and sprayed a short burst, the bullets hitting Nash in a tight arc from his chest to his head, sending him falling backwards onto the dock.

Tony put the gun down, then dragged Nash's body toward the end of the dock; halfway out, he thought better, and just rolled him off the side. With a splash, the body hit the shallows next to the swamp boat.

Tony picked up the Tec-9 and looked at the shed. Next!

Just as he stepped off the dock, the light in the shed went off.

Ugh. Were there going to be heroics?

God love 'em – there's only so much you can do against a man with a machine pistol.

Tony opened the door a crack and poked his head into the gloom.

"Yoo-hoo. Anybody home?"

He opened the door wider, and in the half-light sensed rather than saw something shiny whipping toward his face.

The big steel fishhook at the tip of the rod caught Tony just under the eye, slashed his face open, carving across his nose, opening up his forehead. The blood gushed instantly down his face like a black veil. He staggered backward blindly, gasping in surprise and trying to sweep the blood from his face, his gun firing randomly into the dark for about a half-second before Jenner slammed the canoe paddle into his groin, then again into his head. Tony dropped, Jenner sprawling on top of him, punching at his face, driving his knee repeatedly into his belly, into his groin, into his hip.

Jenner kept smashing Tony's bloody face, and when Tony's arms stopped trying to block his blows, when they finally sank to his sides, Jenner rolled off him and scrabbled around the floor in the pitch black, desperate to find the gun. The hot barrel seared his fingers; he shoved the weapon around and grabbed the butt. He stood quickly, pointed the pistol down at the man and pulled the trigger. Nothing happened.

Deb swung the door open, and now Jenner saw Tony beneath him, a dazed man with a bloody mask where his face should have been. But he was still moving, now slowly, rolling himself onto the mud in front of the shed. Jenner followed him, lifted the heavy pistol high, smashed it into Tony's face with all his strength. He felt the bones buckle in like cardboard under the blow, the recoil force knocking the gun out of Jenner's wet hands.

Jenner grabbed the handle of Tony's knife, pulling it out of its sheath, a big steel blade with strips of sawtooth on its upper edge, a big fucking shark of a blade. And he knew the knife and he grabbed a fistful of blood-matted hair and yanked Tony's head way back, and carved open Tony's throat with that big fucking shark of a blade, and felt the blood pour over his arm, hot and heavy as water from a bath tap. And it felt good, and Jenner cut again, pulling the blade back as hard as he could.

Behind him, he dimly heard Deb saying feebly, "*Jenner! No, stop!*"

But she didn't understand: the man lived to kill and torture, and he'd butchered Marty, and he was there to kill them, and Jenner had no choice but to kill him, and if you're going to kill someone you don't stop killing them until they're dead. He knew this, he had killed before – he was a killer. He let the head drop and stabbed the back of the man's neck from the side, driving the blade in until it hit bone.

Jenner lifted his arm again, but Deb caught his elbow and sank down to her knees against him in the mud, crying, holding on to him and murmuring, "Enough – please, Jenner, stop it! He's dead."

Jenner kneeled over Tony's body, crying, feeling the emotion and effort and fear inside him, feeling Deb's head against his, her hand holding his swaying forehead, her breast against his back. His body shook as she held him, her arms pulling him away from Tony's body and against her.

He wiped the tears and the blood from his face, looked down at the body.

Tony wasn't breathing. Jenner shook Deb's arm off, reached out for Tony's wrist, felt for a pulse. There was none.

Jenner turned to Deb and said, "Go back inside the shed, Deb. Try to stay dry, okay? I'll deal with him."

Deb stood. She was looking at Jenner differently now, but he didn't see her at all.

He needed to get rid of the body, get it out of sight. Get it out of *his* sight.

It was darker now, between the rain and the clouds that blacked out the setting sun, and Jenner knew they were hidden from the farmhouse by the shed. But he still needed to ditch the body.

Tony had been a big man in life; in death he was astonishingly heavy. Jenner struggled to drag his carcass across the muddy grass. He pulled the body down the slope to the short boat-ramp; the rain flowing down the ramp made it easier, but Tony's clothes caught on the rough concrete and it took all Jenner's strength to get the corpse down to the water.

And then Jenner was knee-deep in the brackish water, and the water supported Tony, and it got easier, and Tony floated a bit as Jenner pulled him out deeper, his feet sinking in the mud, slimy and membranous and rooty, until he was almost waist-deep in the water and Tony was floating up against him as if Tony were a drowning man and Jenner a lifeguard saving his life. Then Jenner let Tony go, pushed him out into the dark mangrove river; the body drifted forward, but sank quickly under the rain-splashed surface.

And Jenner had killed the man who had killed his friend.

And now Deb and Jenner would get away.

113

In the dull light in the shed, Deb was sitting up, her head leaning back against the bench, her arm across her belly. She'd stopped crying. When Jenner came over to her she clutched herself with both arms, as if she was cold, and looked up at him. When he leaned over her she seemed to pull away.

Jenner understood.

"What did you do with his body?" Deb asked.

"I put him in the water. We're pretty close to the sea here, I think – the bottom of the farm ends in a mangrove swamp."

Deb nodded dully. "I'm a park ranger, Jenner – I know how the farm ends."

She looked him up and down. "The blood's gone."

"I had to wade him out to make sure he was deep enough."

"Are you okay?"

"Yes. He was too surprised to really hit me back – all he did was try to defend himself."

Deb was crying again. "I went to kindergarten with Tom Nash."

"Deb, I know he was your friend." Jenner sat next to her, his back against the bench. "I don't know why they killed him. I think maybe he refused to kill us."

"You . . . you think he did?"

"I don't know. But I think maybe."

He sat back and watched her cry.

"We have to go, Deb. We'll take a boat, make our way down the channel to the sea."

"They'll see us." She looked exhausted, pale and weak.

"Not if we're quiet. Not if they're busy. Not if it's dark."

"Then they'll *hear* us."

Jenner stood, and went to the window to check the farmhouse. The men were still there.

Deb said, "If it's dark, we'll get caught in the mangroves. We need to think this through. Have you ever even driven a boat?"

He murmured, "No."

There was movement up on the porch. One of the men stood quickly as a ground-floor window swung open. A small girl climbed through it and ran past the men, hands clamped over her ears. She ran to the Volvo, climbed inside and slammed the door shut.

The dome light inside the car stayed on for about thirty seconds. The men on the porch were all standing now, staring at the child as she scrambled around the passenger compartment; Jenner realized she was locking all the doors.

Lucy Craine.

Christ.

114

They had to get moving. *Now.*

Brodie would notice he hadn't heard from Tony and come down to check. More men would come for them soon.

Jenner felt Deb's pulse: faster than the last time he'd checked, but not weak. She seemed to be holding on, but she was weakened from blood loss and stress. He'd help her move.

And Lucy Craine – what could he do for her? Her grandfather had to be in the farmhouse – the Volvo was in the driveway. What was Chip Craine doing in there? Did he know about Jenner and Deb?

Shit.

First things first. They wouldn't hurt Lucy – she was with her grandfather – but they'd be coming to kill Jenner and Deb. Soon.

Deb first, then Lucy.

Jenner cracked the door and peered out. He saw no one.

He slipped out into the rain, crouching as he neared the dock. Two boats – a shallow-draft swamp boat with a large outboard motor, and a big airboat – were tied to the dock; the airboat was half up on the grass bank.

If he took either, he'd be caught. By the time he got the outboard running Brodie's men would have sprinted down the slope and across the field. Then they'd just hop in the airboat and hunt them down. Besides, what if the outboard wasn't even gassed, or if he couldn't start it?

And, even beyond the deafening roar of its huge aircraft engine, the airboat was a complete non-starter – it was controlled with a stick, like a World War One fighter plane, and Jenner had no clue how to pilot it.

Jenner saw a large green canoe lying face down alongside the boat shed, and a canary-yellow kayak next to it. The deep grass around the canoe gave it a neglected air, but it could hold two people, whereas the slender kayak was built for one.

The canoe, then. There would be risk – it was partly exposed to the farmhouse – but he didn't have any choice. He'd be paddling alone so it would be slow, too, but it would be silent.

He went back in, told Deb the plan. She listened and, when he'd finished, nodded somberly.

"I'm going to bring the canoe down to the water first, then come back for you, okay?"

"Be careful, Jenner."

He smiled and nodded, and went out into the dark and the rain.

115

Brodie watched Chip Craine, shirt untucked, face ruddy and glistening with sweat, talk with his granddaughter in the Volvo. He'd been in there five minutes; Brodie, disgusted by the whole thing, had called dinner, and the men were eating in Bunkhouse B.

What could that fucker possibly say to her? The girl knew what she'd heard, would've recognized the whimpering of another little girl.

But Craine had been working on Lucy for her entire life, and Brodie couldn't comprehend the isolation and vulnerability Craine had engineered. A few minutes later, Chip led the sobbing child from the car, holding her little hand in his. Despite the rain, they walked to the farmhouse slowly.

As they passed Brodie, Craine gave the foreman a vulpine smile, teeth bared in triumph. He'd clearly won – or was about to win – a major victory and was ready to move on to a new stage in his relationship with his granddaughter.

It made Brodie's skin crawl. He watched the door close behind Craine and lingered on the deck. He thought about ringing the bell and telling Craine about the mess in the boat shed, knock the wind out of his sails, maybe buy the little girl a chance for a few more days of innocence. But his instructions were clear – completely hands-off with Craine. And even he didn't cross the people who'd made the rules.

Brodie told himself that, had it been anyone else, he'd have gone in there and killed the man. This was certainly true, but it had never occurred to him to question his role in supplying Craine with girls. And even if it had been pointed out to him, he'd have replied that it was Bentas who arranged the girls for Craine, that the girls were older than Lucy, got paid for what happened in the basement, and usually came to the farm with the consent of their guardians. Besides, they were Mexican.

116

From the shadows along the shed, Jenner watched Craine lead Lucy into the house. Good: he didn't like the idea of the girl being out there among those scumbags. At least she'd be safe with Craine.

He crept to the canoe; it was wooden, and much heavier than he'd expected. Or maybe his reluctance was because of the exposure – most of the canoe was visible from the porch, several hundred feet away, and he couldn't move it without risking being seen by someone at the farmhouse. If anyone upstairs was watching, Jenner would be spotted instantly.

He'd just have to hope that the rain and the gathering dark hid him.

He knelt up and slowly tipped the canoe sideways, supporting it with his arms, straining to keep it from rolling and banging as the bow hit the ground. There was an audible thump; Jenner lay alongside the boat, sprawled on his stomach, staring up at the porch, watching for movement. He saw nothing.

Indeed, he could no longer see anyone on the porch –

where were they? Were they coming for Deb and Jenner now?

Jenner crawled quickly toward the water, then turned to drag the canoe. It slid forward slowly, inching toward the ramp.

When the bottom of the canoe hit the concrete, the noise grew louder, a dull, sawing scrape that sounded to Jenner like it would be audible in Miami. But there was still no movement up at the farmhouse.

He squatted, lifted the bow and walked backwards to the water supporting it. This method was quieter, but he was now completely exposed and if anyone was sitting in the shadows of the porch, Jenner was a dead man.

But there was no outcry, no alarm.

He tied the rope to a cleat on the dock and left the bow of the canoe to float in the water.

Then he went to get Deb.

117

The hierarchy at the farm was preserved at dinner time as strictly as if they were aboard the *Titanic*. The field hands ate in Bunkhouse B, the dormitory bunkhouse, while Brodie's core team ate in the farmhouse. Tonight, with Craine at the farm, Brodie's crew were eating on the porch; the meth cooks rarely left Bunkhouse A during a cook cycle.

Brodie pushed away his plate of chicken – too fucking spicy, even without his ulcer. His crew was chatty tonight – they were always that way near a pay weekend. Bentas was cracking jokes, Smith was fake-laughing in response, and Tarver was whining.

Brodie hadn't announced that they'd be closing the operation down – they didn't need to know yet. And not all of them would be going on to the next location.

His cell phone buzzed in his lap. He pushed away from the table and went outside. The rain had eased; in the gloom a low shroud of pale mist hung over the fields, floating out over the road and down past the shed to the water.

"You're being raided. You've got maybe twenty, thirty minutes."

"Thanks for the heads-up. Who is it? How many?"

"Locals, Port Fontaine law enforcement. Maybe six, seven, led by Bartley – you were right about him. They'll be SWAT; they'll be wearing body armor."

"That's not a problem." Brodie said.

"Good. Blow what you can, then get out."

"Okay."

"If you can clean up and get out without engaging them, do it; but we don't think you'll have time. We figure Bartley will go for the money, and he'll go after you – he can't let you survive. He's leading this – take him out first."

"Of course."

"Are you prepared for an assault? Our information is that the county doesn't have a tactical vehicle."

"We're all set."

"Good. Where are we with the cook-up?"

"Bad. We'd need another day at least."

"Forget it. We've heard the feds are on their way, too. They're mobilizing in Miami, so you have some time there. Just blow it and get out. No witnesses, no one gets taken, okay?"

"Okay."

Brodie's bags were packed, sitting in the trunk of his car. He had cash, too, stashed in a storage locker in Port Fontaine, hidden in neatly packed cardboard boxes filled with books, the boxes marked LIBRARY in Magic Marker. And he had someone who'd ship the boxes to him in Costa Rica. He was clean and ready to go.

In front of the far bunkhouse, several field hands sat drinking beer. One had a guitar and was singing a *narcocorrido*, a ballad about the life of the drug trafficker. Brodie grinned; this night would give musicians something to sing about for years.

118

Bartley finished strapping on his body armor standing inside the open door of the impounded black Expedition. He pulled his lucky Saint Christopher out of his shirt, kissed it, then carefully tucked the saint down inside the Kevlar vest.

He walked back to the black Escalade parked on the bridge and shook each man's hand in turn. The officers – tan, crew-cut young men in camo pants, khaki T-shirts and modular bulletproof vests – knew the mission was exceptional. When he'd called them up, Bartley had explained that neither the captain nor the lieutenant had signed off on this: they were on their own here.

They stood by the bridge railing, looking over the

mangrove forest to the farm beyond. The target was the farmhouse and two bunk houses at the top of a low hill built from the mud dug from the swamp to create the river. The approach would be over open ground, slightly uphill, with small outbuildings providing limited cover during the attack; the approach from the north, across freshly plowed fields was not an option – it was longer and offered no cover.

Bartley gathered them into a circle around him. He looked at them gravely, then began.

"This is the real deal, people. You've trained for this, and now it's here. Forget serving warrants, forget bank robberies – that's penny-ante stuff. We're moving on a well-armed force, approaching a fortified, possibly booby-trapped stronghold uphill over open ground. Resistance may be strong; we're likely to encounter automatic-weapons fire. Cover will be minimal.

"The target is a meth lab located on a farm belonging to one of this city's richest citizens. This man has deep ties in the community, so our chances of getting a no-knock warrant through the usual channels are pretty much zip.

"This is unacceptable. I can now tell you that this target must be penetrated urgently for two reasons: first, we have established that the individuals responsible for the murder yesterday of Detective David Rudge are presently on site. Second . . ." He paused and looked around the circle grimly.

"This afternoon, these same individuals took fellow DCSO deputy Tom Nash. I was able to speak with Deputy Nash twenty-five minutes ago by cell phone; he is being held by these men, and is unable to move. He has informed me that his situation is becoming increasingly untenable, and asked that I gather the team and respond ASAP."

Bartley looked around again. "I knew when I put out the alert that you'd show, and show quick. I'm proud to see just how right I was. I need you to understand that this action is not officially sanctioned. Anyone who wants to drop out should just do so; there will be no penalty, no retribution."

No one moved, no one spoke.

"However, if you're coming with us, well . . . it's time to get the fucking show on the fucking road . . ."

Bartley held up a fist. "And one last thing: every worker on that farm is involved in the manufacture of meth. Every one of them will shoot you dead if he sees you coming. Gentlemen, this mission is shoot to kill. Understand me when I tell you this: your goal is to kill these drug dealers before they kill you . . ."

119

Brodie was relaxed. He'd been waiting for this moment for some time. He'd spent the last fifteen minutes making sure that he was all set. He'd spoken quietly with Smith and Bentas, and had told Tarver to round up the Mexicans and take them all into Bunkhouse B and stay there with them. There was to be no argument: if they resisted, even slightly, he was to shoot one to make sure the others knew he was serious.

It went like clockwork: less than five minutes later he heard the sharp crack of a pistol shot from somewhere in the bunkhouses – Tarver taking care of business. Where had Tony got to?

At every operation that Brodie had conducted, he'd had a five-minute exit strategy – a simple scorched-earth policy, involving a little explosive, a few blasting caps, a spool or two of det cord, and the remote-detonator box. Which he needed to get from the farmhouse.

He rang the bell. Craine opened the door; he appeared surprised and unhappy to find Brodie standing there.

"Mr. Craine, sorry to bother you, but we have a problem." Leaning slightly to his right, Brodie saw the ghostly little girl sitting at the dinner table.

"What's that, Brodie?"

"Your pal Nash brought in the medical examiner and a female park ranger."

"*What*?"

"He shot the ranger. He's got them locked up down in the boat shed."

"My God! He *shot* the ranger?" Craine looked like it was him who'd been shot.

"Yes, sir. I, uh, thought you'd want to know."

"Why did he shoot a ranger?" Craine was standing at the window, staring out. Through the thin mist, the pale shape of the Taurus was a ghost next to the shed.

Brodie said, "Mr. Craine, you'll have to ask him yourself. I'm sorry, but I'm dealing with a number of issues right now. I don't know what the hell's going on there, but it needs your urgent attention."

"Yes, of course. You're right. I'll go down right away."

Brodie nodded; he was thinking he should just kill Craine, just do it right now. Follow him down the hill, pop him once in the head. Come back up, send the girl somewhere safe, grab Craine's cash and just fucking go.

He'd give anything to see the look on Craine's face when he got down to the shed to find that Tony had killed Nash, the doc and the cop.

"Sir, I just need to get down to the basement for a second – I need to pick up the remote-detonator box."

Craine's eyes bulged, and he stammered, "Mr. Brodie, now's not the best time. I tell you what, I'll go down there for you, bring it right back up." He was so flustered that he didn't even ask why the foreman wanted ordnance at this time of day.

"That's mighty nice of you, Mr. Craine! It's a yellow plastic box, about yay big, in the wall cupboard in the boiler room."

Craine disappeared downstairs, leaving Brodie peering through the crack in the doorway at the girl. She was reading a book – the same Harry Potter book that Tony was reading. It must be new.

He remembered his own daughter in her Brownies uniform, making some damn thing out of construction paper and glue at the table in their condo in Santa Cruz. That summer, word leaked out that one of the den mother's boyfriends had done time for making child pornography. One Sunday in early August the boyfriend set out for a stroll on the boardwalk and was never seen again. Not that the police looked for him very hard.

But if Brodie felt he'd done some things right, he'd screwed up in the end – no way you can count yourself a good dad if your daughter's doing a fifteen-year bit for distribution of a Schedule 1 narcotic, particularly if she'd been working for you when she got busted.

He cursed himself for fucking up as a parent. He'd

coasted along, doing his work, doing his time, confident that sooner or later he'd get it right. Then one day he was a fifty-year-old ex-con, and his daughter was a twenty-three-year-old convicted felon.

It might be too little, too late, but at least tonight he'd be curing her of her Tarver problem, which counted for something. Even if she might not agree.

Craine's steps sounded on the stairs. Lucy straightened, then flipped the page. Brodie realized she wasn't really reading the book: she was just looking at the same page over and over again. She'd read it, turn the page, then a couple of seconds later jump back to start over again.

The girl wasn't as calm as she looked. Brodie shook his head.

When Craine handed him the yellow box Brodie said, "A word of advice: you should probably think of getting the little girl out of here soon. Word is that we may be raided. And the feds have started poking around."

Craine blanched. "When?"

"Within the hour. If I were you, I'd get out of here as soon as you've taken care of your little problem."

Brodie nodded, said, "Evening," then set off toward the bunkhouses at an amble, leaving Craine gaping in the doorway.

120

Deb draped her arm over Jenner's shoulder and together they moved quickly down the bank to the dock. It was dark now, and the mist that had settled over the swamp

404

was thick enough that he didn't think they could be spotted from the farmhouse. It took them less than a minute to get down to the water.

The canoe was gone.

At first Jenner thought he'd mistaken the side on which he'd tied it, then that his knot had failed, but as he got closer he saw that the canoe was still there, just half submerged. The back of the boat had sunk and now only the rim of the bows stuck above the surface, like a cup in a sink full of water. Either the canoe had already been leaky, or he'd damaged it when he'd dragged it down to the river.

It didn't matter which – the thing was fucked.

Deb looked at the Go Devil swamp boat and at the airboat, then back up at the farmhouse. She looked pale, and felt heavier on Jenner's shoulder.

She saw a shadow in the mist and whispered, "Jenner – there's someone coming."

Whoever it was would go to the shed first, and there was nowhere to hide there. He whispered urgently, "Into the water . . ."

He guided her down the bank and on into the black river, pressing close to the foundered canoe so she had something to hold on to. He led her deeper and deeper into the channel, trying to support her.

Deb was tough. Every step must have hurt like a bitch, but she never made a sound. Jenner took her deep, right to the end of the dock; he felt the kick of her feet, churning slow currents to keep her head above water, but he himself was still just able to stand.

He whispered, "Try to conserve your energy. Hang on to me, tilt your face up – I'll help keep you up."

Jenner held on to the wood at the end of the dock, and helped Deb to clasp her arms around him; underwater, she wrapped her legs around his and clung on to him tight.

It was just one man coming down the slope, Jenner saw. He was in shirt sleeves and carried a flashlight, the light bouncing through the drizzle.

Then Jenner recognized him. He held Deb close and, putting a finger to his lips, pointed ashore and mouthed, "Craine." She ducked her head into the hollow of his neck.

Craine stopped first at the car, shining the light into the compartment, then trying the doors. Finding them locked, he tried the trunk, swore softly when he couldn't open it, and came on down the slope to the shed.

He turned the corner and stopped, finding the door open.

Then Jenner saw his pistol, something small and dark – a Glock, maybe, or a Kahr.

Craine opened the door wider, pointing his gun inside. He pressed his back to the door and moved slowly inside, calling out "Nash?" into the darkness.

He reached a hand in, then fished around to find the switch. The light revealed an empty shed, the floor smeared in blood.

Craine's voice was panicky now. "*Nash!*" There was no reply.

Craine came out of the shed and faced the swamp, his eyes scanning the river. He walked halfway out on the dock and stopped. Jenner held Deb's head against his neck, pointed down; they took a breath, then slowly sank together under the water.

Jenner kept his fingers pressed to the side of the dock. He felt the vibrations of Craine's footsteps as the man walked out further, closer to them. Five seconds turned to ten, then to fifteen, and then Jenner felt Craine's footsteps again, faster now, moving away. He slowly brought Deb to the surface, held them both against the rotting wood of the dock, where they silently gasped at the air, breathing in as deeply and as slowly as they could.

Jenner floated out slightly to look up at the dock; Craine was in the middle now, deciding what to do. He stared at the swamp boat and the airboat, turned to look back at the empty shed, then up at the farmhouse.

He began to run, loping up the dock to disappear into the shed. He emerged a few seconds later with a concrete cinder block, he smashed the window of Nash's Taurus and opened the driver's-side door.

Craine rummaged around in the car but didn't seem to find anything. Then he leaned under the dash, and the trunk door opened.

He walked around the back and began to go through the trunk's contents, immediately finding the garbage bags of money. With obvious dismay, he pulled out the leather bag that Jenner had eviscerated; he brushed away at it for a second, then massaged it back into something approaching its original shape. Then he began to fill it with wads of cash; he moved quickly and erratically, jamming the last of the money into the bag. He'd almost finished when Jenner saw him pull up the white plastic laundry bag, open it to find the hundred thousand, and stuff that into the overnight bag too. He reached into his pocket, pulled out two passports and dropped them into the bag, then tried to zip it shut. It was too full to close; he'd have to repack it, but now was not the time.

Craine hefted the bag and was about to cross the road to the field in front of the farmhouse when he saw two big black SUV's moving silently along the drive, their lights off.

121

Bartley was in the Explorer with three of the team members, one of them holding the heavy tactical shield ready for deployment, the ram at his feet. There were four men in the Escalade behind – between them they had two Baker batshields, one in the driver compartment, the other in the passenger compartment.

Under a misting rain, the two cars rolled slowly under the white arch, all lights off, though they had no illusion that their attack would be a surprise one. They'd begin with the protection of the cars before switching to tactical-shield equipment.

They moved in several hundred yards before Bartley called the stop. He radioed back deployment instructions to the car behind, then slipped out onto the road.

The men gathered behind the front car. They could hear Norteño music from the bunkhouses; they were lit but no one was outside, maybe because of the damp.

Bobby Bartley thought to himself: this just might work . . .

This would be a direct approach uphill, with little cover if a true firefight broke out, so stealth was critical. A sniper would stay down by the cars to lay down cover fire as necessary. Behind the Escalade he'd be almost invisible to shooters up at the bunkhouses; from his protected position the sniper would be strong support against an enemy who held higher ground.

The other six men would move up in three teams, two men to each tactical shield. They'd fan out across the field and converge on the first bunkhouse; two teams would enter the bunkhouse. Barley had stressed that the bunkhouse closest to the farmhouse should be approached with extreme caution since it contained highly explosive chemicals.

If a firefight broke out, the shooters might evacuate Bunkhouse B and move first to Bunkhouse A, then to the farmhouse. SWAT would sequentially secure the bunkhouses, then hit the farmhouse, which was where, Bartley announced, Nash said they were holding him; it was likely this was where they'd meet the greatest resistance.

The eight men gathered into a circle, dropped to one knee and bowed their heads. Bartley led them in prayer. Then they shook hands, nodded solemnly at each other, split up into their teams and began to move.

Bartley led the two teams for the attack on Bunkhouse B; he'd been on-site several times, and knew that this bunkhouse was where the field workers lived.

The men moved silently, like the well-trained pros that they were. They crawled up the slope, fanning out slightly and moving toward their assigned targets. The steady rain helped hide them, but the grass on the slope was slippery and muddy.

One by one, they moved into position, almost unable to

believe that their luck had held. They settled and lay still, all looking to Bartley for the start signal.

Then Bentas, who'd been waiting patiently, hidden behind the lower field slop trough, stepped up behind the sniper and shot him in the back of the head.

Bentas moved quickly into position, pressed the sniper-rifle stock into his shoulder, and peered through the scope.

The SWAT teams were on the edge of panic; in a fraction of a second they'd learned that their arrival had been expected, lost the security of sniper cover-fire, and had their flank completely exposed.

Bentas now began to fire on the SWAT team members arrayed on the hill, as shooters in and around bunkhouses opened fire, pinning them down so that Bentas could pick them off.

Bartley gave the order to scatter and began moving across the slope, trying to get cover before the new sniper destroyed the entire mission. He scrambled across the grass toward one of the pens.

As he reached the enclosure, the corrugated metal surround by his head banged as the bullets smashed into it. From inside the structure, he could hear the frantic grunting of pigs, hear them running around wildly. Someone was firing at him in short bursts; he couldn't tell whether it was coming from the shooter down on the road or from the bunkhouse. He kept his head down and crawled to the enclosure entrance.

Inside the pen the pigs were in full panic, squealing in terror, slamming into each other and smashing against the metal surround until it shook. Bartley lifted the gate and stepped back as the pigs stampeded out, shoving and squealing.

He raised his weapon, fired once, and the stream of hogs veered briefly away from him. Within seconds they were battering him again as they poured out past him.

As soon as he discharged his weapon the shooters focused their attention on him. The metal structure was raked by a blizzard of bullets, the rickety panels shredding apart, clanging like a bell.

There was a pop and then a hiss as an incendiary flare streaked up into the sky over the field. The whole area was flooded with silver light, and in an instant Bartley saw all his men spread out across the field. They huddled under the shields, lying flat to minimize their exposure, returning fire toward the bunkhouse shooters. But the shields didn't cover them completely, and under the white-metal light Bartley saw quick puffs of red, saw limbs jerk and heard screams as bullets hit arms and legs.

The pigs now spread out in panic, careening across the field, running in all directions. A shooter targeted the pigs trying to flee the enclosure; in the bright light, the pigs' skins were a washed-out pale gray and each hit triggered a spray of blue-black blood. The wounded pigs fell at the pen's entrance, kicking and struggling, blocking the path of those still inside, rushing now in a chaotic, churning mass through the small space, terrified by the roar and rattle of bullets slamming the enclosure. The frenzied animals were still battering Bartley as he tried to move along the wall.

As the flare drifted lower, and the lower slope lit up down as far as the road, Bartley saw the man behind the cruiser, sighting calmly through the sniper rifle's scope. Bartley knelt against the concrete base of the enclosure, extended the stock of his MP5, cradled the gun against his shoulder and pointed it toward the man. He held the man's head and torso neatly in the circle of the sight, breathed out fully, paused, then squeezed the trigger, spraying a full burst of fifteen bullets in his direction.

Bartley lowered the gun as the flare died out; he couldn't see the man any more, but was sure that he'd seen blood spattered on the hood and roof of the cruiser; he'd blown out the windshield, too.

He yelled out "Sniper from the road is *down!*"

A fresh hurricane of semiautomatic and submachine-gun fire clattered through the enclosure as Bartley dropped into the muck. He rolled onto his back, pulled out his phone and dialed 911.

122

Craine stood on the dock, staring up over the fields, watching the unfolding slaughter. His granddaughter was up in the house, but what could he do?

He made up his mind quickly: he could *leave*.

He tossed the leather bag into the swamp boat, untied the boat and jumped in. He grabbed the wheel, hit the ignition button. The engine sputtered, then came to life in a small cloud of blue smoke. He lowered the long axle of the propeller into the water, pushed the throttle gently, and moved the boat slowly out onto the river. The sound of the engine was muffled by the noise of gunfire. He made his way out into the dark water and steered toward the open channel. Beyond it the sea.

As he was nearing the highway bridge the sky lit up.

Craine turned to look back at his farm and saw the men scattered on the slope up to the bunkhouses, men shooting down at them. He saw Bentas drop, shredded by machine-pistol fire; he recognized the killer as Bartley, one of the cops supposedly bought by the cartel.

His pigs were getting shot as they ran through the battle, falling in the withering hail of bullets. Craine watched one of the larger hogs sprinting across the grass suddenly skew and tumble, rolling into a slide down the hill, hitting two men hiding behind a shield. The men slid downhill with the pig, and Craine saw one of them shot in the head before the three came to rest just by the road; one of the men crawled out of the pile and onto the road to lie on the berm. He lay still; his partner was clearly dead.

The daylight flare died out, but Craine had seen enough to be able to make his way under the bridge safely. The sound of the boat's engine reverberated against the metal struts and the rock foundation, and he pushed the throttle, jammed it forward. The bow rose a little as the propeller dug deep, and soon Craine was skimming out over the Gulf of Mexico.

123

Jenner lay by the road toward the north end of the property. To his right the battle was raging over the slope; he'd positioned himself well to the side of the fighting.

He looked back toward the dock; he couldn't see Deb anymore. As they'd watched Craine head toward the ocean, Jenner had helped her into the kayak and quietly pushed her out into the water, telling her to avoid the main river, to paddle away from the ocean and into the swamp using one of the feeder channels instead – heading towards the highway would be too obvious.

She'd wanted him to leave with her, but he wouldn't. He couldn't, not until he'd found Lucy.

After the flare went out the shooting became intermittent, then stopped. There was moaning, audible moaning coming from the field, and the occasional low grunt of a wounded animal.

How many of the cops were still active? The police sniper was dead, and Jenner had seen another cop killed as he slid down the slope with a shot pig. He'd counted four other cops pinned down on the hill; he couldn't see Bartley, but he'd spotted him in the pigpen when he'd killed the sniper with his machine pistol. Jenner assumed that he was still there.

It grew quiet on the slope.

He decided to make his way uphill, find Bartley, warn him that Craine's daughter was in the farmhouse. No one had been shooting from the farmhouse; it might be safe.

Jenner crossed the road at a crouch, knowing that if another flare went up he was a dead man.

He made it onto the upper field, climbed the fence, then squatted. The enclosure was barely three hundred feet away, but there was a new problem: Bartley had vanished.

Jenner hung back, realizing that not only might Bartley have moved but that if he were still there he might try to kill Jenner if he approached. He swore under his breath.

Movement. Beyond the bullet-riddled enclosure, Bartley was crawling across the slope to his men.

Jenner moved again toward the farmhouse; he'd find Lucy, get her out. He climbed the fence, crossed the road again and followed it up on the far side until he came to a parking area with a handful of farm vehicles, a couple hundred yards from Craine's Volvo. He moved between the cars, edging closer to the farmhouse.

Jenner paused. It would take him a few seconds to cover the distance to the Volvo, during which he'd be in plain sight. If there was anyone in the farmhouse he'd be cut to ribbons before he reached the station wagon.

He scanned the windows, looking for movement, looking for light, looking for anything.

But the lit windows stayed lit, and the dark windows stayed empty, and nothing moved.

He would sprint. He would count to ten, then he'd book it across that space, just keep his head down and run full tilt.

He counted, tense behind the pickup.

Ten.

Nine.

Eight.

To Jenner's right, the assault team across the field began to shoot, firing short bursts up at the windows. They were moving forward now, firing, then running. Creeping up, sometimes moving behind shields, sometimes taking cover behind the pig carcasses.

The shooters in the bunkhouses returned fire, but in the poor light, without the sniper to harass them, and now spread out across the width of the field, the cops were harder targets.

Bartley was crawling up the slope; he'd move forward, then mutter an instruction to one of the other SWAT team members, who relayed the command with hand gestures.

The team had lost two men, and several had sustained superficial limb wounds, but their action was coordinated now, and they were moving efficiently, really covering ground. It seemed to Jenner that they were meeting less resistance as they got closer. Someone with a submachine gun in the far bunkhouse was raking the field, but the cops kept on moving.

Jenner stared up at the farmhouse. Judging from the firefight on the slope Brodie had been expecting the cops and had stationed shooters in the bunkhouses; no one had fired from or fired at the farmhouse. Craine would be keeping Lucy somewhere safe: a basement, if there was one, or maybe a bathroom – some place deep inside, anyway.

The cops had reached the top of the slope and were readying their bunkhouse assault; Jenner took advantage of the distraction. He crouched down again, then edged up on his toes and focused on the shadow behind the Volvo. He tilted forward, then thought, *Oh, fuck it! Two, one . . .*

He launched off and sprinted full pelt, stare fixed on the Volvo; he'd made it about fifteen feet when Brodie punched the detonator.

124

The bunkhouses exploded into a single curtain of orange flame, fire spraying out horizontally and then rushing into the sky, shredding walls, blowing off the flimsy roofs, shattering the windows in a blizzard of powdered glass. The chemical tanks in the bunkhouses exploded and vaporizing gases howled through the twisted metal carcasses of the buildings, instantly igniting into huge geysers of fire.

Within seconds, the huge propane tank buried between the farmhouse and the bunkhouse detonated. The buildings disappeared in a vast ball of orange and blue flame, and shredded clapboard slats and roofing tiles rained down on the slope.

The buildings at the top of the slope were all ablaze, an almost continuous line of billowing flame, melting tar paper and blackening clapboard. Despite the damp ground, the burning gases turned the grassy slope into a tilted pyre, the bodies of men and pigs charring in the intense heat, thick, acrid smoke twisting up into the sky and floating to hang in a pall out over the swamp.

The rain had stopped. The column of dense smoke rose into the sky like a knotted black rope, visible for miles. Behind it, the silver moon turned the edges of the parting clouds luminous.

Brodie walked back toward the burning buildings, bemused and fascinated by the scene of complete annihilation. Craine's Volvo was charred and shattered, the windows blown out, the paint scorched and blistered, the car as riddled by wood and metal shrapnel as if it had been ambushed with a Gatling gun. Beyond it, the farmhouse lawn had been showered with destroyed furniture – a refrigerator door here, the headboard of a sleigh bed there.

He walked across the slope. The wreckage from the bunkhouses was less refined – dented pots, shredded jeans, the neck and strings of a guitar. The grass fire was burning itself out, and the debris field was scattered with all kinds of charred, smoldering objects, from mattresses to corpses.

Brodie quickly and systematically searched the slope for survivors, moving back and forth across the field like a weaving shuttle, his pistol cocked and ready at his side; there would be no survivors tonight.

He found Smith's left arm, the idiotic tattoo of Mickey fucking Minnie immediately identifiable. Halfway down the slope, near the periphery of the debris field, he found the rest of him. The man was barely alive, the burned skin of his face and torso so pasted with soot that Brodie only spotted him when Smith opened his eyes and Brodie saw the whites. Smith seemed to recognize him, so Brodie muttered, "It's okay, the ambulances are coming" – and, when Smith closed his eyes, he shot him in the head.

Brodie stood. That left Tarver, who should've been in Bunkhouse B, with all the Mexies; with a bit of luck, there wouldn't be much of him left at all. Brodie had a moment of satisfaction when he found the remains of Tarver's camcorder, but he needed to find the remains of Tarver himself; as soon as he caught sight of that mop of stringy yellow hair, Brodie would be able to pronounce the site cleaned, climb in his car and go.

He moved back up the slope, skirting the heat of the

flames still pouring from the bunkhouse foundations. He was moving faster now – he should get going. It looked like he'd set half of Florida on fire, and someone would soon call 911, if they hadn't already done so. There was no way anyone, let alone Tarver, could've survived the explosion and the fire.

He was going to call it a day and head on home. He was crossing the ridge of the hill, imagining his pool in Costa Rica, when he heard, "Yo, boss . . ."

Brodie turned to see Tarver, one hand raised in greeting, not thirty feet away. Brodie raised his pistol.

"Wait! It's me – *Tarver*! I got out!" He put both hands up, and moved closer so Brodie could see that it was in fact him. "I know you told me to stay and guard the Mexies, but I went out the back window to try and flank the cops again like Bentas, and then the whole fucking thing blew!"

"Come closer."

Tarver took a wary step toward Brodie. "You okay, boss?"

"Closer still."

Tarver stared behind Brodie and said, "Someone's over there!"

Brodie glanced quickly down the slope and saw Jenner running across the road towards the boat shed. He'd forgotten all about him and the ranger girl.

"Get him!"

125

Jenner sprinted the length of the dock and then dove. He swam out under inky water warm and thick as blood, away from the highway, away from the sea beyond it. He was swimming upstream to lose himself in the safety of the mangrove maze. He came up for air, a quick gasp before ducking underneath again. He'd have barely a minute before they reached the dock; the less wake he left, the safer he and Deb would be.

He came up again, swimming now to the shallows of the nearer tributary, the channel he'd told Deb to take. The broad river was fed by many smaller streams that ran through the mangrove forest: in the shadows, the men following would have a tough time tracking them, particularly if their pursuers were in the big airboat.

He wondered how far upstream Deb had gone – she could go anywhere in the swamp with the kayak.

Light jerked out over the water from the dock. Jenner sank back under and pushed into the shallows, hiding among the cascading mangrove roots.

The beam of light skidded across the surface; they seemed to be sizing up the situation at the dock more than looking for him. He recognized Brodie and another man, heard their voices across the water.

"He got the Go Devil!"

"It's slow, we'll catch up. Start up the airboat, and let's go."

The airboat's engine coughed twice, then rose to a deep, humming roar. The beam of light scattered over the surface towards Jenner, then bounced away, and then the airboat was skimming across the surface; it picked up speed, heading downriver towards the highway bridge and the sea.

They'd soon realize Jenner didn't have the swamp boat. He moved deeper into the mangroves. The tributary was shallow enough for him to stand, the water reaching his mid-chest. The smell was stale and vegetal – the dark, muddy reek of rotting plants and brackish water – the air humid and his sweat salty under the thick canopy. The banks were not earth but the hard, tangled roots of the trees, big knots of spindly rootlets leaping off the mangrove trunks to plunge into the water. Under the surface, the roots grew together into a wall as dense as the tangle of branches above; the going was slow and hard.

Jenner kept moving. Swimming was no easier – the dark waters looked still but they were moving quickly, swollen with the rains; he found himself standing and walking, pushing forward into the stream, holding the mangrove roots like handles. He called out for Deb; by now, Brodie would be far enough away for it to be safe. In any case, even if they were just a hundred feet away the vast airboat engine would drown out all other sound.

But there was no answer. He was moving deeper and deeper into the mangroves, the branches and leaves and mud and water slowly swallowing him. When he called Deb, the sound died out within a few feet, stifled by the thick baffle of the low canopy.

Jenner had kept the river to his right, but had now lost sight of it as he followed the channel. Particularly in Deb's condition, how far could she have gone?

Jenner stopped, let his feet down, cupped his hands around his mouth to amplify the sound, and yelled her name again. He didn't know how far he'd come, how fast he'd been swimming and walking. He couldn't see the orange light of the burning farm, he couldn't even smell the fire in the trapped air of the swamp.

He should just stop. Stop and wait in the shadows, then in a while go back to the farm: there'd be a police and FD response. They were probably already there – it was probably already safe.

He just needed to find Deb first. The men in the airboat wouldn't keep looking downstream much longer.

126

Ten minutes later he still hadn't found her.

Jenner was getting desperate. Where *was* she? The sweat poured down his face, his mouth parched and bitter, sunk to his chest in muddy water, nothing to drink.

He pressed forward. He felt the full burden of his fatigue now; when he shouted for Deb, his voice cracked and broke from the strain and from the dehydration.

Light swung through the undergrowth, the brilliant white beam of a spotlight, diffracting through the maze of pale trunks and branches, the mangroves a shifting kaleidoscope of silver roots and black shadow. Now Jenner could hear the low throb of the airboat as it came nearer.

He pulled himself up against the edge of the stream, in among the roots. The sound was louder now, the light brighter. The spotlight operator was moving it slowly, sending the beam through the mesh of mangroves, trying to pick him out.

Jenner lay against the roots, gasping, smelling the black fetid swamp mud, feeling moisture – sweat, water, he couldn't tell – trickling down his face.

It hadn't taken them long to turn around and come back to look for Deb and Jenner. He was exhausted now, his muscles burning, his joints on fire, his sodden clothes weighing a ton. He didn't know how much farther he could go.

The light moved past him, and as the airboat moved forward, he saw his channel through the mangrove forest taper and die two hundred yards upstream, the dense curtain of trunks and leaves sealing off his escape.

Deb must have taken the tributary on the far side of the river.

To reach her, Jenner would have to make his way back toward the dock, get past the airboat, swim across the river, and head back up the tributary on the other side.

127

Deb held still as the bright light cut through the mangroves. The airboat was much closer than she'd expected – ten, fifteen yards at most. She'd thought she'd moved far away from the river, but now she saw that she'd simply been rowing parallel to it.

The airboat was idling, not moving forward, not moving back, staying still while the searchlight beam crept slowly through the undergrowth, picking its way through the stunted trees like a steel dental hook, poking into the crevices to winkle her out.

Why weren't they moving? They must have seen something – her silhouette, maybe, the yellow of the kayak.

The light crawled toward her. Deb made her mind up quickly.

She pressed her hand to her wounded side to brace it, then tipped to her right to roll the kayak. Her torso slipped into the water; she struggled to extract her legs, to kick out of the cockpit silently. The salt water roared into her wounds, red-hot pokers jabbing into her flank.

She could barely stand. She pushed the kayak down, opened the front deck hatch and pressed the little boat under until water flowed into the cockpit and hatch. She let the kayak half fill, then shoved it over into the mangrove roots, wedging it there.

Then she swam out into the channel, her eyes desperately searching for a hiding place in the thick wall of mangroves opposite.

From the river, the airboat searchlight was still combing the undergrowth.

Deb was almost halfway across when the airboat engine revved up loud, and the light swung around. The boat flew off back in the direction of the dock.

Had they given up? Were *they* on the run now, not her?

She let herself slow down, rolling onto her back to look up at the sky, her breathing easier. On her back she could float better, let her arms do the work, which hurt less than when she kicked.

She let her neck tip back into the water, and as she did she heard a high-pitched metallic grinding. She knew instantly what it meant: they'd doubled back into her tributary, and were now flying toward her at high speed.

She swam hard. Each time she came up for breath, the

bright searchlight seemed to shoot a straight silver line right at her, right up the middle of the channel from the airboat to her; no matter how hard she swam, it followed. But it was an illusion of her focus; the searchlight operator hadn't spotted her, she had spotted the searchlight.

Afraid they'd catch her splashes, Deb dipped below the surface, tried to make herself go deeper, pulled herself under, clutched the underwater roots to hold herself down until her lungs were bursting. Finally, when she could take it no more, she let her mouth and nose break the surface.

They were a hundred yards downstream. The searchlight was now picking its way along the opposite bank. They *must* have seen her earlier – they were looking right where she'd been.

She swam under the branches of a clump of young buttonwoods lodged among the mangroves. The branches hung out over the water, but if the searchlight hit her they'd see her instantly.

Deb clutched a thicker branch and pulled herself up, gasping with pain as the muscles of her left side tightened to steady her. She rolled through the undergrowth, falling backwards onto the branch-ribbed carpet of rotten leaves and roots and shrubs, wriggling until she was hidden by the dense boughs of the buttonwoods.

The airboat drew nearly level; she pressed her back down into the leaves in the shallow depression behind the buttonwoods.

There was the crack of a gunshot, then the airboat jumped forward, and there were two more quick shots as they pulled up to the kayak. There were two men on the boat, an older man on the stick, a younger one in the bows near the kayak; she'd seen neither of them before. The younger man tugged loosely at the kayak's yellow hull with the gaff in his left hand; he held a .45 in his right.

He put the gun down on the seat and lay on the floor of the airboat to reach out and unsnag the kayak from the mangroves. The kayak bobbed free, then sank quickly.

He stood to speak to the older man, then sat back down behind the searchlight. The engine powered up again, and they crept slowly along the far bank, raking the dark trees with the light, hunting Deb like a heron hunting a frog.

She lay back. If she kept this position they wouldn't see her; all she had to do was just keep still until they left.

Deb breathed slowly. She couldn't get comfortable, roots and branches prodding her back, each movement of her hips or shoulder twisting her wound.

She tried to distract herself by making a list of things that made her happy, but the fear kept cutting in so she focused instead on each pain she felt – the root under her left calf, the torn stump poking her back, the dull burn of her injury when she moved. She told herself four or five minutes tops, and then they'd move on: time would be tight for them, too. She just mustn't budge, or they'd see her.

Something moved across her leg.

In the dark, Deb couldn't see it but she was sure she'd felt something. It wasn't just the scratch of a branch or a fold in her clothing settling – something had actually moved across her leg.

Her breathing came faster. Light gilded the leaves around her as the airboat swung round and began to search her side of the river, moving closer to her hiding place.

There was more movement, a slow rustle, a light, twitching pressure as something else wriggled across her thigh.

Now there was one on her leg, and another inching along the skin of her flank where her shirt had ridden up. Deb was afraid to touch it, afraid to see what it was. It's too small to be a snake, she told herself, it's too small to be a snake.

The light was close now, flooding the trees, a magnesium-bright dawn enveloping her. She had to hold still – any movement, any jostle of a branch and they'd spot her. She breathed in, and tried to ignore all the small things crawling over her body. There was one under her shirt, slithering up her belly; her wound burned at the thought of this thing moving across her stomach, attracted by blood, finding the hole, poking inside her wound . . .

And then she heard it: a desultory, hollow clicking right next to her ear, so close that it was like someone had leaned in to whisper to her, but had instead shaken a rattle.

The light grew brighter, and Deb let her head turn to see that she was in a nest of snakes. Young snakes were crawling over her belly, her thighs, her calf; slender gray snakes, hours old, with a hatched yellow pattern across their backs. And next to them, belly grotesquely bloated with eggs, was their mother, an Eastern diamondback rattler about five feet long.

Deb didn't move, didn't flinch. The rattler was two feet from her head. Light poured through the buttonwoods; she saw the snake's tail lift slightly, saw the sequenced ripple of muscle as the big snake squeezed out a

427

glistening, transparent egg sac, the fetal snake inside coiled tight, the lethal diamond pattern already clearly visible on its silvery scales. It wriggled inside the clear gelatin until it tore through the membrane and seeped limply out onto the earth next to her.

The hollow was bright as day. In the roar of the airboat engine, she stopped breathing. The newborn snakes on her belly and legs were still now; *It's the warmth*, she thought, *they're attracted to my body heat.*

The rattler's body shone in the light, shaking with effort as she expressed another watery, gelatinous egg sac, the brilliantly illuminated little killer inside twisting and writhing in preparation for freedom. The twisting motion of the swollen belly and tail made a stuttering rattle, the sound that Deb had heard earlier.

The snake seemed barely aware of Deb. But would that change if she moved? Rattlers were fast – the snake could coil and strike before Deb could even swing her legs out.

She'd managed two rattlesnake bites in the Glades. The first man had lived, but the second, a German tourist bitten when he'd left his designated campsite to pee, had taken hours to reach the ranger station. By the time he made it his entire leg was glossy and boggy with liquid blood, bruised the color of eggplant. He'd died in the back of her jeep on the way to the hospital.

Deb lay immobile, her lips not moving as she prayed.

128

Brodie, up on the bench behind the airboat's stick, peered into the press of branches and leaves. The ranger had to be on this tributary; the other channel quickly dead-ended, and she wasn't on the river where they'd found the kayak. She'd have started paddling before they'd chased Jenner to the water; it was unlikely that he'd have caught up with her, so where was he? Maybe they'd gone in different directions.

What had Jenner been looking for on the farm? They'd got out of the boat shed – why didn't they just run? Brodie needed to find him, learn just what the hell he was up to.

But they'd catch him, all right. A man could move pretty easily through the mangroves on the water, but the forest was an impenetrable tangle of branch and root and sapling and shrub: no way could Jenner get through on foot. He had to stay on the water. And if they could find the ranger girl, Brodie had a feeling they'd find Jenner, too. And when they did . . .

Brodie spat. He could've used Tony, but Tony wasn't there – fled or dead now, he figured.

He wondered if the cops were already at the farm. Securing his passport and his money were one of the private errands he'd taken care of before he blew the building. He could leave his rental car at the farm – the cops would be piecing burned flesh together for months, and they'd never be able to say for sure whether or not they'd found any bits of Mr. James Brodie of Mendocino, California.

As soon as they found Jenner, got him to talk, Brodie would be on his way. Get rid of Jenner, the girl, too, if they found her – she didn't matter so much since she didn't know his name. Then kill Tarver.

It was all still doable. He could do it. He could get away free now.

Free and rich.

He pushed the stick forward and the airboat jumped a little, then slipped downstream. He was surprised at how far back they'd come – the current was sliding them along.

Brodie turned and glanced downriver; the dock and boat house were in sight.

And, suddenly, so was Jenner – the unlucky bastard had chosen to move at just the wrong second. He was creeping around the spit of forest that separated the river from the channel that the girl had taken. Brodie would never have spotted him if Jenner hadn't moved as he glanced toward the dock.

He said nothing to Tarver and looked back at the bank in front of them, pretending to look for the girl. But he nudged the stick slightly, revved the engine, and let the airboat move faster.

Less than a minute later – a quick swooping turn, a couple of gunshots to show Jenner that they'd spotted him – and they had him. Tarver dragged Jenner up onto the boat, kicked him in the ribs to help him focus, and then, while he lay there winded, tied a noose of yellow nylon rope round his neck, tying the loose end to one of the seat stays.

Jenner lay on the floor of the boat, unable to move.

129

Above the engine, Brodie yelled, "Where's the girl?"

"What girl?" Jenner grinned feebly.

Brodie nodded, and Tarver kicked Jenner in the flank. He doubled up, gasping as the cord bit into his neck, trying to get his fingers under the rope. He lay there, gasping and retching from pain.

Brodie turned the airboat around and cut the throttle, moving back to the edge of the river opposite where they'd found the kayak; he was sure that the ranger girl was in there somewhere and he wanted her to see what he was going to do.

"Two questions. One: where is the girl? Two: what were you doing at the farm?"

Jenner had caught his breath now. "I was looking for Lucy Craine; I saw her go into the farmhouse, and I was trying to get her. Then the place exploded."

Brodie shrugged. "Eh. It didn't 'explode' – I exploded it." He grinned slightly. "So no need to worry about the Craine girl anymore. Where is the ranger, the one that Nash shot?"

It was Jenner's turn to shrug. "I don't know. I put her in the kayak, told her to head to the sea. By the time I got back, she was long gone . . ."

Brodie looked at Jenner for a minute, then shook his head. "I sure wish we were playing poker tonight, doc – you can't lie to save your life!"

130

Deb could feel the big snake moving now, the thick slab of dry muscle uncoiling up over her hip and on up by her elbow.

The light from the airboat had gone, and now she couldn't see the snake, only feel it. It was twisting next to her, its coils, thick as a grown man's calf, curving up her side as the baby snakes wriggled around her.

They were all over Deb now – she didn't know how many. Seven, nine? Twisting awkwardly in her hair, sliding up under her shirt, between her breasts. And the mother now, pressed against her. All of them touching her, pressing her, tickling her, burrowing on her, as if she were being caressed by the fingertips of a dozen deranged men, men who'd kill her if she made the slightest movement.

The big snake pulled back; Deb felt its coils gathering, imagined the head raising.

Then she heard a small splash from the river; something was coming toward them.

The slow rattle began, then got louder.

A weak light shone into the buttonwoods from the water; there was a sharp intake of breath, and Deb saw the snake rise up, its rattle, lifted above the coils, shrilling quickly now. The deadly narrow head swayed as the snake prepared to attack.

She mustn't move. Whatever she did she mustn't move.

The light grew brighter, and Deb closed her eyes. She anticipated the strike, the snake's body driving straight at her, recoiling in a fraction of a second, blood and venom and death in its wake.

The light flared through her eyelids and she saw orange and Deb heard the rattle reach a crescendo, a high buzzing as dry as a cicada on a hot summer's day. Something hard nudged her leg.

She opened her eyes and saw the shotgun blast, the snake's head explode into a cloud of blood, the headless body thrashing and knotting, rolling over her hip to smear blood across her stomach. And when her ears could hear again, the first thing Deb heard was the shimmering rattle, still shaking as the snake's headless body writhed and twisted.

A small man, a shadow behind the glare of a flashlight, was leaning into the bushes, the shotgun now pointing at the ground. The light shifted as he reached in to grab Deb's wrist, and she saw that the lower part of his face was covered by a bandanna, bandit-style.

131

Brodie's eyes scanned the banks of the river. Nothing. It was probably just thunder out over the glades.

"Okay, enough of this shit." He turned to Tarver. "Throw him over the back."

Tarver was confused. "What?"

"Make sure he's tied to the seat rail, and toss him in! Jesus! Don't you even speak English?"

Tarver, muttering, dragged Jenner to the stern. Jenner struggled, tried to clutch onto something, anything, but Tarver moved him too quickly, pushing him against the low rim at the side of the boat, then rolling him over.

Jenner hit the water and was immediately dragged back behind the boat, choking and gasping as he tried to get his face above the surface, fighting to jam his fingers under the noose around his neck.

He'd just managed to get his palm under the rope when Brodie gunned the airboat; the rope snapped tight and they shot forward, Jenner bouncing and spinning behind. He had one hand wedged between the yellow rope and his neck, and with the other fought to hold onto the tow rope for all he was worth, feeling his biceps tear as he fought to give his neck some slack.

The water banged against his back, flailing him from side to side, gasping and spluttering, gulping in water, vomiting it back out. The rope dug deep into his hand as the noose locked tight around his neck. His fingers went numb, his neck on fire as the rope cut a deep groove into his skin.

The airboat slowed abruptly to an idle and Jenner's momentum slammed him against the low transom.

On the deck, Brodie was standing, facing the dark mangroves.

He yelled. "Officer! You want me to do him one more time? This next one will kill him, I figure . . ."

He waited.

"Up to you. I promise you I'll let you go; you probably doubt me, but I'm a man of my word. You don't know my name, you don't know who I am, and within hours I'll be gone, and no one in this country will ever see me again. This isn't about you."

Tarver was moving the searchlight's beam along the

bank, shifting shadows through the foliage.

Jenner had worked the noose a little looser. He grabbed the back rail of the airboat, pulled himself a little bit out of the water, then croaked, "His name is Brodie! Listen to me, his name is Brodie, he's Craine's foreman at the farm, he's a drug dealer. Stay where you are!"

Brodie rolled his eyes. "That's all wrong – do you actually think I'd use my real name?"

They stared into the mangroves.

Brodie sighed, and climbed back up onto the stick.

"Tarver: push him away, and let's finish this."

A hundred feet behind them some branches swayed, and Deb appeared, slipping waist-deep into the water, hands above her head.

Brodie nodded at her. "Thank you, officer. You'll see that I'm a man of my word."

He turned to Tarver. "Get him on board, then help her in."

Jenner lay on the floor of the boat. When he lifted his hands to loosen the rope he saw that his fingers were torn open, a grooved burn across the soft flesh of his palms where he'd fought the rope.

Deb grunted in pain as Tarver dragged her over the rail into the airboat. She lay next to Jenner.

He said, pointlessly, "You shouldn't have."

"It'll be okay, Jenner. They were going to kill you."

"They're still going to kill me. And now that I've told you his name he'll kill you, too."

132

Brodie let the engine idle.

Jenner held Deb close on the floor, Tarver watching, pistol in hand. Tarver was getting antsy, peering back toward the farm, prodding Brodie about when they could leave, when they could just get the fuck out of there.

Deb shook her head and whispered to him, "It'll be okay, Jenner. Just wait, it'll be all right, you'll see. They just need a little more time."

Brodie squatted next to them.

"Okay, doc. Let's just do this. And let's save some time – we both know how this is going to go. I'll ask you some questions and you either answer or you don't. If you don't answer, I hurt you, or maybe her, until you *do* answer. In the end, you'll answer – trust me on this."

"What's in it for us?"

Brodie shook his head. "Enough. You know how this is going to play out – it's a question of whether or not there's pain."

Jenner nodded. "Okay. No pain."

"Good. We've all had enough of that." Brodie spat into the dark water. "Who did you tell, and what have you told them? Call anyone in Port Fontaine?"

Jenner shook his head. "I called a friend in New York – he's bringing in the D.E.A."

Brodie sat back in the seat and grinned. "You're smart to avoid the locals – I mean, don't think Feds aren't for sale, but, yeah, you can buy a hick cop for the price of a doughnut and a pack of smokes."

He looked at the girl. She was lying close to Jenner, her eyes closed.

"Sorry about your ranger friend, doc. I'll make it quick."

Brodie looked at Jenner again. "Oh, one last thing – there was some money, Craine gave you some money – I don't suppose . . ."

"He took it back."

"Yeah, figured he would, that fucker. The rich get richer, eh, doctor?" He glanced over to Tarver, and nodded, then looked back at Jenner. "Anything else I should know?"

And at that moment the night turned into day.

133

They came out of nowhere, two boats, big searchlights flooding the whole estuary with light, Tarver and Brodie and Jenner blinking in the blinding glare. Brodie threw an arm up to shade his dazzled eyes, and Tarver lifted his pistol; a shotgun blast blew his knee out from under him, and he collapsed, howling, on top of Jenner.

Jenner pushed out from under him and rolled onto his back; shielding his eyes, he saw Brodie calmly lift both his hands up and place them on his head.

He whispered to Deb, "Deb, the Feds . . . Hold very still; we're all suspects until they straighten out our stories."

She shook her head. "It's not the Feds, Jenner."

He struggled to sit up, his back braced against the front-row seat struts.

The searchlights dimmed, and Jenner saw more boats

arriving, sliding downriver, and out of the feeder channel came three smaller boats, not much more than canoes with outboards. And the boats, small and large, were full of people – all told, Jenner figured, probably twenty men. They were short and dark, all wearing bandannas pulled up over their noses. Their faces were broad, their hair black, skin mahogany from days in the sun. Some carried cane machetes, others held pistols and shotguns; most of the shotguns were pointing at Brodie, who was grinning wryly.

The boats formed a ring pontoon around the airboat. A man stepped onto the airboat, followed closely by the only big man in the flotilla, a hulking giant whose David Beckham T-shirt bulged like a frying sausage about to pop; the shotgun seemed like a squirt gun in his hands.

The first man ignored Tarver's moaning and turned his back on Brodie to squat next to Jenner. He peered at the rope burn on Jenner's neck and shook his head, then lowered his bandana to speak. His English was heavily accented but fluid, and he spoke with an almost elegant intensity. "Doctor, this is not your fight now. We will take you to land safely; you have no cause to worry."

He looked at Deb. "Your lady . . . She is okay?"

Jenner said, "She's lost some blood; she needs to get to a hospital."

The man spoke urgently to some of his followers in a dialect that Jenner didn't recognize. The other men began to redistribute themselves among the remaining boats; Jenner realized they were making room for him and Deb.

"We will take you to land. We have a . . ." He turned and spoke to the man behind him in the same dialect.

The big man thought for a second, then said "Pickup trock."

"Yes, we have a pickup trock; we will take you to the hospital. We can only take you at the entrance, you understand?"

Jenner nodded.

"There is one thing we must ask of you."

Jenner looked up at him expectantly.

The man gestured loosely to Brodie and Tarver. "This human filth, this *ordure*, they do not exist now. They are gone from the world. You do not see them." His speech was measured and even. "You make your way to the land all by yourself, thanks to God, and a good stranger drives you to the hospital. You do not know what happen to this scum, this animal. You understand, gentleman?"

Jenner nodded.

The man said, "Lady? You understand what I say too?"

"Yes." Deb said. "And thank you."

The man tucked his pale gray bandanna higher up his face and shrugged, his eyes narrowing. "I do not know what it is you are talking about."

He held out a hand to Jenner and helped him to his feet, then had his men move Deb to one of the outboards. He watched Jenner get into the smaller boat, then nodded to the man at the helm. As the boat picked up speed, he nodded at Jenner, then lifted one hand high in salute, fingers clenched into a fist.

The last time Jenner saw him, the man was turning to deal with Brodie and Tarver.

134

On the Promenade, the heavy rain had started late enough to make no difference, spoil no plans – the restaurants were all already empty, the shops closed, even the fairy lights in the trees were dark as Jenner drove to Stella Maris. The smaller pastel houses along the Promenade's commercial strip gave way to the big white mansions, many now deserted as their owners made the annual summer pilgrimage to their cooler homes in East Hampton or Edgartown or Kennebunkport. To his left, the Gulf was vast and black and empty, the waves, silent and cold, sliding onto an empty beach.

Between the slow swoop of the windscreen wipers, the Sebring's headlights lit up the open black gates of Stella Maris; the security team was gone, the fish-eye CCTV lens still and unseeing. Jenner parked on the carriage circle in front of the house; the driveway was empty.

He sat, seat belt still fastened, listening to the hushed rustle of rain on his car roof, feeling the exhaustion eating his bones like acid.

Deb would be clean now, in a hospital bed in the small urgent care center in Bel Arbre. He'd helped her into the reception area and had rung the bell. She'd hugged him, her arms tightening around his neck when he first started to pull back. She shook her head and murmured, "Please, please, just call the sheriff, Jenner." But he couldn't do that.

He'd turned to look at the Mexicans waiting out on the road in their pickup truck, and she felt him start to turn, and clutched on to him; she knew they were taking him back to his car, and that she couldn't stop him from going.

She told him to be careful and kissed him on the mouth, a soft, sad kiss, and then he pulled back, away from her. When he turned to look at her through the glass doors the nurses were coming to her.

Jenner moved his seat back, pulled the Beretta out and lay it across his lap, feeling the seriousness of its weight.

He looked up at the house, golden and bright in the garden floodlights. He saw no movement, but they'd be in there now, both of them. They'd have heard his car, seen his headlights.

He walked down the path, down the steps past the pool to the lower of the terraced lawns. He stood at the white balustrade, looked out over the dock, where the swamp boat was moored.

The house looked huge from the bottom of the garden, its immaculate surfaces coffered by rectangles of light pouring from the windows. Jenner climbed the steps, remembering the first time he'd seen it, how perfect it had seemed, how luxurious, every man's dream.

He crossed the broad veranda, stripped of its furniture, now a barren plaza of slick marble; he went in through the open sliding doors that led to the ground-floor breakfast room. Lucy Craine's passport lay on the low glass coffee table; behind the table the garbage bags had been flung onto a couch. Jenner opened them to check; the money was still there.

The kitchen was tiled in clinical white. It was larger than most restaurant kitchens, with glass-fronted SubZero fridges and wall-mounted ovens and under-cabinet wine coolers and an eight-burner Wolf range; a child could dog-paddle in the huge soapstone sinks.

Jenner stepped out into the back of the huge entrance hall. The floor was a checkerboard of large black and white marble tiles that shone under the light of an enormous crystal chandelier.

He heard the sound of muffled speech from upstairs, movement too, someone passing rapidly back and forth between rooms. He lifted the Beretta and climbed the wide stairs, the conversation growing louder as he neared the landing.

On the second floor, his footsteps were silent in the deep pile of the carpet. The sound was clearer now, and he recognized the rhythm and crackle of a police radio scanner; Craine was listening on the sheriff's frequency, listening to the operation up at the farm.

The sound came from the half-open door of the master bedroom, just off the stairwell. Jenner stood in the doorway, the Beretta in his hand.

There was an open carry-on bag on a large four-poster bed. Craine stood in the middle of the room, his back to the doorway, packing his beautiful handmade shirts into the bag. His pistol, a small Walther, lay on his bureau next to the chattering scanner.

"Craine."

He straightened slowly, and glanced toward the dresser.

"Don't," Jenner said. "I'm not the world's best shot, but at this distance I won't miss."

Craine raised his hands, and turned slowly to face Jenner. He was smiling slightly.

"I like you, Jenner! You've got . . . *gumption*!"

Jenner shrugged. "More importantly, I have a Beretta."

"Yes", Craine said. "Yes, you do."

He backed over to the bed and sat. "Do I have to keep my arms up?"

"Suit yourself."

Craine lowered his arms. "You know, you can still walk away from this a wealthy man."

"It's too late for that."

Craine laughed. "Good God, doctor! It's never too late for money!"

"Your granddaughter is dead because of you."

Craine's smile slackened a little, and a tremor of emotion passed across the man's face; it could've been real. "You can have no possible idea of what a nightmare this is." He paused a second, then said, "But of course, you have to understand that I had no way of knowing what would happen there tonight."

Maggie Craine said, "What would happen where?"

Both men turned. She stood shivering in the doorway, her hair wet, skin flushed; there was something ominous, feverish in her expression.

Jenner turned to Craine and said, "Tell her."

Craine stood; he looked at his daughter, but stayed silent.

"Tell her or I will."

"Where is she? Where's Lucy? For the love of God, what did you do?"

Craine said, "Maggie, listen . . . You need to pull yourself together. This is hard on all of us."

"Where's my daughter?" She was shaking violently now, the words chattering out of her mouth.

Craine looked at Jenner. "Doctor, I think we should get her to a hospital."

The scanner crackled, and an urgent voice said,

"Sheriff, this is Weeks. We're in the basement now . . ." The voice grew hesitant. "You maybe oughta see this. We have the body of a young female, a girl. She's pretty charred up, but . . . I'm sorry, sir, but she's a skinny little thing, and with the backpack, I'm pretty positive we got Lucy Craine here."

Maggie screamed out, "You fucking *bastard*! How *could* you! How *could* you?"

Craine shook his head helplessly. "Maggie, I didn't know what was going to happen. I just wanted to . . ."

"You wanted to what? You wanted to WHAT??? What were you doing with her in the basement?"

He smiled thinly. "I just took her to the farm for a nice evening with her Papaw."

Maggie pulled the pistol out of her purse so quickly that Jenner had no time to react. She fired once; there was a spray of red from Craine's neck, and the string went out of his spine and he collapsed vertically, folded into himself and on down to the floor. He lay there, gasping, eyes open but not moving, blood pulsing rhythmically out of the hole in his neck.

Jenner dropped to his knees, threw his gun aside and said, "Jesus Christ! Jesus!"

He hovered helplessly over Craine, saw the blood pulse out. He covered the wound with his hands – he had to do something. He pressed firmly, feeling the shredded muscle beneath the skin rippling under his fingers.

Over his shoulder, he said, "I think it hit his spinal cord. Please call 911, Maggie. Please, they can help him."

"Move, Jenner."

He looked up at her. She was pointing the gun at him.

"Move now. Don't make me."

"If I let go now, he'll die, Maggie. You'll be a murderer."

"Let go, Jenner. It'll be on me."

"This is a death-penalty state, Maggie. He's not worth it."

She lifted the gun slightly and fired. A shower of pulverized veneer and mahogany erupted from a dresser.

"Let go." She pointed the gun at Jenner again.

Jenner looked down at Craine, at the blood welling over his fingers, the muttering lips. He couldn't make himself lift his fingers up, couldn't just let the man die like that. He said, "I . . . I don't think I can."

Maggie stepped closer, leaned over Jenner, pointed the weapon down and fired two more shots into her father's face.

"You can now."

135

"Maggie? It's over." Jenner stood. "Put the gun down – now."

She looked down at the pistol, at the fine white smoke trickling from the hot muzzle.

"I had to, Jenner. He wouldn't have left her alone."

"What do you mean?"

"I found her journal. He was calling her, talking to her – he'd given her a cell phone, I didn't know, I swear, or I'd have stopped it." A big tear welled up in her left eye and spilled down her face.

"He was calling her most nights, Jenner. He was making her . . . do things. To herself."

She sat on the bed and looked up at him. "He was making her sick, you know? He told her she was fat, even when she weighed ninety-seven pounds, Jenner. When she was just a little paper bag of tiny bones, he told her that she was fat. He gave her a kind of anorexia prayer list, sick little prayers, horrible things to make her hurt herself."

Maggie held the gun loosely in her lap. "He was calling her most nights, calling when I was painting shitty paintings, or out with shitty men at the Polo Grounds."

Jenner said, "It's finished now. Give me the gun, okay? Let me take it . . ."

She shook her head. "There's one thing left, one more step to get rid of everything that man polluted."

"What do you mean?"

"Oh, Jenner, don't even! I know you know. You figured it out pretty quickly; I could tell you knew when you came to my house this afternoon."

He was silent.

"Say it. I know you know. Say it!"

He knew. "He said he just wanted to go away with his daughter, but he took her, not you."

She sneered. "Oh, I'm his daughter, all right! One hundred percent Craine DNA . . . Can't you tell?"

"And Lucy?"

Maggie smiled, her face suddenly calm. "You're getting warm . . ."

"Lucy was his daughter too?"

She crumpled, put her face into her hands, the pistol nuzzling her thick hair, her shoulders curving and sagging as though she was a wingless angel trying to fly while the sobs rocked her body.

"It was the worst thing that ever happened to me, and the only good thing I ever did!" Behind her hands, Maggie face was red and wet.

"Tell me what happened."

She sat up, wiping her eyes. "Well, it wasn't a stork!"

Jenner sat next to her.

"What happened, Maggie?"

She was crying hard again, her knuckles white around the gun, her fingers wet with tears.

Jenner waited.

She calmed and said, "It's so fucking banal . . . it happens every day to some girl somewhere in the country. I was twenty-three, and I'd come home from grad school for Spring Break. And we went to the Polo Grounds, and we got drunk, both of us, real drunk."

She sat straighter, and wiped the damp hair from her eyes.

"We were in the kitchen alone, and 'Stand by Me' came on the radio, and he hugged me, and we were dancing in the kitchen. And then I felt him pressing against my leg, and I pulled away, but he wouldn't let me go. He dragged me into the breakfast room, and he was kissing me, trying to get his tongue in my mouth, but he couldn't, so he was licking my neck. And he was too big for me to get him off of me. And it was like, you know . . . It all went quiet inside me. I just let him do it, I stopped fighting and just let him do it."

Maggie shook her head. "When he finished, he rolled off me and went to the kitchen and got a bottle of wine, and asked me if I wanted any. And that was that.

"I mean, I washed myself as best I could, but there wasn't a morning-after pill back then. And when I told him I was pregnant, he wasn't mad or even upset – he was . . . *intrigued*. He took me out of school, brought me back to Stella. He took me to a clinic in Gainesville to have an early amnio, and when it came back all right he promised me all sorts of things. And I kind of just let it happen."

She noticed the photo of the girl on the bedside table and picked it up, running her thumb softly over the little face.

"She was pretty much perfect – she had some hearing problems; the doctor didn't know – he said I probably had a viral infection while I was carrying her. But she was beautiful, and sweet, and a good girl."

There was crackling on the police scanner. Maggie stood abruptly, flicked the scanner off.

"But she's dead, and my father's dead – my turn now! Sorry."

She smiled helplessly at Jenner, lifted the gun to her temple, and he shouted "No!" – and she pulled the trigger.

She fell back against the bed, and slipped to the ground as he tried to gather her in his arms. Blood soaked her hair. She wasn't moving.

Jenner laid her flat. He touched his fingers to her neck, felt for a pulse. He pressed harder, felt nothing but the beat of his own heart in his finger tips.

He pressed the heel of his palm into her breastbone and began to pump, felt the give of her chest wall, the recoil of her lungs. He pumped for a minute, then felt for a pulse again.

And there was none, and he knew it was hopeless.

He stood, looked around the room. Craine lay dead on the floor, his daughter by the bed, four feet away from him.

Jenner went to the scanner and tried to find a microphone to call for help, but there was none. He switched the scanner on, and the overheated chatter from the farm filled the room. In the moment, confronted with the carnage and the loss, the deputies had given in to chaos, abandoning ten-code and just blurting whatever was going on out into the airwaves. The sheriff was on the scene now, shouting out orders to establish a perimeter, to keep the press at a distance.

Jenner walked down the stairs. In the kitchen fridge he found a carton of apple juice. He poured a tall glass, sat at the counter and drank it, tried to figure out his next step. He had Maggie's blood on him, both her blood and her father's; God only knew what else he'd touched in the house.

He finished the glass of juice and poured another. He drank, then rinsed the glass and put it back in the cabinet.

He took the bags of cash from the breakfast room and walked out to his car with them. He jammed them into his trunk, pressed them as flat as he could get them, then covered them with his clothes.

In Craine's bedroom the air smelled of blood and metal and gun smoke. Jenner stood in the doorway, looking at the bodies. Maggie Craine lay stretched next to the bed, her right leg draped over her left; she looked like a mannequin now, as if she'd never drawn breath.

He listened to the noise of the scanner for a minute, then went out to his car and drove to the farm. Just north of Bel Arbre Jenner stopped, threw the spare tire into the irrigation ditch by the side of the road, hid the money in

the tire well, then laid the trunk carpet back down on top
of it.

136

At the farm, it was pandemonium. Jenner parked on the
bridge over the mangroves and stared out across the fields
at the charred wreckage of the distant farmhouse. The
approach road was clotted with rescue vehicles, fire
trucks, ambulances and patrol cars from as far away as
Fort Myers – and with white news vans, their microwave
antennas red and blue in the turret lights. They were
already live, the on-air talent standing in isolated pockets
of white light in the dark, sharing with the nation rumors
of the carnage gleaned from returning paramedics and
firemen.

He drove on, parked at the mouth of the approach road
and walked the rest of the way, passing unrecognized
through the throngs of emergency personnel and news
people. Parked up near the white gate was a furniture van:
the D.E.A. response team, he figured. A young uniformed
deputy stopped him at the gate; he identified himself and
she pulled up the sheriff on the radio, then let him
through.

The sheriff stood in the middle of the slope, surrounded by a knot of SWAT cops in black uniforms and
body armor. The bodies of his men had been cleared from
the field; those who hadn't been removed by ambulances
lay in a row of body bags at the foot of the rise, with a
small honor guard.

The stand lights turned the slope into a floodlit nightmare, strewn with the battered and burned bodies of men and pigs. Anders had sent an officer round to put the wounded animals out of their misery; periodically, a gunshot rang out as he came across another.

The sheriff was pale and sweaty, juggling priorities as fast as he could. When he asked what Jenner was doing there, desperation had driven the animosity out of his voice. Jenner suggested they speak privately; the sheriff followed him across the field, relieved to be out of the spotlight, if only for a moment.

"The Miami pathologists are on their way, Doctor Jenner. I think it's best we just let them get on with it, keep it local."

"I was here."

"What?"

"I was here when this happened. With Deb Putnam, from the Park Rangers."

"Why were you here?"

"I was looking for Lucy Craine; her mother called me after Chip Craine took her without permission."

"Just what happened here? I'm running blind."

"What do you have so far?"

"Nothing. Zero. This got called in by a motorist who saw it from I-55; he dialed 911 to report a farmhouse fire. It's an underserved rural area, so both Douglas and Lee County FD respond. They find multiple fatalities, evidence of multiple explosions, and dozens of dead or wounded pigs. Just after we get here, a D.E.A. Response Team shows up; they're not saying anything about who put them onto this, or why they responded."

451

Anders squinted at Jenner, noticing for the first time the state of his clothes, soiled and bloody.

"Drugs, right? It's drugs if the D.E.A.'s here."

Jenner nodded wearily. "I'll fill you in on it as much as I can in a second, but first there's something else I have to tell you."

Jenner glanced over at the D.E.A. agents talking among themselves – they were an outside agency, and behaved like one. They were professional and respectful, but Jenner could read them well enough to sense their exhilaration.

Beyond them, all four Douglas County Crime Scene Unit operatives stood at the foot of the field, looking overwhelmed. Jimmy Squire, the chief, had just arrived; he was breaking down the scene for initial mapping and documentation.

The sheriff said, "I'm listening. What is it?"

"Sheriff, I'm sorry I have to tell you this, but . . . Maggie Craine is dead."

"*Dead*?" Anders looked like a Clydesdale had put a hoof through his chest.

"Yes. And Chip Craine. She killed her father, then she killed herself. I was there in the room, I saw it all. "

The sheriff bent forward, then sat down heavily. His legs dangled down the slope like a little boy's; he rubbed his eyes, then looked out over the slope, toward the dock and the water and the mangroves.

"Why? For God's sake, *why*?" He said it not so much with surprise that it had happened but that it had finally happened that day – why now?

Jenner sat next to him. "She was angry because Chip had taken Lucy without her permission. When we got out

452

of the farm, I went back to find Craine and to tell Maggie – I was here when they blew up the buildings, and I knew that Lucy was in the farmhouse when it burned."

The sheriff started to interrupt, but Jenner cut him off. "Sheriff, let me get this out. It'll only take a second.

"When I got to Stella Maris, Craine was getting ready to run – he'd been working with a Mexican cartel to make and distribute methamphetamine along the East Coast and in the Midwest. They had a high-volume operation in one of the buildings, and a funeral director was helping them move product inside dead bodies, mostly to the Northeast, up I-95, and by air. Dr. Roburn found out about it, so they killed him.

"When Maggie came in, she was pretty much hysterical about her daughter. Craine had a police scanner; when word went out over the radio that you'd found Lucy's body in the farmhouse, Maggie just lost it. She shot her father in the throat; there was nothing I could do for him.

"She was really upset – her daughter was dead, she'd killed her father. I guess she didn't see any other way – she just put the gun to her head and pulled the trigger. I didn't have time to do anything."

The sheriff sat there, shaking his head slowly. "Oh my God . . . Oh my God."

"Really, there was no way I could've stopped her. She had the gun, and she'd made up her mind; I think she'd been working up to it for some time – killing her father, I mean. She . . ."

"She what?"

"She said he raped her one year when she was home from college – that Chip was Lucy's father."

453

Anders's head whipped around to Jenner, the incredulity in his face quickly replaced by dawning understanding as he thought about everything he knew about the Craines.

"My God. I . . . I didn't know." He cradled his forehead in his hand. "I just didn't see it. I must've been blind. When she dumped me – really suddenly, no reason – I just assumed it was another guy. I mean, I'm no George Clooney, and she ran with a pretty rich set, so there were always lots of better-looking rich guys for her to go with, so I never really thought I'd last with her anyways. And then she was pregnant, so I figured . . ."

Jenner said, "She couldn't tell anyone. She was completely dependent on Craine, she had no money of her own, no marketable skills or anything. You know, Chip *wanted* her to have the baby? He stopped her from getting an abortion, built a little honey trap for her at Stella . . ."

The man was crying. Jenner said, "You can't beat yourself up about this. She had a rough deal, and she played it out."

Anders wiped his eyes with the back of his hand. "After she dumped me, I didn't speak to her for almost five years."

"You didn't know. She wouldn't have told you."

Anders, snuffling, pulled himself awkwardly to his feet. "Want to know the funny thing about this?"

Jenner said nothing.

"About half an hour ago, we found Lucy Craine alive and well. She said some guy named Brodie put her in the piglet shed at the bottom of the ranch before everything happened."

"She's *alive*?" The pit of Jenner's stomach began to crawl.

"Not a scratch on her. The shed got dinged up a bit, but the thing is basically corrugated metal wrapped around stacks of feed bags – it was like a bomb shelter. She stayed there, didn't make a peep until the D.E.A. team went in. She's just fine."

"What'll happen to her now?"

Anders raised his eyebrows. "Well, she'll be one rich little girl. Even if the State Attorney goes ahead with asset forfeitures, she'll inherit her mom's property, and will get Chip Craine's share of Stella Maris, as well as this farm. Plus any shielded accounts, insurance policies, annuities."

"I meant more the next few days and weeks."

"They're checking her out at Port Fontaine General as we speak. I guess I should call Gabe Caine now."

On the slope they were rolling up the last of the hoses. The firemen milled around, in no hurry to leave. Two fire marshals with clipboards compared notes in front of the shell of the farmhouse; the bunkhouses had been reduced to tangled heaps of siding and soot-covered cinder blocks, and a deep chasm gaped between the foundations of Bunkhouse A and the farmhouse. One of the fire marshals was waving the sheriff over.

Anders put a hand to his forehead. "I don't know how I'm going to do all this. We lost almost our entire SWAT team tonight. I don't even know what they were doing here – I never authorized any SWAT action!"

"I think some of your men were on the take. Tom Nash took me and Deb Putnam to the farm at gunpoint on Chip Craine's orders; one of Brodie's men shot him."

455

"Oh Jesus."

"There may have been others – I don't know. The D.E.A. operation was mobilized by a friend of mine, a New York City cop. I saw the SWAT attack but I don't know who notified them. Nash, maybe, or maybe they had someone inside. And I don't know if they were trying to save Nash, doing a straight raid, or looking for cash."

There was a loud crack as another hog was shot.

Anders looked over the field, up toward the smoldering rubble, then down at the jam of journalists beyond the gate.

"I don't know what to do, doctor. I don't even have anyone left to send to the Craine house."

"Listen to me: the forensics here aren't going to be as big a deal as they will be at Stella Maris. You need to send someone good there; it's going to take days to process this scene, but the Craine deaths will be huge – this is one of America's Blue Chip families. You can't afford to screw up either investigation. Also, I don't want to get jammed up for something I didn't do.

"I have a weapon on me; it's my own personal side arm, a .40-caliber Beretta. It hasn't been fired since my last visit to the range last week. Marty Roburn submitted my carry permit; it's still processing. I'll surrender my weapon willingly, but I want it back when you're finished with it. Also, I'm prepared to speak to your investigators without a lawyer present, with the condition that the entire interview is videotaped. I consent to a DNA sample, and I am willing to take a polygraph."

Anders's face was wide and empty as a field of winter wheat. "A polygraph?"

"I'm saying I'll comply with whatever investigational

procedures you use. I didn't shoot Chip Craine and I didn't shoot Maggie, and I want your office to understand that from the get-go – it'll save us all a lot of time and hassle."

Anders jumped as another shot cracked across the field.

He turned to Jenner and said, "We better get this started."

137

It was two days before they let Jenner leave Douglas county. They interrogated him for hours, but the forensic reconstruction of the scene and the pathologist's evaluation of the bodies supported his story; besides, he'd had no motive to kill either Chip or Maggie. They didn't bother with a lie-detector test.

In the end, Chip Caine's paranoia sprung Jenner from Port Fontaine. The director of the security company that Caine had used at Stella Maris contacted the police to tell them the estate had movement-triggered video surveillance. He sat with them in a darkened room and showed them digital video of Maggie Craine arriving; at the front door she'd hesitated a second, opened her purse and pulled out her pistol, then had finally put it away before going inside.

At autopsy, the pathologist documented visible gunshot residue on Maggie's hands, as well as blood spatter on her right arm and clothing consistent with a self-inflicted gunshot wound. Initial evaluation showed that the bullets recovered at the autopsies were similar; Ballistics would eventually confirm that all four had been fired from the same gun.

And that was that.

When Jenner stopped by Port Fontaine General to say goodbye to Deb Putnam he found her dressed in street clothes, chafing to be sprung. She'd become a celebrity in the Park Ranger world and had a small retinue of deeply tan men and women in green uniforms sitting by her bed.

She excused herself to walk with him.

"Well, that was something, right, Jenner?"

He grinned. "Eh. In New York, this kind of thing happens to me all the time."

"I hear New York's pretty nice this time of year."

"Someone's lying to you. The city's a pit in the summer – hot, sweaty, smelly, filled with tourists . . ." Jenner draped an arm gently around Deb's shoulder. "But, you know, the restaurants have air conditioning, and I know a great place for swordfish. If you don't really care about the planet, that is . . ."

She laughed, then looked up. He'd walked her to the entrance lobby. She laughed again, and punched him softly in the shoulder. "You bastard! I can't believe I'm the one who got shot, yet you make me walk you out!"

They hugged, and he left. An hour later he was on Pelican Alley, heading for Miami. The dog, his chest bandaged, a protective plastic support cone around his neck, snored in the back seat.

He made good time. At the Midpoint gas station, in the middle of the Glades halfway between Port Fontaine and Miami, a big bald man in a Winnebago told him Michael Jackson had died. Jenner turned on his radio, but out there in the wild, he could get nothing but static.

Back on the road, the rain started again. The car's wipers beat the drizzle away, and the sky was silver over the endless green expanse of the Glades.

When Jenner had first arrived in Port Fontaine, the region had been in near-drought conditions, but the past month had completely reinvented the wetlands. The sedge was vibrant green, and now there was water everywhere, flowing around the hammocks and through the sloughs, turning the Glades into a drowned world.

EPILOGUE

At sunset, they flocked to the wild edges of the farms where they worked, to the places where the fields gave way to marsh. The organizers waited three days to let people gather; some had come all the way from Chiapas. At first the atmosphere was cruelly festive, fueled as much by tequila as by the adrenalin of revenge: many were drunk before the boats even went out on the water.

It was a ragtag little flotilla, roughly fifty men in a dozen boats, mostly canoes and cheap fishing boats with puny outboards. At the head of the fleet was the large airboat from Craine's farm.

As the smaller boats drew near, they finally caught sight of the men on the airboat, many of them for the first time. The mood changed palpably, the antic excitement replaced by grim purpose. There was little talk now. Some still drank, but the men were silent, reflecting on

459

the things they were about to do, on the events that had brought them all there.

The airboat pilot was unfamiliar with the controls but was learning quickly. The two men sitting next to him navigated, calling the left or right shifts as necessary.

The sun came out, a yellow, nostalgic light settling on the river of grass that flowed around them. The pilot tipped the stick and the airboat swung into a wide arc to the right.

The two men tied to the front seats were immobile. The younger one was weak; he'd been shot when they'd caught him, and now his wound stank. When they'd carried him to the boat he'd begged and wept, but he was quiet now. The older one hadn't spoken a word since he'd been taken, hadn't reacted, no matter what they did to him. Both had bags over their heads, and their necks were tied together by a length of gray rope.

One of the navigators nudged the pilot's leg and pointed. Up ahead, a large island of mahogany and gumbo-limbo rose from the water like a surfacing whale. In the golden light of the sinking sun, huge black vultures floated over the dense canopy of leaves, sometimes breaking away to drift off over the marsh, but always coming back to settle in the high branches and wait.

Acknowledgements:

I hate writing acknowledgements, not because I'm an ungrateful bastard but because I always leave out critically important people; if you're one of the people I'm about to leave out, please just go ahead and start working on forgiving me now.

First off, thanks to my friends and colleagues at the New York City Medical Examiners' office – I couldn't ask for a smarter, more supportive or better-looking bunch of pathologists to work with. A similar shout out to the many fine men and women of the New York Police Department with whom we work on a daily basis; I recently heard a lecturer tell an audience of mystery fans that cops almost never use the F-word – thank you all for proving him epically wrong, time and again.

On the topic of the F-word, my thanks to Jesse Sheidlower for seeing fit to cite me several times in the new edition of his encyclopedic work on the subject, *The F-Word*. While impeccably polite in decent company, I'm drawn to the profane, and am proud of the legitimization provided by Mr. Sheidlower and his cronies at the Oxford University Press. (Readers of my first novel *Precious Blood* are already slightly familiar with Mr. Sheidlower; a prominent lexicographer, he was the inspiration for the Simon Lescure character.)

My thanks also to my friends in the District Attorney's Office of New York County, particularly the Sex Crimes/Special Victims folks, who insist that one sees even the most lovely of neighborhoods as open cesspools where horrifically violent crime is always just about to strike. Those people are also my only openly Republican friends, and thus allow me to claim fairness and impartiality during arguments about politics.

Speaking of Sex Crimes, I'd like to thank Linda Fairstein for her kind support of junior novelists – me in particular, but she's tireless in helping all beginners out, even those who weren't forensic pathologists working with her back when she was running the division. And speaking of crime fiction writers, Patricia Cornwell has been more than generous with her advice and insight.

Who else, who else? Lots of important people. Research assistance came from Anya McCoy, a Florida-based friend from natural perfumery circles. Ira Stone, DVM, gave me great feedback about emergency management of canine injuries. Mike Caffrey hooked me up with an insider's perspective on EMS work. Brian Womble stopped listening to the Butthole Surfers long enough to share his vast knowledge of South Florida flora and fauna, including the two-legged kind. Lacey Burke, the junior wine director at the Gotham Bar and Grill in Manhattan, was an amazing source of wine and lingerie gift advice.

In Florida, special thanks to the Major Crimes unit of the Collier County Sheriff's Office, and a particular thank you to Lieutenant Rob Maxfield, director of the Collier

County Crime Lab. And most of all among Florida peeps, my thanks to Rob, Stephen and David Coburn for putting up with me, and letting me drag them into the Glades and through the mangrove swamps. And to their wife/mom Marta, who has been my best buddy way back since we trained together in Miami, as well as being the Chief Medical Examiner for Collier County.

In New York, I have been sustained by a variety of individuals and organizations. My core providers have been the Village branch of 'wichcraft, Momofuku Milk Bar, the East 10th Street branch of Spice, Stand Burger, and most importantly Alfred Portale's restaurant the Gotham Bar and Grill, where I've dined pretty much weekly since I first moved into the East Village in the early 1990s. Like all regulars there, I'm treated like family, except without the arguing; it makes me suspect that bickering at holiday family meals could be eliminated by having everyone pay to attend.

Speaking of family, mine have been great, too, almost embarrassingly proud of me, which is its own kind of burden, really – the sense of unworthiness is crushing. Thank you all of you, particularly the ones who're still speaking to me.

Thanks to the people who make it all possible: at Random House, Oliver Johnson has been infinitely patient, diplomatic and funny, and a sharp reader; Nick Austin's copy edit was nothing less than a lesson in novel writing. Charlotte Haycock and Katie Duce wrangled the logistics with style and grace. Back in the US, Claire Wachtel and

Heather Drucker at HarperCollins have looked after me wonderfully, and I both couldn't and wouldn't take a step forward without consulting my brilliant agent Sarah Burnes of the Gernert Company. Other Gernert Allstars include Courtney Gatewood (née Hammer) and Stephanie Cabot.

Jill Bresler and Jennifer Cassetty have worked hard at holding me together. And I've been blessed with an excess of great friends, all of whom have looked out for me – Cricket, Mame, Lisa, Whitney, Barbara, Jim, Jen, Sophie, Pauline, Shahla, Christine, Jane and so many more people – thank you (shades of the B-52's song "52 Girls" – not you, Jim Heckler). And special thanks to Kate, who left me a little scorched around the edges, but probably better for the experience.

I'm stopping there – if you've read all the way to the end just to see your name in print, and didn't find it, I'm sorry! Look me up in person and I'll apologize. Offer me a bribe, and I'll include you in the acknowledgements section in the next Jenner book; next time, I'm hoping to stretch it to chapter length.

Precious Blood

Jonathan Hayes

'They found her in the East Village, nailed to the wall of a railroad flat'

Dr Edward Jenner is a New York forensic pathologist: he has attended countless murder scenes and performed thousands of autopsies but the killing of 21-year-old Andie Delore is different. The naked body is marked with an indecipherable ancient script and is arranged in the shape of a ritual sacrifice.

The murderer poses as a cop. The sole eye witness is Andie's flatmate, Ana da Jong. She can't trust the police anymore. Instead she turns to Jenner for help.

But then a second victim is found in rural Pennsylvania. Her head has been placed in a puddle of milk.

And then the third. Another decapitation: her naked torso is decorated with exotic bird feathers . . .

Both corpses have the same mysterious script. The killer is leading Jenner and Ana into his own private nightmare. A place for which there will be no escape.

'Taut and chilling . . . a fast-paced thriller written by a real player in the game of forensic sleuthing' Kathy Reichs

arrow books

Hannibal

Thomas Harris

Seven years have passed since Dr. Hannibal Lecter escaped from custody, seven years since FBI Special Agent Clarice Starling interviewed him in a maximum security hospital for the criminally insane. The doctor is still at large, pursuing his own ineffable interests, savouring the scents, the essences of an unguarded world. But Starling has never forgotten her encounters with Dr. Lecter, and the metallic rasp of his seldom-used voice still sounds in her dreams.

Mason Verger remembers Dr. Lecter, too, and is obsessed with revenge. He was Dr. Lecter's sixth victim, and he has survived to rule his own butcher's empire. From his respirator, Verger monitors every twitch in his worldwide web. Soon he sees that to draw the doctor, he must have the most exquisite and innocent-appearing bait; he must have what Dr Lecter likes best.

'Worth the wait . . . look no further for the chiller of the year'
The Times

'Readers who have been waiting for *Hannibal* only want to know if it is as good as *Red Dragon* and *The Silence of the Lambs* . . . It is a pleasure to reply in the negative. No, not as good. This one is better'
Stephen King

arrow books

Hannibal Rising

Thomas Harris

In Thomas Harris's previous novels, which include *The Silence of the Lambs*, *Hannibal* and *Red Dragon*, readers learned that Dr Lecter saw his entire family killed during World War II in Eastern Europe. *Hannibal Rising* chronicles the early life of Dr Lecter, and sheds more light on the circumstances of those deaths.

Thomas Harris has written the most compelling psychological suspense of our time. In Dr Hannibal Lecter, he has gone beyond creating a master villain to present one of the most irresistibly brilliant and disturbing characters in all of literature. Now, in *Hannibal Rising*, readers will at last learn of Lecter's beginnings and will see the evolution of his evil . . .

Praise for *Hannibal*:

'A masterpiece . . . Chillingly brilliant' *Observer*

'Quite simply this is the best-written thriller to dominate the market in years.' *The Times*

'A gut-churning, nail-biting, skin-crawling, often lyrical triumph – addictive on every level' *Daily Express*

arrow books

Play Dead

Richard Montanari

In each soul, a secret . . .

Philadelphia homicide detectives Kevin Byrne and Jessica Balzano's first assignment from the Cold Case files is the brutal murder of a young runaway. The lifeless body of Caitlin O'Riordan was found carefully posed in a glass display case in the desolate Philadelphia Badlands but, as Byrne and Balzano rapidly discover, she was just the first pawn in the killer's twisted game . . .

A mysterious phone call leads them on a scavenger hunt for a second victim. This time a young girl has been dismembered, her body parts left in three boxes in the basement of a deserted house. More clues lead to other victims and, as the body count rises, it becomes clear that there is a serial killer on the loose, hell-bent on completing the 'performance' of a lifetime.

As more runaways vanish, Byrne and Balzano come to realize that the homicidal mastermind plans to complete seven depraved tricks in his dark and dangerous magic act. With Balzano increasingly obsessed by a case that haunts her, and Byrne struggling with a loss of his own, the stakes are mounting. But this is one game they can't afford to lose . . .

arrow books

The Skin Gods

Richard Montanari

Philadelphia is blistering in the summer heat and detectives Kevin Byrne and Jessica Balzano prowl the streets with growing unease. Suddenly, a series of crimes shatters the restless city. A beautiful secretary is slashed to death in a grimy motel shower; a street hustler brutally murdered with a chainsaw. Piece by piece, a sickening puzzle presents itself: someone is recreating famous Hollywood murder scenes and inserting the clips into videos – for an unsuspecting public to find.

Investigations reveal a violent world of underground film, pornography and seedy nightclubs, hidden to all but the initiated. None of *The Actor*'s victims are as innocent as they appear, though, and Kevin and Jessica soon discover they're not just chasing a homicide suspect. They are stalking evil itself . . .

arrow books

The Rosary Girls

Richard Montanari

Only a killer hears their prayers . . .

In the most brutal killing crusade Philadelphia has seen in years, a series of young Catholic women are found dead, their bodies mutilated and their hands bolted together. Each clutches a rosary in her lifeless grasp.

Veteran cop Kevin Byrne and his rookie partner Jessica Balzano set out to hunt down the elusive killer, who leads them deeper and deeper into the abyss of a madman's depravity. Suspects appear before them like bad dreams – and vanish just as quickly. While the body count rises, Easter is fast approaching: the day of resurrection and of the last rosary to be counted . . .

'Be prepared to stay up all night' James Ellroy

'A specialist in serial killer tales . . . a wonderfully evocative writer' *Publishers Weekly*

arrow books

Bones to Ashes

Kathy Reichs

**Under the microscope, the outer bone surface is a
moonscape of craters . . .**

The skeleton is that of a young girl, no more than fourteen years old
– and forensic anthropologist Dr Temperance Brennan is struggling
to keep her emotions in check.

A nagging in her subconscious won't let up. A memory triggered,
deep in her hindbrain – the disappearance of a childhood friend; no
warning, no explanation . . .

Detective Andrew Ryan is working a series of parallel cases: three
missing persons, three unidentified bodies – all female, all early-to-
mid teens . . . Could Tempe's skeleton be yet another in this tragic
line of young victims? Or is she over-reacting, making connections
where none exist?

Working on instinct, Tempe takes matters into her own hands. But
even she couldn't have predicted the horrors this investigation
would eventually uncover . . . Can Tempe maintain a professional
distance as the past catches up with her in this, her most deeply
personal case yet?

arrow books

ALSO AVAILABLE IN ARROW

Break No Bones

Kathy Reichs

A decomposing body is uncovered in a shallow grave off a lonely beach . . .

The skeleton is articulated, the bone fresh and the vertebrae still connected by soft-tissue – it's a recent burial, and a case forensic anthropologist Dr Temperance Brennan must take.

Dental remains and skeletal gender and race indicators suggest that the deceased is a middle-aged white male – but who was he? Why was he buried in a clandestine grave? And what does the unusual fracture of the sixth cervical vertebra signify?

But just as Brennan is trying to piece together the evidence, another body is discovered – and before long Tempe finds herself drawn deeper into a shocking and chilling investigation, set to challenge her entire view of humanity . . .

'A brilliant novel . . . Reichs's seamless blending of fascinating science and dead-on psychological portrayals, not to mention a whirlwind of a plot, make *Break No Bones* a must-read'
Jeffery Deaver

arrow books

ALSO AVAILABLE IN ARROW

Bare Bones

Kathy Reichs

It's one of the hottest summers on record and forensic anthropologist Dr Temperance Brennan is looking forward to a long overdue vacation. But it's not to be . . .

First, the bones of a newborn baby are found in a wood stove; the mother, barely a child herself, has disappeared.

Next, a Cessna flies into a rock face. The bodies of the pilot and passenger are burned beyond recognition, and covered in an unknown substance.

And then a cache of bones is found in a remote corner of the county. But what happened there, and who will the next victim be? The answers lie hidden deep within the bones – if only Tempe can decipher them in time . . .

'The forensic detail is harrowing, the pace relentless, and the prose assured. Kathy Reichs just gets better and better and is now the Alpha female of this genre'
Irish Independent

'Reichs has now proved that she is up there with the best'
The Times

'Better than Patricia Cornwell'
Sunday Express

arrow books

THE POWER OF READING

Visit the Random House website and get connected with information on all our books and authors

EXTRACTS from our recently published books and selected backlist titles

COMPETITIONS AND PRIZE DRAWS Win signed books, audiobooks and more

AUTHOR EVENTS Find out which of our authors are on tour and where you can meet them

LATEST NEWS on bestsellers, awards and new publications

MINISITES with exclusive special features dedicated to our authors and their titles

READING GROUPS Reading guides, special features and all the information you need for your reading group

LISTEN to extracts from the latest audiobook publications

WATCH video clips of interviews and readings with our authors

RANDOM HOUSE INFORMATION including advice for writers, job vacancies and all your general queries answered

Come home to Random House
www.rbooks.co.uk